PRAISE FOR DOON

Other books in the Doon series

Forever
Doon

Carey Corp and Lorie Langdon

BLINK

BLINK

Forever Doon
Copyright © 2016 by Carey Corp and Lorie Moeggenberg

This title is also available as a Blink ebook.
Visit www.zondervan.com/ebooks.

Requests for information should be addressed to:
Blink, 3900 *Sparks Dr. SE*, Grand Rapids, *Michigan 49546*

ISBN 978-0-310-74237-1

Thank you to the Alan Jay Lerner Estate and the Frederick Loewe Foundation for
use of the premise.

Cover design and photography: Magnus Creative
Interior design and composition: Greg Johnson / Textbook Perfect

Printed in the United States of America

16 17 18 19 20 21 /DCI/ 20 19 18 17 16 15 14 13 12 11 10 9 8 7 6 5 4 3 2 1

*To our Doonians all over the world, you
are Called to a great purpose!*

*And for Mary Sue Seymour whose quiet passion
continues to change the world for the better.*

CHAPTER 1

Mackenna

I collapsed to my knees in the wet sand, staring at the vast, empty expanse of beach without a mountain in sight. Behind me the waves of the morning tide roared like a voracious beast. Soon they would devour the land and we would return to Dunbrae Cottage having failed to find a way back to Doon for the twenty-second day in a row.

Balling my hand into a fist, I willed the silver and emerald ring on my finger to react. It had opened the portal to the secret back door into Doon before. But despite wanting it to work more than ever before, it remained cold and lifeless on my finger as if mourning the loss of its counterpart, my best friend's gold and ruby one.

According to Duncan, Vee's ring had fallen from his finger when Eòran pushed us toward safety during the bridge collapse. It had most likely been swept downriver with the rubble. Although Fiona and several others continued to search for it, I feared it was lost for good. And all of us with it—the unfortunate Doonians trapped on the wrong side of the Brig o' Doon as our loved ones battled against a wicked witch for their very lives.

Duncan's warm hand rested gently on my shoulder. "Come away, woman," he murmured. The heat of his touch caused me to realize how miserable the weather was—much cooler than the first time we'd visited the beach. That had been another lifetime ago. Duncan's first legit trip to the ocean—his first time feeling the surf around his feet and exploring tidal pools. Despite the threat of zombie fungus and the urgency of returning to Doon, we'd had a perfect "Summer Nights" moment, getting friendly in the sand and all that. Later, when we were safely home, I'd given him a petrified starfish to commemorate the moment.

But the days of singing about our true love vow were over. It turned colder, *that's where it ends* . . . Now our kingdom was under siege and we were as useless as a classically trained Shakespearian actor at a *Hairspray* audition.

No! I cut off the hopeless thought. We'd find a way back to Doon, help our friends save the kingdom, and live happily ever after. All we had to do was believe and not give up.

I sighed internally. Easier said than done.

"Ready, lass?" Duncan's hand slid down my shoulder to curl around my bicep. But instead of rising to my feet with his support, I shrugged him away.

"Just a few more minutes." I clenched my fist tighter, squinting at the horizon where I willed mountains to appear. *Please*, I pleaded silently. *We need to get back to Vee and the others. We need to save Doon.*

My plea seemed to disappear into nothing; the sand remained unchanged, flat and desolate except for an old Scotsman who lumbered across the beach in our direction. There was something vaguely familiar about the old guy, but Duncan interrupted before I could figure it out.

"Mackenna. Perhaps it's time we admit the truth. Aye?" Although he didn't touch me again, I could feel the heat rolling off him as he stood at my back.

Without warning, I lurched to my feet and whirled to confront him. "Which is?"

His velvety brown gaze held mine. "Mayhap we're no' meant to return to Doon through the mountains. At least no' right now."

The words weren't easy for him to say—I knew Duncan well enough to be certain of this. Every bone in his body yearned to reunite with his brother, as mine ached to return to Vee. Neither of us ever spoke of the possibility that one or both might already be dead, or that it might be our fault for abandoning them.

Despite the human heater facing me, my teeth began to chatter. "What if we're not meant to go back at all? What if this is how Doon survives, through our memories? I suppose we should just get on with our lives then. Maybe move out west to Santa Fe—I hear it's sunny and nice."

I'd flung my response at Duncan carelessly and had the uncomfortable satisfaction of seeing the pain in his eyes as my verbal darts hit their mark. He paled, his brows pinching together as he struggled not to react. "I'm no' sayin' we give up—or relocate. Just that we look for Doon another way."

"Like rebuilding the bridge?" I asked, doing my best to not sound critical about his fixation with restoring the Brig o' Doon.

"Aye."

I shook my head before he even finished speaking. "And how much longer is that going to take? It not like erecting a Taco Bell—it's an historical replication made of stone and built by master craftsmen. Anything could be happening in Doon while we're waiting here in limbo."

"Don't ye think I know that?" He turned and stalked up the beach.

I followed at a jog, closing the distance between us. "I know . . . And I'm sorry. But if I stop coming here, it's like I'm giving up. We need to have hope, now more than ever." Slipping my hand in the crook of his arm, I leaned into Duncan, drawing from his strength and giving him mine. "I wish the Protector would give us some sort of sign."

His lips pursed in a crooked smile. "Perhaps he's trying to, but we're too busy arguin' instead of listenin'."

Ever sunny and optimistic, my boyfriend had a point. Letting go of Duncan, I stepped away so I could fling my arms wide. "Okay," I shouted toward the heavens as I turned in a slow circle. "I'm listening."

The old guy who'd been wandering along the beach stopped to gawk at my outburst. He gaped at me, then Duncan, and then back at me again. As he stared, my mind began to place him as the storyteller from the tavern in Alloway, a lifetime ago. It was through him that Vee and I first heard the legend of the MacCraes and their enchanted kingdom.

Being a distance off, the old man gestured toward the empty beach and shouted, "Hear this then, lassie. You'll no' get ta Doon through the mountains. Not this time."

CHAPTER 2

Duncan

Mackenna Reid could break a fellow's heart in a hundred different ways without realizing it. Like now, gray eyes wide and shimmering with hopefulness, mouth set against the possibility that something good was on the verge of happening, and eyebrows knit together in uncertainty—her bonnie face a map of contradictions that worked in tandem to reveal the secrets of her heart. Secrets that I would protect at any cost.

I stepped between my love and the modern-world stranger who'd just professed knowledge of our hidden kingdom. Motioning with my left hand for Mackenna to stay behind me, I rested my right hand lightly on the hilt of my dirk tucked into the waistband of my blue jean trousers. "Identify yourself, sir," I demanded.

Mackenna's hand lightly brushed my arm. "It's okay, Duncan. I know him."

"You do?" I asked, my eyes never leaving the man.

"Yes," she replied. "Well, sort of. He's the storyteller who first told Vee and me the legend of Doon. He works at the Tam O'Shanter pub."

The storyteller in question was steadily closing the distance between us. In another moment I would need to make a decision . . . Unsheathe my weapon or no. Unfortunately, Mackenna's account of the gentleman didn't aid in that decision. "And jus' how did he come to know the legend of our kingdom?"

Her voice faltered. "I, uh, never thought to ask. It was just a story at the time. I had no idea it was real." She emitted a soft sound of revelation. "Actually it was the Witch of Doon who introduced us, when she was pretending to be Ally."

I knew from conversations with Mackenna that her and Veronica's first encounter with Adelaide Blackmore Cadell had been in Alloway, when they'd been on vacation. The witch had been posing as both the caretaker of Dunbrae Cottage and the caretaker's daughter. In those capacities she'd set the girls on the trajectory for Doon, which had eventually granted her the power to take the kingdom by force with dark magic.

With that latest revelation I pulled my dirk from its scabbard and ordered the stranger to halt when he was less than a dozen paces away. Wishing I had a proper blade, I took quick mental inventory. Besides the eight-inch dagger in my hand, I had my wee sgian dubh tucked into the hosiery of my right leg—utterly useless beneath the stiff, modern trousers. At Mackenna's insistence on remaining inconspicuous, all my other weaponry had been left at the cottage. What I would have given in that moment for a cutlass or broadsword.

The man, face as leathery and blemished as aging cowhide, came to a standstill. While leaning heavily on a walking stick of driftwood, he blinked at me enigmatically. "I couldna help but notice that you're looking for Doon, friend. But try as ye might, ye'll no' get those mountains to appear."

For the next few seconds we took one another's measure. Dressed in crumpled, overlarge tweeds and woolen cap, the auld man gave the impression of a shrunken version of his former self. His rheumy eyes and the burst capillaries of his sagging face indicated he'd seen the bottom of plenty of cups. Overall, he appeared innocuous. But appearances, especially where known associates of the Witch o' Doon were concerned, could be misleading.

"What do you know of Doon?" I asked lightly, noting that Eòran had quietly circled round behind the stranger with his dagger at the ready.

"Mayhap more than ye, Yer Highness." He cleared his throat. "Please call off yer man. I mean ye and yer lassie no harm."

I signaled for Eòran to pause in his advance but remain at the ready. The man's face cracked slightly into what I surmised to be a smirk. "Ye see, I've been watching you for the past fortnight. And waiting for you much longer, for lifetimes . . ." He shifted his attention over my shoulder, to Mackenna. "When Adelaide first brought you American lassies inta the tavern, I knew it had begun."

My grip tightened on my dirk. "Explain yourself, sir, and how ye came to be acquainted with the Witch o' Doon."

"How did you know Ally was the witch?" Mackenna asked.

The auld man chuckled. "Adelaide Blackmore Cadell has gone by many aliases in her long walk on this earth . . . and I have known them all. Ye see, lassie, I'm the only person who's been alive as long as she has. Her fate and mine were the same— trapped on the outside, unable to cross the bridge. But tha's all different now. As yer Obi-Wan Kenobi might say, 'There's been a change in the force.'"

As a young lad, I'd heard the stories. An auld wives' tale of a cowardly man fleeing Doon at the exact moment the miracle happened. The legend went that the man, giving into his fear, had attempted to flee across the Brig o' Doon as the Protector enacted the blessing. He was then caught between realms and suspended on the bridge. The benevolent Protector appeared to him with a choice to return to Doon or continue his flight into Alloway. But before the foolish man could make up his mind, the witch snatched him into the modern world and Doon was lost to him forever. "You're the Suspended Man."

"Worse 'n that, laddie. I was King Angus Andrew Kellan MacCrae's only brother and yer kinsman, Alasdair MacCrae."

Squinting against the rising sun, I tried to picture the auld, blue-eyed man as a strong, ruddy youth. Edging a small step back toward Mackenna, I groped for her hand. Her chilled fingers found mine, intertwining with a reassuring squeeze. "You lie, sir. Besides ruling Doon, the MacCraes are known for two things: siring sons and dark eyes."

With a fragile, blue-veined hand, Alasdair scratched at the side of his nose. "I suppose tha's true, laddie. But many generations back, a young lass by the name o' Shoshanna Haldane became queen by marrying the MacCrae. She was the village Seanachaidh—its storyteller—and she had the same blue-gray eyes ye see before you. She was my mum."

Now that he spoke thus, I did see the resemblance between Alasdair and Doon's current Seanachaidh, Calum Haldane. But hailing from Doon did not necessarily make him a friend. Or a MacCrae.

As if the man could read minds, he spread his hands wide, palms up in supplication. "Yer Highness, I have no magick and no allegiance to the Witch o' Doon, but that doesna mean ye should readily believe me. I have valuable intelligence—information ye need to know."

Letting go of my hand, Mackenna rushed from my side toward Alasdair before I could stop her. "Please? Do you know how to get back to Doon?"

My heart began to pound as I calculated the likelihood of the auld man doing her violence and whether I could get to her before he did. To my relief, Eòran crept within a pace of them. Without his queen to safeguard, Eòran had decided it was his sacred duty to guard the queen's best friend. I knew with absolute certainty the good man would protect my love with his life. It's what Veronica would want.

Alasdair grinned, splitting his leathery face nearly in two. "Aye, lassie. I know how to get back to Doon. And tha's not all I know."

"I just want to know how to return to Doon. I don't care about anything else."

"Well, ye should care," he replied with a delighted snort. "If you knew what I know, ye'd care a great deal."

Stepping closer to Alasdair, within reach of Mackenna, I let my hand rest lightly around my lass's soft hip. "Stop talking in riddles, man. You will curry no favor if ye dinna answer our questions."

"Apologies, Yer Highness. You see, I not only know how ta get back to Doon . . ." He paused self-importantly, his enigmatic smirk reminding me of a great-uncle I had not been overly fond of. "I am perhaps the only soul who knows how ye kin defeat the witch."

"How?" Mackenna demanded as I scrutinized my supposed kinsman. What was his game? And why speak now after we'd been in Alloway for nearly two fortnights?

"Not so fast, lassie. I know how to defeat the witch, but I'll only be sharin' that information with the queen."

I dug my fingers lightly into her hip to quiet her. "Which queen?" I asked, feigning ignorance.

Alasdair's shrewd, watery eyes moved from Mackenna's to mine. "The American lass. Wee thing, dark hair, goes by the name of Veronica."

"I know who my best friend is—" Mackenna's pocket chimed, cutting through the tension of the auld man's revelation. She removed her mobile phone and glanced at the screen. "Fiona says we need to return to the cottage right away." Turning halfway toward the parking area, she paused as if suddenly remembering we had unfinished business on the beach. "What do we do with him?"

With a series of gestures, Eòran indicated caution. Addie had magically removed the faithful guard's tongue and given it to her lackey, Sean. Despite being a mute, Eòran had no issue with making his sentiments known. Regarding Alasdair, Eòran was of the opinion that this was possibly another trap set by the Witch o' Doon. I agreed. The only way Alasdair could've known about Veronica is if the witch had told him.

But if he truly had intelligence about how to defeat her . . .

Both the guard and Mackenna looked to me to determine Alasdair's fate. If there was the slightest possibility the auld man had information that would help us not only return home but ultimately defeat Adelaide, we had to take that chance. "He comes with us."

With a delighted chuckle, Alasdair nodded his consent. With Kenna at my front, the auld man at my back, and Eòran bringing up the rear, we solemnly made our way across the beach to our waiting sedan.

When we arrived at Mackenna's ancestral home, Dunbrae Cottage, the front door was ajar. Not only was the door open, but the library windows as well. Our people spilled out of the doorway onto the front walk and garden. Those outside huddled in groups near the windows, whispering to one another. The posture of their bodies and severe expressions made it easy to discern that something of great importance was happening in the library.

As Mackenna pulled the sedan to a stop, I ordered Eòran to stay in the car with Alasdair. Fixing my stare on the auld man, I said, "If ye know what's good for you, you'll stay put until I tell ye to move."

Alasdair's rheumy eyes crinkled as if amused. "Yes, m'Laird."

By the time I exited the car, the Doonians standing out of doors had turned to face the road. They all shared the same expression of unease mingled with hopeful expectancy. Mackenna slipped her cool hand into mine. Her brows pinched in confusion. "What do you think's going on?"

"I dinna know." I squeezed her hand in reassurance. "Let's go find out."

Wordlessly, the crowd clustered around the doorway parted so we could enter the cottage. The interior contained more human beings than I would've imagined possible in such a cramped space. Friends were pressed against one another in the foyer and up the stairwell, their bodies angled toward the library. As we appeared, heads swiveled in our direction. Each one regarded us with that same disquieting expression.

Despite the mass of bodies, the crowd managed to step aside so that we could get to the library. The focal point of the room seemed to be a divan—or rather a person perched on the divan with her face downcast. At first sight, the figure appeared to be a child. Slender and petite, the girl had sleek ebony hair and copper skin. The slight trace of makeup on her fine-boned face indicated that she was not a child, merely small in stature.

Caledonia Fairshaw, Fiona's mum, sat to one side of the girl while her daughter sat on the other. After a grim look in our direction, Fiona put a hand on the girl's knee. "Ches, these are the friends I was telling ye about, Duncan and Mackenna. Do you think you could tell them what you told me?"

The girl nodded and raised her head to address us. Despite the confusion in her dark eyes, she radiated intelligence. She cleared her throat softly before speaking. "My name is Cheska Ann Santos. I'm fifteen."

Her accent sounded similar to Mackenna's, with slightly crisper enunciation and an undercurrent of something exotic. Cheska closed her eyes as she drew in a deep breath; after a slow exhale, she opened them to regard us fiercely. "I can't account for what happened, exactly, or how . . . but I believe I was sent here from my home, the City of Tayabas, in the Philippines."

Fiona nodded, prompting, "Tell them how ye came to be in Scotland, Ches."

She fixed her grave eyes on mine as if daring me to doubt her veracity. Without so much as a blink of hesitancy, she replied, "I crossed a bridge."

Chapter 3

Veronica

The snow fell in relentless sheets that blocked out the sun. The kind of snow that made you forget there was ever a world without it. I trudged down the forest path and embraced the biting wind that nipped at my exposed face and slithered beneath my cloak. The pain of the cold felt good, better than the hideous monster that lurked inside, waiting to consume my sanity.

"Majesty, 'tis just around the next bend!" Ewan Murray shouted over his shoulder. The boy's green eyes sparkled as if we were on some great adventure instead of tromping through a blizzard to find a blackberry patch. Ewan was incorrigible, just like the time he'd asked me to dance at my first weekly feast when most of the kingdom still believed me a witch—including Jamie.

The monster reared its ugly head and I tripped over a lump beneath the snow, pitching forward. But before I could fall, strong hands grasped me from behind.

"Och, lass!" Fergus set me on my feet, and then let go of

my arms. "Only the good Lord knows why ye had to come on a blasted mission for *berries*. But at least refrain from injurin' yerself in the process, eh?"

My giant friend wasn't quite himself. Not that any of us were, but Fergus in particular bore the burden of failing to save his future king. No matter how many times I reassured him that there was nothing he could've done, he continued to blame himself. And it didn't help that his wife, Fiona, and who knew how many others, were trapped outside of Doon because I had sent them there.

Before the Brig o' Doon disintegrated, Fiona had been seen making it to safety in a group that included Eòran, Kenna, and my successor, Prince Duncan. At least if something happened to me, the heir to the throne would be safe, and perhaps, someday, find a way back.

Fergus and I continued down the path side by side, walking fast to keep up with Ewan's quickly diminishing form. "I can see you didn't forget your grumpy pills this morning," I jabbed, trying to coax out the old Fergus, so full of joy that no circumstances could dim his light—the friend I so desperately needed. But so far, my banter had been rewarded with grumbling and sour glares, much like the way he looked at me now.

"Veronica," he whispered, to ensure no one heard his use of my given name. "Why do ye keep insistin' on endangering yerself by gatherin' firewood, goin' on supply runs, and any other menial task ye can latch onta? Yer the only hope we have left—"

I whipped my head around. "What hope am I, Fergus? I have no plan, no idea how to defeat the witch." My voice rose above the wind, drawing the attention of the guards behind us. I didn't care. "The least I can do is be useful. I have nothing! No ring, no crown, I—"

My throat closed as Jamie's words from another world

echoed in my head. "Yer crown is no' what makes you a queen. And you are betrothed to me, even without a ring."

That may be true, Jamie, but without you my crown means nothing.

I didn't know how I was supposed to survive without him. The years following my father's abandonment had shown me how to stand on my own. I'd learned independence the hard way. But after knowing what it felt like to have Jamie by my side, I knew standing alone and feeling alive were two very different things.

Fergus grasped my arm and pulled me to a stop in the middle of the path. "You are our *Called* sovereign and whether ye choose to act like it or no', you are our leader! I know yer grieving. But so are most of yer people who lost loved ones across the brig or in the quake, and even to that blasted witch." He leaned down, the cowl of his cloak casting shadows that sharpened his cheekbones and emphasized his glittering blue eyes. "We. Need. You! Not as a worker bee, but as our queen!"

A hand shot out of the trees and grasped my arm. Fergus pulled his sword, but before he could unsheathe it, a face popped out of the darkness. Ewan pushed back his hood, red hair falling over his eyes. "A patrol is headed this way. We dinna have much time."

With a flurry of movement, we left the path. I glanced over my shoulder to see one of the guards sweep our footprints with a pine branch, fresh flakes quickly disguising the shallow grooves left by the needles. As I followed Ewan, the forest closed in around us, cutting off what little sun filtered through the snowstorm. He reached back and took my hand, whispering guidance and lifting branches out of our way. We entered a circle of pines and Ewan stopped. "We should be safe here for the moment."

After Fergus and the guards joined us, we stood in a circle, each one of them focused on me. I met their gazes in turn; Ewan's verdant and gleaming, both guards' stoic, and then the giant Scotsman, whose pale stare cut into me with unbearable expectancy. Fergus had been my first friend in Doon, the first to believe Kenna and I were innocent. I'd once referred to him as my guardian angel. But his belief in me now didn't make a bit of difference.

When I remained silent, Fergus pushed out a heavy sigh, and then turned to Ewan. "What did ye see of the patrol?"

"No' much. I heard footsteps . . . more like marching, as if they were moving as one. Then I ducked off the path and circled back."

"Camp is less than a league from here." Fergus frowned and shook his head. "We'll need ta move."

"And leave the Brig o' Doon?" Ewan asked the question that dominated all of our thoughts. We'd made camp in the forest nearest to the bridge—at least the spot where it used to stand. Grief tied us to the place where so many of our loved ones had been lost.

Fergus's gaze burned into mine, and I searched my mind for the right thing to say—the queenly thing. Following a pregnant pause, I gave a single nod. "After sunset. We'll move under the cover of darkness."

Back at camp, our blackberry mission an epic failure, I approached the teepee-like tent I shared with sisters Sofia and Gabriella Rosetti, and Analisa Morimoto—the girls who kept me sane through my grief. Things were beginning to mend between Ana and me, despite the British thief's refusal to pledge to me at the coronation ceremony. But I couldn't deny the support she'd given me in this time of crisis, regardless of her reservation regarding the monarchy; she'd taken a knee and made the vow on a cold forest morning just days before, along with anyone in our Doonian camp who'd missed the opportunity the first time.

I still missed Kenna so badly I refused to even think about it, but Ana's pragmatic nature was a perfect contrast to Sofia's quiet compassion and Gabby's unwavering merriment. At night, the four of us jammed in the narrow tent like sardines, willing to sacrifice legroom for warmth and companionship.

As I neared our new home, a single curl of smoke rose through the hole in the teepee's roof, dispersed by the trees overhead. Not everyone had the luxury of a fire inside their tent. We'd had to make do with what we could scavenge from Jamie and Duncan's well-fortified Brother Cave and a covert mission into the village, where we gathered food staples, livestock, clothing, a few tee-pees, and some smaller tents. Lean-tos had also been built from animal fur and sticks. The most unlucky slept on pallets on a patch of cleared ground or tucked beneath the pine boughs.

Ready to dry my socks by the fire and lose myself in Gabby's lighthearted chatter, I opened the flap and ducked inside. But none of my roommates awaited me. Sofia and Gabby's mother, Sharron Rosetti, sat, legs folded like a pretzel, roasting a pheas-ant over the flames. My mouth watered and my stomach twisted simultaneously.

"Please sit, my queen." Sharron eyed me the way only a mother of seven could. "I've prepared us a meal."

I moved to a pallet away from the door and sat. "I'm not hungry."

She removed the crisp bird from the flames and bile rose in my throat. Eating had been next to impossible. As had sleep-ing. I spent my days helping around camp wherever I was needed the most. The night before, I'd nursed the injured until the sun began to crest the horizon, then fallen onto my pallet hoping my exhaustion would keep the dreams at bay, but I still saw *him* there. The dream could be as mundane as walking through the forest, or as terrifying as facing Addie down in the throne room, but Jamie was always there. Casually leaning against a tree, arms crossed over his broad chest, one booted foot in front of the other, intensity drawing his brows into a scowl. Or his dark eyes shining with mischief as they caressed my face, my cheeks, my lips. He never spoke. But I awoke drowning in fresh sorrow.

"With all due respect, Yer Majesty." Sharron tore off a leg of the bird and held it out. "Sofia told me ye haven't been eatin'. Ye need your strength."

I took the warm drumstick by the knobby end and stared at it. "You can call me Veronica."

"All right then, *Queen* Veronica."

Her emphasis on my title caused me to lift my eyes to her challenging gaze. "Did you need something, Mrs. Rosetti, or did Sofia send you in here to give motherly advice?"

She ignored my tone and continued as if I hadn't spoken. "Yer Majesty, many of us have lost loved ones these last days. Mags Benior was a dear friend." Sharron's voice broke. The earthquake had injured and killed many, including the French chef who made the best blueberry pancakes on the planet. Mags had been my friend too, but I didn't have room in my soul to feel that loss.

I focused on stripping pieces of skin from the bird. Maybe that was why I spent so much time in the infirmary tent. Doc Benior understood me. We didn't speak, because there were no words to express losing your Called partner. Your heart.

Her voice once again strong, Sharron continued her speech. "We must go on. Not despite our loved one's deaths, but because of them."

Easy for her to say; her husband was injured but alive. Pinching off a piece of dark meat, I slipped it between my lips and forced myself to chew and swallow.

"Look at me, sweet girl."

Almost against my will, I raised my eyes to meet Sharron's shimmering gaze. "Love never dies. And because of that, we live on." My nose stung as she reached over and took my free hand, squeezing my fingers tight. "Honor him, Vee. As much as you loved Jamie, honor him with an equally passionate life."

A shudder tore through me, and I pressed a fist to my mouth. I couldn't let it out. If I did, I might not ever stop. Shooting to my feet, I dropped the drumstick and stumbled out of the tent. And I ran. Ran as fast as my feet would take me, past groups of staring people, past the makeshift paddock full of livestock, and into the burnt-out countryside beyond. Leaping a jagged tear in the earth, I sprinted past gnarled trees burnt to a crisp by the righteous fire that had destroyed the witch's curse, the Edritch Limbus; their blackened carcasses in relief to the pristine snow made it appear as if the color had leached from the world.

I pushed my legs faster, running until I reached the edge of the River Doon and the chasm where the Brig o' Doon had been, and then fell to my knees. My grief went deep; past bone and sinew, permeating my organs and blackening my soul. It soaked the earth beneath me and echoed in the mists that coiled among the treetops every morning, moaning on the wind.

But not me. I'd refused to give voice to the pain, to let it take me. Now it rose up—the monster I could no longer control— and I lifted my face to the snowfall, a cry tearing from deep inside. Balling my hands into fists, I sobbed his name. "Jaaamiiieee!"

I cried until the tears closed my throat, and I collapsed in on myself. I'd always thought if a loved one passed on, they could visit you in spirit—that God would allow it in times of need. But I didn't feel Jamie's spirit lingering with me. In fact, it seemed as if he himself might actually appear any minute. Like I could glance over my shoulder and he'd come sauntering up, that too-confident smirk tilting his lips. But that would never happen again.

Lifting my head, I stared across the empty chasm and at the river rushing below. Water roared and churned in angry swirls over sharp rocks, their jagged points beckoning, promising a swift death. A shudder vibrated through me. If the fall didn't kill me, with my heavy clothing, the current would suck me under and I wouldn't fight it.

Fight. The word echoed in my head until it morphed into the last words Jamie spoke to me. *"Verranica, one of us will live to fight another day, and that must be you."* He'd then pressed his lips against my forehead. *"The Protector will be with you."*

He'd wanted me to fight. Clutching the wet grass where the river spray had melted the snow, I leaned forward and peered over the edge of the ravine. Stubby trees and limestone shelves jutted out from the slope. But if I took a running leap, I could clear it. Jumping would be quick and easy . . . and horribly selfish.

Giving up was not an option. I'd always said my dad took the easy way out, the completely self-serving path, by leaving when things got hard. I refused to do the same.

I leaned back and balled my hands into fists. The Protector had chosen me. Jamie had chosen me. No matter how much it hurt, I would find a way to honor that by choosing to live, to fight, and be the queen he believed I could be. Not some cop-out Juliet who couldn't live without her Romeo. I'd always hated that story.

Reclining back on my haunches, I took the multicolored ribbons I always carried from my pocket and tugged the purple one from the knot. When I'd researched handfasting, I'd read that the purple represented strength, honor, and sanctity.

Stretching an arm over the ravine, I held out the ribbon, the purple strand flying in the breeze as the words ripped from my chest like a vow. "I promise you, my heart." My voice broke on a sob, but I pushed through. "By whatever means necessary, I *will* defeat your murderer and save our kingdom!"

The sun broke through the clouds as I released the ribbon. It floated, suspended for a moment before a gust of wind caught it, taking it up, up, up. Astonished, I watched it fly against the fall of flurries and then curl into a spiral and drop. Scrabbling on my hands and knees, I peered over the edge and searched the cliff face until I spotted the scrap of purple resting on a rock shelf.

The clouds shifted again and a ray of light glinted on an object buried in the snow beside the ribbon. Falling flat on my stomach, I strained to reach the ledge, rocks and dirt tumbling with me. Unable to see, I rifled through stones and hunks of frozen mud until something hard and cold brushed my fingertips. I scooped it up along with a handful of snow. Yanking my arm back, I sat up and fell on my backside, opening my trembling fist. Gold and crimson sparkled with flecks of ice. I gasped as tears streamed down my cheeks, and I stared in wonder at the most beautiful sight I'd ever laid eyes on—the ruby Ring of Aontacht.

Perhaps Jamie's spirit was with me after all.

CHAPTER 4

Jamie

MacTavish, Campbell, Lockhart...

I recited the names of our people in my head, a trick Duncan and I had devised as kids to distract us when we were sick or in pain.

MacG—

Knuckles smashed into my nose and my head snapped back with a crack. I straightened and licked the warm fluid gushing over my lips. After days of being beaten to a bloody pulp, I'd become disturbingly accustomed to the metallic taste. I swallowed, and for the hundredth time considered why I wasn't dead.

While I placed considerable faith in the Protector to keep me alive, the irony of escaping the gallows only to be pummeled to death by a mindless dimwit had not escaped me. Before I could brace, Sean MacNally's fist slammed into my already massacred ribs like a hammer, pushing the air from my lungs and stealing my vision.

Saints! I bit the inside of my cheek, forcing myself to stay alert. *Rosetti . . . MacPhee . . . Fairshaw.* Blacking-out was not an option. The last time I'd lost consciousness, I'd awoken as a knife sliced open my chest. That was when the true torment began.

"Good Lord, MacCrae, would it kill ye to show a bit o' weakness," Sean hissed in my ear before he rammed the butt of his knife in the precise spot where he'd just fractured my rib. My knees buckled as the bone broke loose, ripping a path of fire through my insides. Slowly, the pain fanned out, less sharp but no less horrendous, and I became aware of the shackles ripping the flesh from my wrists as they bore my weight.

I sank lower and lower until I floated weightless, swallowed by warmth. The agony abated, and I opened my eyes to aqua blue, sunlight shimmering through translucent waters. Just like the postcard of the Caribbean Sea Veronica had shown me. Weightless, I moved my arms through the silken texture and spun in a circle to find her there, floating, eyes shining brighter than the turquoise surrounding us, her dark hair fanned around her face in mermaid-like waves. Then she smiled; that beautiful smile that had the power to ignite my soul. She reached out. My arms moved with excruciating slowness as red drops descended like rain. Faster and faster, their crimson spread through the blue. I kicked forward and yelled her name, water flooding my lungs.

With a gasp, my eyes popped open and I choked as icy liquid cascaded over my head and into my mouth. The loss of her felt like a tiny death. But she still lived and I would keep fighting. For her.

"I'm awake, blast it!" I regained my feet and shook my soaked hair, droplets of water and blood flying.

"So he does speak." Sean dropped the bucket with a plunk.

"There's a difference between speakin' and cryin', MacNally, as ye'll do well to remember when I get my hands on ye." For days, I'd kept my silence, afraid if I made a peep I may never stop screaming.

Sean's beady eyes narrowed, his mouth taking on a cruel set that should've had me shaking. The man had caused me more suffering in the last days than a body should experience over a lifetime. He stalked forward, grasped my shoulder in one hand and my arm in the other, and wrenched them in opposite directions, effectively tearing the ligament around my collarbone. I let the pain drive me. Leaning into his face, I growled, "I will kill you."

"Now, now, my sweet prince, Sean is only followin' orders."

Relief washed through me at the sound of the witch's voice. And I hated myself for it. Hated my weakness. The part of me that knew she brought respite, however brief, and craved her presence.

Sean pushed a single finger against the arm hanging limp in the shackles above my head and laughed. I swallowed a groan as black closed in on me again. Inhaling as deeply as my busted rib would allow, my head began to clear. I could not let my guard down now.

"That will be all, Sean darlin'." Addie caressed Sean's bearded face and gazed into his bloodshot eyes. He reached for her waist, but she stepped back. "Not yet, young man. But ye've earned a meal and a rest. Run along." She flicked her fingers toward the door and turned, her violet gaze raking over me. "It's my turn to play."

Sean marched out the door and shut it behind him. Clearly, he was under her spell, but his hatred for me was real, which served to fuel the witch's evil inside him and likely strengthened her hold on his mind.

Addie slinked toward me and my heart accelerated. She seemed to want to take her centuries-old grudge against

Doon out on me personally, as if hurting me could bring back her mother and sisters, or her perceived claim to the throne through the affections of King Angus. Underestimating her would be a grave mistake.

And yet, with every step she took, my anticipation grew for the magic that would mend my bones and flesh, and take away the agony of the injuries clawing through me with unbearable intensity. Muscles trembling, I closed my eyes against her, drawing on the vision of Veronica's face. Her smile.

The witch stopped so close, I could feel her breath on my neck. "I know . . ." Fingers trailed down my cheekbone to brush against my lips. "I know you want what I can give you, James. I feel you shaking. But first, tell me . . . Gideon just completed an extensive search of the catacombs, and they're clear. Tell me where she is. Where are your people hiding?"

"I've told ye. I dinna know. Your men caught me before I could find them myself."

She pressed close, and the heat of her body against my damp skin made me shudder. "But you must have some ideas. Hmm?"

When I was silent, she walked her fingers along my chest, up to my injured shoulder. The heat of her magic penetrated muscle and bone, her painted nails digging into my flesh. I clamped my teeth together to keep from sighing in relief as the ligaments and bones snapped back into place.

"I have more where that came from, young prince." She took a step back and smoothed her hands down the silk hugging her hips. At first glance she was beautiful, but all one had to do was look beyond the surface to see her true nature—the evil lurking beneath the façade. I knew her plan, had figured it out the first day Sean had beat me senseless and she'd then healed me with her sick, sweet words and a wave of her hand. She couldn't enthrall me like the rest because I'd already pledged to the true queen, but she could condition me; break me down and then build me up until I became her slave.

Much like I'd trained Veronica's pup with a sharp word and the reward of a bit of bacon, the witch had me salivating for what she could provide. But I was no dog. I would accept her healing, if only to stay alive, and then I would turn on her with a vengeance.

Addie must have seen the set of my jaw or the renewed determination in my eyes, because she ran her fingers down my bare chest. "If it's possible, I think ye are even more attractive beaten down as ye are now. All covered in blood and sweat."

Her touch left a trail of fire, scorching my flesh. I hissed through my teeth and stared at the arched beams above her head, reigning in my reaction. I refused to give her the satisfaction, but the trick of reciting Doonian names was of no help. The burning continued in loops and swirls across my left pectoral muscle as the witch muttered under her breath.

Exhaling the stench of my melting flesh, I lowered my gaze to the corner of the antechamber where I'd kissed Veronica for the last time, right after I'd given her the ribbons for our handfasting. It was a moment I'd relived over and over again in this room to push out my new reality, but as much as it grieved me, the memory had lost its sharpness, becoming fuzzy around the edges like a dream I'd invented in my head.

"There, all finished." Addie lifted her hand from my smoldering chest and brushed her palms together in satisfaction. "Take a look at my masterpiece, young James."

When I leveled my gaze on the witch's face, her smile resembled that blasted fictional cat from one of my brother's books—wide and satisfied. Shutting out all emotion, I met her eyes, but did not look at her handiwork on my chest.

"I do so enjoy the strong, stolid Jamie, but I need the care-free young man to appreciate my art." She waved her hand and the scalding pain faded to a residual sting. "I have more healin' where tha' came from, and I'll remove your shackles and perhaps give ye a real bed for the night. All I ask is that ye look."

At the mention of healing, all my wounds throbbed in a symphony of agony. My legs buckled and the metal cuffs cut into my lacerated wrists. An end to the torment and a good night's sleep was more than I could resist. Regaining my feet, I glanced down at my chest to find a snake swallowing its own tail branded into my skin. An ouroboros. The serpent in a perpetual circle had been a symbol for witchery in Doon for generations.

Anger erupted from my core, pure and hot. I could not endure having her evil mark upon my flesh forever. With a swell of strength, I surged toward her, the chains screeching as I strained against them. "Take it off, now!"

Startled, she stumbled back a step. I bared my teeth in a growl that was more primal than intelligent, and a dark smile lit her face, her eyes glowing vivid violet. My reaction had been her goal; the outburst that Sean, with his continuous beatings, had not been able to evoke from me.

Breathing heavily, I clenched my jaw and stepped back, fighting to regain my internal equilibrium. *Protector, help me. I cannot let her turn me into her animal. I am Prince James Thomas Kellan MacCrae, the fourth. The queen's betrothed and the future king of Doon. My soul belongs to you. My heart belongs to Vee. And my life belongs to Doon.*

"Are you *praying*?" Addie spit out the word like a rancid piece of meat, causing a droplet of her spit to hit my face.

Realizing too late that I'd been mouthing my plea, I clamped my lips shut and raised a challenging gaze. Nothing she could do would stop me.

She gave her wrist a quick flick and a black, scaly snake with fangs bared flew from her hand. I jerked back as it coiled around my arm, sinking its tiny, dagger-like teeth into my skin. With my arms positioned above my head, I was eye-level with the animal wrapped around my bicep. I bit the inside of my cheek as the muscles of its body contracted and it attacked me, fangs sinking in over and over, chewing through my flesh.

I turned away. *It isn't real. It isn't real.* The gnawing stopped, and when I looked back, it was as if the snake had fused with my skin, leaving another ouroboros branded around my bicep.

"I could cover your body with them to remind you that you are mine."

She dragged the tip of her fingernail around the fresh brand, and all the fight left me. Crashing after my rush of adrenaline, I slumped in exhaustion. Unable even to keep my head upright, I let it loll against my shoulder as Addie continued her rant.

"Your Protector will no' save you, nor will your tiny queen, because she believes ye are dead. She's probably already chosen some other young buck to be her consort. Girls like that cannot bear to be alone."

Whether Veronica assumed me dead or no', I knew better than to believe she'd moved on. But Addie had no conception of the Calling, love, or family. "Duncan will come for me."

Her laugh grated like stone against stone. "That's right, you don't know!" She clapped her hands together, her smile widening before turning into a sneer. "Your brother is gone."

Panic squeezed my chest and I lifted my head. "What do ye mean, gone?"

"He abandoned you. Crossed the Brig o' Doon wi' a third of your precious kingdom."

"Yer lying." But as soon as I spoke, I remembered Vee's vision. The Protector had shown her that either Duncan or I would need to leave in order to save Doon. "He'll come back. My brother will come back for me."

"With the Brig o' Doon destroyed? Doubtful."

"The mountain pass . . ."

"Blocked." She shrugged and pivoted on her heel. She was halfway across the room before she turned back. "Don't you see, James? You're completely alone."

I didn't respond, but my gut tightened as I watched her slink away, taking my hope of relief with her.

She lifted the single lantern from its hook by the door and then said over her shoulder, "I've changed my mind about healing you tonight. You can hang there and rot."

Ensconced in utter darkness, I tried to fight off desperation. My entire body ached from being unable to move more than a few inches. My wounds and broken bones throbbed with every beat of my heart, and panic began to set in. No one knew I'd survived. They weren't coming for me. The flame of hope that had fired my resistance dimmed.

I let my head fall between my shoulders, the strain on my arms and back near unbearable. I didn't know how much more I could withstand. But I knew I could no' let Addie use me as a weapon. Death would be preferable to becoming her pawn.

Squeezing my eyes closed, lest my addled brain play tricks with the shadows, I pleaded with the Protector. *Please, protect my brother and those with him on the other side. Keep Veronica in your care every moment. Give her wisdom and strength to lead and find a way to take back our kingdom.*

My queen was captivatingly beautiful, but she was also the most pig-headed, determined, brilliant woman I'd ever met. If anyone could keep Doon from ruin, it was her.

Even if it is without me.

CHAPTER 5

Duncan

Mackenna's fingers tightened around mine. Her cool touch caused my heart to speed ever so slightly, and I suppressed a shiver. So as not to be intimidating, I sat on the divan in the parlor of Dunbrae Cottage opposite the wee lass claiming to have materialized from half a world away.

"Tell us what transpired," I coaxed. "Be as exact as you can in your account. Any detail—no matter how small—could be of importance."

Cheska Santos nodded and raised her delicate hand to sweep the dark fringe of hair from her eyes. Despite the nervous gesture, her gaze was clear as she began to tell her story.

"This morning I woke up in my bed in Tayabas, which is a little over three hours from the capital. Although I didn't have anything specific I needed to do, I felt an urgency to go out. It was colder than usual, so I dressed in layers. My parents had already left for work, so I wrote them a note to tell them not to worry—that I was fine and that I loved them. I knew it was an odd thing to write at the time, but it seemed right."

She paused, her somber gaze darting between Mackenna and myself as if daring us to contradict her. Mackenna offered her an encouraging smile. "Please don't stress out about what you did. No one's going to judge you. Everyone here's been down the rabbit hole at least once."

The girl laughed in response. "I do feel like Alice right about now. What happened next was curious indeed. When I left my house, I walked until I reached Malagonlong Bridge, which crosses the Dumacaa River. It's a historic landmark because it was built during the Spanish colonial era, but the stone arches are stained from age and overgrown with plants.

"When I was a small child, my cousin told me that the ghosts of our ancestors, who were forced to build the bridge, still roamed the structure. So I always went out of my way to avoid it. But this morning, it called to me . . . It might have been the ghosts, or possibly the bridge itself. Either way, I felt compelled to cross."

Cheska stood, as if caught up in the moment. At full height, her dark head was level with my abdomen. Having no people of Filipino ethnicity in Doon, the closest person to her coloring was Sofia Rosetti. The girl's skin was darker, her hair straighter, eyes more exotic in their almond shape than the Scotch-Italian girl from home, but like Sofia, her diminutive stature contained a brave spirit.

"As I stepped onto the ancient stones, disembodied voices began to wail. I wanted to turn and run but I couldn't move, except to walk forward. When I was about halfway across, the bridge began to shimmer with light. The wailing turned to thunder, and as the light took shape I realized I was not in the presence of ghosts but of angels. The light and noise grew with each step until I had to shut my eyes and cover my ears to continue." The girl lifted her hands to her face in demonstration. "My body felt light, as if I were about to float way.

"At some point, I must have dropped to my knees. I remember laying my face against the mossy stones. I'm not sure how long I stayed prostrate on the bridge—it felt like both hours and seconds. As if the laws of time and nature no longer applied.

"Suddenly, the sensations stopped. When I looked about, I was kneeling on a grassy bank, facing an unfamiliar river and Malagonlong Bridge was nowhere to be seen. The air was much colder than in Tayabas. Although clearly not Wonderland, I knew immediately that something fantastical had happened. And that's when Mrs. Fairshaw found me on the banks of the River Doon in Scotland."

Caledonia, who was nearly a full head taller than Cheska, stood and placed a matronly arm round the girl's shoulders. "The poor, wee thing asked where she was, and I told her."

Cheska nodded. "I could scarcely believe it."

Stepping up behind us, Fiona said in a low voice not meant to be overheard by our new guest, "Despite her experience, she seems remarkably clear-witted."

Maybe a wee bit too clear . . . The soldier in me cautioned against accepting the girl blindly at her word. Squaring my shoulders, I leveled my gaze on the foreigner. "Does what happened scare you?"

"A little." She burst into a wide, earnest smile. "But, you see, I'm addicted to this video game, Tussle of Tribes. It's set in this medieval/Middle-Earth-type fantasy world. The first time I played it, I knew I was destined for something great. This is it. I can't explain how I know, but I *am* certain."

The force of her conviction helped to alleviate my concerns. After all, Mackenna and Queen Veronica had arrived in Doon much the same way—suddenly, but with a sense it was where they were supposed to be. If Cheska Santos had been called here, then she had an important role to play in saving our kingdom. As to what that role was, hopefully the Protector would show us in due time.

In the pause that followed, Mackenna looked from Cheska to me to Fiona and then to Caledonia. "What do we do next?"

"I'd like to get Ches settled," Fiona stated. "At Rose Petal Lodge."

Upon our arrival in Alloway, Fiona had readily taken up the tasks of feeding and sheltering our group. Using funds from the MacCrae trust, she'd rented several cottages in the vicinity, a paddock and barn for Mabel, a patch of land for a garden, and a large dining hall where the people would take their meals. She'd also made a roster of the Doonians who had managed to cross the Brig o' Doon before the collapse, complete with an inventory of skillsets—not that there was much useable among the forty-odd group of mostly children and elderly citizens. Still, Fiona made the best of what we had, dividing countrymen into groups for cooking, cleaning, and laundry.

Not only did she run things, she also pitched in at every opportunity, often engaged from sunrise until well past sunset. I recognized the avoidance tactic all too well. I'd used it when Mackenna had abandoned me on the Brig o' Doon to pursue her career in the modern world. I'd erroneously thought if I stayed busy enough, I wouldn't have to think about the possibility of never seeing her again. It was the same way now with Fiona in regards to Fergus.

I wanted to tell her it wouldn't work. But from the determined gleam in her green eyes, I suspected she already knew. Instead, I rose and thanked my dear friend for her service.

As Fiona and Cheska prepared to leave, Caledonia, obviously reluctant to abandon her new charge, hesitated in front of me. "By your leave, Your Highness, I'll go with them. Help the lass settle in."

It took me a moment to comprehend that Caledonia Fairshaw had addressed me, as unaccustomed as I was to thinking of myself as a ruler. As the second son, I'd made peace long ago with a life of military service. But with things in Doon unsure, the people looked to me for guidance. To lead them.

"Of course," I replied, hoping the preceding pause hadn't been as awkward as it felt.

As the two women led Cheska from the library, the small girl halted at the doorway. She turned back to regard Mackenna and me with her unwavering gaze. "There is one more thing you must know. The unseen voices . . . The angels weren't just wailing. Their sound of warning and thunder—it was a battle cry. War is coming."

Cheska set her shoulders and, with a nod of parting, left Dunbrae Cottage. Despite her size, the newest addition to our group possessed the heart of a lion . . . of a Doonian.

Once they were out of earshot, Mackenna frowned. "What do you think about Cheska? I know that video game she's talking about—it's got castles and witches and stuff. What a crazy coincidence."

Before I could reply, she continued. "Do you think Fiona told her about Doon?"

"Fiona wouldna. She'd defer to me," I replied. "The girl does tell a compelling story, but even if we believe her, we should figure out what's going on before we reveal the secrets of our kingdom."

The Doonians who had been watching the exchange began to disperse. Some went to market, some to oversee the progress of the bridge, while others tended to the planting of a garden. The dozens of children who'd crossed the bridge before its collapse settled in for their lessons, which were held at Dunbrae Cottage under the astute tutelage of Mrs. Alsberg, the baker's wife. She had managed to escape with her twin daughters, but the fate of her husband, who'd been a few paces behind, was still uncertain.

As Mackenna and I stepped into the mottled sunlight of the cottage garden, I remembered the other stranger the day had brought us: Alasdair. Were both the auld man and the foreign girl the signs we'd asked for on the beach? Or was one of them a decoy sent by our enemy to confuse and distract us from our purpose?

The more I thought about it, the more certain I felt that Cheska was who she claimed to be. But Alasdair was a puzzle that needed solving before any more lives were placed at risk. As if Mackenna was privy to my thoughts, she tugged my arm so that I stopped. Leaning into me, she whispered, "What are we going to do with the mysterious man? I think we should keep him on lockdown until we figure out what his agenda is."

"Agreed. I'll assign a couple of the guard to watch o'er him." I mentally reviewed the handful of auld yet able-bodied men who made up my new guard and choose two that would be conscientious and discreet.

Incapable of hiding the eagerness in her voice, she suggested, "You could ask Eòran to do it."

"I could," I replied, pretending to consider the request. "But he won't."

She snorted. "A girl can dream."

Since coming to Alloway, this was the longest the guard had let my girlfriend out of his sight. If he'd been a wee bit younger and taller, I might have been suspicious of his motives. However, Eòran's diligence as self-appointed protector, while it annoyed Mackenna to no end, provided me with immeasurable comfort.

Toward the end of my musing, I realized Mackenna was waiting for me to look at her. When I did, she searched my face, her fathomless gray eyes boring into me as her features twisted into concern.

"Duncan," she began, "we haven't really talked about what happened before we crossed the bridge. Are you still mad at me?"

"What for?" I asked cautiously.

Letting go of my arm, she paced toward the stone bench in the center of the garden and stopped, facing away from me. The wind buffeted her motionless body, tugging at her shawl and hair. "Because you couldn't go after your brother. Because Vee forced you to lead the people out of Doon."

She turned to face me. There was a question in her eyes— the same one that was there every time she'd looked at me since our arrival in Alloway, the one we were both afraid to speak. *Do you think Jamie is alive?* The truth was, until I saw his grave with my own eyes, I could not afford to believe otherwise.

Other unspoken questions tumbled into the space between us. What of Veronica? How many people had died trying to escape? Would we ever return home, and if so would there be any Doonians to greet us?

I had no answers to give, only questions of my own . . . about the strength of my faith and the purpose of this new trial.

My stomach twisted, tangling my insides. I stuffed my reaction into the hole in my spirit—I didn't want to think about this. Not now, not ever.

Instead I watched as a shiver trembled its way up Mackenna's spine. Going to her, I pressed my chest against her back. My heartbeat synchronized with hers as I wrapped my arms around her shoulders and brushed my lips against the side of her neck.

After a moment, Mackenna discarded her unspoken questions with a small sigh. "So we're okay?" She twisted in my arms so that we were toe to toe.

"Aye, woman. We're *okay*."

Her enchanting lips curled into a half smile. "Prove it."

My pulse stuttered as she reached for me. Although her hands were perpetually cold, her fingers inflamed my body as she wound them around my neck.

I caressed the downy skin of her jaw with my hand. Mackenna was so soft and elegant, at times I felt overlarge and awkward when I touched her with my rough, fumbling hands— like the giant who went about grunting *fee-fi-fo-fum*. But each time my mouth pressed against hers, the self-awareness drained away as I dissolved into her, evaporating into nothing so that her love could rebuild me one atom at a time into the best version of myself.

Maybe this version would be able to let go of his secret resentment. If not, the least I could do was lose myself in what she offered.

Sometime later, after my universe had been decimated and rebuilt multiple times, she pulled back with a contented "Holy Hammerstein." Her glorious eyes were large and shining as she rested her hand against my pounding chest. "I love you."

It was a sort of miracle, that this vibrant, talented lass had accepted my heart and given me hers in return. I'd been seeking her for nearly the whole of our lives. I still remembered the first time I saw her, not as part of the Calling but in the flesh at Castle MacCrae. I'd heard that two foreigners had been apprehended near the coliseum, a dark-haired lass and her brash, ginger-haired friend. I instantly knew it was her. I'd been planning to go find her at the Centennial, but somehow she'd come to me first. Perhaps our love had been too strong to wait for the opening of the Brig o' Doon . . .

I barely recalled rushing down the castle corridors to the antechamber where Jamie was interrogating her.

Pausing at the doorway, I tried in vain to collect myself. It was then that I heard Jamie's accusations of witchery. A strange female voice challenged him and Jamie ordered the lasses back to the dungeon. Next, I heard her voice—a voice I would recognize in any world, in any age, and in any circumstance. My love.

Mackenna hadn't come to Doon as an agent of the witch; she was here because she was mine.

I burst into the antechamber—"A word, brother"—intent on setting Jamie straight and fully expecting Mackenna to make a gesture of recognition, to gasp or call out "Finn," the name she knew me by as a child, but she remained mute.

My brother did not. "Not now, Duncan."

I wasn't fooled by his expression. He'd been practicing his impassive face ever since he understood he was to be the future ruler of Doon. "These wee lasses are—"

Jamie's face turned as dark as a thundercloud. He shot to his feet and grabbed me by the arm. For an instant I imagined punching him in his sanctimonious face, but my second thought, that of Mackenna, enabled me to control my temper and allow him to pull me into the alcove.

As soon as we cleared the room, Jamie leaned in, hissing, "What are ye doing, Duncan?"

"They're no' who you think," I whispered back.

"Who are they, then?" He glared at me impatiently. "If ye know, speak."

I opened my mouth to explain, but words failed me. As boys, Jamie had made fun of the wee friend I played with at every opportunity, who was not only invisible but also female. I never questioned why I was the only one to see her, or why, when she appeared, the small creek and bridge in the Royal Gardens seemed to transform into a raging river and the Brig o' Doon.

"Well?" Jamie barked.

He didn't believe in Callings—our belief that your true love could be called to you across the portal that hid our kingdom from the rest of the world. During lessons in Doonian history, he'd been very vocal about his thoughts on the matter. Why would he put any credence in my Calling? "Well," I hedged, careful to keep my voice low. "I've a feeling those lasses are not in league with the Witch o' Doon. I think they were sent here on purpose."

"Duncan, I can't risk the safety of our kingdom based on your feelings." He moved to brush passed me, but I blocked the doorway. *There were advantages to being the little-yet-big-in-stature brother.*

Jamie sighed. "Get out of my way."

"Please dinna send those lasses to the dungeon. I'll be responsible for them. Remand them to my care—and to Fergus's. Please, brother."

He hesitated. *The only thing I did more infrequently than oppose him was beg. I was content to serve my older sibling and future king, and was loyal beyond measure. Jamie knew this.*

With a nod, he waited for me to give way and let him pass. Reassembling his impassive expression, he stepped into the antechamber, stating, "I'm releasing you both into the custody of Fergus and my brother, Prince Duncan, until such time that your trial can be conducted."

"But Laird—" Gideon sputtered.

Jamie's gaze shut him up. "Gideon, I require your assistance with the king." He strode from the room with Gideon following obediently at his heel. *True to his word, he'd handed the lasses over to Fergus's and my care. My heart began to thunder with anticipation. Suddenly I was so nervous that I had to approach the dark-haired girl first to give my nerves a chance to settle. I extended my left arm to her before turning toward the lass with the glowing red hair.*

"Fear not, m'ladies. You are under the protection of Duncan Rhys Finnean MacCrae, Prince o' Doon, and no harm will come to you. I swear it on m' life." I reached for Mackenna, who swatted my arm away.

"Ugh. Get away from me, you big ogre." Rather than gratitude, she surveyed me with contempt. For a moment I just stared at her luminous gray eyes searching for some sign of recognition, no matter how small. But alas, she had no idea who I was. I wasn't sure if she had truly forgotten me or if some aspect of her stubborn memory refused to see what was right in front of her.

As I led her and her friend away, I realized that it didn't matter. We were destined to be together and, therefore, I would make her fall incurably in love with me. Soon, she would look at me, her eyes shining with affection as she confessed her love. And we would live happily ever after, just like in the best of stories.

Mackenna's cool hands clasped the sides of my face. "Hey. Where'd you go?"

I gazed into her shining eyes and chuckled. "I was thinkin' about the first time I saw ye in Doon—before I escorted you to my chambers—when you swatted me away and called me an ogre."

"Oh, gosh." She ducked her head, burying it against my chest. Her ginger hair smelled so strongly of strawberries that my mouth began to water. "I'm so sorry about that."

Caressing her hair, I murmured, "Dinna let it trouble ye, woman. I love you too."

Mackenna Reid was mine and there was nothing in any world, in any age, or in any circumstance that would break us apart.

CHAPTER 6

Mackenna

Kissing Duncan was like losing and finding myself in the same instant. The moment his lips touched down, the mysteries of the universe—like quantum physics and the intricacies of Sondheim musicals—were within my grasp. But as the kiss went on, his presence pushed all other thought away until there was just him and only this. The boy was seriously addictive.

I came up for air, my heart bursting with one of my favorite songs from *RENT*. "Can we just stay like this?" *There's only now.* I brushed my mouth against his, once . . . "I'm not talking forever—" *There's only here.* Twice . . . "Just today." A third time . . . *Give in to love or live in fear.* "Maybe tomorrow too."

"Aye." Tucking me against his chest, Duncan rested his head on top of mine with a sigh.

Usually I tried to curb my PDA impulses out of respect for Fiona and the other Doonians, but we seemed to be plagued by an abundance of Scots and not nearly enough alone time. When we were newly stranded in Alloway, Duncan's displaced countrymen had followed him around like a flock of theater intern newbs. Not that I blamed them. They were scared, wounded, separated from loved ones, and each coping with the trauma of the situation in their own way.

As the shock wore off, a few others, like Fiona, Caledonia, and Rabbie, stepped up to help bear the burden of leadership.

Raibeart MacGregor—affectionately known as wee Rabbie—had been the only other soldier to make it out. Although he'd been Duncan's apprentice with the guard for less than a month, like most Scotsmen, what he lacked in experience he made up for in enthusiasm. Wee Rabbie was built like a boulder—a super-nice, very conscientious boulder.

Said boulder cleared his throat loudly as he focused pointedly away from where Duncan and I were swapping saliva. Like many Scottish boys in their late teens, Rabbie's natural complexion was a mottled shade of pink that had a tendency to turn scarlet with emotion. As someone who'd battled the curse of the ginger all my life, I took pity on the blushing guard and broke away from Duncan with a hasty apology.

"M'Laird," Rabbie stammered, pretending that I didn't exist. "Eòran sent me for ye. The gentleman in his custody is in need of relief."

From the street beyond the garden's privacy hedge, a voice clarified, "I've got ta see the wizard."

Laughing, I explained the use of slang and the euphemism. Alasdair certainly had inherited the MacCrae wit.

With a sigh, Duncan ran his hand through his hair so that it stuck out at odd angles. It was longer than he typically wore it, but my boyfriend had more important things on his mind than a haircut—like being responsible for a hundred-plus people in a strange new land and finding a way to return home.

From across the hedge Alasdair's voice whined, "I'm gonna wet m' trousers if ye don't get me to a privy, m'Laird!"

A nod to Rabbie sent him scurrying away to prevent Alasdair from doing something drastic. Still smirking over the old man's cheeky response, Duncan captured a tendril of my hair and tucked it behind my ear. "What do ye think—should we leave Alasdair to wee Rabbie and pick up where we left off?"

Tempting as it was, we still had no idea whether the old man was friend or foe. Reluctant to transition back into real life, I leaned in for one final kiss. "You should go. Why don't you take Alasdair to Oz, and then get him settled in the guys' dorm. I'll go check on Cheska."

Duncan open his mouth, but was cut off before he could speak. "Unhand me, laddie," Alasdair insisted. "I mean ta relieve m'self one way or another!"

With a groan of regret, Duncan jogged off. Not wanting to know if Alasdair made good on his threats, I waited in the garden until the guys were good and gone.

The girls' dorm, Rose Petal Cottage, was in the opposite direction of the guys' housing, Thornfield Lodge, with Aunt Gracie's place right smack between the two. The journey to Rose Petal took less than five minutes. It was a lovely walk down the path that overlooked the river, but one I would forever associate with my best friend.

In a weird way, the journey reminded me of summers between seventh and twelfth grades spent at drama camp. Those six weeks were the longest, most exhilarating weeks of my life. Exhilarating because I got to perform in the camp showcase, first in the ensemble then as a soloist; long because I missed Vee every minute of every day.

Each time I made the trek, the construction of the new bridge reemphasized the absence of Vee, as if the two things were one and the same. I guess in some ways they were. They both symbolized Doon and both were inaccessible. Although restoration work had begun simultaneously on both banks, the construction had been cordoned off with police tape to keep the gawkers and everyone else back.

The media had attributed the disappearance to a freak earthquake that broke the bridge apart and caused a river surge that carried off the debris—which, to me, sounded more preposterous than an evil witch making it vanish.

After another dozen steps, I veered away from the river, following the trail that would lead me to the cottage's back door. Before I could knock, Greta flung the door open, nearly running me over in her rush to get outside.

"Whoa! What's the rush? Is it SpaghettiOs day or something?"

"Sorry," she chirped as she skidded to a halt with an infectious smile. "Canna be late fer afternoon lessons."

Without Lachlan, Greta had stepped up as the leader of the Crew—the Doonian equivalent of a mini-me service organization sponsored by Jamie himself. Her number-one responsibility was getting the other members to attend our improvised school. Which was easier said than done, especially when it came to those over the age of nine. Although the lure of SpaghettiOs did wonders to keep them in line.

"Do you need some help rounding the others up?" Tween wrangling had become one of my unofficial tasks.

"Nay, ma'am. Everyone's in attendance. We canna wait to start the new course after dinner." Despite her throat nearly being slit by Adelaide's henchman when the witch had overtaken Doon, the girl had bounced back from the near-death experience without any discernable scarring. She beamed at me, waiting for me to take the cue and ask what had her pantaloons in a bunch. I knew what would do it for me—Broadway karaoke—but Greta was not a drama geek.

"What are you learning this afternoon?"

"Well," the girl drawled as she bounced on the balls of her feet. "Missus Alsberg said we were unmanageable in the classroom, so Prince Duncan suggested we take up physical education in the afternoons."

Really? That's what all the fuss was about? PE? In my world, PE had been a punishment straight from the pits of Mordor.

"Okay. You'd better hurry then." I swallowed a laugh as Greta bolted past me. "Have fun."

"I'm sure we will, ma'am," she replied as she jogged down the path toward the river. "We're learnin' combat trainin' with actual weapons!"

What? By the time that little grenade registered in my consciousness, Greta was long gone. Had I heard her right? Had Duncan suggested teaching children to fight with *real weapons*? Prince or no, the boy had some explaining to do. Deciding Cheska could wait, I set off to find my boyfriend.

As I backtracked along the river, I saw them—two boys, sitting on the bench at the mouth of the Brig o' Doon where Vee and I had sat just moments before we'd crossed over for the first time. I can't say what first captured my attention, perhaps it was the way these two sat huddled: close and woefully underdressed for the temperature, their dark complexions ashy from cold.

As I moved closer, I noticed one boy was older than the other. His feet were bare, while the younger one wore discolored slippers. Their clothes appeared to be a hodgepodge of mismatched, threadbare hand-me-downs that were either too big or too small. Nobody dressed that way unless they were homeless, not even in the Midwest.

"Excuse me—" I began, and then paused as two dark heads slowly turned to stare at me, their bloodshot, ebony eyes wide with amazement. "Are you guys okay?"

The older boy swallowed so that his Adam's apple bobbed against his chalky throat. "Please, miss, is this heaven?"

"Heaven?" For a moment, I was dumbfounded by the oddness of the question. "No, you're in Alloway."

The same boy, whom I deduced was the spokesperson for the duo, frowned. "Is that in Africa?"

Something clicked. The clothes, the odd cadence to their English—these boys were definitely not from these parts. "No. Scotland."

The older boy turned to the younger one, his eyes and smile bright. "Did you hear that, Jeremiah? We are no longer in Africa. We are saved."

CHAPTER 7

Veronica

When I was ten years old, we were forced to move from the candy-colored Victorian home I'd lived in all my life—forced because my father had lost his umpteenth job. As we packed, Mom and I agonized for weeks over which belongings to sell, keep, and store, wrapping each treasured possession with special care, only to find out months later that Dad had sold them all to feed his escalating addiction. I'd mourned for weeks, not for the loss of our things, but the life I knew we'd never get back.

This move was nothing like that.

In the dead of night, as quickly and quietly as three hundred men, women, and children could manage, we threw things into crates, wagons, and animal skin bags strapped to our backs. When we were packed and ready, I climbed atop a flatbed wagon and called our caravan to gather round.

I cleared my throat and took a deep breath. I had no crown and no royal regalia; in fact, I still wore the baggy tunic and leggings Kenna had scavenged from the Brother Cave before we went our separate ways. Fiona would've been appalled. But when the people clustered around my makeshift podium, I lifted my chin and addressed them as their queen.

"Earlier today, we crossed paths with one of the witch's patrols. To avoid splitting up or moving continuously, we will camp in a place she will never expect to find us. Behind the old Blackmore cottage."

Cries of outrage rose up, but I was prepared for such a reaction. I lifted my fist high above my head and the Ring of Aontacht shone bright, silencing their exclamations.

"The Protector has brought the ring of your ancestors back to us! It sheltered me from the Eldritch Limbus and it will guide us around the cursed ground." I didn't share that the ring had also protected me and Kenna when we'd entered the witch's cottage and retrieved Addie's spell book.

I lowered my arm. "I know many of you do not wish to leave this spot. That it makes us feel closer to those we've lost, across the bridge and to the quake. But a wise woman once told me"—my eyes searched the crowd and found the bright gaze of Sharron Rosetti—"that we must go on. Not despite the loss of our loved ones, but because of them."

I swallowed hard as Jamie's face filled my vision. But instead of letting his memory overwhelm me, I chose to draw strength from it—his charisma, confidence, and empathy were what had made him a great leader. I would work hard to follow in his footsteps. Straightening my shoulders, I raised my voice. "Because of the gifts they have given us, we will choose to live, to fight, and take back what is rightfully ours!" A cheer rose up, the cry so loud that snow shook from the branches overhead. Fergus jumped up beside me and pushed his palms through the air in a shushing motion. The Doonians quieted, but the determination shining from their faces didn't wane as I continued. "What we must do will be uncomfortable and difficult at times, but if we work together and follow the Protector's guidance, the witch cannot stand against us!" The cheer was subdued, but fists rose into the air, pumping in unity. Grime-coated faces mirroring my own exhaustion, beamed with new purpose.

Now, if I could just figure out how to accomplish that purpose.

Determining I could only take it one step at a time, and right now that step was to guide my people to safety, I jumped down from the wagon and led the way on foot with Fergus and two of my remaining royal guards flanking us on either side. The journey wasn't far, but we would need to tread carefully. Keeping to the borders, we tromped through the snow, the soft powder muffling our movements, its relentless fall covering our tracks.

Almost an hour later, I swiped snowflakes from my lashes as we sloshed through a recent fall of slippery sleet, and excused Fergus to check the line. He'd known most everyone here his entire life, and they trusted him implicitly, so I'd tasked him with ensuring no one was left behind.

"Yer Majesty." Lachlan stumbled up beside me, tugged by the ever-growing Blaz, whose head now reached my thigh. I ruffled the pup's ears and he rubbed against me.

I missed having Blaz at my side, but Lachlan needed him more. The boy who'd once won a mock sword fight against Jamie to win my favor had ended up stealing a piece of my heart. Both of his parents had gone missing during the quake, but Lachlan refused to believe they were dead. Even with his brave face, I knew the dog brought him much-needed comfort and companionship. In fact, he'd given up a chance to escape to Alloway when he chased Blaz down during the quake.

"What's up, Lachlan?"

His head slanted and his moss-green eyes reflected in the moonlight, taking on an amused look that said he didn't quite understand what I'd said. "I was wonderin'." He paused in thought. He couldn't be more than ten years old, but he had the natural confidence and maturity of a born leader. "Perhaps hoverin' near the dragon's lair isna such a brilliant idea."

I tilted my chin in his direction and arched a brow. Not the look Kenna had dubbed the Evil Highney, but close.

Wisely, he backpedaled. "I dinna wish to question yer judgement, 'tis just that the Crew wanted me to ask." He shrugged and his voice trailed off.

I looped my arm through Lachlan's and tugged him close, our joined momentum making our progress a bit easier. "Thank you for being my ambassador, Lachlan. Every member of the Crew is important to me. So you can tell them that because it's forbidden by Doon law to approach the witch's land, it's the safest spot in the kingdom at the moment."

"Will we use the old cottage for shelter, then?"

"No. There are artifacts inside that hold dark power." As I'd learned the hard way when I'd removed a royal amulet and worn it for courage, not realizing it was slowly poisoning me with the remnants of an ancient curse. "But if we stay clear of the witch's cabin, we'll be fine."

"But how will we know where her property starts? What if we accidently walk into it?"

Such a smart boy. "First of all, you'll feel it. Dark magic is very heavy and there are wards surrounding the cottage. But there is also a border of enchanted black petunias. I'll be sure to have them uncovered every morning so there is no mistake."

"Right-o." He lifted his hand in salute. "I'll tell the others!"

I grinned at his use of slang. Clearly he'd been spending

time with our resident Australian, Oliver Ambrose. Lachlan unhooked his arm from mine, and while tugging Blaz behind him, called over his shoulder, "Thank you, Yer Majesty!"

My hood flew back off my head, whipping strands of hair into my mouth and eyes, but I didn't reposition the cloak. The air was still hard with cold, but the snow had softened to light flakes that melted like butter on my skin. "Ewan."

The boy appeared at my side seemingly out of thin air, his hair swept off his narrow face in damp auburn waves, his slightly turned-up nose red from cold. Odd that I hadn't had to look behind me to know he'd be there.

"Yes, my queen?" The left side of his top lip hitched up in a smirk that would've appeared cocky on someone else, but Ewan only conveyed good-natured mischief.

"I have a mission for you."

"I'll do anythin' you need." His eyes met mine, radiating eager energy. If he'd been born in the modern world, I could picture him as an extreme sports fanatic; snowboarding down a mountainside, carving up a half-pipe, hang gliding at six-thousand feet. Just the kind of throw-caution-to-the-wind person required to help me.

"I need to learn to protect myself."

He gave a quick nod.

"Fergus refuses, and my guard—" I lowered my voice. "My guards placate me by saying they'll keep me safe, but I want to do more than hide behind them."

Ewan gave an appreciative nod, so I continued, "Darkness is coming, a great battle that the Protector has shown me in a vision." If the undead monster Kenna and I had faced inside the limbus was any indication, it would be a horrific battle indeed. "I want to fight *alongside* my people."

The angular plains of his face fixed in sharp determination.

"I'm small and have no training." I gestured to my petite stature. "I need weapons I can handle. Something that won't slow me down or take me months or even weeks to learn to use." A memory of coming upon Jamie working out in the Brother Cave caused me to falter—dark-gold hair flying, powerful muscles glistening with sweat as he wielded his massive sword through a labyrinth of obstacles he'd designed himself. I'd thought him invincible.

With a colossal effort, I kept walking. My prince hadn't just been a figurehead who spoke eloquently and looked gorgeous in royal regalia; he'd trained every day for hours, building his skill and stamina, mock fighting with the guards or anyone who would take him on, all to prepare himself to protect his kingdom. That was the kind of leader I wanted to be, but I didn't have time to gain that level of skill. An attack could happen any day, any hour.

I focused back on Ewan's expectant face. "Can you help me?"

His lip quirked up again, this time showing a line of straight, white teeth. "Aye. I know just the thing."

After this was all over, I vowed to find an occupation better suited to Ewan Murray than farmer.

🏵 🏵 🏵

The following morning, I awoke with the dawn lighting up our teepee like a flame. We hadn't seen the sun in days. With a stretch and a yawn, I soaked up the warmth like a budding flower, careful not to wake Sofia sleeping close by. Eager to feel the naked rays on my skin, and find Ewan to get started on my training, I wrapped my cloak around my shoulders and slipped on my boots. When I opened the flap and ducked through, the air was clear and bright.

Just beyond the trees, the white expanse of a snow-crusted field reflected the sun's rays, melding from buttercup to gold to russet. I blinked and then blinked again, looking up at the clear sky. The snow had stopped for the first time in weeks.

Voices and soft laughter pulled my attention to the center of camp, where a group of early risers had gathered around the fire pit. I recognized Lachlan and Gabby Rosetti, with her shiny blonde waves, along with the other new members of the Crew. They sat with the Seanachaidh, Calum Haldane—Doon's resident storyteller. The balding man's movements were exuberant, his face animated.

I wandered over, my boots sinking into the squishy, half-frozen earth. The entire encampment had been cleared of snow and ice. As I approached, Lachlan let out a wide yawn and rubbed his eyes, and I knew. The Crew had stayed up all night to clear the grounds—just as Jamie would've expected them to.

"Yer Majesty! Do join us!" The storyteller made a beckoning motion. "I've just begun a new tale."

I approached, noting the slumped shoulders and red eyes of the teens and preteens gathered around the circle. Deciding not to embarrass them by making a big deal of their sacrifice, I determined to find some way to reward their efforts later. As I stepped into the circle, a soft breeze caressed my face, the first one in weeks that didn't hurt my skin. "Mr. Haldane, do you understand this sudden change in the weather?"

His gaze met mine, his eyes conveying something I couldn't read. Then he grinned. "Nay, Yer Majesty. But let's enjoy the respite whilst we may, eh?"

Unsatisfied with his answer, I sat on the log next to Lachlan and gathered my cloak around me. Despite the lack of snow, the sun hadn't yet reached the fire ring and the air was cool enough for me to see my breath.

Gabby, more subdued than usual by her obvious fatigue, handed me a steaming mug and offered a smile. "Tea?"

"Yes, thank you." I gathered the heat of the cup in my palms and inhaled the fragrant steam. Blaz, who rested near the fire with his head on his front paws, cocked one eye, and then stood up and stretched his long body. As he walked around the circle, every person he passed ran their hands over him, until he stopped and laid down on top of my feet.

"Now where was I, then?" Calum began.

"Saint Sabastian arrived on the Isle of Skye," a brown-haired boy suggested, who I recognized as one of the young Rosetti twins.

"Nay! He's past that part, Fabi. Sabastian had just found the Fairy Pool."

My gaze bounced between the brothers. The second one must have been Luciano. I studied him; his hair had more of a wave and red spots of acne dotted his forehead.

Fabrizio, whose face was slightly leaner, narrowed his eyes at his brother and opened his mouth, but Calum silenced him with a raised hand. "Yer both right." His gaze darted between the twins. "Shall I continue?"

There were affirmative responses all around as a warm body sat down next to me.

Ewan's eyes danced, his hair a tousled shock of red sticking out all over his head. "I found the . . . items we discussed. When do ye wish to start?"

"Right after breakfast."

The corner of his mouth kicked up. "Aye, my queen."

I turned back to Calum, and tuned into his story. ". . . the pool was crystal clear and surrounded by rocky cliffs covered in lush foliage. Sabastian Demetri had never seen anythin' so lovely. His spirit quickened. He knew everything he'd heard about the magical waters was true. Surely, they could cleanse the soul, drive out evil, and even heal his young sister, Meg."

Warmth saturated my right side and I realized Ewan had pressed up against me, our arms and thighs aligned. I stiffened, but quickly relaxed into the larger body. Under the circumstances, a brother or a friend would share his body heat, just as Blaz had done.

"As Sabastian bent to gather water inta a glass vessel, a scream caused him to start and drop the tiny vile. Watching it sink through the clear water, he debated whether to retrieve it or investigate the cry. He'd only brought four containers. So he reached into the frigid aqua-blue water up to his elbow. But then the voice cried out again. Followed by harsh, male voices.

"Sabastian jerked his arm from the water, secured his satchel containing the other empty vessels across his chest, and set off around the edge of the glistening pool toward the sound. As he rounded a rocky outcroppin', Sabastian's heart hammered against his ribs. He'd heard the tales of fairies in the pool making mischief with visitors. Lurin' men under the water and holdin' them down until their souls were trapped forever as their playthings."

Ewan bumped my shoulder with his and I turned to find his auburn brows wiggling. He was eager for me to share his excitement. I smiled and gave him a nod. Calum painted a beautiful story with his words, but I couldn't help imagine Ewan's reaction to watching *Star Wars* or *Jurassic Park* on the big screen. Would he ghost the movements of the actors while picking apart the logic, like Jamie had during his first movie experience when he'd been trapped with me in Indiana? Or would Ewan immerse himself in a new world? I suspected the latter.

Jamie.

The memory that had casually entered my thoughts ripped its way through my consciousness—Jamie's large fingers wrapped around mine, his other hand digging into the pop-corn as the movie began. Jamie leaning forward, jaw tense, elbows braced on his knees during the Ringwraith's pursuit of Arwen. Me, nestled up against him, hearing his heartbeat quicken as Aragorn said good-bye to his elven princess with no hope of a reunion. Then Jamie's golden-brown eyes holding mine.

I bit my lip against the rising sob. Now that I'd unleashed my grief, it was never far from the surface. The gaping loss inside me was eager to swallow me whole. But I'd made a choice—a choice to go on without him, no matter how much it hurt. I let the tears flow, and straightened my spine as leather-clad fingers encased my clenched fist. Silent and reassuring, Ewan held my hand as tears streaked down my face and Calum continued his story.

". . . Sabastian watched a group of rough lookin' boys gaff and encourage one another as they pushed a young child under the water, her golden hair fannin' out on the surface. Sabastian ordered them to stop and the boys brought the sputtering child out of the water. *'Tell him, little witch,'*" one of the boys taunted. *'Tell the good man we're tryin' to drive the demon from your soul!'*

"But the girl only cried, choking on her own tears." Calum paused and met the eyes of everyone in the circle. "Sabastian knew there be evil in the world, but watchin' these wicked boys harm a child, even in the name of witchery, could no' be tolerated. So he rounded the pool, drew his blade, and gave them one last opportunity to release the girl. Several of the boys brandished their own knives and a scuffle ensued. In the chaos, the girl escaped, but not so for Sabastian. The boys were larger and stronger than he'd realized and they eventually dis-armed him."

Lachlan shifted, leaning forward, his narrow shoulders stiff.

"Outnumbered and weaponless, Sabastian was forced into the pool, the icy liquid instantly slowin' his reflexes. As the boys held him down and water flooded his lungs, his last thought was that he'd failed. Failed to collect the enchanted water and take it back to save his sister."

Calum lifted his mug to his lips, and I wiped away the moisture from my cheeks, waiting for the rest of the story. Every Scottish fable I'd heard in Doon had a silver lining. My eyes shifted around the silent circle and I noticed Gabby had fallen asleep on her brother Luci's shoulder. She had to be one of the oldest members of the new Crew. My respect for the girl grew exponentially. Calum continued in a rumbling whisper, drawing my attention back to the story.

"Sabastian Demetri's murderers fled as his lifeless body floated to the surface of the sparkling pool. The waters didna contain magical properties, so there was no healin' that could keep him from his destiny in heaven. But that was all about to change."

Calum paused, his eyes widening as he leaned forward. "When the angel lifted Sabastian's soul from his body, he resisted. The angel tightened her hold. *'Why do ye fash, Sabastian Demetri? You've shown great faith and strength of character. I'm takin' you to paradise.'*

"*'My sister is dyin'.'* He jerked against the angel's grasp, to no avail. *'I've failed to save her! I must go back!'*

"*'Brave Sebastian, young Meg will be healed. And because of your sacrifice, this pool will forevermore contain the properties you sought in it.'* And so it was that the waters of Saint Sabastian's pool became an elixir that has driven out evil and healed all those who seek it with honest integrity."

Everyone in the circle clapped and Calum crossed an arm in front of his waist to take a mock bow, but something about the tale had caught my attention.

"Why are ye no' clappin', Yer Majesty?" Ewan asked. "Did you no' like the story?"

Since coming to Doon, the lines between fiction and reality had blurred. I'd seen the impossible happen before my eyes over and over. The magic and miracles woven into daily life had forced me to see the world through an entirely different lens. Finding the answer to our dilemma couldn't be that easy, but I had to ask. "Is it possible"—I glanced at Ewan—"that a pool like that could exist in Doon? A blessed place with waters that hold the power to drive out evil?"

Ewan tilted his head and I saw the moment comprehension clicked in his gaze. But then his face fell and he shook he head. "No' that I'm aware. And I know this kingdom just about as well as anyone."

"We used to have a bit o' Saint Sebastian's elixir." I spun around to find Fergus standing behind us. "In the royal chapel."

I dropped Ewan's hand and sprang to my feet, searching my giant friend's face. I felt kind of ridiculous asking about a magic potion from a fairy tale, and part of me wanted to forget I'd even asked. But something deep inside, that might have been intuition, pushed me on. "If it's still there, do you think it would be strong enough to impact Addie's evil?"

"'Tis blessed by God, so aye. But—"

Lachlan finished for him. "It's inside the castle."

"The castle's surrounded by Addie's bewitched guards," Fergus unnecessarily reminded me.

I shot him a glare and then turned to the boys who were less jaded. If this thing existed, I had to get my hands on it. "There has to be a way in . . . through the catacombs or the dungeon entrance."

"She would have all of those entrances well-guarded, lass." Fergus's face flushed and he clamped his hands behind his back. "I mean . . . um . . . Yer Majesty. And I dinna know for certain the elixir is still there."

Calum walked over and joined in, his hazel eyes shrewd. "But if it were, it would certainly hold the power to do what you wish."

Fergus, Calum, Lachlan, and Fabrizio began to debate the probabilities, their voices growing louder as they talked over one another. But I wasn't listening. Hope burned inside my chest, stealing my breath with its intensity. Could the means to defeat the witch have been under our noses all along? It almost seemed too good to be true.

"I know a way." Ewan, who'd been oddly silent up to this point, spoke with quiet conviction. When his words failed to reach the others, he hopped up onto the log. "I know a way!"

His voice finally cut through the argument, and all our eyes focused on the fearless farm boy whose gaze fizzed with excitement. "It's risky, and probably a long shot, but I can get us into the castle."

CHAPTER 8

Jamie

Time had lost all meaning. With no way to track the sun, the seconds scraped by with every agonizing throb of my pulse. I focused on the single source of light, a sputtering torch just outside the bars of my cell, and assessed my injuries. At least three fingers on my right hand were fractured, both eyes had swollen to slits, my ribs on the left side pierced my insides with every breath—likely broken again—and the rest of me ached with bone-deep bruises. But worst of all, the brands on my chest and bicep failed to heal, the constant burn a painful reminder of the witch's power over me.

After multiple refusals to cooperate, the witch had me removed from the relative comfort of the antechamber to a freezing cell in the bowels of the castle, where Sean visited frequently but Adelaide did not. A part of me wished to hear the click of her heels on the dusty flagstones. Longed for the respite that only she could provide.

I could not give in to those base instincts, that weakened part of myself that begged for a second of relief. Or the logical side that reasoned; if only I could give her what she wanted and earn her trust, she would heal my pain and return my strength. *Then* I could defeat her. In truth, there were no circumstances in which I would beg that demon-woman to liberate me.

I pushed up on the vermin-ridden hay pallet with a groan, the clatter of the chains attached to my wrists clanging in my already throbbing skull. Every movement took great effort. I leaned my head back, the icy stones helping to lessen the ache. I despised weakness. Could never understand people who chose the easier, more comfortable path. Now, after only a few days, I was as weak as a child, all of my preparation and training useless.

Carefully, I lifted a hand to the filthy strands of my hair. I'd told Vee that I'd cut it for battle. What a joke. Judging by the severity of Adelaide's supernatural quake, hundreds of Doonians must be dead, hundreds more pledged to serve *Her Evilness*. This wasn't a battle, it was a massacre.

I had to find a way to escape, find the survivors and my queen.

My lips curved and I held tight to the image of Veronica's face. A tilt of her lips, the arch of a dark brow, and my world slipped off its axis. How had I ever doubted the validity of our Calling? The Protector's ultimate gift. Veronica was the sun breaking through my dark sky.

These last torturous days, that light had fed and sustained me, but the night had begun to creep into my heart, stealing my hope. Vee would tell me to get off my arse and find a way out of this prison. Like the great story we had watched in the modern world, Aragorn never gave up, never allowed evil to corrupt his mission. He'd overcome insurmountable odds to reclaim his kingdom and his love.

My eyes opened in narrow slits and I assessed my surroundings. All I had to do was find the herculean strength to break out of my manacles, pick the lock on my cell door with a piece of straw, sneak past Adelaide's preternaturally enhanced guards, and somehow escape the castle and find the others before the witch could stop me—again.

Laughter, frantic and perhaps a bit deranged, surged up in my throat. When it passed my lips, paralyzing pain shot up the side of my face, black wisps surging into the edges of my vision. Desperate to stay conscious, I yanked my right arm forward, and tugged the chain through the iron rings above my head. The ungodly racket had the desired effect and I blinked back the wee ghosties, while adding broken jaw to my list of injuries.

Drawing a steadying breath, I focused on the single key glinting on a hook nailed into the support beam in the corridor. Its curves glinted in the torchlight, beckoning like a siren to a storm-tossed seaman—promising what it refused to give.

My freedom so close, yet forever out of reach.

I fisted my unbroken hand. There had to be a way. There was always a way.

I glanced around the cell, empty save my makeshift pallet and a rickety bucket for refuse. Mayhap I could disassemble the wooden pail and use one of its nails to pick the lock on my cuffs. The peg would likely be too short to reach the mechanism, but I had to try. Rolling to my hands and knees, I crawled to the reeking vessel, saturated with decades of human filth, and drew back on a gag.

Get out and find Vee.

The simple mantra repeated in my head, and I leaned in, turned the bucket until I found a loosened pin head, and dug my fingernails into the grooves surrounding it. Already crusted with blood, as they were, a little more filth couldn't hurt. If I could unlock my cuffs with the tack, I was confident I could then use the length of my chain to snag the key.

I'd just about wiggled the nail free when I heard foot-steps. Long, heavy strides. *MacNally.* I gave the nail one last tug and it came loose. Once removed, it was much larger than I'd imagined, with a sharp, jagged point. Palming the metal, I leaned against the wall and slumped over, pretending to be too weak to hold myself erect.

A metallic click sounded, followed by the squeak of hinges and Sean's shadow loomed over me. "Oh, how the mighty MacCrae has fallen."

Rough hands grabbed my hair, pain screamed across my scalp, and I saw red as he tugged me to my feet. I forced myself to remain limp, my head lolling to the side as he shoved me up against the wall.

Sean rubbed his hands together in excited anticipation of the beating he was about to administer. Bile rose in my throat and I swallowed hard. The first punch landed in my gut. But Sean had become predictable, and I'd hardened my muscles the second before it landed.

"Oh, think yer smart, do ye? Let's see how ye defend against this." His fist slammed into my broken ribs and fire engulfed my consciousness. The pain so intense, I couldn't breathe or see. Words escaped my throat as an unbidden plea, "*Squir. Sguir.*"

"Slippin' inta Gaelic now, are we? I must be gettin' some-where. But I willna be stoppin' this time." He moved so close I could smell sweat-soaked leather and unbathed skin. His voice lowered to a hiss. "If yer wee queen could see yer weak hide now, she'd toss ye over for a real man. I'll be more than happy to take the position when yer gone."

Sean's words penetrated the fog clouding my brain and I forced my head to lift and focus on his beet-red face. His eyes danced with bloodlust and something else . . . something like madness. Alarm skittered down my spine. Had Adelaide's enthrallment finally unhinged his brain? I forced myself to meet Sean's shifting gaze. Perhaps I could pull him back from the edge. We'd known each other all our lives. He despised me, but surely he remembered our long history.

"Sean, you *know* me. Our horses were foaled the same day. I helped ye come up with the name Titus."

Sean froze. And that's when I saw the glint of metal as he glanced down to the knife in his fist.

"Sean," I barked, but he didn't look up. "Remember the time we raced across Farmer Tavish's field and tore up his crop? Our fathers almost skinned us alive."

His gaze jerked to mine, his brows drawing down. "Aye, my father *did* skin me. And you won. You *always* win. Even her. Yer all she talks about. How to break yer will. How to win yer loyalty. As if it's some great prize!" He stepped close and clamped a hand onto my throat, choking off my air. "But you will no' win this time. Let's see her heal you from this."

As I struggled, Sean's blade sliced into my side, sharp and cold, cutting deep. Instinct took over and I swung with all my strength. My fist connected to flesh and the rusted tip of the nail tucked between my fingers slammed into his temple. His eyes flared wide and he stumbled back. I grabbed him and spun his back to me as I looped a length of chain around his throat. He lurched away, but his momentum only tightened the metal links around his neck. He gagged and dropped to his knees.

White-hot fury pushed out everything but the memory of Sean breaking my bones, laughing as he cut my skin, his fists smashing into me over and over as I stood helpless to stop him. It was time for him to feel the pain. I yanked the blade out of my side, and watched ruby blood splatter the floor. I was probably dying, but I would take MacNally with me. I lowered the knife to his throat, but froze with the blade pressed against his flesh. Adelaide stood watching through the open door of the cell, her violet eyes caressing me with open hunger and appreciation.

"Do it," she cooed, those two small words tempting me like nothing else had.

My muscles shuddered as I fought the weeks of buried rage boiling through my veins, urging me to end the man who had caused me unending pain. I'd never experienced true hatred before, but the anger rolling through me felt almost inhuman.

"Do it now." Her voice shook as her eyes locked on mine. "He hurt you, cruelly and savagely, more than I ever gave him permission to. Kill him, Jamie, so he can never hurt anyone else again."

Sean jerked away from me, but I yanked the chain hard, forcing his head back against my legs. She was right. He'd harassed and bullied countless innocents for as long as I could remember. Started an uprising against Veronica that led the kingdom into hysteria. Tied me up and made me watch as he forced Vee and Kenna to walk into the deadly Limbus. This had to end. *He* had to end. I couldn't allow someone with a heart so corrupt to exist. With one swift motion, I drew the knife across my tormentor's throat and he slumped forward.

Adelaide stepped closer, her eyes glowing as they swept over me. "You are more worthy than I imagined."

I removed the chains from Sean's neck and watched him fall to the stone floor, his lifeless eyes wide. Brilliant red leached from the line on his throat, still flowing even after death. I'd killed him.

But I felt nothing. No remorse. No relief that Sean could no longer hurt me or others. No sorrow at taking a human life. Nothing.

Dizzy from blood loss, my head spun and the room tilted.

The witch stepped over Sean's prone body and stopped in front of me, the train of her deep purple gown draping over his face like a shroud. I didn't move as her hands reached up and caressed my face, my jaw, my arms, my chest, my side. Healing me. A reward I didn't deserve.

She moved to unlock my chains, her movements uncovering Sean's sightless gaze, and I couldn't look away. A man I'd known my entire life. A son. A brother. A victim of the evil standing before me. *A citizen of Doon.* I squeezed my eyes closed. Bone-deep cold seeped into the soles of my feet and spread to the tips of my fingers.

Who had I become?

CHAPTER 9

Mackenna

Sometimes musical theater—even Jason Robert Brown—doesn't fit the somberness of the situation. There isn't a show tune for every circumstance, and some things can never be fixed with song. In fact, some situations are so unthinkably horrific they kill the music in your soul.

That's what it felt like as I watched Ezekiel and his younger brother, Jerimiah, devouring food in the kitchen of Dunbrae Cottage. The minute I set out a loaf of bread and steaming bowls of Mrs. Fairshaw's savory lamb stew, the boys attacked as if they hadn't eaten a real meal in months. Perhaps they hadn't. The plaid blankets that I'd bundled them in on the way from the foyer to the kitchen now pooled on the floor, forgotten as the two traded warm bodies for full bellies. What kind of world had they come from where a kid had to choose one over the other?

Ezekiel broke the last chunk of bread in half and handed the larger piece to little Jerimiah. I waited for them to scrape the stew dregs from their bowls before pestering them with questions. I'd made the decision to keep their discovery a secret for now. Although I had yet to learn the specifics of where they'd come from or what they'd gone through, I didn't want to add to their trauma by turning them into a spectacle. After I heard their story, I would decide what to do next.

Easing into an open chair, I poured tall glasses of milk for my guests before starting my interview with a simple question. "How old are you guys?"

"I'm thirteen," Ezekiel answered before indicating his brother, who hadn't said a word since I found them. "Jerimiah is eleven."

The younger boy nodded, head tilted downward toward the table, fixated on his empty bowl. I briefly thought about offering them seconds—we had plenty—but if they were truly starving then they needed to pace themselves. At least that is what I thought I remembered from history class. Instead of giving them more, I asked another question.

"Are you able to tell me what happened?"

"Yes, mum." Ezekiel's unflinching gaze met mine. Despite the fact that his eyes were bloodshot and the whites tinged with yellow, they radiated intelligence and determination. "My brother and I are from a village near Chibok. Do you know where that is?"

"No." Geography hadn't been one of my best subjects.

"It is in northeastern Nigeria, in Africa." I nodded to let him know I was following. "My parents were schoolteachers. They were educated in London. After earning their degrees, they returned home to teach."

The boy paused to scratch the side of his nose. As he did so, his eyes refocused on the tablecloth. "They were killed by rebels in an attack on their school. After that, it was just me and my brothers.

"Isaiah—our older brother—took care of us. Together, we continued to teach the others for a time . . . until the rebels came again. They said, 'Join our army or die.' My brother made a deal with them. He would join, if they spared Jerimiah and me. That was the last time we saw him—nearly a year ago—as he rode away with the militia."

Tragic. I couldn't imagine being orphaned and raising my brother amidst such violence and uncertainly. In that moment, I felt ashamed that I had paid more attention to *Playbill* than to CNN. "Wasn't there any safe place you could go?"

"We heard about a UNICEF camp in Cameroon. Some of the people in our village decided to go there. We were to join them, but the night before we were to leave, my brother had a dream that we should stay put. So we did not go . . ." The younger boy bobbed his head in corroboration.

"Days later, we found out the group was slaughtered before they reached the camp. That is when we decided to establish a system to protect our people. The women of the village, the mothers and daughters, volunteered as sentries. When the rebels would come, they would wail in prayer and the warning would pass from group to group until it reached the village. When we heard the signal, the young men and boys would scatter to hidden bunkers in the fields.

"It worked for a time. But then the rebels caught on. They always came in daylight, but this time they returned in the middle of the night when there were no sentries to watch out for them. They took the boys and girls and shot the rest of my people. Then they burnt our village to the ground."

Ezekiel paused briefly in his narrative to get his emotions under control. "They separated the girls from the boys. I heard later that our sisters were sold into marriage with rebel supporters.

"The rest of us were taken to military camps. When we arrived, the general informed us that Isaiah was dead. He said we must join their cause or die." The boy's demeanor, which had been mostly impassive up to this point, turned fierce. "I tried to make the same deal as Isaiah—to save Jerimiah—but he refused."

"I'm sorry." It seemed like such an insufficient thing to say. Like the Black Knight in *Spamalot* missing both arms and legs and dismissing it as a flesh wound. The truth was I couldn't imagine what these boys had been through. "You don't have to talk about it if you don't want to."

"But I do, Miss. Some stories need to be told. Is this goat's milk?"

"No, cow." What a strange question.

Ezekiel took a sip, his nose crinkling as he processed the unfamiliar beverage. A moment later, he nodded in approval before taking a bigger drink. When he had drained the glass, he wiped the resulting mustache away with the back of his hand—such a normal thing for a teenager to do that I nearly burst into tears. To keep myself from bawling, I ladled more stew into each of the boys' bowls.

"The first night in the rebel camp, I prayed for a means of escape. If not for myself, for Jerimiah, but we were so closely guarded that it was impossible to get away. Then one night Isaiah's spirit woke me from sleep. He said, 'The general plans to make you kill your brother in the morning. You must take the others and flee. Now!'

"Suddenly, a great roaring, like that of a hundred lions, came from the opposite end of the camp. When the guards rushed toward the noise, I woke Jerimiah and the rest of the boys. We slipped under the back of the tent and into the tree line. Thankfully we were able to evade capture and the seven of us made it to the UNICEF camp a week later."

At UNICEF, they would have been clothed and fed—certainly in a better state than they'd arrived in. Which begged the question: "How did you get here?"

Ezekiel flashed me an easy smile. "Once our group was safe, my brother and I decided to go back and get more. We were able to liberate boys at two other camps and a large concentration of girls that had been sold to the same village. That's how Jerimiah came to be in possession of his slippers. One of the girls gave them to him for his feet."

Busy devouring his second helping of stew, Jerimiah mutely nodded in testament to his brother's story. I wondered if all the violence he'd experienced made him immune to the horror.

"That is how the soldiers caught up with us. The village had trackers who helped the rebels follow our trail. We were less than a night's walk from the border of Cameroon when the gunshots began. One of the older girls fell down dead. The rest began to panic. They were saying they would rather die than go back to the village.

"That's when Isaiah's spirit returned to me. I was doubting that any of us would survive when my brother appeared. He said, 'They will make it. You must send the girls on ahead and lead the rebels away.' So that is what Jerimiah and I did. We told the girls to run while we led the trackers away.

"And it worked. The soldiers followed us for most of the night. But toward dawn, they caught up. We had no weapons, so we ran as fast as we could manage. That is when Isaiah's spirit said, 'You must cross the bridge.'"

Chills trembled up my spine, radiating across my skin in the form of goose bumps. "Cross the bridge?"

"Yes, miss. His spirit said, 'Cross the bridge and you will be safe.' So we scrambled along until we came to a river. The river was shallow, so my first instinct was to wade across, but Isaiah cried out to me, 'Stop, Ezekiel! You must cross the bridge.' At that moment, light, like from a great fire, blazed in the distance. We ran toward the blaze and discovered two angels flanking each side of a bridge like sentinels. As we approached, their voices became a mighty roar that shook the ground."

He paused, visibly paling. "I was terribly afraid and dropped to my knees in fear until Isaiah's voice urged me forward. Clinging to Jerimiah's hand, I ducked my head and ran between the angels. The light grew brighter and brighter and then we were across. It was no longer night, but midday. And although we were on a riverbank, there was no bridge in the direction we'd come from.

"Still clutching Jerimiah, I collapsed on a bench. I felt sure we were in heaven and that Isaiah would come to welcome us home. Then I saw you. When you told me we were in Scotland, I knew what had really happened . . . a miracle."

The coincidences between Cheska's and this boy's stories—angels beckoning them to cross a bridge—gave me chills. Wishing I had thought to grab a plaid for myself, I crossed my arms over my chest in an attempt to control my shivering. "Did the angels say anything to you? Did they send a message?"

Ezekiel shook his head. "No, mum. I could not understand what they said. The light and sound invaded my body in a way that filled me with fear and made my senses burn. I was barely conscious. I am sorry."

"It's okay. I'm just glad you're here and safe."

I reached out, intending to refill Jerimiah's bowl, when the younger boy grabbed my hand. He lifted his head and his haunted eyes bore into mine. "The angels want you to rebuild a bridge."

"Excuse me?" How did the angels know I'd been questioning the purpose of rebuilding the bridge?

"It is called the Brig o' Doon. They cried, 'Restore the Brig o' Doon to its former glory. Rebuild the bridge and prepare a mighty army.' That is the message we were to give you. Rebuild the bridge and be ready to fight."

CHAPTER 10

Duncan

I walked down the street next to the auld man who claimed to possess singular knowledge that would help us defeat the Witch of Doon. Kinsman or not, I needed to determine what Alasdair's game was. Until I knew that, I would have no idea if the information he supplied was false or true.

Despite his spry, cheeky demeanor, Alasdair grimaced with each step of his left leg. "Might we stop on the way back to see your bonnie horse?"

"Of course." Although both of us were loaded with the meager possessions we'd just retrieved from his flat, he didn't need to ask twice. I'd eagerly accept any reason to lavish attention on Mabel. Since being stranded in Alloway, I'd been hard pressed to make time for my second-best girl. Not that I'd ever admit to her that Mackenna came first in my heart. Still, I suspected she knew—some beastly feminine instinct for competition.

Cutting away from the village center, we headed toward the parcel of land we'd acquired for our improvised garden and dining hall, and the adjacent paddock and barn just beyond.

"Have you always lived in Alloway? I mean, since the miracle?"

"More or less." He shrugged. "I've adventured out into the world—seen many a wonder—but I always come back in the hopes that Doon will call me home."

"If you are King Angus MacCrae's brother, you would've been a young man when the miracle happened."

"Aye, that I was. Like you, I was a great, strapping lad." The auld man preened like a rooster. "A favorite of the village lassies too."

"How did you come to be so—" I paused, belatedly realizing the rudeness of my question.

"So old?" Alasdair's leathery face cracked in two as he laughed. "You can say it. I know what I am. Not havin' the benefit of magick like Adelaide to stay young, this world has taken its pound of flesh from me. I'm aging, ye see. Just more slowly than others. 'Tis not natural for a man ta live in such a suspended state. I'm ready ta go home . . . ta be at rest."

The hall was packed with Doonians taking their dinner meal. Knowing the bairns would be anxious to start combat training, I skirted around the building, careful to stay out of view of those within. My stomach grumbled in protest.

When Alasdair and I entered the barn, I reached for a bag of green apples. After tossing one to the auld man, I grabbed two more, one for me and one for my bonnie steed. We munched in companionable silence until there was nothing left but cores, which Mabel accepted with a grateful whinny. As she finished our meager meal, Alasdair took the hoof pick and comb from a shelf on the side of the stall. He handed me the pick and waited patiently as I dislodged stones and dirt from her shoes. Once finished, I exchanged the pick for a hard brush. Now it was my turn to wait as my relative combed Mabel from neck to rump.

Often in Doon, the grooms in the royal stable had lamented that my horse was intolerant of any touch that wasn't mine. She was known to nip and pass wind as the stable boys attended her. To my astonishment, she took to Alasdair as if she were his own. Under his cooing affirmation, Mabel gentled, as compliant and eager to please as a young mare.

I followed behind my relative with the hard brush. As soon as I reached Mabel's barrel, she rewarded me with a pinching bite on my left hip. While I scolded my beloved horse, Alasdair sputtered with amusement. "Mayhap ye've neglected this fine beastie too long, lad."

"She's been well taken care of," I assured him.

"And none too happy about it, I see." He laughed again as he moved around to her other side. As he combed her neck, he peered at me over her broad back. "Since ye've got so much that needs lookin' after, perhaps you'd allow me to tend ta her daily ministrations. My gnarled hands are not good for much, but she seems to take to 'em just fine."

I watched Alasdair for a moment, trying to make my mind up about him. "May I ask ye a question? Why did you run—as the miracle was happenin'?"

He paused in tending to my horse. "We were at odds—the king and I. He desired to petition the Protector for sanctuary. I wanted to flee. Ye see, I dinna believe his prayers would work.

"But even in my lack of faith, as I ran away like a coward, the Protector still gave me another chance—when I was suspended on the bridge with one foot in Doon and one in Alloway."

I nodded. I'd heard this story at every clan gathering since I was a wee bairn. "That's when the witch pulled you into the modern world."

"It wasn't her fault. 'Twas mine. Even in the face of a second chance, I hesitated. All Adelaide did was seize the opportunity.

She was cast out of the kingdom forever and I was the final blow she could strike at the king. My brother and I were close, and she saw to it that we'd be apart for all of eternity. Running away—leaving my brother when he needed me most—is my greatest regret."

His words shattered the serenity of the stable. I began brushing Mabel's rump, my eyes on my task to avoid letting the man see the full weight of my emotions.

Alasdair worked his way down Mabel's side until we stood face to face. "What eats at you, lad?"

I continued to avoid his gaze . . . Because I couldn't tell him how I really felt about abandoning Jamie. I couldn't tell anyone. But there were other matters I could discuss.

"Our people." So many lives were dependent on Mackenna and me—and not just for their happiness, but for their very survival. "Is it right to return to Doon when I could be leadin' them into slaughter? Mayhap it's better if we can't make it home. We could build a life here in Alloway . . . But if we don't go, are we sealing the fate of those left on the other side of the Brig o' Doon? I don't know what to do. Jamie was groomed to make these types of decisions; I wasn't."

"I see your point, laddie." Alasdair switched the comb for a soft brush as I moved to Mabel's other side. Again on opposite flanks, we worked our way down the horse. After a heavy pause, he said, "As someone who's been challenged with patience for thousands of years, I've learned that the Protector reveals what we need to know exactly when we need to know it."

Noting my frown, he cleared his throat. "Put another way, it's all right for ye not to have all the answers at present. Have faith that the course will be made clear when it is time to take action."

As I pondered the auld man's advice, the barn door flew open and Greta burst inside.

Red-faced, the girl panted as she stopped in front of the stall. "There ye are, m'Laird! Fiona sent me to fetch ye. More have come."

At first I thought the girl was referring to the afternoon's combat lessons. But the agitation in her face hinted at something else. Something monumental. "What do ye mean?"

"Four lasses an' two lads. Two of the lasses are from a place called Toronto, Canada; one's from China; and one from Pakistan. The girl from Pakistan is missin' part of her face. She survived somethin' known as an honor killing, but Fiona says we're not ta ask her about it.

"The two lasses from Toronto are best friends, their names are Lee and Natasha. An' the one from China is in trainin' fer the Olympics. She does archery."

In her excitement, Greta talked so fast that I could scarcely follow. "One lad's from New Zealand—that's near Australia. He's an activist for the rights of humans. The other came from Central Park in New York City—he's American, like Queen Veronica and Miss Mackenna. His name's Jeremy an' he does magick tricks. Not bad magick, like the witch, but illusions for television. He pulled a shiny coin, a quarter, from my ear."

Despite her incredibly detailed account, most of the information she shared lacked relevance. "How did they get here?"

"Like Cheska, they crossed bridges in their own lands and suddenly appeared here." Greta grabbed my hand. "They each claim they were *called*. The two lasses from Toronto crossed together—just like Kenna and Vee. Fiona says to come quickly!"

Alasdair rubbed his old hands together. His pale eyes gleamed almost maniacally. "Just like I predicted. It's happenin'."

"What's happening?"

"Don't ye see, lad? When Adelaide demolished the Brig

84

o' Doon and consequently the portal—it didn't disappear, it splintered. Piece by piece, it's returning ta Alloway, and as it re-forms it's bringing a mighty army with it."

For the first time since our exodus, my chest swelled with hope. An army? If that was truly what was happening, then we might stand a chance of taking back Doon. But surely Adelaide wouldn't have been so reckless as to do the one thing that could give us an advantage over her.

"Go on, laddie. I'll finish up here for ye." Alasdair took the brush from my hand and turned toward the side of the stall.

I grabbed the auld man's bicep, stopping him. "Why would the witch fragment the portal just so it could rebuild and amass an army?"

Alasdair blinked up at me, his leathery face still cracked in a toothy smile. "Because, m'Laird, she might not o' known that splintering the portal was only temporary. She might have thought that the particular spell she used would demolish the portal fer good."

In my experience, Adelaide had been careful, patient, and above all precise in her cunning. Her plans were carefully laid with centuries of planning to perfect them. I said as much to Alasdair. "So why on earth would she believe that the portal could be destroyed forever?"

"Because"—the old man crowed, clearly delighted by his own cleverness—"that's precisely what I told her."

☭ ☭ ☭

CDACKENNA

I filled Duncan in on the two brothers from Africa and he told me about the new arrivals everywhere else. They'd all crossed bridges in their hometowns and ended up in Alloway with visions of a phantom castle and an unwavering sense of destiny. If Alasdair was to be believed about the army, this was just the overture to the opening act. Many more were coming.

"So is the old guy working with Addie or not?"

"I dinna think so." Duncan scooped a spoonful of stew into his mouth and made a blissful noise somewhere between a grunt and a groan. "Tha's good." Compared to Ezekiel and Jerimiah, who'd recently been escorted to the guys' dorm, Duncan towered over the other side of the table, giving the impression that the kitchen at Dunbrae Cottage had been designed for hobbits.

Feeling more anxious than hungry, I toyed with my spoon. "Why would Addie listen to him if they weren't allies?"

"He claims he spent centuries earning the witch's trust and seeding the idea that if she returned to Doon, she could destroy the Brig o' Doon for good. He called it a 'long con.'"

"That makes no sense. What would Alasdair have to gain from lying to her—except her wrath? No offense to your great-great-great-great-great whatever, but I don't see the old dude risking getting turned into a toad. He's too wily for that."

"Since the Miracle, Adelaide's been obsessed with returning to Doon and taking her revenge. Alasdair felt his best chance of not only getting home, but also of the Doonians defeating the witch for good, was to play into it.

"According to him, shortly after being pulled into the modern world, he became despondent to the point he was considerin' taking his own life. Tha's when the Protector spoke to him in a prophecy about the Brig o' Doon. The bridge would be destroyed but he would rebuild it from the shards and, in the process, bring forth a mighty army to defeat the witch."

"That would certainly fit with what Jerimiah told me. Like Cheska, he saw angels as he crossed the bridge in Nigeria." I explained to him what the boy had told me about the angels' message to rebuild the bridge and prepare an army. "It made little sense at the time, because we are hardly an army, but considering Alasdair's dream and the other recent arrivals, I guess the army is coming to us."

Duncan nodded. "We need to get ready. Prepare housing and supplies. I'd planned on using part of the paddocks to train the bairns in the art of combat, but I think we'll convert the entire south field into a training camp."

"About that. Are you actually using real weapons to teach the Crew to fight?"

"You heard about that, did you?" I arched my brows and nodded as he grinned sheepishly back at me. The boy was so busted. After a second, he looked away. "Jamie and I were accomplished swordsmen by their age. And I asked Rabbie to dull the training swords. They canna do much damage with blunt weapons, except for a few bruises."

As much as I hated to admit it, Duncan was justified in what he was trying to do. These weren't modern kids; they were Doonians. If it came to a battle, I doubted we could keep them out of it. The best thing we could do for them was make sure they were trained by the best, and that was Duncan MacCrae. "You should expand the training to the Destined."

He smiled gratefully and reached across the table for my hand. "Aye. Rabbie and Eòran can start military drills in the morning while you and I go to see the solicitor."

"What for?"

"To see if we can accelerate the rebuilding of the Brig o' Doon."

The MacCraes' lawyer had pulled out all the stops in cutting through the red tape that hindered rebuilding the bridge. Apparently, permits and special approvals were inconsequential when you had more wealth than a small country.

Being crazy rich also came in handy as inspiration for the most qualified architectural firm around to drop everything for the Scotland job, at ten-times their quoted rate. But no amount of money could get their team—their master craftsmen and masons—to work faster than humanly possible.

When I said as much to Duncan he laughed. "Oh ye o' little faith, woman. We canna make them work faster, but we can add a second shift of builders—utilize all twenty-four hours in the day. We'll have the solicitors negotiate the terms."

"Will the local officials sign off on that?" Initially, they'd been a huge barrier with their concerns about private financing, until Duncan's lawyer pointed out the obvious—they were getting a historical re-creation for free!

"I dinna see why not. Especially if we make another donation to the parish." He paused, his magnetic eyes sparkling with hope. "Do you realize what this means, love? We might be able to return home in as little as a fortnight."

Despite Duncan's elation, chills crawled across my skin. Restoring the bridge and training an army meant that in two weeks' time we could be fighting to take back our home. Although I'd thought about that moment a thousand times, and even pictured my friends fighting to the death, I'd never thought about my role. What would I do, what *could* I do? Stage fencing wouldn't keep me or those I loved alive.

I stood and stepped around the table as Duncan gracefully rose to meet me halfway. "I want to ask you for something. It's really important to me."

Duncan smiled his bone-melting crooked grin and pulled me into his arms. "I will give ye anything. The moon, the stars. I'll tether the sun and stop it in its orbit if that be my lady's pleasure."

"It's nothing so dramatic." I chuckled. His fingers caressed my back in soft, warm circles. "When we return to Doon, I plan on fighting alongside you. I want you to teach me."

The lopsided smile melted from his face as he released me. "No."

Then he walked away.

CHAPTER 11

Veronica

Ignoring the damp hair whipping around my face, I focused on the weight of the carved bone handle in my palm and leveled the blade, envisioning Addie's face as my target. Not allowing another second for doubt, I threw the dagger. It spun end over end, silvered edge catching a glint of late-afternoon sun before sinking into the tree with a thud. The engraved hilt vibrated at the edge of the target. I'd hit it. Again. We'd been at knife-throwing practice for a good hour, and I now rarely missed.

Ewan let out a whoop and jogged to retrieve the knife. Before he could remove it, I followed in his wake to inspect the impact of the weapon. As I suspected, it had barely pierced the ridge between two strips of bark, and would likely fall to the ground if I breathed on it hard.

I lifted a finger and pressed down, letting the handle drop into my open palm. "This isn't good enough."

"What do ye mean? You're a natural!" Ewan stumbled back as if I'd wounded him, his brows arching comically.

Oliver approached. "Your aim could use a bit of refinement, but that will come with repetition." I'd recruited our resident genius to join our retrieval mission to the castle and help with my training, but his perfectionism had begun to wear on my nerves.

I didn't have time for repetition. We were breaking into a literal fortress in less than five hours, no matter who tried to talk me out of it. I gripped the knife handle and shoved it under Oliver's nose. "What is this little knife going to do against a supernaturally powered zombie? When we faced Drew in the limbus, he wasn't even alive. And I have no doubt Addie's cooking up some similar undead weapon against us. Zombies don't stop if a tiny knife sticks in their chest. They just keep coming. Cut off their arm—they keep coming. I could throw a hundred of these daggers at one of Addie's minions and—"

"It would keep coming, eh?"

I whipped around to find Analisa watching our exchange, arms crossed, head cocked in her usual arrogant manner. We were on the outskirts of the camp in a partially wooded glen, but apparently privacy didn't exist in our tight community.

I gave Analisa a tight nod and then turned back to Oliver. "Stop coddling me. I need a weapon that will do real damage."

"Aye, Yer Majesty." Oliver's chin bobbed, but I could tell he had no clue what to do with me.

With an impatient huff, I stalked away. Ewan followed. "Perhaps the arrow machine the Laird purchased in the modern world?"

As we'd packed up our camp near the site of the Brig o' Doon, the Crew had found the items Jamie and I had purchased at the mall in Indiana when we'd been trapped outside of Doon. There were bags of baseball caps, bats, gloves, Royals and Giants jerseys—enough equipment to outfit two entire baseball teams. When we'd returned that long-ago night, we'd had to abandon the bags at the edge of the bridge, and in the chaos that followed, the purchases had been entirely forgotten.

The moment I'd opened the first bag, all I could see was Jamie's dimpled grin as he tugged a cap low over his eyes and dragging me off to eat churros. We'd never had the chance to form our teams for the epic World Series of Doon.

It had taken every bit of strength I possessed to hold it together as I'd asked Fergus to distribute the items as needed. The bats in particular could be of use in battle. But I'd forgotten about the weapons from the sporting goods store.

I stopped to consider Ewan's suggestion. "The crossbow is a last resort. I'd like to conserve the arrows. If it comes to a battle, we'll need to give it to our best archer and position them as a sniper."

Analisa joined us. "Good plan. What you need now is a masakari, isn't it?"

In no mood for the girl's cryptic comments, I arched a brow. "Contrary to popular belief, I am *not* a ninja. Interpretation?"

"A small throwing axe," Analisa explained. "Light and perfectly balanced, but deadly."

"A hatchet, ye mean?" Ewan's eyes lit and he bounced on the balls of his feet. "Aye! I know just the thing." He spun away, but hadn't gone three steps before he turned back and dipped into a hasty bow. "Pardon me, my queen."

"You're fine, Ewan."

He stayed bent at the waist.

I waved him away. "You may go."

He straightened with a grin, and then took off at a sprint.

"Looks like you have a mate for life," Oliver commented.

My stomach did a tight roll before I quipped, "I hope you mean the Australian version of mate."

He shrugged. "That too."

I set my jaw and lifted my chin. "Ewan is a loyal friend, and I need all those I can get at the moment." I leveled my gaze on him until he nodded.

"Speaking of which." Analisa cleared her throat, her features tightening with resolve. "Will your plan accommodate a fourth?"

I blinked and tugged down the hem of my tunic. Our mission to sneak into the castle and retrieve the elixir wasn't common knowledge. "How did you—?"

Ana rolled her dark eyes and shook her head until the long side of her asymmetrical bob covered half of her face. With an impatient puff, she blew the hair out of her eyes. "Thief, remember? Which is precisely why you need me, eh?"

The girl had grown up on the London streets, blending in and stealing to survive. I had no idea how she did it, but she always seemed to know things before I wanted her to.

"Need you fer what, Ana?" Ewan jogged up beside me and lifted a canvas bag with a triumphant grin. I could only assume the sack contained throwing axes.

"Ana wishes to join us tonight." The advantages of her going on a mission to rob the castle were undeniable. I turned to Ewan in question.

"The supply boat 'tis small and will only accommodate three of us because we'll need ta lie flat on our belly's to remain undetected."

Ewan's plan to enter the castle involved a pontoon-like wooden boat that delivered goods to the castle via a little-used door beneath the kitchens. As the providers of farmed goods to the royal pantry, his family members were the only ones who knew where the key was hidden.

"Then I need to go in your place . . ." Analisa hesitated before bowing her head in a rare show of deference. "Your Majesty."

"Or Oliver can stay behind?" Ewan suggested.

Oliver looped his thumbs into his belt and widened his stance. "I'm the only one who can unhook the generator and collapse the wind turbine without damaging it."

I nodded. The power generator he'd built on the southeast battlements could be invaluable for our small camp. I wasn't sure how, exactly, but with Oliver's brain for invention, the possibilities were endless.

"I've stolen for you before." Analisa's gaze didn't waver. "Let me do this. You're too valuable to risk."

A light mist began to fall and I blinked the dewdrops from my lashes. Part of me knew Ana had a good point, but another, stronger part argued that if I had the elixir in hand, I might be able to end Addie and this nightmare once and for all. But Oliver and Ewan's plan didn't account for me searching the castle for a witch. They had our steps mapped out down to the second. In and out in twenty minutes. Any more and we were less likely to come out alive. Which brought me back to the logic of Ana's point.

"I can't deny that your particular skill set would be of use, but . . ." I hesitated. When she'd vowed fealty to the throne, she'd earned an additional level of protection from Addie. It didn't make my subjects immune to the witch's spells, but somehow we were able to resist her enthrallment and could not be killed directly by her magic. Unfortunately, none of us were immune to death by non-magical weapons, including me. "I need to do this."

Ana shot me a cocky grin. "I swear I can get in and out without being seen."

The girl was stealthy for sure, and yet, something inside me rebelled at letting her take my place. I had two objectives in life—two things that got me out of my bedroll each morning:

1) Keep the Doonians safe. 2) Take out Jamie's killer no matter what the cost.

I could trust no one else to accomplish either. But this particular mission was only a step toward those goals.

Pain shot into my temple, and I forced myself to unclench my jaw. "I'll think about it."

Ana gave a single nod and then took the weapons bag from Ewan. "Then let's start ninja training."

۞ ۞ ۞

My neck and shoulders burned like fire and my right arm felt dislocated from my body, but I kept throwing. Analisa was a relentless taskmaster, which was exactly what I needed. The sun would soon set and then we'd have a few hours to eat, rest, and go over the plan one last time. The question was—would I be a part of it?

"Throw it again, Highney. This time, try to hit somewhere in the vicinity of the center."

Too tired for a snappy comeback, I glared at her, wishing my best friend were there to put the smart-apple in her place. Kenna had a way of letting me fight my own battles until she sensed I needed her, then she'd jump in with both feet. I missed her something terrible. Letting my sorrow fuel my next throw, I chucked the axe with all of my strength. But I forgot to anchor my feet, and the moment the handle left my fingers, I toppled forward. The hazy sun winked out and in a snap I was back on my feet with an axe, poised to throw.

"Check out the Warrior Princess."

Sure I was hearing things, I lowered my throwing arm and turned toward the sound of my best friend's voice. Kenna, in her favorite *Playbill*-covered pajama set, sat on a nearby crate, elbows on knees, face propped in her hands.

"What are you doing here?"

"It's your dream, silly." She straightened and then glanced around. "I'm proud of you."

My chest ached with longing. I wanted to run and throw my arms around her, but I knew she wasn't really there. Desperate to talk to my BFF, even if she was imaginary, I took a step forward and asked, "Why?"

"Winter is gone."

The snow turning to rain, the warmer air, the line of lavender and yellow crocuses sprouting by the stream, had been in the back of my mind all day. The clues were right in front of me, but I didn't put it together until I met Kenna's smoky gaze. "The ruler of Doon is tied to the weather."

She smiled. "Her *strength* dictates the weather."

Because I'd chosen to lead and stop allowing my grief to dominate me, the Protector had rewarded us all. That thought made my heart beat faster. I had to continue to make right choices. But in the case of sneaking into the castle, I didn't know the best course. Ana had skills, no doubt.

I took a step closer to my best friend. "Should I let Ana go on the mission for me?"

Kenna tossed a lock of red hair over one shoulder and shrugged. "Do you want her to?"

"No." But maybe what I wanted wasn't the most important factor. "Ana is way more qualified in breaking and entering. And if something happens to me, who's going to lead the people? Take out the witch?"

Kenna's virtual doppelgänger began to blur at the edges. "I have faith that you'll figure it out." She waved. "See ya later, Wonder Woman!"

I stumbled toward her fading image. "Wait! Please, don't go . . ."

The scene reset and I lifted my arm to throw the axe at the target.

"Straighten yer wrist, Verranica."

The blood froze in my veins. I'd recognize that honeyed brogue if I were six feet under and had worms crawling in and out of my ears. I shifted my gaze to see Jamie, in all his kilted glory, leaning against a tree, one booted foot crossed in front of the other. His intense, dark gaze captured mine, connecting to my soul. In that way only he could.

And my heart imploded. *This isn't real. It's just a dream. It isn't real. He's gone.*

"'Tis no' a dream, love. We are connected by our Calling."

Not anymore. I forced my gaze away from him, straightened my wrist, and threw the axe. It hit the target dead center.

"Tha's it."

"You need to go. I can't handle this." My voice broke before I could continue. "In my dreams is one thing, but a waking vision . . . I . . . that's something else." I couldn't start seeing him around every corner, like I had before I came to Doon. My precarious sanity—my fragile strength—couldn't take it.

"I'm here for a reason." He pushed off the tree and strode forward, extending his hand. "To show ye somethin'." He reached toward me.

I stared at his strong fingers, broad palm marked by a map of callouses—real in every vivid detail. I lifted my gaze to the glow of his golden-brown eyes and his lips quirked, drawing out a dimple in his right cheek.

Forget strength! If this wasn't real, I never wanted to wake up.

I rushed forward and reached for him. The moment our fingers touched, images exploded across my eyes.

I'm in the shadowed antechamber of the royal chapel.

I turn in a slow circle.

There are walls and walls of cubbies, sealed with hundreds of tiny doors.

Jamie's voice echoes inside me. "Use the ring."

I lift my hand, and the ruby ignites.

One cubby glows red, and then the door springs open.

Inside is a single vile of crystal-blue water.

My eyes snapped open to Ewan's grinning face, his hand extended. Analisa appeared beside him. "That was quite the spectacular dismount, Highney."

Oliver laughed. "But she hit the mark, didn't she?"

I had to have been unconscious for quite a while. I'd spoken to Kenna. Then Jamie appeared. And then the vision. The vision! "How long was I out?"

Ewan cocked his head. "Out?"

I took his hand and allowed him to pull me upright. "Yeah, how long was I unconscious?"

My friends exchanged anxious glances above my head, and then Analisa squatted down in front of me, her sharp gaze searching my face. "You fell only seconds ago."

Chills raced over my shoulders. The vision had been real. The Protector brought those I trusted most to show me the way. They'd bolstered my courage and strength. More than that, they'd banished my lingering doubts over the best course of action.

This risk was mine to take—to do anything less would be bowing to my fear.

Only I could lead the mission to the castle.

chapter 12

Jamie

I awoke on my stomach, my face pressed into something soft and clean. A slow smile stretched my lips. Vee had visited my dreams, just as she had before coming to Doon. Her hair was pulled tight off her heart-shaped face, and she'd looked especially appealing as she bit her bottom lip just before throwing a wee axe.

My eyes popped open to darkness. I'd shown her how to find a specific item in the royal chapel. What, I couldn't recall, only that it held great significance. But her reaction to seeing me had been off. She'd appeared angry, almost belligerent, and worse . . . unbelieving. Had Addie told the truth about Veronica believing me dead?

Raising a hand to comb the hair from my eyes, my arm moved without restraint. Pain free and well rested, my body hummed with energy. An unexpected blessing, and one that I was sure did not come without cost.

Cautiously, I pushed myself up, expecting soreness or broken bones. Though the brands on my chest and arm still throbbed, nothing seemed seriously injured. I reclined on a double bed in an unfamiliar room. The curtains were drawn tight, allowing a narrow sliver of sunlight to slant across the stone floor. A washstand, small table, and straight-back chair made the room feel sparse. Perhaps one of the old servant rooms in the south wing?

I moved to a seated position, the quilt falling to my waist. The blanket shifted to reveal clean trousers, my filthy, blood-stained kilt and shirt long gone. Someone had changed and bathed me, and I didn't remember a moment of it.

That's when the memory hit. *Sean.* I slumped back, my arms refusing to support my weight as something inside my chest fell away. I'd killed him. Not in self-defense or in the honor of battle. He'd been helpless at my feet when I'd slit his throat. I pushed my palms against my eyelids, trying to block out the image of his lifeless body, his sightless eyes staring up at me in accusation. I'd murdered a fellow Doonian, and then I'd been healed, given a soft bed and a good night's sleep as if I were a child rewarded for good behavior.

Springing up, I swung my legs around and my feet hit a wall—an invisible barrier. I kicked with all my might and my legs bounced back toward my chest. Unsurprised she'd caged me like an animal, I rose on my knees and pounded against the magical cell with my fists—a sting of pain buzzing through me with every punch. I didn't care. I deserved more than a bit of physical discomfort for what I'd done, but I wasn't her pet monster to lock up and gawk at, either. "Blast it, Adelaide! Let me out of here. Now!"

When no response came, I slumped back onto the bed. My thoughts shut down and I just stared for a good long time. How could *I* have done this? The crown prince—the boy who'd been raised from birth to lead his kingdom and put his people's needs before his own? My mother's sweet voice echoed in my head, "Never forget, my son, that there is a price for everythin'. And as our future leader, your decisions weigh heavier than most."

I'd lived that adage, been willing to give up my Calling and sacrifice my happiness for the sake of my kingdom if necessary. But Mother never told me what to do when I made the wrong choice. When it was too late to reverse what you'd already done.

A soft click sounded and I arched up, facing the door as it slowly swung open. Addie never entered a room with caution. Perhaps it was a servant bringing food, one I could coerce to help me. A dark-haired girl peeked into the room—a girl whose face was imprinted on my very soul. It couldn't be. My muscles froze as the name tore from my throat: "Verranica?"

She shut the door behind her and threw the lock. A plain, black cloak covered her from neck to feet, but could not disguise the innate grace of her movements, the familiar tilt of her head as she allowed her eyes to adjust to the gloom. "Jamie?"

My heart pounded with such force, it muffled my reply. "Aye, Vee. I'm here!"

She stepped forward, searching. Her eyes were wide with fear, but the line of her jaw remained set in determination. "Jamie?"

Could she not see me behind Addie's magic? She stumbled over to the window and threw the curtains wide. I raised my arm against the onslaught of light, but when she turned back, she looked right past me. "Use the ring. I'm behind a spell, right in front of you."

She raised her hand and a flash blinded my already sensitive eyes. Before I could recover, I felt her slight weight on the bed, her thin arms around my neck. "I found you. I found you . . . They told me you were dead, but I refused to believe it."

For one delicious moment, I allowed myself to hold her. I

ran my hand down the silky length of her hair and pressed the soft skin of her cheek to my neck. I breathed in deep. But her usual sweet scent of honeyed berries was absent. Perhaps the cold air and days camping in the wild had masked it.

Gripping her arms, I pulled back so I could see her face. Saints, she was even more beautiful than I'd remembered. "I could hold ye forever, but we need to go. Who did ye bring with you?"

She gave one slow blink, her eyes shifting away and then back. "No one. But we'll be fine for now. The door's locked. I just need to touch you." She reached her palm to cup my face.

But the weight of what I'd done made me turn away. I didn't deserve the worshipful look in her eyes. If I told her the truth, would she still look at me the same way? Or would she rear back in fear and disgust?

"What is it, babe?" Her thumb moved in slow circles against the stubble on my jaw. "Everything will be all right now that we're together."

"No." I moved away, her normally soothing touch grating against my raw hurt. "Nothin' will ever be the same. I'm not who you thought I was . . . not who I thought I was." My throat tightened as I stared at my hands, the hands that had wrapped the chain around Sean's neck. The hands that had pulled the blade from my own side. The bloody hands that had held his head and slit his throat. And I didn't think I could ever touch her again.

Gently, she lifted my chin, forcing me to return her steady blue gaze. "I don't care what you've done. You are my perfect match."

Lost in the deep, crystal pools of her eyes, my guilt began to ease and I could breathe again. She rose up onto her knees and leaned toward me, her stare fastened on my mouth, her face filled with longing. A fierce need awakened within me. This is what I needed—to lose myself in her, in us. I rose to meet her, grabbed the back of her head, and captured her lips with mine.

And almost gagged.

I jerked back, my head slamming against the wall with the force of my retreat. "What in all that's holy?" My chest heaved up and down. I blinked and rubbed my eyes, trying desperately to clear my vision. "You're no' Verranica."

"Please, don't be afraid." She lifted her palm to me. *Veronica's delicate palm.*

I tried to get away, but I could no longer move a muscle, frozen by magic from the neck down. That's when I knew the girl wearing Veronica's exquisite face was really the Witch of Doon. "Why?" I sputtered. "*Why* have ye done this?"

"To show you that we can be happy together." She tilted her head, and her perfectly-shaped lips curled into a serene smile.

The familiar expression hit me in the gut, my own lips longing to respond in kind. Bile rose in my throat. *She* was not my Veronica.

"The moment you had Sean on his knees at your mercy, and then met my gaze just before you cut his throat, I knew. I knew you were my equal. The one I've been searching for my entire immortal existence." A violet spark ignited deep in her eyes, transforming the clear turquoise into an unnatural lavender-blue.

"A Calling canna be—"

She sprang forward and stopped inches from my face. "Do not speak to me of Callings," she spat. "They are for the weak-minded who refuse to choose for themselves. Do you really think that yer Calling is valid now that you've broken the covenant with your Protector? That your righteous little queen will still want you after what you've done?"

I stared at her hard as Veronica's musical voice dripped words of poison. "Quiet your blasphemy, witch. I willna hear it."

She leaned back on her haunches and took my lifeless hand in both of hers. "Jamie, you murdered one of your own. Committed the gravest sin of your faith. Do you truly believe you'll be accepted back as the golden crown prince? The shining specimen of honor and virtue?"

My breath caught and I worked to prevent the impact of her words from showing on my face. A part of me knew she was right, that I could never be the leader I'd been, once confident that others would follow my example.

She moved closer, her thigh pressed against mine, and she reached up to hook a strand of hair behind my ear. "You've been fighting your base impulses for a long time, Jamie. I've been watching. So much delicious anger rolls just beneath the surface. But I accept you with all your flaws. I embrace them."

I shook my head and forced my gaze away from her beloved face. "I dinna want your acceptance." But with every word she spoke, my heart crumbled under the tremendous weight of my guilt. The images of Sean's brothers and his sweet ma, whom I'd known my entire life, flooded my vision. What would I tell them? How could I explain?

Veronica's wee hand brushed along my cheek, igniting a tingle across my skin, and I clenched my jaw against my body's betrayal.

"We could be happy, you and I. We could lead the people into a new era of freedoms and pleasures they've never been allowed. We would rule side by side as equals." Her gaze ran over me from head to toe, her eyes heavy, her lips pursed. "I can be the Veronica you've always wished for—uninhibited, compliant, yet powerful. And I can share that power with you."

I closed my eyes, my only defense when I longed to wrap my hands around her throat. "Get away from me, witch."

"I can see that you're hurting. But through every trial and torture, you've remained stronger than I believed possible. You're a god among men, Jamie MacCrae, and for the first time in my life, I know what love feels like."

Love? Surely she was jesting. Desire, maybe, but she was incapable of love.

Her odd periwinkle eyes glistened in the sunlight and her mouth turned down at the corners, just like Vee's when she fought back tears. I bit off the words of comfort that rose in my throat.

"This is a lot for you to accept, I realize. I'll let you get some rest. I shall return on the morrow, my beautiful warrior." She leaned in, strands of silky, dark hair clinging to her cheeks as she brushed her lips against my forehead, and I had to work hard not to weep like a babe. This was not Veronica. Not *my* Veronica. But my soul ached for her so desperately that I watched her every movement like a starving man at a banquet as she crawled off the bed and glided across the room.

At the door, she turned back, and her eyes narrowed in a purely Addie expression. "I've endured unimaginable loss. Plotted and schemed for centuries in order to gain vengeance and sit on the throne of Doon. I can wait out one strong-willed prince. Inevitably, you will see that you belong to me." She blew me a kiss and then slipped out. I heard the bolt slide home and her spell fell away, my capacity to move returning by slow degrees. But when I scooted to the edge of the bed, the invisible wall had returned. Apparently, her claim of love didn't extend to trust. Not that Adelaide Blackmore Cadell had the slightest grasp of true love—the kind of love that would sacrifice anything for the other person.

I sagged against the mattress; the interaction with Addie-Vee had drained what little energy reserves I'd gained after my ordeal. Perhaps I could win Addie's confidence, let her believe I cared for her, and then stop her once and for all. Even if she took me down with her, the loss of my life would be well worth what Doon would gain.

Eventually, my morose thoughts drifted into a dreamless sleep, and sometime later three knocks in quick succession startled me awake. I responded without thinking, "Come in." As if I had a choice in the matter.

The door swung wide and Gideon's bald head caught a glint of the setting sun as he brought a tray of food into the room. He stopped at the foot of my bed, grinning like a jackal, then practically shouted, "Oh, how I love the sight of the powerful Laird brought low!"

I pushed up to a sitting position. "Come to rub salt in my wounds, Gideon?"

The ex-commander of the royal guard nodded, the smile never leaving his disfigured face as he set the tray on a table beside the bed. He glanced over his shoulder and then said in the conversational tone of one discussing the weather, "I've no clue how ye think ye're goin' to defeat her, when she's beginning to amass an undead army."

Straightening, I watched the older man arrange the silverware on the tray. What drivel was he spewing now? He met my gaze, the smile melting into a resolute stare. "She plans ta release them in a fortnight."

Was he feeding me information? My pulse quickened as I thought back. At the coronation ceremony, when Addie revealed herself, Gideon had jumped to join her side before she could enthrall him. He'd taken young Greta captive at knifepoint, but he hadn't hurt her. "What are ye tellin' me, commander?"

He stepped closer, his voice hushed. "A mass grave of Druids near the southern tarn is bein' unearthed. But I've determined she needs souls to feed her power. For every human she drains, she can reanimate at least a dozen cadavers." His eyes darted to the door. "She'll need more souls, and soon. The dungeons are near empty."

I searched his face, a terrible hope growing inside me. "Why are ye divulging this to me?"

Gideon glanced at the still-open door and then dropped into a low bow. When he rose, his hazel eyes burned with fever. "I am loyal to Doon still, my Laird."

Nearly choking on my surge of emotion at his confession, I swallowed and forced myself to think. "So she's desperate to find whatever Doonians remain in the kingdom and convince them to pledge to her so she can use them to raise her army?"

"Aye. She'll herd them and capture those she can without killin' them. She needs people left to rule, after all."

I nodded, several pieces clicking into place all at once as I remembered Vee's vision the night of the Fairshaw cottage explosion. "Verranica sent my brother across the bridge with the others to save them, dinna she?"

"That is my belief, aye."

"Do we know how many Doonians escaped?"

"Nay. Between the quake and the destruction of the bridge itself, we—"

"What?" I sat straight up.

"Tha's right, ye didna know." The old man shook his head. "The witch destroyed the Brig o' Doon, Laird. Whilst people were attemptin' to cross it."

My shoulders slumped. The loss of life could be far worse than I'd imagined. Duncan and Kenna . . . Nay, I had to believe they'd crossed safely, and would someday find their way home.

My brother, I could do nothing about, but those left in Doon were a different story. "We need to warn them. I have to get out of here!" I smacked my palm against the invisible shield, and received a sharp sting for my stupidity.

Footsteps sounded from down the hall and Gideon's eyes darted to the door. Hastily, he turned back, picked up the tray and slid it onto the bed, then withdrew his arm and nodded with satisfaction. "Tha's what I thought. The spell only keeps you in. But it does no' keep things, such as weapons, out."

I returned his grin as another thought occurred. "Report back to the witch that I'll need a way to use the privy, unless she intends for me to sleep in my own filth. Then perhaps she'll lower this shield."

"Aye, I shall." Gideon nodded as the footfalls grew louder. He backed away from the bed, whispering, "Hold on a bit longer, my prince. She watches me still, suspicious of my loyalty. But I vow, I will find a way to free ye, so that, together with the true queen, we will liberate Doon."

CHAPTER 13

Duncan

Since the first time I crossed the tiny bridge in the castle garden and ended up on the much larger Brig o' Doon, face to face with an auburn-haloed angel, I'd worried about losing her . . . to the modern world, to her ambition, to some fancy theater lad, even because of my own mule-headed stupidity. At times I obsessed over it. But in all that time, I had never pondered what it would be like to lose Mackenna to the grave.

I could feel her wounded gaze on my back as I walked out the back door of Dunbrae Cottage. Despite the crispness in the air, I felt like I couldn't breathe—as if my chest was caving in. Moments later, I stood over the Brig o' Doon construction site. Panting, I tried to recall how I got there. It was obvious from my body's labors that I'd been running, but I couldn't recollect doing so.

My face stung. I lifted a trembling hand to my cheek and discovered I was crying. Surrendering to the emotion, I dropped to my knees and sobbed. Everything within me raged that I must keep Mackenna safe at all costs. But the truth of the impending battle was that each person's best chance at survival depended on his or her ability to fight. They needed the best training possible—including the one who held my heart.

But I feared I wasn't up to the task.

Sometime later, when the tears had subsided, after my body had gone stiff from posture and cold, I spied Rabbie and Eòran coming up the path from Dunbrae Cottage. I dropped my head to my chest, closed my eyes, and waited. When they arrived, I tried to stand but my frozen body wouldn't comply.

Kneeling on either side of me, Eòran and Rabbie lifted me to my feet and helped me hobble to the nearby bench.

After a few more minutes, Rabbie broke the silence. "Mackenna's told us what happened."

I looked up in time to see Eòran nod for the lad to continue. "M'Laird, we want ye to know that we'll train her personally."

"Thank you." My voice creaked from expended emotion. Suddenly I was exhausted but I felt certain that if I tried to rest I would be plagued with visions of Mackenna being massacred in front of me. Our best chance at happily ever after, and my only hope of peace, was to ensure she got the best training possible.

Rising to my feet, I addressed the two men I was entrusting with my love's life; tenacious, badger-like Eòran and loyal, diligent Rabbie. "Starting tomorrow, every able-bodied person, young to old, Doonian and Destined, starts training for battle. We have roughly two weeks to prepare an army to defeat whatever the Witch o' Doon throws at us. That's not enough time to properly train soldiers, so we have to be clever and make the best use of the time we have."

◉ ◉ ◉

Over the next week, we turned our ragtag group into a highly efficient operation. Part of Mabel's barn had been annexed for a war room and the western paddocks repurposed for military training. For convenience, barracks had been set up in upper lofts of the dining hall and in tents erected in a temporary camp on the surrounding grounds. All the Doonians took shifts training and doing chores like cooking and cleaning, the prospect of going home lighting a fire in their souls and filling their days with joyful determination.

The Destined had a similar routine, but instead of chores they had lessons in Doonian history concerning the witch and the havoc she'd wreaked on the kingdom. With new Destined arriving every day, Fiona had been put in charge of what Mackenna dubbed "intake"; getting their histories, which bridge they'd crossed to get here, and a detailed inventory of their skillsets. So far lads and lasses had come from every continent except Antarctica, called from places like Mexico, Thailand, France, Brazil, Australia, Germany, India, Greece, Argentina, Italy, Puerto Rico, and many more. There were also scores of Americans, Canadians, and modern-day Britons.

Each new arrival appeared with a sense of purpose and a similar story—crossing a local bridge, the battle cry of angels, a message from the Protector, and a yearning for a kingdom that didn't exist in their world. If I'd had a moment to catch my breath, I would have marveled at how easily the Destined accepted the existence of Doon, their instant belief in magic and evil witches, and especially how ready they were to defend a kingdom they'd never set foot in to the death. It was as if the Protector had created them with a kingdom-shaped void that only Doon could fill.

The only person who seemed to be struggling was Mackenna. We'd had little opportunity to talk since I'd walked out. I'd managed to apologize and discuss her training plan, but I hadn't been able to offer an explanation as to why I'd reacted as I had. She didn't understand why I wouldn't personally train her or my inability to explain myself. But I knew that any justification I could offer would likely degenerate into my begging her to stay safely behind in Alloway—which I couldn't ask her to do.

With Rabbie and Eòran's help, I'd kept her in a training regimen that began before sunrise and ended long past sundown. While the others gathered around bonfires, the Doonians entertaining the newcomers with tales and songs from home, Mackenna engaged in night combat, learning to use senses other than her vision to locate and track her enemy.

This particular evening, I had Rabbie working to enhance her sense of smell. Blindfolded and wearing earmuffs, Mackenna was about a thousand paces outside of the camp in the woods. Her objective was to sense the approach of her assailant and successfully defend herself against an attack.

As Missus Alsberg led the camp in a chorus of "Ye Banks and Braes," I slipped out of the camp to observe Mackenna's progress. The inky sky held the faintest ghost of a crescent toward the east. Earlier at supper, when I'd commented the new moon would be perfect for tonight's exercise, Mackenna had joked about hoping that a bare-chested wolf would appear and save her from her sparkly boyfriend's domineering oppression.

Although I didn't understand the reference, the inference had been clear. She was having a difficult time with the rigorous schedule but doing her best to, in her own words, suck it up.

Armed with a wooden knife, Mackenna stood in a small clearing in the heart of a copse of trees. Blind and deaf, she turned in a wild circle, exploring the immediate space around her. In the early stage of the exercise, Rabbie stood a dozen paces upwind. Unable to help myself, my inner soldier began to assess her errors. *Stop moving. Identify which direction the wind is flowing. What do you smell?*

I'd deliberately selected Rabbie because the boy hadn't bathed in a while. Standing upwind as he was, his stench should have been easy for her to identify from her current position. If only she would stop whirling about.

After a couple of minutes, Rabbie crept toward her. For a youth still growing into his large body, he was surprisingly stealthy. He stopped at arm's length, patiently waiting for her to figure out his position. But she continued to thrash about as oblivious as the village drunk.

Quietly, Rabbie stepped in to tap her on the shoulder. Mackenna gasped and spun in a frantic circle, wielding the knife with both hands as if it were a hostile animal. The boy moved around her in a wide arc, going the opposite direction until again she was downwind. After a moment's hesitation he reached out and tugged her ponytail, earning him an "Ow!" and more frantic twirling in response.

The blood coursing through my veins began to boil. The lad was toying with her, playfully baiting her like a schoolboy. Adelaide and her evil minions would have butchered her by now—*just like Jamie . . .*

No! I didn't know for sure that he was dead. *Concentrate on something else.*

Waving Rabbie off, I slipped into position just out of arm's reach and waited until Mackenna came to a stop. Cocking her head to the side she said in an overly loud voice, "What's the matter, Rabbie? Afraid to get your butt kicked by a girl?"

I rattled a bush and stepped to the side as she charged the noise. Without benefit of sight, she crashed into a low-lying tree limb. Her feet flew out from under her and she landed hard on her back. I was on her before she could react, flipping her over and wedging my knee into the small of her back while I plunged my fingers into her kidney. Terrified, she began to fight for her life in earnest.

After a couple moments of futile struggle, I let her go. As soon as I stepped back, she scrambled away. Sitting up, she ripped off the earmuffs and blindfold. Blinking up at me, she tried to comprehend the information in front of her. "Duncan? What the heck?!"

The way she looked at me, I thought I was going to toss my supper. Forcing my emotions away, I replied, "If I'd been the witch, you'd be dead now."

"But you're not the witch," she huffed. "You're my boyfriend."

"Not in combat." I willed my face to remain expressionless. "In combat, I'm either your ally or your adversary." I watched the thunderclouds gather in her expressive eyes. Before she could explode, I dismissed Rabbie, saying, "Go back to camp, lad." The boy gratefully slipped away without a word.

I watched him go and turned my attention back to Mackenna, who was clutching her throat. Staring daggers at me, she spat, "You let that branch clothesline me, you stupid ogre."

"And you were stomping about like a drunken moose. I think I've made a grave error in judgment. You should stay in Alloway when the army returns to Doon."

She scrambled to her feet, wincing as she put weight on her right leg. "Over my dead body. You don't get to decide that."

"Tha's what I'm afraid of. You're no soldier. And if ye canna handle yourself, that makes you a liability."

"Then teach me, you egotistical jerk." She crossed her arms obstinately over her chest. "Make me ready."

Try as I might, I could not escape destiny. I was the only one who could transform her into a warrior, because I was the only one who loved her enough not to cut her any slack.

"You're no' going to like it."

She arched her brow, giving me the Evil Highney. "I already don't like it."

To keep her alive, I would push her beyond her endurance, well past her breaking point. "You're no' going to like me." *By the time I'm finished, you might hate me.* But it was a price I'd gladly pay to keep her alive.

Mackenna tossed her head, her ponytail whipping behind her in ginger fury. "Doesn't matter. All that matters is that I'm ready for battle when the bridge is finished." She glared at me for another moment. "So are you going to train me, or what?"

My inner soldier bellowed at me to be dispassionate. The way her feelings for me might change was a small price to pay to insure her life. "Aye. But remember, this was your choice."

"Fine."

"We're done for the night. Let me escort ye back." I reached for her arm, forcing my expression to remain impassive as she jerked out of my grasp.

"Don't bother. I can find my own way."

As I watched her walk away, I fought back the emotions threatening to erupt. Last time I'd kissed her good and proper, I'd thought that nothing could ever break us apart. I was naively and sorely wrong. Making her over into a soldier, giving her the best chance at survival, might possibly break us both.

CHAPTER 14

Mackenna

Food. Glorious food . . . cold sausage and mustard. I speared a piece of meat, marshaling the willpower to lift my fork to my face. It was hours past the regular time for dinner and all I really wanted was to collapse into bed and sleep like Princess Winnifred, minus the armor between the mattresses. But if I was going to keep up with Duncan's sadistic training regimen, I needed my strength. That meant eating.

Plus, I was waiting for Fiona to give me the rundown on the newcomers being called to Alloway. More arrived on a daily basis. At last count we were up to sixty-seven Destined from all over the globe.

As I toyed with the congealed mass of root vegetables on my plate, my father's voice projected into my head. "Now Kenna, there are starving kids in China who'd be grateful for such a feast."

And Africa, I amended, thinking of Ezekiel and Jerimiah. Whenever I felt like throwing a diva-sized hissy fit about my boyfriend's training tactics, I thought about the brothers from Nigeria—becoming guerilla liberators at the ages of eleven and thirteen. Life-and-death struggles were their reality, so what right did I have to complain about anything, especially a nutritious meal after a long day of voluntary exercise?

I lifted my fork, my arm shaking from the effort, and shoved the sausage into my mouth. Chewing and swallowing as quickly as possible, I ate half the sausage and several bites of tepid turnips and cabbage.

"Holding your nose really does work."

Vee stood in front of me, chuckling. She'd learned that the hard way when her mom, Janet, had run out of money before payday and therefore concocted a culinary specialty she called "freezer casserole." Which basically consisted of whatever remnants were in the freezer mixed with cream of chicken soup. The recipe varied; one week green beans and cream of chicken topped with bits of frozen waffle and baked at 375 degrees until golden brown; or peas, carrots, and cream of chicken topped with freezer-burned french fries and broiled to a crisp. No wonder Vee was such a foodie. She had a whole childhood of crappy meals to make up for.

"Darn right, chica," Vee said, popping a morsel of scone into her mouth.

Surely I was hallucinating from the intense combat training I had endured at the hands of my boyfriend. I blinked my eyes, but the apparition of my bestie remained.

"Duncan has your best interests at heart. And from the looks of you, he's doing a great job." Sometimes I really hated that we shared a brain.

She reached for my hand. "Come on."

I rose from the table and let her lead me to the door. "Where are we going?"

"To storm the castle, silly."

I hesitated. "Isn't that dangerous?"

"No." She shook her head, grinning mischievously. "It's fun. After all, why do you think they say, 'Have fun storming the castle'?"

She tugged at my hand, but I refused to budge. "Nobody says that."

With a musical laugh, she jerked me forward. "Stop stalling. We're already late."

Half expecting her to turn into a white rabbit, I stumbled forward. The ground beneath us began to sway. Suddenly, we were surrounded by wisps of mist, gliding along a glassy surface like a snake. I crouched down and discovered water on all sides. We were on a tiny raft, bobbing along on something infinitely calmer than an ocean.

The panic of the sudden scene shift must've shown on my face, because Vee squeezed my hand. "Relax, silly. We're exactly where we're supposed to be."

"And where's that?"

Pointing ahead, she replied, "See."

The mist parted to reveal a wooden dock at the base of a massive stone wall. Craning my neck toward the night sky, I noted turrets complete with gargoyles. The castle was straight out of a Disneyland nightmare and bigger than anything I'd seen in real life. And just like in Sleeping Beauty, it was surrounded by an impassibly thick, thorny hedge.

The hedge wrapped around the base of the walls in both directions as far as the eye could see. "How are we going to get past the shrubbery?"

"I know a secret entrance." She stepped off the raft onto the dock. "I just need the magic key."

The minute Vee's foot touched dry land, the hedge changed. Tiny black flowers—petunias—began to sprout along the base of the brush. The thorns began to pulse with an eerie violet light. Their tips began to crackle and hiss as drops of purple liquid oozed forth. I covered my mouth against the smell— rotting meat, moldy compost, and month-old garbage.

Zombie fungus! The hedge wasn't a hedge at all, but one of Addie's spells.

Now I could clearly see that the decayed shrubbery was really a magical barrier surrounding the castle. And just like when we'd faced the witch's curse along Doon's border, Vee seemed oblivious to it.

"Wait!" I gagged out a warning. "Stop!"

Vee set her jaw, determination radiating from her blue-green eyes. "I'm doing this with or without you."

"You can't," I gasped, my nose and throat burning from the foul stench. "It's a zombie hedge! You have to go over it!"

But it was too late. Vee was already reaching into the hedge. For a millisecond she stared at her hand as the skin turned purple and fell off in putrid chunks. Then she began to shriek.

"Kenna!"

"Go up! Go up!" I shouted.

The boat began to rock, and I blinked up into Fiona's startled face. The stench of rot gave way to the earthier aroma of roasted root vegetables.

Cold slime dripped from my face as I pushed back from the table, my fatigued arms twitching from adrenaline. "What happened?"

Fiona handed me a napkin, her sympathetic face pinched with concern. "Ye fell asleep in your plate again."

I wiped my face, trying to shake the image of Vee's melting hand. *It was only a dream,* I told myself. *You're okay. Vee's okay. After all,* I continued to reassure myself as I worked to shed the clinging tendrils of my nightmare, *she would never do anything as reckless as storming the castle.*

CHAPTER 15

Veronica

"Go up! Go up!"

Kenna's voice vibrated with urgency as she shook my shoulder.

Instantly wide awake, I sat up and clutched my right arm. In the low light of the banked fire, I shoved up my sleeve. The skin from my elbow down burned like it'd been drenched in acid. But when I ran my fingers up my arm, the surface appeared unmarred and the ache eased. *Just a dream.* I blew out a quiet sigh and glanced around the tent to see Sophia, Gabby, and Analisa still asleep in their bedrolls.

My pulse revved up from the nightmare, I pushed back my blanket and began to finger-comb my tangled hair. Ewan would sound the call to wake me any second now. But as hard as I tried to go over the steps of our plan, I couldn't focus. The dream played over and over. I'd reached out toward a door, something metal clutched in my fist, and a zap ripped up my fingers, melting the flesh from my bones.

I shuttered. What were Kenna's exact words? Get up? Or *go* up?

A warbling call, like a cross between a duck and a whippoor-will, echoed through the camp. I sprang to my feet and pulled on the pair of gray-and-blue baseball pants and long-sleeved Royals jersey I'd found among the purchases from the modern world. Somehow, wearing them made me feel closer to Jamie. After plaiting my hair in a long single braid, I stepped into the night.

It was time. An image of a giant, a Spanish swordsman, and a pirate climbing the battlement walls to save the princess made me smile. Just like in *The Princess Bride*, I had a castle to storm.

Ewan waited by the fire circle, shifting from foot to foot. When I approached he handed me what looked like a leather holster in the shape of an x. "Place this across yer . . . er . . ." His eyes stuck to the cursive writing of my Royals jersey as his hand flapped in the general direction of my chest. Impatient with his modesty, I handed him my cloak and grabbed the holster, then drew it over my head. "I got it, Ewan." Funny that Jamie had been raised in the same medieval-like kingdom, but never suffered from such old-fashioned propriety.

Ewan cleared his throat and passed me a leather sack. "Thank you, Yer Majesty. Buckle the belt and then place the hatchets, blades down, in the holsters on either side of yer waist."

I pulled the weapons from the bag, careful of their razor-sharp edges, and tucked two axes into each pouch. Then I straightened and pulled the straps tight. "Where did you get this?"

"I made it."

My gaze jerked to his red-tinged face. "When?"

The side of his mouth quirked. "Tonight, my queen. I couldna sleep."

And yet the boy buzzed with barely contained energy as if he'd just downed five cups of espresso. I returned his grin and reached out for my cloak. Ignoring my hand, Ewan shook out the fabric and then swirled the cape around my shoulders.

Unsure if I'd get another chance after the suicide mission we were about to embark on, I whispered, "Thank you."

He tilted his head. "Fer what?"

"For the holster, for risking your life to find the elixir . . . for always taking care of me."

His eyes narrowed and latched onto mine. "Somebody's got to, eh?"

The moment drew out into awkwardness and I realized he stood so close that I could feel his body heat. I stepped back. Had Oliver been right, that Ewan had feelings for me? I hoped not. I valued his friendship, and would never wish to lead him on. But the part of my heart capable of romantic love had died along with Jamie.

"Let's get this party started, mates!"

I whirled on Oliver as he strode into the circle. "Hush! If you wake my guards, or, heaven forbid, Fergus, this ends now."

His dark eyes widened. "Sorry," he mumbled. "Guess I'm a bit nervous."

The man had weapons fastened all over his body. A broadsword—that I doubted he knew how to use—was strapped to his side, there were knife holsters on both his legs, and various metal objects hung from a leather strap around his waist. "What's all this?"

"I fashioned a tool belt of sorts." He lifted a stick, whittled to a point at one end. "A screwdriver. Not exactly a Phillips-head, but it should do the trick." He showed us a small hammer and a wood-and-metal saw.

"Let me guess. You didn't sleep either?"

He shook his head. "Not possible."

Without saying the words, we all knew the likelihood of us coming out of this alive. But we also knew we'd never defeat Addie by playing it safe. "Let's go over the plan one more time."

Icy liquid sloshed up toward my mouth and nose, and I strained to draw breath. With the loch freezing and thawing so quickly, water had leached into the bottom of the supply boat. We were halfway to the castle when Ewan cheerfully announced the vessel was leaking; i.e., we were sinking. He claimed that, with the cloudless moon reflecting on the mist-shrouded loch, we were better disguised sitting lower in the water, but the panic tightening my chest didn't agree with his logic.

Kenna had begged me to take swimming lessons with her during our tenth summer. I'd used cheer and dance as my excuse when, really, I despised water—the communal pool slimy with kiddie pee and too much chlorine; the painful chills puckering my skin when I emerged into the cooler air; and most of all, the deep end.

A surge of panic completely blocked my airway and I lifted up on my hands. The castle loomed, its shadowy turrets stretching into the sky beyond my range of vision. We were close. I glanced behind me and met Oliver's strained expression. The corners of his mouth rose along with his eyebrows in what could've been an encouraging expression had it not melted into a scowl so quickly.

Oddly, the apprehension written on his face gave me strength. As their queen and leader, my mood would dictate whether we faced this impossible mission with courage or cowardice. Stuffing my own fear deep into the recesses of my soul, I shot Oliver a jaunty smile and watched as the crinkles on his forehead smoothed in relief.

Wood scraped against wood, vibrating through my bones as our tiny craft shuddered to a stop. Ewan grabbed the rope attached to the prow and leapt onto the dock. I sat up, ignoring the protest of my overworked arm muscles and the sodden fabric of my cloak chilling my skin, and ran through the steps of our plan. This was it. No mistakes.

Ewan helped me out of the boat with Oliver following quickly behind, tying the second rope to the dock. Ewan disappeared into the scrub of short trees and bushes bordering the lake while Oliver and I searched the area. No sign of Addie's guards, or anyone else, for that matter. Perhaps Ewan had been right in saying this entrance had been forgotten by all but the servants.

I checked my weapons and noticed the holster on my left side had dislodged, now hanging loose against my hip. Ewan returned holding a ring of ancient-looking keys and eyed me as I struggled to reattach the pouch.

"Here, let me help ye." He handed the key ring to Oliver and stepped close, soon tying two strips of leather together in triple knots. I swallowed my impatience as he fixed the holster.

"I'll unlock the door, mate," Oliver whispered.

"Pull the knob to ye as you turn." Ewan knelt down to get a better view of his repairs, and as I watched Oliver approach the dark wooden door, apprehension clenched in my chest and rose into my throat—that anxious feeling that I had forgotten something vitally important but couldn't quite place it. As Oliver struck a match and held it close to the keyhole, something made me look up. Expecting to see zombified minions dropping down on bungee cords, I was relieved to only find the night-darkened stone of the castle and an empty balcony two stories above.

"Go up. Go up!" Kenna's voice echoed in my head.

Ewan sprang to his feet. "That should do."

My ring pulsed heat up my arm. Kenna hadn't been telling

me to wake up. Her words had been a warning. I rushed forward, my hand extended. "Oliver, stop!"

But I was too late. Violet sparks exploded from the door. Oliver convulsed like he'd touched a 10,000-volt electric fence, and then flew through the air and landed flat on his back. I rushed to his body and dropped to my knees on the dock. His eyes stared blindly back at me. I didn't need to touch him to know he was gone.

"No . . . no . . . no!" I leaned in and positioned my locked hands over his chest. Before I could make the first compression, Ewan jerked me back.

"Stop! The magic could still be in him."

"I don't care!" I jerked out of his grasp, but his arms locked around me and he tugged me away. That's when I noticed the flesh of Oliver's right arm had turned purple, with bloody blisters cracking open all over his skin.

"Ye canna save him now, Yer Majesty."

I struggled against the cage of his arms as he dragged me down the dock. "The magic shouldn't have been able to kill him! He pledged fealty to the true throne and the Protector."

Ewan stopped, but kept his hold on me. His breath was harsh in my ear as we both stared at our friend's inert body. Tears welled in my eyes. This was my fault. I'd concocted this whole crazy, impossible scheme. And I'd missed Kenna's warning. Somehow, she'd known about the deadly force field and tried to tell me in my dreams. "I have to try to help him."

Slowly, Ewan released me. "Let me try. Tell me what to do."

"You . . ."

Oliver blinked and sat straight up with a gasp.

"Oliver!"

We both ran to his side, and Ewan caught the dazed man from behind as he fell back with a groan. "That was a rush."

His words were mumbled, but after several tries he focused on my face. "What happened?"

I laughed and swiped the moisture from my eyes. "Just a little run-in with the forces of darkness."

Oliver tried to stand and collapsed with a grimace. Clearly, he was too weak to continue on with the mission. Ewan and I helped him hobble over to a spot behind a stand of pines. I had to trust that he would be okay when we left him behind, just as I trusted Kenna had come to me for a reason. *Zombie hedge!* Her words made perfect sense to me now. To get into the castle, we would have to go up.

Quickly, we pulled the small boat onto the bank and removed the ropes, tying them into one long cord, and then found a towering yew close to the second-story balcony. Ewan climbed as high as he dared, secured the rope to a branch, and swung over. I held my breath, bracing for his violent collision with Addie's force field. But he landed on the terrace without mishap. Maybe Addie only had enough power to cover the lower entrances to the castle. The thought that she couldn't be everywhere at once gave me hope. Maybe we could do this after all.

Ewan threw the line back and I swung across to join him. After knotting the rope to the balcony rail, we slipped along the shadowed corridors.

The air felt thick, like walking through dense fog, but without the visual impairment. The effect was disconcerting to say the least.

"Do ye feel that?" Ewan whispered as we entered a back servants' staircase.

"Yes, it's magic. Dark magic." I stopped at the bottom of the staircase and raised a hand for Ewan to wait. When I didn't hear anything beyond the threshold, I peeked into the hallway.

Torches illuminated the corridor with flickering violet flames, throwing monstrous shadows against the walls. Living in the castle had always felt a little like Hogwarts to me, but the witch had stripped my home of its epic mystery, and replaced it with harsh, unrelenting despair.

Anger buzzed through me as I lowered my hand and Ewan followed me into the hallway. We'd only made it a few feet when voices floated to us from around the corner. I tensed and yanked an axe from my belt, more than ready to fight. But before I could position the handle for throwing, I was jerked sideways into a darkened alcove. I shot Ewan a glare as he leaned in and murmured, "Axed guards will draw unnecessary attention."

His words skittered across my brain without registering, adrenaline coursed through my veins, filling me with reckless energy. The voices drew closer and I wrapped my fingers around the handle of my axe. Taking out two of the witch's minions would mean two less people to protect her. Two less people to do her bidding. And it would send a message that we'd been here. That we'd penetrated the witch's defenses. My hands shook with need and I gripped another axe with my left hand. I could do it—throw the first hatchet before they could react, and the second before the guard could draw his sword.

But these were people who had once been Doonians, possibly guards from my own detail. My chest felt tight, as if I couldn't get enough air. Steady footfalls drew closer. I sucked in a deep breath. And I knew I couldn't do it. Couldn't murder one of our own, even if they'd switched teams mid-game. The patrol passed without even glancing our way. I exhaled long and slow.

My thoughts clear again, I led the rest of the way. We reached the enormous double doors of the royal chapel without meeting anyone else. Half expecting the room to be locked, I breathed a sigh of relief as the handle turned with a soft click.

We stepped inside and moonlight bled through stained glass, washing the stone columns and arching vaults in shades of watered blue, magenta, and gold. Memories assaulted me everywhere I looked. The pew toward the back where I'd been gripped with temporary madness as I'd watched Jamie go through the rituals that would make him a king. The altar, where Aunt Gracie's cursed journal flamed, and where the surge of the ring's power had flowed through me for the first time as I destroyed the evil spell.

So much had changed.

With effort, I turned from memories to face the vault door. I reached for the handle, smacked into something hard, and stumbled back. Ewan walked around me, but I yanked him back. "Stop. The door's guarded by magic."

I lifted my hand and focused on removing the enchanted barrier. My ring glowed scarlet, and then winked out. I stared down at the dull red stone as a wave of dizziness swept over me. My gaze jerked up to meet Ewan's. My legs wobbled and I reached out for something to steady myself.

"Yer Majesty?" Ewan grabbed for me, but I toppled, my hip striking the wooden pew as I dropped to my knees.

I focused all my energy on raising my arm, but my limbs were made of lead. My stomach lurched with the sickening realization that the spell guarding the door had latched onto me like a parasite, gnawing away at my strength. My muscles trembled, and I slumped to my bottom.

Ewan knelt beside me. "What is it? Are ye hurt?"

"There's a spell . . ." I sucked in air. "It's inside me . . ."

Ewan followed my gaze to the door, his eyes flaring wide as they turned back to me. "What do I do?"

I fell back on my elbows and he cradled my head in his lap. Panting as if I'd sprinted a mile, I stared up at him, panicked. I didn't know what to tell him. I knew Addie's magic couldn't kill me, but could it put me in a coma? Make me a vegetable for the rest of my life? "I don't . . . I don't . . . know." I blinked. What would Jamie do? "Pray . . . just pray."

I squeezed my eyes closed and focused on my breath.

Deep inhale. Slow exhale.

I reached out with my consciousness to the Protector, but with every breath my throat squeezed tighter and the words wouldn't come. I heard Ewan pleading above me, "Show us what to do . . . Save her."

My fingers and toes tingled and then went numb, and that's when I began to shake, not with fear but with white-hot anger. After every challenge I'd overcome, all the hard-won battles, that witch still had the upper hand. She'd earned my trust as my assistant Emily while killing innocents behind my back. She'd deceived good people—men, women, and children who had become my family—into pledging their lives to her. She'd forced me to send my best friend out of Doon. Then she'd killed countless others with the earthquake, destroyed the bridge, and murdered the only boy I would ever love.

And there was no way on God's green, blessed earth she was getting away with it. I focused all my strength into sitting up and drew in a deep breath. "Help me stand." Ewan searched my face, but hooked an arm around my waist and complied. My knees buckled and he tightened his hold.

Spreading my feet, I anchored my legs and lifted my clenched fist. This was *not* how it ended. I would live to make Addie see that taking Jamie had not weakened me, but turned me into a dragon.

The ring sparked and I focused every ounce of power left in

my being at the invisible barrier in front of me. Crimson waves shot down my arms and legs and then exploded from the ring, hitting the door like a bazooka. Addie's spell disintegrated in a burst of violet embers, and the door flew off its hinges and slammed against the wall.

"Holy Saints!" Ewan's arm tightened around my waist, but as I lowered my arm, I pulled away from his grip, realizing my full strength had returned.

"We need to hurry. Someone may have heard that." Feeling like I could lift a car with my bare hands, I strode into the vault.

The elixir was mine, and this dragon was about to swallow a witch whole.

CHAPTER 16

Jamie

The moon had set and the sun was yet to rise, but I couldn't sleep. Every time I closed my eyes, my dreams were haunted with nightmarish images of Veronica, pale and frozen like a cursed princess from a fairy tale. Danger hovered all around her with fangs and horns and bloody claws.

There is nowhere you can go, nothin' that can keep us from finding our way back to each other.

It was a vow I intended to keep.

By the flame of a single lantern, I lowered a sliver of wood toward the lock in my ankle cuff. I'd already snapped a dozen shards, but this one was sturdier than the rest. With my elbow propped on the inside of my knee, I inserted the narrow end into the hole and carefully felt around for the lever that would release the latch. I closed my eyes, felt the pressure and slight give of the mechanism as a trail of sweat trickled down the side of my face.

Gideon had managed to have the magical shield removed from my bed, and replaced by an ankle cuff. When he'd suggested to Adelaide that the only other option was a nappy, the witch had readily agreed to give me more mobility. The chain, attached to a support beam, only allowed me to reach the loo and the bed. I couldn't even glance out the window. And as far as I knew, Adelaide possessed the only key.

Life with *the thing* that spoke like Adelaide and looked like Veronica had become unbearable. Every visit, her voice, her touch, her face assaulted my sense of reality, defiling my memories. Even worse than when Sean broke my bones and starved me. At least then I could escape inside my head to my safe place—to Veronica. The witch had stripped me of that comfort. Every time she entered the room, my soul lifted at the sight of Vee's beloved face, and then crumpled like a dry leaf in the witch's fist as she opened her mouth. If I didn't get away from her soon, my sanity would break.

Crack.

"Blasted saints of Midar's army!" I slammed the splintered stick onto the coverlet.

After permitting myself a moment of anger, I stood and gathered the slivers of wood, then dropped to my hands and knees. Peering under the bed, I tucked the fragments between the mattress and bedrail with the rest of my failed lock-picking attempts. But as I reached under to dig out another sliver, I paused. Sturdy wooden slats, as wide as my palm, were nailed at even intervals beneath the mattress. I lowered to my back, the stone icy-cold through the thin cotton of my shirt, and wiggled into the tight space underneath the bed.

The middle slat bowed with the weight of the bedding, the nails worked partially out. I gave the board three good whacks with my palm and the right side came free with a shattering pop. Dust and bits of straw rained down, settling in my throat. I coughed as I gripped the other end of the plank and broke it loose.

Yanking one of the nails from the board, I pushed it into the keyhole on my manacle, but it was too large to fit through the narrow opening.

Nail-studded slat in hand, I crawled back out and dusted myself off. Then I tucked back under the covers, hiding my makeshift weapon at my side. The next time the Addie-Vee thing entered my room, I would do whatever it took to escape.

Just as I drifted off to sleep, footsteps sounded outside my door. The witch had already made her evening visit, and although she didn't make a habit of returning in the dead of night, I clutched my makeshift weapon tight. I thought about jumping up to hide behind the privy door, but there was no sense in it when the chain on my ankle would ruin the element of surprise. Brute force it was.

The door swung inward and my muscles tensed as a shadowed figure entered the room. Tall and lank. Movements careful and stilted.

Not the witch.

I let out a relieved breath. "Gideon?"

"Aye, my prince. We must hurry. Ye have a small window durin' the change o' the guard."

The beautiful sound of jangling keys filled the room as I threw back the blankets. Gideon's brows rose at the sight of the nail-studded plank in my fist. "Plannin' an attack, I see."

"Aye, I'm bloody well finished bein' that witch's plaything." My voice came out in a deep growl.

Gideon leaned over and unlocked my shackle. The moment the metal released my foot, I sprang from the bed and rolled my neck, getting the circulation flowing into my limbs in preparation for battle. "Did ye bring me a weapon?"

"Nay, ye'll need ta take the board. The keys were all I could manage, and I'll have ta return these ta Adelaide's chamber before she rises." He lifted the ring of iron keys and then dropped them into his sporran.

I leveled my gaze on the old man. "Ye're no' comin' with me." It wasn't a question.

"I'm o' better use ta ye here, eh?"

The captain knew the nooks and crannies of Doon better than just about anyone, but I couldn't deny that having a spy close to the witch could prove invaluable. "If ye have information, we'll need to establish a drop-off point and a signal."

"Aye."

"Could ye manage to reach the royal cemetery without detection?"

"I could use the catacomb entrance."

"Right. If ye need to communicate, tie a strip of plaid in the oak next to my mother's stone. I'll send a scout every day at dawn. But only use it for vital information. If the witch catches you . . ."

He gave a tight nod.

"I canna guarantee I'll return for ye before the battle begins."

Gideon lifted his chin, his watery eyes searching mine, the corner of his left pulled down by red, puckered tissue. His battle scars. "Jamie, I've served ye since you were a lad. Dinna ye know by now tha' I would die for ye?"

My chest tightened as I met his determined gaze. The thought of leaving him behind in this living perdition was too much. "Gideon, come with me. We'll find a way to defeat her."

"Nay, m'Laird." He bent at the waist in a low bow, and when he straightened his demeanor changed to the gruff tone I was accustomed to hearing from him. "We're out o' time. The first level o' the castle is surrounded by a deadly curse. Ye'll need ta leave by the east. There's a balcony above the kitchen entrance wi' an overgrown yew nearby. If ye're lucky ye can jump to it."

Realizing I had no shoes or cloak to guard against the wintery chill, I grabbed my makeshift weapon and let him guide me to the door. Would my father have left his trusted captain of the guard behind for the sake of the kingdom? Without a doubt. Doon always came first. But this price hit me right in the gut.

Gideon peeked out into the corridor and then turned back. "One more thing. I heard whispers tha' the witch is sendin' a contingent o' magically enhanced guards ta the mountains in the mornin'. A spy returned with information that a large group o' Doonians is campin' in the caverns to the west of the Muir Lea. They move every few days, so Adelaide is hopin' to catch them before they disappear again."

There were hundreds of caves scattered throughout the mountains. It was a smart strategy. "Is Veronica with them?"

"No reports o' the queen's location. Now go. Ye dinna have much time."

I glanced up and down the corridor. It appeared empty. I stepped outside of my prison and turned back to Gideon as he locked the door behind us. Transferring the bed slat to my left hand, I lowered the end against the slate floor, stiffened my spine, and snapped a salute. "*Gratiam et fortitudine*, Captain. May the Protector be with you."

Eyes glistening, Gideon stood at attention and lifted his hand to return the salute. "And with you, my prince." He snapped his heels, lowered his arm, and then rushed away.

The hallway I'd walked at least a thousand times loomed dark and menacing as I plunged into the shadows. Up ahead, a recessed alcove contained an oil painting of a summer pasture, helping me orient myself. The third floor of the south turret consisted of servants' quarters; the floor below me, guest rooms and a secret passage tucked behind a tapestry that led straight to the east wing above the kitchens. I cocked an ear, and when I didn't hear anything, I quickened my pace to a jog.

None of the torches were lit, but my foreboding stemmed from more than the darkness—the bright, joyful castle I'd lived in my entire life hung heavy with malevolence, like a corporeal presence. If I turned quickly, I could almost see the magic slithering down the walls, and gliding above my head. I ran faster.

My pulse ratcheted into my ears as I reached out to open the staircase door. The witch's sentinels could be anywhere; a single touch to an object covered in her spell could alert her to my presence. I couldn't overthink every move I made or I wouldn't survive. Setting my jaw, I grasped the handle and slipped into the pitch black stairwell. Chills raced over my skin as I pressed against the damp stone wall, my bare feet aching with cold. After several moments of silent prayer, my heartbeat regulated and I felt my way down the winding corridor, one step at a time.

At the door, I stopped to listen and review my path. A short jog down the hall, past the fairy pool tapestry, and through the passage. I was as good as free.

The door swung open, bringing me face-to-face with two men dressed in royal guard blues and greens; two men I'd sparred with in the lists, two men I'd trusted with Veronica's life—before they took a knee and pledged to serve evil. They were no longer the men I knew.

"Hello, gentlemen."

Guard one's empty eyes blinked and then flared just before I smacked the bed plank into the side of his head. He toppled, out cold. Guard two grasped for his sword. But before it was unsheathed, I slammed my fist into his throat, dropping him to the ground. He clutched his neck with both hands, gurgling and choking for air. I shook my head. "I taught you better than that."

Releasing the board, I dragged the unconscious guard into the stairwell and then returned for the second, who had slumped to his bum, his face turning blue. I'd likely damaged his larynx, but he'd live. I pulled his sword and leveled the tip against his chest. "Get up, or so help me, I'll run ye through."

He scrambled to his feet and I directed him into the stairwell. Before the door had shut behind us, I conked the sword hilt against his forehead and he crumpled beside his mate. Making a quick assessment, I tugged the boots off the first man and slipped them onto my feet. A bit snug, but they would do.

After stripping the broader guard of his green coat and the *sgian dubh* blade from his stocking, I crept back into the main hallway. I jogged to the tapestry, ducked behind it, and opened the panel. Wind moaned through the passageway, the cobwebs so thick I had to use my sword to clear a path. The webs were a good sign that the passage had remained secret.

I paused at the exit. Footsteps sounded on the other side, moving fast. Two sets, by the sound of them. Were they searching for me? Had the castle itself betrayed me to Adelaide, as I'd feared?

It was a risk I'd have to take. Armed, I could easily take two more guards and make my way to the east terrace. I eased through the opening and shut the panel softly behind me. Voices echoed down the hall and I followed their urgent whispers. One male. One female.

Keeping to the shadows, I drew closer. The female voice held a familiar cadence, and by her tone, she was clearly the one in charge. Even if she were a Doonian, someone I'd known, she'd chosen to pledge to darkness. I would need to take her out first.

I slipped into the alcove as their backs were turned. They leaned over the balcony rail, searching for something, or someone—probably me. The woman straightened and my heart galloped into my ears. The grace with which she moved, the solid set of her narrow shoulders . . . Vee, but not Vee. The witch. And with only one guard.

The Vee-Addie thing turned, and I crossed the room in two long strides. Blood-red rage ripped through me, and then turned ice cold, stealing all thought but one—*kill her.* I smashed the hilt of my claymore into the guard's head, he dropped and I whirled, grabbing *the thing* by her throat. She gasped my name, her eyes wide aqua pools in the starlight, the perfect mix of shock and wonder swirling in their depths.

Not Vee. She's not Vee.

I squeezed, crushing the delicate cords of her neck. "Ye will no' fool me this time, witch!" I drew back my sword. Not even Adelaide Blackmore Cadell could survive a blade through the heart.

CHAPTER 17

Mackenna

Du-dut-da-dut-dut-dut . . . Again!
    Advance step, thrust, step, kick, thrust . . . Again!
Advance step, thrust, step, kick, thrust . . . Right!
That connects with . . .
Retreat step, parry, step, retreat, duck.
Turn, turn, forward, back, jump, step.
Got it? Going on . . . And—

"Mackenna!"

The blunt edge of Duncan's sword smacked me across the back and I stumbled forward. Somehow, I managed to turn the momentum of my impending face-plant into a roll. Springing back to my feet, I swung around to face my boyfriend with my sword at the ready.

"Good. That was a brilliant recovery." Despite the positivity of his words, he continued to scrutinize me with narrowed eyes. Since taking on the role of my personal drill sergeant, he'd lost all sense of humor, and although I'd sworn not to complain, I missed his "Chuckles the Ogre" side.

He tipped his head from side to side, cracking his neck. "What do ye say to takin' the rest of the night off? I think you've earned it. If ye hurry, you can make it to the hall 'fore supper is through."

I wasn't the type of girl who needed to be asked twice. Before he finished the sentence, I was shucking off my weapons belts and protective padding, which flopped onto the dewy grass like a slug. Although I'd been given a reprieve from Duncan's rigorous training, I still had to clean my sword and return everything to the armory, aka Mabel's barn. That would take at least another half hour.

Sighing, I reached over to gather my things, but Duncan's soft voice stopped me. "Leave them be, woman. I'll take care of your gear for ye."

"Oh." I'd assumed he would come to dinner. I couldn't remember the last time we'd had a meal together. "I'll wait."

"Tha's all right. I have much to do here." His eyes skimmed over me and continued on to the tree line. "Then I planned to check the progress of the bridge. They were beginning the apex of the arch this morn."

I followed his gaze, wondering when we'd stopped looking at each other. "I could—uh—go with you."

"Nay, lass. As you Yanks say, go blow off some steam. I heard that some o' the lads have planned a proper gathering after the meal—dancing and everything. Enjoy yourself."

Apparently, while I wasn't the type of girl who needed to be asked twice, I was the type who needed to be told twice. Duncan wanted me to get lost . . . and not in the good way that involved his deep brown eyes.

"Well," I drawled, as a sinking feeling settled in my chest. "See you tomorrow, then."

In a daze, I headed toward the dining hall. On the short walk across the meadow, the sweat cooled on my skin. And although I started to feel the evening chill, it was nothing compared to the blizzard in my heart. Something had happened between Duncan and me—a shift too subtle and vague to give a name to, but too substantial to dismiss. Ever since he took over my training, it had felt like he was disappointed in me; like he'd lost interest because I wasn't a good enough pupil. And he still wouldn't talk about why he hadn't wanted to train me in the first place.

As I stepped into the ginormous barn, the sounds of pipers and fiddlers reverberated from stalls across the room as they began to tune their instruments. Our converted dining hall, which consisted of a primitive kitchen at one end and long tables and benches filling the length of the space, had been decked for festivities. Boughs of purple-and-green heather wrapped artfully around the walls, interspersed with flickering golden candles, transported me to a certain Scottish kingdom in a galaxy far, far away.

Dressed in store-bought plaids, the newcomers easily outnumbered the tartan-clad Doonian refugees. Nearly everyone who had crossed the bridge from somewhere in the modern world seemed to be in their late teens or early twenties. Yet despite all their differences, the two groups intermingled like they'd know one another forever.

At a table on the opposite end of the room, I spotted Ezekiel and Jerimiah in animated conversation with a group of guys. From his gestures, I surmised that quiet little Jerimiah was telling a story—a good one from the looks of it. Both of the boys were laughing, their carefree smiles radiating across the hall.

Experiencing a touch of high school cafeteria déjà vu, I shuffled into the dinner line wondering if, after I got my food, I should insert myself into an existing group, or just go for the first open spot and eat alone. If this had been school, I'd be eating with my bestie, which I'd done from kindergarten through junior year. My friendship with Vee had, among other things, saved me from a decade of lunches eaten in a bathroom stall.

"Beautiful evening, dinna ye think so?"

I blinked out of my glory days reverie and into the smiling face of Fiona's mom as she handed me a plate heaped with stew, bread, and some sort of greens. Since I'd started training with Duncan, I'd taken most of my meals at Dunbrae Cottage, so the change in dining wear caught me off-guard. The plate was one of those fancy disposable, three-section deals that I remembered from picnics. "Paper plates?"

Caledonia Fairshaw made a sound of correction that was uniquely Scottish. "Not paper, lass. Recycled sugar cane. They're biodegradable and a mite easier on the cleanup than traditional plates. They just go in that tub and then at the end o' the evening we put 'em on the composting heap. Flatware too—on Prince MacCrae's recommendation. Such a time saver."

For a millisecond I thought she meant Duncan, until Alasdair's face appeared over her right shoulder. Of course, he was the Prince MacCrae she was referring to—I'd have to get used to there being two of them around the camp. "I've been introducin' the good ladies ta the conveniences o' the modern world. No sense in not enjoyin' them while we're on this side o' the bridge, right, Missus Fairshaw?"

"Oh, m'Laird," she chided, spearing him with a sidelong glance as she batted her eyelashes. "How many times must I insist ye call me Caledonia?"

Leaning in so that his bulbous nose practically grazed her neck, Alasdair replied in a low voice, "I'll call ye Caledonia, *Missus* Fairshaw, when ye start callin' me by my God-given name. *Alasdair* . . . Say it just once in that temptress voice o' yours."

Fiona's mom ducked her head in an effort to hide the blush that was spreading across her face. Without meeting my eyes, she said, "Enjoy your meal, Mackenna. And please forgive *Alasdair*. I'm afeared all this modern livin' has made him far too cheeky for his own good."

Thoroughly creeped out, I hurried away from—whatever that was. Scanning the room, I spied Fiona sitting with Cheska, Greta, and a few others. As I approached, Greta and Cheska slid apart, making room directly across from Fiona.

Before I sat, Greta pointed to the backs of the two girls at the two girls on the opposite of her. "Lee and Natasha," she mouthed. Apparently crossing the bridge as besties had elevated them to rock star status.

I slid into the open spot and let Greta handle the introductions. After greeting the newcomers, I cast a playful look at Fiona. "So . . ." I drawled. "Your mom and Alasdair . . . What's that about?"

Fiona rolled her eyes. "Dinna get me started on those two." She nibbled on a cracker. "My da's barely cold in his grave and my mum's taken up with a man old enough to be her—her—I canna even wrap my mind around him ta figure out what he is!"

"At least he doesn't sparkle in the sunlight," I replied. Fiona and the rest of the Doonians stared at me as if I'd started speaking in tongues, and I realized my smart remark had been for Vee's benefit . . . only she wasn't around to hear it. My throat tightened as tears began to well in my eyes.

Suddenly Cheska's hand covered mine. "I was always more of a Jacob girl. Now my best friend Danissa, she loooooves Edward."

Greta leaned in with a frown. "Who are Jacob and Edward? I've not met them. Are they newly arrived?"

Cheska giggled as she lifted her hand from mine. "No. They're from a book series—and some movies."

The dark-haired girl sitting next to Greta, whose name I couldn't recall, paused mid-bite. "Like Harry Potter?"

Greta and her friends had discovered Vee's copies at Dunbrae Cottage, and after reading the first book, the series had spread through the Crew like wildfire. If she'd been here, Vee would've been geeking out right along with them.

Fiona pushed aside her plate. "Ches, would ye and the other girls give me a moment in private with Mackenna, please?"

As the table cleared, I indicated Fiona's full plate of uneaten food. "Feeling okay?"

"Aye," she said, taking another bite of cracker. "Jus' a wee bit of a tummy ache. It'll pass."

Seconds later, Fiona and I were alone. In my experience, private hardly ever equaled good. With Duncan's recent dismissal and Vee's absence casting a shadow over me, I didn't think I could handle anything else tonight. I just wanted to eat my stew in peace, and then slink back to Dunbrae Cottage and collapse into bed.

"I've been thinking about something." Attempting to redirect the situation, I leaned in and asked in a hushed tone, "Do you think the boy from Sofia's Calling is one of the Destined? Like maybe Jeremy?"

Fiona smiled. "I've been wonderin' the same thing."

"I hope so," I replied, truly meaning it. "She deserves to be happy."

"Aye. She does."

We lapsed into silence. But as Fiona continued to scrutinize me with her shrewd, hazel eyes, I knew I wasn't going to get off that easily. For several minutes, she let me eat in silence. Then she asked, "What's on your mind, Mackenna? Besides Sofia's love life. You're not yourself this evening."

If my bestie was sitting across from me, I would have spilled my guts. That's how easy it was between us. Tired of feeling alone, I replied, "Duncan and I are having some issues. I mean—I'm having issues with him. I have no clue whether he's having issues back. Which I guess is part of the problem. Ever since he took over my training, we don't seem to be in sync."

NSYNC . . . I smirked down at my plate, remembering just how much Vee loved JT. "And I miss Veronica—so much that she's practically all I think about. She shows up in the middle of my training to crack jokes, and every night we're together having adventures in my dreams."

"What kind of adventures?"

"Crazy stuff, like visiting parts of Doon I've never been to." That reminded me of the most recent episode in the nocturnal escapades of K & V. "Is there really a cattle entrance at Castle MacCrae off the lake?"

"Aye. Ye didn't know that?"

"Not before last night's dream. Vee and Oliver and some other dude were going to storm the castle like something out of *Princess Bride*—it's a movie. Anyway, when they got to the castle, they couldn't see that Addie had placed a spell around the lower level. Vee touched it and got zapped and then I woke up."

Fiona bit at her lip. "When did these dreams start?"

"The first night we returned to Alloway." I remembered because I dreamed that Vee was sharing a teepee with Sofia and Gabby Rosetti.

"And they're regular occurrences?"

The more I talked, the better I began to feel. "Pretty much every night. It's not *always* the castle—first it was in the woods near the bridge, and then it was a different part of the woods near the witch's cabin—where, I assure you, I've never been before. They're so vivid—the smells, the textures—it's like I'm

145

almost there. And they seem to last all night. Which is crazy, because the way Duncan is training me, I ought to be sleeping like the dead."

As I unburdened myself, Fiona's eyes grew wider. She stared at me open-mouthed, and for the second time since entering the dining hall, I felt like a total weirdo. "What?"

"Mackenna. I dinna think those are merely dreams. I think you're havin' a Calling with Queen Veronica."

"Aren't Callings usually—uh, romantic? I'm not having *those* kinds of dreams."

"Nay. You misunderstand. Callings can be romantic in nature, and traditionally have been, but they all serve the will of the Protector and are for the good of Doon. Like Doc and Mags Benoir, who were called ta Doon together because the kingdom had need o' them—and o' course, all of the newly arrived Destined were called to save Doon. Those Callings aren't romantic."

I hadn't thought about the newcomers as having a Calling, but she was right. "So Vee and I are having a Calling? Cool."

She continued to gawk at me as if I were the village idiot. "Dinna ye realize what this means?"

"Kind of—I mean, sort of—but not fully, I guess."

"It means that the two of you are connected despite being on opposite sides of the portal. You can communicate."

CHAPTER 18

Duncan

Mackenna's footsteps sounded on the cobbled stones behind me. For a lass, she had a sure, strong gait—not like that of a dainty damsel in distress, but the presence of an Amazon warrior. Now, thanks to her dedication, she was beginning to fight like one.

As she approached the bench, she stopped. It was endearing that she assumed she could watch me without my knowing it. And I allowed her that misconception, although, in truth, I was attuned to her presence in a way that was almost supernatural.

I remembered how it felt when I landed in Chicago with the purpose of escorting her back to Doon to face the Eldritch Limbus. The instant I stepped off the plane, I could feel my heart—the one that beat inside her chest—pulling me on an invisible tether. By the time I got to the theater, my entire body vibrated with the need to reclaim my soul mate.

Mackenna's name on the marquee and her face on the color advertisements beckoned to me. The performance was sold out, so I paid a young couple six times the price to get their tickets. As I walked through the lobby, my hands began to shake so badly I could hardly manage to hold the program.

From my seat in the darkened third row, I could feel her in the wings—and when she made her grand entrance, I had to bite my lip to keep from calling out. Although her dialogue was humorous, I fought the urge to weep. After months of being numb, every nerve in my body sprang to life. Suddenly, I was alive again to experience the excruciating agony of loving Mackenna Reid.

"Boo!"

I started, causing Mackenna to chuckle as she leaned over the back of the bench. "Guess you didn't hear me sneaking up on you. I'm getting good at this."

"Come and sit with me." As she rounded the bench, I turned away, pretending to stare at the moon while I surreptitiously wiped at my face with the palms of my hands. For what needed to be done, it would serve no purpose for her to see me teary-eyed. Thankfully, she was too preoccupied to notice.

She reached over and grasped my hand. "Guess what?"

"What?" I asked. I focused on the river lest my emotions betray me.

"Your hand's all wet. Duncan, are you sweating? Maybe you're getting sick." She touched my forehead with the back of her free hand. "You don't feel hot."

"I'm not. Come here and warm a lad up." I wrapped my arm around her and pulled her close to my chest. As she rested her cheek against my shirt, I felt her heart beating for the both of us. "What am I to be guessin'?"

Mackenna sighed, and I felt her exhalation sweep through my body down to my toes. "I've been having these crazy dreams about Vee, and Fiona thinks we're having a Calling. Do you know what that means?"

She paused as I processed the information with growing excitement. "That you should be able to communicate."

"Geez!" She sat up and twisted in her seat to face me. "Am I the only one who didn't know this?"

The mock outrage on her face was adorable. "Apparently, woman."

She swatted at my bicep. "Don't you 'woman' me. I'm a modern lass, remember. There's no way I should be expected to know all your crazy Doonian hoodoo."

"It's not hoodoo. It's destiny. The bridge should be ready by the day after tomorrow." I pointed toward the darkened construction site where scaffolding supported the recently completed bridge. "But we only have one of the Rings of Aontacht. Without the other, we won't be able to cross."

I had dropped the other ring, the ruby encircled with gold, when we'd fled Doon. After an extensive search of the river-bank, I was fair certain that it hadn't ended up in the modern world—which meant it was still in Doon. I just hoped that one of my kinsmen had found it and returned it to Queen Veronica. If the witch had it, we were in serious trouble.

"Son of a Sondheim! I didn't think about Aunt Gracie's ring."

I took both her hands in mine. Her flesh felt chilled to the touch, so I gently rubbed her skin. "Why would ye? But we need to find out if the queen is in possession of it. Can you test your Calling tonight and try to communicate with her?"

"Yep. That's the plan. If she does have it, what should I tell her?"

I had given the matter of our return to Doon a lot of thought each night as I assessed the progress of the bridge. "I think we should be cautious for the first crossing. Tell her to be ready the night after next and that we'll be a small party," I replied.

I wanted to suggest that she remain behind for the first trip across the Brig o' Doon but knew the request would be futile.

Confirming my thoughts, she asked, "Who should we take—besides us, I mean?"

"Alasdair. I'm not comfortable leaving him behind."

"And Mutton Chops?" She lifted her eyebrows, causing me to smile at the pet name she had for Queen Veronica's most devoted guard. "I don't think he'll stay behind."

"Aye," I agreed. "We'll take him too."

"What about Fiona?" Mackenna bit her lower lip in a most distracting way, her concern for our friend as plain as the freckles on her face.

Forcing my eyes away from her bewitching mouth, I met her troubled gaze and wished I could ease her distress. "I'd love to take her with us, but I'm afraid it's not practical."

"But Fergus is on the other side," she insisted.

Although Mackenna had become more than adequate in the art of combat, her heart still held dominion over her head. With her emotions ruling how she fought, she was unpredictable and reckless . . . which made her a danger not only to herself but to those around her as well.

"Say something, Duncan." She tried to pull her hands away but I refused to release them.

Calmly, I replied, "I too wish to see her reunited with Fergus, but I fear this place would cease to function without her."

She rolled her eyes, clearly still unhappy but unable to argue away my point. She let out a small huff before agreeing. "I suppose that's true. Can you at least ask her not to go over-board while we're gone? She keeps getting sick, and of course she won't stop to take care of herself."

"Aye. I'll speak with her." I waited for her to look at me. Instead, she watched the moon.

"I'll see if she would like us to deliver a note to Fergus. That is, *if* we can get across the bridge." She shook her head from side to side. "Ugh! I can't believe I forgot about the other ring."

I continued to hold her hands, unwilling to break the physical connection between us. "Don't beat yourself up, woman."

"Speaking of beatings," she drawled as she glanced at me and away again. "What's on the rehearsal schedule for tomorrow's training?"

I'd been giving that much thought as well. "Tomorrow we're going to exploit your weaknesses."

Finally meeting my gaze, her breathtaking eyes narrowed in curiosity. "Such as?"

"Anything that makes you vulnerable or distracted. In battle, you have to shut out everyone and everything except the fighting around you. That's what we are going to focus on tomorrow. Revealing your weaknesses."

Mackenna arched her brow. "And once they're revealed?"

"We eliminate them." I shrugged in a way designed to minimize the importance of my words.

"Sounds fun." She flashed me a smile that was all pearly teeth and sunlight. I couldn't help but smile back. She leaned in to kiss me and, in a moment of impulsiveness, I turned away so that her lips grazed my cheek. Instantly, I wished that I could take it back, but it was too late.

Pulling away, she asked, "Are you okay, Duncan?"

Unwilling to witness the hurt I'd cause her, I looked into the starry expanse of sky. "I'm fine."

"Really?"

"Aye." I held back the words that threatened to indicate otherwise. "Now ye best get your rest so that you're refreshed for training in the morn."

"Okay. Well . . . goodnight." Her cool fingertips brushed my cheek in a butterfly caress that was over far too soon.

"Goodnight." The unspoken words I wanted to say caught in my throat. Swallowing them back, I listen to her retreating footsteps, my spirit dropping with each one.

She thought that exploiting her weaknesses sounded fun, like a drama game. But I knew all too well what waited on the morrow's horizon. How many times had I lectured to soldiers in the lists that they were only as good as their weaknesses? These flaws were so important that a fortnight had been dedicated to the identification and eradication of them. Because a warrior's weaknesses would get him, or in this case her, killed.

Since the instant Mackenna had broached the subject of fighting, I'd known that this moment would come. Tomorrow would confirm what I'd suspected from the start, a terrible fact that I would have rather not faced . . . that her fatal weakness was me—just as she was mine.

CHAPTER 19

Veronica

Staring into a face I never thought I'd see again, I didn't feel the pain of Jamie's fingers digging into my throat. It couldn't be. *My* Jamie was gone. Fergus had watched him hang. No way the witch let him survive.

Fury contorted my attacker's face and his muscles tensed to run me through. I jerked back and brought my knee up hard, but he twisted away. His lips curled in a dark smirk that was so Jamie, my legs buckled beneath me. His hand squeezed tighter on my throat, keeping me on my feet.

Everything indicated Jamie stood before me, but his actions said otherwise. Could this creature be some reincarnated nightmare Addie had devised to torture me? If so, it was working like a charm.

Cold steel pressed into my breastbone. "Where's your magic, *witch*?" He shoved his face into mine and growled, "This act doesna fool me."

Act? I had no idea what he was saying, but as his hand

crushed my windpipe and he lifted me into the air, I began to beg. "Jamie, please," I croaked. "Don't—"

He cocked his head, his brows drawing together in confusion before he hardened his jaw and drew back his sword arm with fresh resolve. "Usin' her voice will no' save ye this time."

Whoever, or *whatever* he was, he didn't recognize me. Believed I was his enemy. I reached for an axe, but my vision began to fade, my fingers going numb.

A body rushed out of the darkness and tackled the Jamie-creature. I fell in a jumbled heap of tingling limbs. Gasping to pull air into my lungs, I scrambled away as Ewan smashed an unlit torch against Jamie's arm, knocking the sword from his grip. They rolled, fists flying so fast I couldn't tell who was winning. In that moment, I wasn't sure which one I wanted to prevail. The Jamie clone had almost killed me, but it was still somehow, *impossibly* . . . Jamie.

Ewan lost the upper hand, and Jamie, straddling his waist, trapped the smaller boy on his back and locked his arms to his sides. Quick as lightning, a dagger appeared in Jamie's hand. He raised the knife, ready to strike. But before I could choke out a scream, he froze. "Ewan?"

"Aye, ye bloody loon, and that there is her highness, Queen Veronica!" Ewan jammed a finger in my direction. Then he turned back to the large Scotsman sitting on his chest, his eyes widening as realization dawned across his face. "Laird?"

Without answering, Jamie turned to me, our gazes locking through the gloom. Could it really be him? Had Fergus misunderstood what he'd seen? My hearing dimmed and the rest of the world faded away. Without realizing it, I had crawled toward him.

"Laird!" Ewan's voice squeaked in desperation as if he'd repeated himself more than once.

"Aye?" Jamie answered, his eyes never leaving mine.

"I'm happy ta see ye and all, but could ye have your reunion somewhere other than on my chest?"

Jamie rose and Ewan rolled away, hugging his ribs. Jamie rushed forward and dropped to his knees before me, his stare intense and questioning. Inky shadows hung under his eyes and he was thinner, but every line of his face, from his slashing brows to his dimpled chin, was Jamie's. My throat closed and I swallowed, hard. "Is it really you?"

Slowly, as if I might shatter into a million pieces if he touched me, he raised his hand to my hair, his dark eyes turning liquid. Desperate to believe he was real, I threw my arms around him, even as doubts flooded my mind. The witch had fooled me before. She'd disguised herself as Allyson when we first arrived in Alloway, and then Emily to worm her way into my inner circle.

Was I letting it happen again?

"Yer Majesty, we've got company." The urgency in Ewan's tone brought me back to the present with a jolt. Shouts sounded in the distance, punctuated by hurried footfalls. My questions would have to wait. I fingered the teardrop-shaped bottle tucked in my pocket. The elixir was our best hope and we had to get it out of the castle.

Jamie released me. "Escape and then we'll talk, eh?"

I nodded as we rose to our feet, my head spinning with the possibilities. If this were a zombie Jamie, wouldn't he be a mindless killing machine like Drew? His skin melting off like Gregory? Or was that just from the effects of the zombie fungus?

"I'll jump across and throw the rope back," Ewan called from where he perched on the stone rail, knees bent for the dismount.

When we'd first returned to our escape route, we'd noticed the rope had come untied from the terrace. Now it hung useless from the yew tree, fifteen feet way. It was a leap I doubted I could make without the rope, but I had to let Ewan try. I gave a quick nod and he launched himself into the air. For a moment, he appeared suspended, arms spread, dark cloak flapping behind him like a flying squirrel. Then he gripped a jutting branch that bowed under his weight, and he swung to his perch in the tree.

The pound of boots grew louder, intermingled with the yap of hounds. Jamie's warm fingers closed around my bare wrist. His touch rocked me so deeply, I gasped. Refusing to look at him, I grit my teeth and pulled away.

"Ye go first and I'll follow."

I gave a nod, and when the rope slapped into the banister I grabbed it and climbed up onto the ledge. I glanced back to see Jamie retrieving his sword, just as guards rounded the corner.

"Stop in the name of the queen!"

The queen, my behind! Tempted to turn and face my betrayers, I forced myself to focus on my mission and leapt off the banister. I flew through the night, and before I had time to think, Ewan clutched my arms and steadied me on the branch beside him. Grabbing an overhead limb, I spun around, but could just make out flashes of movement in the alcove and hear the metallic clash of steel meeting steel as Jamie fought the witch's soldiers. My heart hammered into my temples. "Throw the rope!"

I grabbed it and tried to jerk it out of Ewan's fist, but he held tight and whispered, "Wait."

"Wait for what?" I hissed, my head about to explode. "To watch him die in front of me this time?" Regardless of my doubts, I couldn't let that happen.

Ewan stepped backward along the branch, his body forcing me to move deeper into the tree. "The witch's sentries may not have seen us. We canna risk lettin' them inform her that ye've been in the castle."

"But we have no idea how many guards are over there. We *need* to help him!" My voice rose in panic as shouts and barking carried to us, followed by what sounded like a bar brawl. Grunts and growls. Crashing metal and the thump of bodies. I stared hard at the shadowed space, but could only see quick bursts of action.

"The MacCrae is one of the best swordsmen I've ever seen," Ewan answered while keeping his gaze glued to the terrace. "In the lists, I've seen him take down five armed guards by himself."

A body went flying over the balcony rail. My breath stopped, until the large man smacked into the water next to the dock, and I recognized that it wasn't Jamie.

"And he fights dirty." A begrudging admiration laced Ewan's words, as if he'd been on the receiving end of his leader's particular brand of attack more than once.

The commotion in the darkened alcove seemed to lessen, and Ewan inched forward along the branch. A familiar sharp command sounded, followed by the cessation of barking and a low whine—Jamie quieting the hounds. I'd always marveled at how he could calm Blaz with a stern noise and a touch to the dog's neck. If he were the witch in disguise or a mindless zombie, would he know to do that?

"Throw the rope."

Just as the words left my mouth, Jamie hopped onto the railing. Ewan rushed forward, tossed the rope, and we both worked our way back toward the trunk to make room on the branch. Jamie swung through the air and landed with the powerful grace of a big cat, the limb dipping gently beneath his added weight.

"We should go," Jamie panted as he swiped blood from a cut on his cheek. "One of the men escaped."

But I couldn't move. My fingers gripped the rough edges of bark at my back as I examined his face. The moon filtered through the scattered foliage, peppering his countenance with blotches of night. Was this my Jamie?

"Yer Majesty," Ewan urged, and then turned to face Jamie. "Laird, as ye said, we must go. There'll be time for makin' cow eyes later."

Jamie tore his gaze away and gave a quick nod before he began to scramble down the tree. I followed and when I reached the lowest branch, dangled several feet from the ground. Before I could drop, hands encased my waist. "Let go, I've got ye."

I released my grip and fell, my stomach jumping into my throat before I felt Jamie take my weight. He lowered me down the strong plains of his body, and despite being in the lee of a cursed castle with enchanted guards on their way to find us, sparks skittered over my skin, leaving me breathless. Could a witch-created Jamie do *that*?

There was an easy way to find out. My hands settled on the back of his broad neck and I stared up into his face as my feet touched the earth. "What's your favorite food?"

The corner of his mouth lifted and he answered without hesitation. "Churros from the mall in Indianapolis."

I blinked at him in awe; only my Jamie had traveled to America and fallen in love with all forms of junk food.

His eyes still guarded, he asked, "What did I give ye before your last coronation ceremony?"

"Handfasting ribbons." I lowered my right arm and pulled up my sleeve to show him the scarlet ribbon, the one that signified strength, tied to my wrist.

"Verranica." His voice broke on my name. "I . . ." He raised his hand to my throat, brushing a thumb over my bruised skin. "I hurt ye . . . almost killed—"

"Stop, okay? You're alive, that's all that matters."

He swallowed and his tortured gaze cut straight to my soul. "I'm so verra sorry."

Blinking tears from my eyes, I squeezed his hand. "You thought I was the witch, didn't you?"

His lips parted in wonder and he nodded before he crushed me to his chest and buried his face in my hair. And the link I thought forever broken snapped into place between us. The Calling's indescribable bond that made us part of one another.

This was my Jamie.

I'd heard once that everyone gets one miracle in their lifetime. A whimper vibrated my chest, and I was unable to draw air as I clung to mine. From the first moment Jamie MacCrae had appeared to me in the modern world, my life had been one marvel after another. But holding him in my arms again topped them all.

He murmured something about honeyed berries before releasing me and turning to Ewan. "I assume ye arrived in that." He hooked a thumb over his shoulder. "Will the boat hold us all?"

"With Oliver, just barely." Ewan took off toward the trees where we'd left our injured friend.

I turned to follow and felt large, warm fingers link through mine. Fresh tears prickled the backs of my eyes and I gently pulled my hand from Jamie's. An emotional breakdown was a luxury I couldn't afford at the moment. And if he touched me again, I might curl into him and never want to move.

Focusing on the task at hand—getting us and the elixir safely away from the castle—I jogged after Ewan's retreating shadow. Jamie followed and we broke through the stand of pines, just as shouts rose from the castle gates. Oliver, only half conscious, staggered to his feet. "Is that you, MacCrae?"

"Aye." Jamie's eyes narrowed on the ragged flesh of the older man's arm before ducking under his shoulder. Ewan did the same on Oliver's other side, and they half carried him out of the forest.

"I'll get the boat in the water," I called as I rushed to the muddy edge of the lake. The steady tattoo of booted feet echoed through the night air, but mist hung heavy on the loch. If we could just make it onto the water, the guards would never catch us.

I pushed with all my might. My feet slipping and sliding in the muck, I only moved the craft a few inches. The odd shuffle of the guys approaching grew louder and I doubled my efforts, anchoring my heels. The prow sank into the lapping current as a cry sounded from the castle. "The intruders are entering the loch on the east side!"

My arms shook as I pushed. Part of me knew that one of the men could get the boat in the water with a single shove, but the thought only made me more determined. I gathered strength from my core, let out a growl, and gave a mighty heave. The boat slid into the shallows, tugging me with it. I stumbled forward, then threw my weight back, just managing to keep the back edge of the craft on dry land.

Jamie lifted Oliver into the boat. "Ewan, take the oars. I'll man the rudder."

Ewan positioned himself between the oars and I hopped in beside Oliver. An arrow whizzed past my face and splashed into the mucky bank.

"Vee, get down!" Jamie yelled as he shoved the boat the rest of the way into the lake and then jumped in. "Get this bucket moving, Ewan!"

Ewan heaved the long oars through the water with as much speed as his thin arms could produce, but moving against the current slowed our momentum. I helped Oliver off the seat and we both sank into the icy puddle at the bottom of the boat as three more arrows landed in quick succession. One missed, but the other two hit dangerously close—the first stuck in the wood near my face, the other in the bench we'd just vacated.

Jamie jerked the rudder, but the boat's slow response didn't produce the evasive maneuver he was aiming for. Why hadn't I listened and brought the crossbow? At least then I wouldn't feel like a duck in a carnival shooting game. The whiff of several more arrows flew toward us, one hitting the oar less than an inch from Ewan's fingers. Frantic, he increased his speed and we entered a bank of fog so thick I could barely see my hand in front of my face.

"Stop," Jamie commanded in a sharp whisper. "Hold us here."

Ewan pulled back on the oars until we floated in roughly the same spot, completely shrouded in a cloud of vapor. The fog blocked us from even seeing each other, and for several moments, we were silent. My brain ran through all the possible scenarios, and by the time Jamie spoke, I dreaded the words he would say.

"We're too large a target. We'll need to swim for it."

I shuddered. Everyone has phobias. This was mine. As kids, when I had agreed to a rare afternoon at the pool with Kenna, I'd watched others frolic in playful oblivion as I doggie-paddled with my feet suspended above twelve feet of open water, terrorized by all the ways I could die. Jumping into a hundred-foot-deep, pitch-black lake teaming with hungry fish, and who knew what else, had to be worse. *Much worse.*

It was a losing battle, but I whispered, "What about Oliver?"

"I can float on my back and kick my feet," Oliver volunteered. "All you'll have to do is tug me along."

An arrow thunked into the side of the boat. I heard Ewan set down the oars and then what sounded like the heavy fabric of his cloak falling as he readied himself to jump into the fathomless depths.

Not as good at following orders, even when I knew they were sound, I turned in Jamie's general direction. "We're still too close to the castle. If we swim back to shore, they'll easily overtake us on foot."

"There's a small island just ahead. It's where I was takin' us. If we stick to the fog, they'll think we headed to shore. Then, when things die down a bit, we can use the small craft we keep on the island to reach the other side of the loch."

Blasted Scotsman! Why was he always right? I jerked the tie at my throat and pushed off my cape. "I suppose we have to abandon our shoes as well?" My boots weren't the custom-made leather creations I'd become accustomed to, but at least they fit my feet. I kicked them off and then pulled the small vile from my pocket. Unsure where to put it, I settled on tucking it into my bra.

The boat shook from side to side and I almost shrieked when Jamie's face appeared through the fog, a cocky grin tilting his perfect mouth. "I willna let ye drown, love."

My heart convulsed in my chest. Whether from the sight of that familiar, infuriating smile, or my mounting terror, I couldn't be sure. Perhaps a bit of both.

I tore my eyes away from his and began to knot the laces of my boots into a handle, planning to take them with me. "I know how to swim."

"The tremor in yer voice says otherw—"

A flurry of arrows hammered into the boat in quick

succession. We had drifted out of the fog bank, into open water. Missiles whizzed past our heads. Oliver screamed, a shaft protruding from his shoulder.

"Saints, Murray! Keep us steady!" Jamie dropped down next to Oliver and snapped the stick end off the arrow. "'Tis buried deep. Keep the head in to staunch the blood flow."

Ewan grabbed and then fumbled the oars, one of them slipping out of its metal ring and into the lake. I sprang over the edge, reaching for the wooden pole as it floated away. I'd almost reached the tip when someone yanked me back by my shirt. I spun around, screeching, "I almost had it!"

Jamie tugged me into the middle of the boat and then pointed. "Look."

At least twenty guards stood on the shoreline where we'd pushed into the lake, reloading their bows. At that close range they'd see us enter the water and could pick us off one at a time. But we had to try to make it to the fog. My throat tightening with fear, I gave the order, "Everyone jump in different directions, then swim under the water as long as you can. Jamie, take Oliver." The arrows flew, smacking all around us. "Now!"

Not giving myself a second to think, I wrapped the laces of my boots around my left hand and leapt into the lake. Water enveloped me with muscle-numbing cold and I sank like a rock. My ears filled with pressure and I opened my eyes to solid black. Deaf and blind, it was like floating in deep space. Forcing down my paralyzing fear, I swam with no idea if I headed up, down, or sideways. I heard arrows slice through the water, losing speed but still lethal.

If I surfaced, the archers would have an easy target, but my lungs squeezed, already begging for air. Death by drowning or an arrow to the face—neither option sounded appealing.

And then the water lit up like dawn. As a moth drawn to

a bug zapper, I swam toward the light and popped up with a gasp. Streaks of fire arched overhead. Treading water, I turned in a circle and searched for the others.

"Vee!"

I swam toward the sound of his voice. "Jamie!"

I rounded the back of the boat and met his grinning face, eyes sparking gold as more flames flew overhead. "The cavalry has arrived."

"What?"

His free hand, the one not holding Oliver, found my arm under the water and turned me to face the source of our rescue. Like something out of a movie, two large boats floated nearby filled with men and women, shooting flame-tipped arrows at our attackers on shore. Legs braced wide, the archers streamed an almost constant barrage of missiles, lit and fed to them by a row of people seated in back. "Duck boats. They snuck across the loch under camouflage. Who else knew ye were comin' to the castle tonight?"

"Analisa." The brilliant girl must have planned on following us all along.

"Hurry!" Fergus's voice boomed across the water as he loaded a bow. "We've got ye covered, but our arrow supply is no' endless."

Clearly, Fergus hadn't spotted Jamie floating in the water beside me, or he'd be freaking out for a different reason.

Bands of light smudged my vision, like the aftereffect of fireworks as we swam through the glowing water to the waiting vessels. Ahead, Ewan pulled himself onto a boat, and hands tugged him the rest of the way out of the lake. The return fire from shore had dwindled to almost nothing. We reached the first boat and hands reached down to lift Oliver. I pushed wet hair off my face and turned to Jamie with my first genuine smile in weeks. "Are you ready to come back from the dead?"

Jamie's eyes locked with mine, and I read something raw and intense in his gaze before he hooked a hand behind my neck and pulled me close. Our bodies sealed together as he pressed his lips to mine in a single, searing kiss. When he pulled back, I felt the heat of his words against my mouth, "I would die a thousand deaths, if it meant coming back to you."

CHAPTER 20

Jamie

A gentle wind caressed my skin as I sat by the banked fire enjoying the sensation of being warm for the first time in ages. Freedom tasted sweet like primrose, and alive, like . . . spring. No sign of the blizzard conditions that had plagued Doon before my capture. Which meant my queen had found her strength, despite our divided nation. Despite camping in the forest, hiding from her greatest enemy. Despite believing me dead.

Pride swelled in my chest. I'd always told her she was stronger than she knew. The Protector would not have chosen her otherwise. But a small part of me grieved that she'd awoken to her potential without me. Not because she'd done it on her own; I just would've liked to have seen it.

"So, I'm curious." Fergus lowered his enormous frame onto the other end of the log, and I felt my seat rise a bit from his weight. I stoked the fire with a long stick, sparks flurrying into the misty air, and waited for my old friend to continue.

After escaping the witch's guards at the loch, we'd hurried

back to camp, where the Doonians greeted me like a returning war hero, tears streaming down many of their faces as they declared my return a miracle.

But not Fergus. The big man had hung back, arms crossed, eyes narrowed to slits, examining me like a sword with a broken hilt that he couldn't decide whether to fix or melt into scrap. Now, as dawn began to sneak up on the horizon, I longed to collapse onto a pallet somewhere—preferably within easy reach of Veronica as she slept. But I'd come to the fire ring to wait, certain my oldest friend would find me.

Fergus cleared his throat, shifted his weight, and began again. "I'm curious how I watched a noose bein' looped around yer neck and *saw* ye drop from the gallows, and yet here ye sit."

"I was wondering the same thing," a melodic voice said behind me. I turned to find Veronica approaching, wrapped in a tattered quilt, hair mussed and eyes heavy with sleep. My heart raced at the mere sight of her, and I patted the log beside me in invitation.

Blaz, a head taller than last I'd seen him, padded up to me. Ears erect, tail down, he paused several feet away. I extended my open palm. Cautious, he stepped forward and sniffed my hand. His tail rose, wagging faster as he licked my skin. With a mighty leap, his enormous paws were on my shoulders and a wet, warm tongue bathed my face.

"Down, boy," I commanded with a chuckle. Following one more quick lick, he settled near my feet, one paw resting on my boot.

When I looked up, I saw that Fergus still awaited my answer. I wasn't entirely sure how to explain what had happened to me without causing him to question my sanity. Veronica sat close, the heat of her side pressed into mine as I let my mind go back over the moments surrounding my near execution. So much had transpired since that fateful night, but I'd had plenty of time to ponder what I'd experienced and to form a theory, no matter how outlandish.

I rubbed Blaz's downy head, allowing his presence to calm me as I relived the nightmare. "When I walked out onto the gallows and stared into the witch's smug face, the hood lowered over my head. I wish I could say I faced death wi' bravery, but it took ever' thing I had no' to scream."

Veronica's breath caught and she looped her arm through mine, squeezing tight. I kissed her temple and then met Fergus's tormented gaze, realizing there was more than curiosity, or even distrust, in his face. If he thought he'd watched me die, then as a royal guardsman he harbored the guilt of being unable to protect me—his prince. His charge.

The best I could do was reassure him with the facts. Such as they were. "I remember my last prayers, beseeching the Protector, and then Adelaide's voice tauntin' me, promisin' my death would break Doon and its queen once and for all." The witch's words echoed in my head, followed by flashes of Sean's fists, the never-ending pain, then Adelaide's voracious gaze as her brand burned into my skin. Fury pulsed inside me, obliterating my focus, taking me back . . .

"Jamie?"

Sharp fingers dug into my arm and I realized my entire body was tense, ready to spring. I blinked at Veronica, her aqua eyes wide with concern, her small hand running over my clenched bicep. But all I could see was the witch staring back at me through my love's face. I tore my gaze from hers and tugged my arm from her grasp.

This was *my* Veronica.

I was safe.

Free.

Like climbing a rope hand over hand, I heaved my mind back to the present and out of the horrors I'd experienced. Then I forced my muscles to relax and turned back to Vee and Fergus.

"Before I felt the drop, hands pulled me back and a deep voice said, *It is not yet your time.* The next thing I knew, I awoke in the castle gardens unharmed."

Tears glistened in Fergus's eyes. "Do ye think . . . could it have been . . . an angel?"

"Aye, that is my belief."

My old friend reached over and clapped me on the shoulder. "A true miracle, then."

"But what happened after that?" Vee asked softly.

"I ran, but the witch caught me within hours."

"So you've been her prisoner this whole time?" Her delicate brow furrowed and she shook her head. "But why didn't she kill you once she got you back? Not that I'm complaining. I just don't understand . . ."

A pain shot up my jaw and I unclenched my teeth before saying, "The witch had . . . other plans for me."

"Jamie, whatever you've been through . . . I'm sorry."

Her sympathy didn't help. Would she feel the same if she knew I'd murdered one of our people in cold blood? I shot to my feet. The weight of what I'd done was suddenly heavy enough to drive me into the ground.

Startled, Blaz let out a deep bark and I jumped, the abrupt noise sending my heart pounding into my ears. I shook so hard, I had to cross my arms to still their trembling.

Vee started to rise. "Jamie—"

I shot her a glare and she lowered back down.

"Where's my brother?" I couldn't trust that what Adelaide had told me was true. But if it wasn't, surely I would've seen him by now.

"He . . ." Vee started and then began again, her voice firm. "I sent him across the bridge with as many Doonians as he could take with him, in accordance with my vision."

I gave a single nod. "And the bridge?"

Fergus answered, "'Tis gone. Disintegrated during the quake. We believe by the witch's magic."

"What of the mountain pass?"

"We don't know," Veronica said.

None of it was their fault. And yet red closed in on my vision and my pulse thrummed in my fingertips. Vee had sent Duncan out of Doon when I needed him most. And with no way to return, I may never see my brother again. Judging from the numbers of those who'd greeted me in camp, our population had dwindled to a third or less. And the witch was raising an undead army of thousands. We were as good as dead.

"I need to sleep." And with that, I stalked off.

I found an empty pallet next to Oliver in the infirmary and collapsed upon it without removing my boots. How long had it been since I'd truly slept?

🟊 🟊 🟊

When sleep finally came, the same dream I'd had for weeks sucked me in . . .

This was it. Our last hope—my last hope.

Because if I couldn't save Doon, I couldn't save her—the girl who had become the sustainer of my soul, my strength, my light—and if I didn't have her, I would never be strong enough to lead what was left of us.

If there is anything left.

Tension buzzed through my veins as strategies and contingencies rebounded through my brain. I rolled my shoulders and bent my head. The prayer was incoherent at best, a mantra of deliver us, give me strength, protect her . . .

I lifted my eyes, and the outline of our beloved Brig o'Doon— our portal to the outside world—shimmered in the malevolent haze. The bitter taste of fear coated my tongue as a rhythmic beating filled the air, vibrating in my chest.

With a resounding ring, I drew my sword. The answering tone of blade, ax, and bow staff being unsheathed rang out behind me. The unity of our people was heartening, but it wasn't enough. Half the guard had been lost in the separation. These soldiers were mothers and fathers, tanners, blacksmiths, maids . . . trained in only the bare essentials of battle.

The bridge solidified with every deafening beat of my heart. Its stones becoming solid once more, I could make out the silhouettes of men on the other side. Glancing to my right, I wished to see the Captain of the Guard, my brother and friend, Duncan. Instead, I was greeted by the ashen face of Gideon MacTavish, his bald head dripping with sweat, his sword quivering as if it had a life of its own.

Saints.

In disgust, I turned back to the ominous sight on the bridge. The rising mist brought the ghostly figures into sharper view. A burst of icy wind pushed against my overheated skin, sweeping away the last of the fog, revealing the witches' army in all its malefic glory. Vacant eyes, glowing with an ethereal violet light, faces void of all expression. The sheer numbers spreading across the bridge and beyond were staggering.

Searching for affirmation—some sign that I didn't lead my people into certain death—I glanced to my left, bolstered to see my mate, Fergus, a fervor burning in his eyes to match my own. Waves of righteous fury radiated from the giant solider as he growled, "I've got yer back, Laird."

I swallowed the last vestiges of my fear, tucking it deep down inside, then nodded my acknowledgment with a grim smile. "Aye, let's do this."

Raising my sword high into the air I shouted, "Archers ready!"

This was it. I'd gotten us into this nightmare, now I would get us out of it—or die trying.

"For Doon and her queen!" I bellowed, pointing my sword toward our enemy. An answering cry echoed all around me and we surged forward as one.

My last thought of Vee, her aqua eyes filled with sorrow and accusation as I shut and locked the door behind me. If I lived, I only hoped she could forgive me for what I'd done.

I sat up and gasped for air. The emotion of the dream still pounding through my heart, I threw back the quilt. I knew what we had to do . . . what *I* had to do.

CHAPTER 21

Mackenna

Not that anyone who knew me would believe it, but I'd actually started to enjoy my morning jog from Dunbrae Cottage to Mabel's barn. Okay . . . maybe "enjoy" was too strong a word. But I did feel a sense of accomplishment that I no longer arrived huffing and puffing like the big, bad wolf. I'd started making decent time too. Not enough that I was in danger of exchanging my tap shoes for a track medal, but enough that I believed I might actually be useful in the impending battle against Addie and her minions.

The morning, though cool, was bright and clear. If one looked closely, not that I made a habit of it, you could see the first green shoots of spring struggling to life. That was another effect of running; my focus on the world around me became sharper as the ever-present show tunes in my brain shut off. Unfortunately, I did enjoy living my life with an internal Broadway soundtrack. When things got quiet, I missed the voices harmonizing in my head.

Still, the early signs of spring gave me hope that whatever

funk Duncan had been suffering from the last couple days was over. In the distance, I spied my boyfriend setting up for training. As I approached, I searched for signs that whatever little, black rain cloud he'd been trapped under was gone.

Skidding to a halt, I glanced at the fitness app on my phone. "Ta-Da! Eight minutes and twenty-seven seconds. A new record." With a flourishing sweep of my arms, I took a bow and straightened up in time to catch Duncan's grimace before he resumed working.

"Were ye able to speak with Queen Veronica last night?" he asked as he placed a stone marker in the grass, completing a rectangle.

No "Good morning" or "Great job, woman." No "You look positively radiant in this light, lass." Zip.

Despite the clear skies, I found myself wishing I'd brought an umbrella for protection against my boyfriend's isolated thunderstorms. "Not really. Last night's dream was weird. It's like we were underwater or something."

He headed into the barn and I followed like Fosca begging for the scraps of Giorgio's affection. "Vee looked like a mermaid with her hair floating around her head. I was swimming behind her, so I don't think she even saw me. But I did see her wearing Aunt Gracie's ring—so I think she has it." I noticed because it sparked to life, lighting the water around her, just before I woke up. Since I didn't have any context for the dream, I felt reluctant to mention that part.

"Tonight, try to speak with her again. If you can, tell her that we're coming home. We'll need her and the ring to be ready."

"Aye, aye, captain," I replied with a little salute.

He frowned again before pointing through the open barn door at two figures in the distance. "Eòran and Rabbie are going to help us today."

"With what exactly?" I asked as I reached for the protective padding that Duncan insisted I wear under the leather gear. When I got it all on, I was more insulated than that kid in *A Christmas Story.*

"Sparring. And don't bother with that," he said, waving at the padding. "We're fighting just like ye would in a battle— leather plating only, no extra gear. And be careful with the weapons, they're extremely sharp."

Great. Battling experienced soldiers with razor-sharp swords and no protective padding. That was like Christine Daaé being ripped from the chorus and thrust into the starring role at the *Opéra Populaire*. Did that make Duncan my Angel of Combat? I had to trust that he wouldn't put me in this position if he didn't think I was ready for it. He wouldn't endanger me unnecessarily. At least I hoped he wouldn't . . .

Rabbie and Eòran strode into the barn. While the former blushed at the prospect of interrupting something, the latter, whom I affectionately thought of as Mutton Chops, scowled as if he were here under duress.

"Thank ye for coming, lads." Duncan picked up two swords, handed them to the guards, and then retrieved the remaining two for himself and me. As he handed me the weapon, he explained, "Rabbie and Eòran are familiar with this exercise. We will spar side by side. I'll partner with you first and then we'll switch until ye've fought all of us. All right?"

I nodded. That didn't seem too hard. I'd sparred individually with each of them a dozen times or more.

Successfully blocking out the other two soldiers, I focused on blocking Duncan's moves. Although he didn't go easy on me, he did hold back—at least at the start. When I finally gained the offensive, he went into Celtic warrior mode, but I growled and snarled right back at him as I swung my blade repeatedly to drive him back.

"Time!" Rabbie called as he lowered his weapon.

Duncan nodded toward the young soldier. "Partner with Mackenna and I'll take Eòran."

Expecting a brief intermission, I tried not to let my disappointment show as I moved to my next opponent. As I faced off against Rabbie, Duncan fought to my right. Suddenly my concentration split in two, and no matter how hard I tried to block him out, Duncan dominated my awareness. So much so that I failed to block Rabbie's sword as it swung toward the leather plate strapped to my thigh. The adrenaline rush caused by the prospect of being amputated like the Black Knight allowed me to twist away, saving my leg, but earning a long gash in my favorite yoga pants.

Struggling to regain my mental focus, I gave myself a little pep talk. *Duncan will be fine. He's the Michael Crawford of battle. Focus on Rabbie. What's his weakness? Find it and use it!*

As I blocked my opponent, I focused on Rabbie's movements. Tall and broad in the shoulders like Duncan, but without the same fighting mastery, Rabbie would be most vulnerable from a quick, agile attack toward his lower body. Since most of his strokes were high and wide, it would take him more time to respond.

When Rabbie's body language announced his next move would be a sweeping down stroke, I hastily blocked a set of counter moves—*fake parry, roll, turn, calf strike.* As his weapon dropped, I feigned a block. Then at the last possible second, I dropped and rolled under his arm. Still in a crouch, I turned to strike.

That's when I saw the blood. Duncan's blood—running down his limp left arm, soaking the shirt under his leather breastplate and spattering the ground as he continued to fight Eòran.

Shouting his name, I dropped my weapon and ran toward him—right into Rabbie's sword. With a "hey," Rabbie checked his swing so that it stopped just short of cutting me in half. Undeterred, I pushed the flat of the sword out of the way and continued forward.

As I approached, Duncan leveled his blade at me. "Halt!"

Feeling like I was trapped in a nightmare, I stared down the pointy tip of the blade at my bleeding boyfriend. "What are you doing?"

Now that he was no longer fighting, a crimson pool began to form around his left boot. Face flushed, his body shaking, he growled, "Pick up your weapon and finish the exercise!"

"No. You're injured." I pointed to his left arm. "We need to stop."

"There's no stopping in battle. Now go get your sword." He swayed on his feet, eyes rolling back in his head as the tip of his weapon lowered toward the ground.

Closing the distance between us, I carefully inspected the gash in his bicep. "This is bad. We need to get you to a doctor."

Duncan's eyes snapped back into focus with a grunt. "Get your hands off me. Continue fighting!"

"I will not!"

In one fluid motion, Duncan dropped his sword and then grabbed me by the hair. Quicker than I would've believe possible, he wound it around his wrist and spun me around so that my back was against his chest. "Do ye think the witch's soldiers will give ye a time out?" he snarled. "Eòran, retrieve Mackenna's sword for her."

Mutton Chops scurried to do as his prince commanded. The badger-like guard handed me my weapon, hilt first. But I wouldn't take it.

When I refused a second time, Duncan released me with

a little push that sent me stumbling forward. "Pick up yer weapon and fight! Rabbie, begin the attack."

The young guard's mouth dropped open as he stared between the two of us with wide, disbelieving eyes. "But m'Laird."

"That is an order, man!"

Rabbie leveled his sword at me, and nervously cleared his throat. "Please pick up your weapon, Miss Mackenna."

"No." I loosened the laces of my ruined top to expose my breastbone. "Kill me or let me tend to Duncan. Either way I'm not picking up my sword."

Poor Rabbie looked at Duncan apologetically. "Sorry, m'Laird, I canna do what ye ask."

"Be off with ye then! You too, Eòran." Duncan waited for the guards to retreat, and then, without warning, he gripped my elbow and spun me around. "That was unacceptable. I'm tryin' to save your life."

"And I'm trying to save yours, you stupid ogre." The blood streaming down his arm had started to pool on the ground. Whatever point he was stubbornly trying to prove would have to wait until after he got stitched up.

"In battle, you can't afford to be impulsive," he snapped, spit flying from his mouth. "If I'm injured, ye canna drop everything and come rushin' to my side."

"You'd do it for me," I insisted.

Suddenly all the rage drained from his face and the coldness that replaced it terrified me in a way his anger never would. "Winning the battle and saving the kingdom is more important than any single life—even mine."

"This is about more than the battle for Doon—and you know it. You never answered my question, back in the garden. Do you blame me for being stranded in Alloway? For not being able to go after your brother?"

His face was granite, features taut like he was keeping himself together through sheer force. "I should've been part of the rescue party. Then I'd have the certainty of knowing that Jamie was alive, or we'd both be dead and it wouldna matter."

Hearing the truth of his confession rocked me on a cellular level. "So you'd rather die with him than survive with me?"

Duncan ducked his head. "Tha's no' what I said."

"It's exactly what you said. Now please answer the question."

"I dunno," he admitted, unable to meet my gaze. "I mean, maybe . . ."

I searched his face. "What happens when we return to Doon, if he's—gone."

A muscle in his jaw ticked. "How dare you."

But I could see the truth of it in his eyes. "You're thinking it too. How could you not be? Let's talk about it."

"No." He released my elbow so swiftly that I lost my balance and fell to my knees—the action seemed almost intentional in its violence. For a moment, I just stared at the small puddle of blood in the grass. When I finally found the presence of mind to get up, Duncan was gone.

🛡 🛡 🛡

I lay in bed, tossing and turning. For hours I'd tried everything in my power to fall asleep: counting sheep, lullabies, even reading. Nothing worked. Every time I closed my eyes, my humiliation and disappointment boiled over in a toxic burst of anger.

I was furious with Duncan for refusing to talk to me—and for walking away. Again. I kept replaying our fight over and over in my head, realizing too late what I could have said and done differently. It was Elaine Stritch all over again.

My final summer at drama camp had been highly anticipated

for a couple of reasons. First, I got to pick my own monologue and song for the soloist showcase. Second, Elaine Stritch was coming as the showcase mentor. I'd spent most of my junior year preparing. Choosing Nina's monologue from *The Seagull* had been a no-brainer—it was my best material, but the solo had been difficult. I'd driven Vee crazy testing songs on her before finally choosing "Still Hurting" from *The Last Five Years*.

Despite my nervousness, I knew everyone at camp had faith in me, and as their resident star, I couldn't let them down. They were sure, as was I, that Ms. Stritch would fall in love with my performance—maybe even insist that I skip my senior year to study in New York as her protégé.

After I finished my pieces, I walked downstage for the interactive part of mentoring, notes from an actual Broadway legend . . . Ms. Stritch regarded me with her critical eye and larger-than-life personae, asking, "What do you know about heartbreak, Ms. Reid?"

"Uh, well . . ." I stammered, my face flushed from my performance and inability to form coherent thoughts. "Not a whole lot."

She nodded and said in her rasping drawl, "I could tell. Next!"

I remember leaving the stage in a stupor, shame blurring my vision. She was right, of course. I'd picked performance pieces that I'd had no life experience for—I'd never had a serious boyfriend, let alone crippling heartbreak.

Now, I could sing that song with enough heartfelt passion to make a cynic weep. Without warning I started to sob—dry heaves that racked my body from the inside out. Eventually tears began to gush, and gush, and gush. I cried until my nose stopped up, my eyes swelled shut, and my throat felt raw. Sometime shortly after, I drifted off to sleep . . .

I followed the orange glow until I reached the campfire. Listening to the crackle and hiss, I sat on an old stump to bask in the heat and aroma of burning wood. Vee sat across from me, sporting her favorite fleecy sleep pants and a tank top. Her upper half was wrapped in her Hogwarts blanket.

Compared to my typical dreams involving Vee, this seemed so chill. "No wacky escapades tonight, Buttercup?"

"Nah." She smiled at me, the firelight causing the planes of her face to move. The shifting shadows reminded me of Vee's favorite quote from J.K. Rowling. The one about everyone having both light and dark inside. "No energy for hijinks tonight."

I chuckled. "Tell me about it. Even the Scooby gang needs a night off now and then."

"Exactly."

The breeze picked up slightly, and I pulled my Les Mis blanket tighter around my shoulders to offset the chill. Outside the fire circle the night was pitch black, making it impossible to decipher my surroundings. "Where are we?"

"In Doon." Shutting her eyes, she stretched her slippered feet toward the fire.

I gestured to my Playbill pajamas. "Why does it feel like drama camp?"

She opened one eye to peer at me. "Because it's a dream, silly." Closing her eye, she wiggled her toes in the heat. "But you can sing camp songs if you want to."

Where I went, camp songs equaled show tunes. Nothing against "Kumbaya," but it couldn't touch "Seasons of Love" for building unity. But this wasn't the time for songs. If this really was a Calling, we had important information to discuss. "I don't think so."

Her eyes popped open and she leaned in to gawk at me. "Mackenna Reid doesn't want to sing show tunes?! Who are you and what have you done with my Ken?"

Another gust of wind ripped through the fire circle. Strands of hair whipped around my face, obscuring my vision. Projecting my voice over the elements, I said, "No. I don't think this is a dream."

"Of course it is." She stood and walked toward me. "Why else would we be in our sleepover jammies?"

But this wasn't a middle school slumber party. I rose to meet her. "Vee, I need to tell you something."

Her smile faded as her eyes widened in concern. "Sure. Anything."

The wind sprang to life, howling like a beast and ripping at our clothes as it sought to tear us into pieces. "We've rebuilt the Brig o' Doon and we're training an army in Alloway. Duncan and I are going to cross first so that we can make a plan."

Shouting to be heard, I grabbed Vee's shoulders and leaned in toward her ear. "We need you to use Aunt Gracie's ring so that we can open the portal on the bridge."

Tendrils of hair escaped her braid. They lashed her face like tiny whips. "When are you coming?"

"Soon. Hopefully tomorrow night. Can you meet us at the bridge?"

She nodded.

Rain started to pour from the sky, assaulting our skin in pellets of icy water. The downpour doused the campfire, plunging us into turbulent darkness. Suddenly my bestie threw her arms around me in one of her trademark bear hugs. "I miss you."

The raging storm snatched her blanket so that it went sailing through the air. When it attempted to take mine, I let go of Vee to hold it tight. "Do me a favor," she yelled. "Next dream, let's envision someplace serene and tropical—like Hawaii."

"I told you," I sputtered as I attempted to speak above the howling wind and salty water coursing down my face. The wind *had given up on stealing my blanket; instead it began to wind it around my body like a fuzzy python.* "This isn't a dream. This—"

Vee's brows knit together in confusion. "I can't hear you."

"This is—a—"

"What are you saying?" *The storm swallowed her words.*

I mimed dialing a cell phone and holding it to my ear. "It's a Calling!"

She answered with a helpless shrug. "I can't hear you."

I sat up in bed, face drenched; my body tangled in my sheet. "A Calling . . ."

CHAPTER 22

Duncan

Training Mackenna had revealed to me that I was both sadist and masochist. I'd promised her I'd never ask for my heart back, and now I was taking it by force—bit by bit, shard by shard. Inflicting emotional and psychological wounds in the attempt to toughen her up. My fear was that by the time I was finished, the damage would be irreparable and the remaining mutilated fragments wouldn't do either of us any good, ever again.

Yet the sacrifice of my heart was a small price to pay in order to give Mackenna her best chance at surviving the upcoming battle. Again, I was possessed with the overwhelming desire to leave her in Alloway, where she would be safe. But my intuition told me that in addition to refusing to stay behind, she was also the kingdom's best chance at survival. The Rings of Aontacht had chosen two American girls for a reason; their destinies and that of Doon were intertwined.

Alasdair and I walked toward the bridge after tending to Mabel. "Yer mighty gloomy for someone about ta go home. If I might say so, Yer Highness."

Yellow tape roped off both sides of the Brig o' Doon to keep people off. Tomorrow was to be the grand opening, during which my solicitor would represent the anonymous benefactors at the ribbon cutting. Hopefully by then, Mackenna and I would be back home.

"Thank you again, m'Laird, for taking me with ye. I can scarcely believe that by tomorra' I'll be laying these weary eyes on our homeland once again."

Watching him out of the corner of my eye, I asked, "So you're ready to go home?"

I still didn't fully trust the auld man, but since he claimed to have information he would only divulge to the queen, I had little choice in the matter of bringing him along. Plus, until his loyalties were revealed, he needed minding.

"Aye." He stared wistfully at the bridge. "You, m'Laird?"

"Yes. I'm excited to see my queen and be reunited with m' brother." The words sounded hollow as I spoke them aloud.

"You think Prince Jamie lives, then?"

Given his familiarity with the matrons of our camp, it shouldn't have surprised me that he knew about my brother's capture and death sentence, yet it did. "I believe he lives."

He cleared his throat. "With all due respect, couldn't Miss Mackenna have used her Calling ta find out for certain if your brother survives?"

"You know about that as well?"

The auld man shrugged. "Miss Fiona might have said somethin' ta her mum, who in turn may've mentioned it to me."

The fact that he possessed such intelligence irritated me, but I did my best not to let it show. "It doesna matter now. Tonight I will see Jamie for m'self."

"Aye, m'Laird."

Truthfully, I'd contemplated the same thing about Mackenna

and Queen Veronica's Calling. But it was like holding tight to the lid of Pandora's Box. Once the truth was unleashed, it could never be put back. And I wasn't ready to know for certain.

My energy was better spent in planning for the return home . . . I just prayed that all our planning had not been in vain. We'd rebuilt the bridge and confirmed that Queen Veronica was in possession of the gold and ruby ring—but we had no assurance that the portal had been reestablished. Perhaps the Witch of Doon's destruction could not be undone so easily.

When I voiced as much to Alasdair, he chuckled. "Dinna worry, Yer Highness. The portal is ready and waiting fer us."

"How can you be sure?"

"Have ye not noticed that the Destined stopped arriving in Alloway?"

Honestly, I'd been so consumed with the completion of the bridge and Mackenna's training that I'd thought of little else in the past fortnight. Rather than confess my preoccupation, I asked, "What do you think it means?"

"That the portal's restored. By my figurin', the final Destined arrived the day before last at the same moment the final stone was laid fer the bridge." The auld man turned to regard me with his pale, watery gaze. "I know yer still forming yer opinion of me, lad. But I swear ta ye, I would stake my honor and my verra life on the portal being ready fer us ta cross."

He might be willing to stake his life—and I could agree with that—but was I willing to stake my life or Mackenna's?

As if being my kinsman made him aware of my innermost thoughts, Alasdair placed a veiny hand on my arm. "Dinna fret, Yer Highness. Go get yer things and yer lass. I'll fetch Eòran. We'll meet back here after sundown."

The auld man headed off in one direction while I went the opposite way to Dunbrae Cottage. Things being as they were, I had no choice but to believe Alasdair knew what he was talking about—the alternative was bleak. If the portal didn't work, then the rebuilding of the bridge, the training of the Destined army, the wedge that had grown between Mackenna and myself would all be for naught.

I knocked on the door to Mackenna's bedroom. We hadn't spoken since the training disaster the previous afternoon.

After a moment, she said in a tight voice, "Come in, Duncan."

There was so much that I wanted to say to her—to help her understand, to make things right between us—but I found myself at a loss for words. I stood silently in the doorway as Mackenna stomped about the room tidying it up—something she only did when she was beyond angry.

She picked up a castle figurine, began to cross the floor but then abruptly stopped to glare at me. (I readied myself on the off chance she decided to hurl it at my head.) "Did you want something?"

"Aye." I fidgeted in place. "We cross the Brig o' Doon at sundown. Pack lightly. Take only what you deem absolutely necessary."

"I know. I'm not an idiot." She crossed to the closet and rummaged around until she found a small knapsack. Opening her chest of drawers, she began sifting through the contents, being selective in the garments she chose. When her arms were filled with clothes, she dropped them in a pile on her bed. One by one she rolled them and stuffed them in the bag. Her packing abilities had come a long way since her flat in Chicago.

Focused on her task, she sniffed, "I'm surprised you're even telling me. I figured you'd try to sneak across the bridge without me."

When I didn't say anything she paused, looking up. "You thought about it, didn't you?"

"Aye," I admitted.

Mackenna squared her shoulders as if she were bracing for the confirmation of her worst fears. "For this particular crossing."

"Aye."

"And the one before?"

"That one too." Now that I'd admitted part of the truth, the rest came bubbling forth. "I never intended to stay with you. After the people were safely across, includin' you, I was going to turn back."

"And how exactly were you planning to do that? Pretend to go with me but then grab my ring and dash back through the portal?" The tightening of his jaw confirmed that I was right on the mark. "You jerk! You would have left me here—left us? How could you be so selfish?"

"Selfish?" He barked. "I'm selfish? The queen made me choose between you and m'brother. An' so did you."

"That's not fair. Vee wanted to keep you safe—not just for me, for all of us. We need you."

"Jamie needed me! If he's dead—if I could've saved him and I didn't . . ." He took a slow breath. "Dinna ye see, Mackenna? I'll never be able to embrace happiness with my brother's death on my hands."

"Are you really blaming me for what happened to Jamie?"

"I'm blamin' myself."

"But Vee's my best friend. Part of you wonders if the only reason she chose you to get the people safely to Alloway was because of me. You think if I hadn't been there, she wouldn't have made you leave. Admit it."

"Fergus could've led them. Then he'd be here with Fiona. And Jamie would be alive."

"Or you'd be in the ground alongside him."

"Aye."

Although I seemed to make an unfortunate habit of hurting her, the degree of pain in Mackenna's eyes was so much worse this time than anything I'd ever seen. I was deeply sorry to be the cause of it, which is why I'd avoided having this conversation.

"You're so deluded, Duncan. To me it sounds like you made your choice—you just didn't get to act on it. You'd rather die with your brother than live with me."

"Tha's not—"

"Save it. I think it's time for you to go. I'll meet you at the bridge at sundown."

CHAPTER 23

Veronica

Soft mist peppered our cloaks as Jamie and I made our way to the Brig o' Doon—or at least the spot where the bridge had stood for centuries. Something had prompted me to return. I'd dreamed of Kenna the night before, which was nothing new. She seemed to visit me every night now, my grief over her making the dreams more and more intense. But this was more of an urging. Almost as if Kenna had implanted the idea in my head, and like a fly buzzing around my brain, I couldn't dismiss it.

"This is a waste o' time. We could be halfway to the mountain trail by now," Jamie grumbled.

"I need to check this out. I just . . . I *know* Kenna's trying to get back to us."

He barreled on as if he hadn't heard me. "According to Gideon's intelligence, the witch's guards left for the mountains already. If they reach our people first—"

Jamie had sent Analisa to the royal cemetery at dawn to check for a message from Gideon. We were both shocked that the old captain had left news so soon. But not surprised to hear the witch's plan. Jamie had explained she needed souls to power her magic in order to raise the undead army she planned to use to destroy us.

He was right, we needed to get to our people before she did. "Kenna can't cross the bridge without my ring. You should—"

"The bridge is gone! You told me so yourself."

And I also knew the Protector could reopen the portal. But Jamie's present mood didn't encourage a discussion on faith. "You should go after our people without me. You know the mountains better than anyone."

Jamie gripped my elbow and spun me to face him. "Blast it, Verranica, I canna . . ." His eyes blazed into mine. "I canna let you out of my sight again. I need you by my side!"

The rain chose that moment to pick up, cascading droplets over our hoods, obscuring my view of his face. The admission that he *needed* me was not like my fiercely independent, iron-willed prince. Not at all. I stepped closer, until I could see the hard set of his mouth and chin. I reached for his hand, but he stepped back.

"Let's go. The sooner we check this out, the sooner we can be on our way."

He headed down the trail and I followed, hanging back. Since his return, he hadn't spoken much, and had said nothing at all about his time as Addie's prisoner. His easy smiles and quick wit had disappeared, replaced by the stoic, impatient boy I'd first met upon coming to Doon. He'd had his reasons then; being the heir to the throne with his father on death's door, and me crossing the bridge unexpectedly—the girl who he'd believed his Called mate until I'd begun starring in nightmares that showed me destroying his kingdom.

But this was different. Almost as if he were stuck in his own head, and every time he tried to get out, memories crowded around, yanking him back. I'd attempted to draw him out by teasing, flirting, even sitting beside him in silence. But nothing had worked. The thought of the suffering he may have endured at the witch's hands burned in my chest like a festering stew of sorrow, dread, and fury. How he must feel, I couldn't even imagine. All I knew was that I had to find a way to pull him back from the dark side before he went full-on Anakin.

A snow-melt stream cut across our path, moving fast. I glanced past floating sticks and debris, but before I could determine an easier place to pass, strong arms swept me up.

I clung to Jamie's strong neck and he carried me across in three long strides. "Why is it okay for your boots to get wet and not mine?"

As he placed me on the ground, his hood shifted back and a corner of his mouth twitched. "Because lasses have delicate feet?"

I arched a brow. "Was that a joke, Prince MacCrae?"

"Mayhaps." A shadow of a smile tilted his lips before his eyes eclipsed and a muscle flexed in his jaw. He jerked his cowl forward, and again set off without me. It wasn't like him to stalk off and not take my hand or at least gesture for me to proceed him. He'd been raised by a queen, after all.

Determined to draw him out, I jogged to catch up. "Jamie, what—" But my voice drifted off. We'd reached the clearing that led to the river's edge. The rain had slowed and I lowered my hood to the sound of water rushing over rock. Ancient yews and oaks stood sentinel, tiny buds sprouting on their limbs. Pearls of vapor rose from the canal like breath on a cold morning.

But no bridge.

I ran to the drop-off and peered over the edge, searching

through the misty fog for . . . what? My best friend in mountain-climbing gear, scaling the embankment. Kenna and Duncan riding the rapids in a big orange raft. A rainbow bridge connecting Doon to Alloway . . .

"I know she's coming. I . . . I feel it . . . in here." I pounded a fist against my aching chest.

Warm arms encircled me. "Are ye sure it is no' wishful thinkin', love? There isna much I wouldna give to have my brother here with me now."

I turned in his arms and clung to him. Maybe the vivid dreams and premonition meant Kenna was trying to get back to us, but she'd been unsuccessful. I brought my right hand up between us and stared at the ruby on my ring for some sign of reaction—a sign that its mate called to it from outside of Doon.

It gave not so much as a twinkle.

CHAPTER 24

Mackenna

N ot so much as a twinkle."

I stood in the center of the newly restored Brig o' Doon, shaking the silver and emerald ring on my hand and hoping for a miracle. One that would get us to Doon, reunite me with my best friend, and confirm that Jamie had been saved. Overcast skies blanketed us with misty rain that coated my bare arms. Little droplets flung in all directions as I shook my hand again.

Nada. Frustration hitched in my chest as I stared at the stone. I wasn't sure what I was expecting—it wasn't like the ring had a supernatural short that could be fixed with a little rigorous jiggling.

Duncan stood on my right side. Despite the fact that he was close enough to touch, the boy kept his hands to himself—a wise move considering his recent confession. The balance of our small crossing party, Alasdair and Eòran, waited to my left.

Throughout the afternoon I'd successfully avoided him by staying in my bedroom and skipping meals. But now, as he stood next to me on the bridge, I could feel the distance between us as insurmountable as a fractured portal.

I looked up and accidentally met his dark scowl. Shifting my gaze to the vicinity of his recently injured bicep, I said, "I told Vee we were coming and to meet us at the bridge."

"And you told her that ye were having a Calling?"

"I tried." Crossing my arms over my chest against the chill, I continued to speak to his shoulder. "That part got a little muddled."

"Never mind," he stated. "All that matters is that you can open the portal."

From his expression—equal parts expectancy, urgency, and frustration—I concluded that was my cue to try again. But I wasn't sure what I was supposed to do. Each time I'd crossed the Brig o' Doon, the rings had done their thing, regardless of what I wanted.

Saying a mental *abracadabra*, I waved my free hand over the ring. When that did nothing, I mentally recited the lyrics to "Defying Gravity," which seemed fitting for the circumstances. And finally, I closed my eyes and in true Veronica Welling fashion summoned my inner Jedi to will the ring into action. Apparently, I was not strong in the Force. "It's not working . . ."

"Mackenna—try again."

Duncan's stern voice made me want to throat punch him. Making a fist, I thrust my hand out in front of me. "Work, you stupid piece of junk! Open the portal."

The mist picked up, but that was the only change. Tears began to fill my eyes. Unwilling to let him see me cry, I stalked away from the others. "Let's just forget it, okay? We're never going to make it back."

"I beg ta differ, child." Mrs. Fairshaw's voice echoed from the riverbank as she and Fiona appeared at the mouth of the bridge. Behind them, barely visible through the mist, stood several hundred people, the Destined newcomers arm in arm with the native Doonians.

As I stared at all the smiling faces, the emerald in my ring began to flicker. It was just the faintest spark of light, but still it was something. "How did you know to come?"

From behind me, Alasdair chuckled. "I sent fer reinforcements. I suspected we'd have need o' them."

I swung around to confront the old man. "Why—I mean, what made you think to bring them to the bridge?"

Alasdair stepped toward me and placed a withered hand on my shoulder. "Lass, don't ye know that everything happens fer a reason—even when it defies our comprehension? When yon newcomers began ta cross ta Scotland, they each brought a fragment o' the portal with them. However, they didn't just appear fer the sake o' restoring the Brig o' Doon.

"Each one possesses a special gift or skill we'll have need of in the upcoming battle—but alas, their role is even more significant than that. These Destined are Doonians sure as you an' Queen Veronica. Have ye not wondered at how easily they accepted their Callings?"

I shook my head. Honestly it hadn't occurred to me. I'd been too preoccupied with my own drama.

He raised his brows in mild reproach. "I've spoken ta each an' every one—an' the one similar thing between them is the feeling that they were meant ta do more with their lives. There's unity when like-minded beliefs lead ta a shared cause an' great power in that unity." He paused. "What I'm tryin' ta say, lass, is that we're no' meant ta do this alone. We need ta help one another—it's our only hope."

With that, he nodded to Caledonia, who reached for her

daughter's hand and then declared in her clear, unwavering brogue, "For Doon!"

Fiona, in turn, grasped Cheska's hand. "For Doon."

Echoing the words, Cheska took the hand of Ezekiel, who took the hand of his brother, Jerimiah. Both boys said in unison, "For Doon."

The pattern continued with each person grasping the hand of the one next to them and pronouncing their allegiance with two simple words: "For Doon." Like the turning of a switch, my ring glowed a steady green that grew with each declaration.

When the chain was completed and the final person had spoken their oath, Alasdair grabbed Eòran's and Duncan's hands. "Fer Doon," he uttered.

Duncan's severe gaze bore down on me as he threaded his fingers through mine and proclaimed, "For Doon."

At last it was my turn. My whole body buzzed with the power of my uncle Cameron's ring and the power of the restored portal. I thrust my fist in the air. "For Doon!"

The green glow emanating from my hand turned white. The beam burned though the mist as Alloway and the people on the riverbank disappeared. Instead of the rainy night, it was a clear spring morning. In the distance, the proud turrets of Castle MacCrae stood out against the purple mountains. And at the opposite end of the bridge, with a radiant smile on her face and her arms open wide, stood the true queen of Doon and my best friend in both worlds, to welcome me home.

CHAPTER 25

Veronica

As the glow of our rings faded, Kenna ran the rest of the way across the bridge and smashed into me. I stumbled back until a firm hand stilled my fall. Glancing over Kenna's shoulder, I saw Jamie lower his hand and then stride toward his brother. Both their eyes liquid, they embraced. Not a one-armed, tight-fisted, back-pounding guy hug, but a full-on, arms-wrapped-around-each-other, rib-cracking squeeze. Overwhelmed with emotion, I stepped back to see Kenna's face.

Tears streaked her cheeks and her body shook with sobs. "I didn't . . . think it was . . . was going to work. We rebuilt the . . . the bridge . . . and the dreams . . . and the people came, just like in *Field of Dreams* but . . . Duncan, he . . . I don't. . . ." Her head whipped around to glare at the MacCrae brothers, who had separated but were gripping onto each other's shoulders, tears freely streaming down Duncan's face.

"Shh . . ." I pulled Kenna back into my arms and stroked her hair, concerned that the deep hurt behind the look she'd given

Duncan indicated more than a passing annoyance. "You're home now. You can explain everything later."

My own eyes were strangely dry, even as my heart felt full to bursting. I lifted a hand to wave at Eòran, who returned my greeting with a rare smile and a bow. Perhaps my reticence was due to the old man standing at the mouth of the bridge watching us all with tender affection. He looked so . . . proprietary, as if he had a right to stand on Doon's soil and share our intensely personal moment. He shifted his gaze to meet mine. Keen blue-gray eyes, a roadmap of wrinkles over his weathered face, and his animated countenance brought to mind a scene from long ago . . . a low-beamed ceiling coated with smoke and grime, the bitter taste of ale on my tongue, and the anticipation that my life would never be the same.

Slowly, I extricated myself from Kenna's arms.

The man nodded at me, and I remembered. *"This tale is not for the faint of heart, lasses."* The Tam O'Shanter Inn. He'd told us the real story of the Brig o' Doon at the request of Ally—the pierced and glittery fashionista who'd later transformed into the Witch of Doon before my eyes.

"What did you do?" I asked Kenna before rushing toward the old man. "You're not welcome here!" I grabbed his sleeve and began to tug him back toward the mouth of the bridge, which was already fading into a ruin. I'd toss him over the edge if necessary. No way would I allow another traitor into our midst.

"Lass, I'm no' who ye think I am."

"Don't call me lass!" I snapped at the old storyteller and raised my chin. "I'm the queen of Doon, and your time here is over."

"One way or another," Jamie threatened as he clutched the old man's other arm and pressed a short blade into his back.

Eòran appeared between us and the bridge, his arms crossed over his boulder-like chest, and shook his head emphatically.

"Get out of my way," Jamie growled as he rammed a shoulder into my guard. Eòran stumbled back before turning an irate scowl on Jamie and yanking a knife from his belt.

"Wait, it's okay!" Kenna shouted as she and Duncan rushed toward us.

Dark rage flashed across Jamie's face as he smashed his fist into Eòran's mouth, snapping the guard's head back.

"Whoa!" Duncan rushed in between the two of them, bracing a hand on each of their chests to keep them apart. "I can explain."

Kenna stepped up and placed her hands on the old man's thin shoulders, halting my attempt to drag the betrayer back to the bridge.

I released his jacket and whirled toward Duncan. "Start talking."

After ordering Eòran to stand down, Duncan took Jamie by the arm and turned him to face the old man. "This is Alasdair MacCrae, our kinsman."

Jamie crossed his arms over his chest and leaned into Alasdair's face with narrowed eyes. "I dinna care if ye're the sainted Bruce himself. Why does the queen no' trust ye?"

"'Tis quite the tale, Jamie," Duncan said. "We can explain on our way—"

The old man's eyes warmed. "So this is yer brother. He's alive!"

Jamie pulled back, but his posture remained tense and he turned to me with brows raised in question.

"It's not so difficult to explain. I met Alasdair through Ally, who turned out to be the witch in disguise."

A muscle in Jamie's jaw jumped as he turned to Duncan. "Ye'll explain now."

And so they did. A crazy tale about how Alasdair, fearing for his life, had fled across the Brig o' Doon at the exact moment the Miracle shielded the kingdom. He'd been trapped on the bridge and the Protector had given him a choice—go back to Doon or leave forever. But before young Alasdair could make up his mind, the witch had snatched him into the modern world.

As Duncan finished speaking, his brows drew together, telling me he had reservations of his own. I would just have to trust he had a good reason for bringing the man with him through the portal.

"You're the Suspended man." Jamie's arms dropped to his sides as his mouth opened in astonishment.

Alasdair gave a tight nod, clearly not proud of his legacy. "I'm also the brother to King Angus, makin' me yer many times removed grandfather."

I shook my head. "But how are you still alive?"

"My life force was linked to the witch, trappin' me all these many centuries so close to my home and yet never able to return."

"Why didn't you cross during one of the Centennials when the bridge was open?" I asked, still not convinced.

Jamie answered for him. "Because he couldna enter until the witch did."

"A day I ha' longed for with both hope and fear," Alasdair replied, almost too low to hear.

I exchanged a glance with Jamie, and then with Kenna, and we began to walk back toward the path. Blackened trees, arched and broken, littered the landscape where the Eldritch Limbus had scorched the earth as it burned away. We stepped over a narrow fissure in the ground and Duncan helped Alasdair across as Jamie answered the old man's questions about the destruction. I glanced over my shoulder to see Eòran hanging back, his eyes glued to the back of Jamie's head, distrust clear on his face.

Before I could go back and speak to him, soft fingers linked through mine and I turned to smile at my BFF. She looked different, a bit leaner and harder around the edges. But I had a more pressing question that needed answering. "How did you tell me you were coming? I woke up knowing I needed to meet you at the bridge this morning."

"Don't you remember all of our dreams, silly? Me calling you Wonder Woman during axe-throwing practice?"

I started and stared at her hard. How had she known about that?

"The icky supply boat and me warning you that the first floor of the castle was cursed? Our conversation—"

"By the campfire in our sleepover PJs!" I finished for her, the revelation hitting me like a smack to the face. "We had a Calling?"

She smiled wide. "Have a Calling. We're connected in here." She pointed to her chest.

And the tears finally came, rushing down my face as ugly sobs racked my chest. I'd felt alone for so many long weeks, grieving for Jamie and my best friend. Resolved to protect our people and be strong on my own. Now they were both here with me.

Kenna pulled me close and wrapped her arm around my shoulders. We'd been through so much, fought so hard for our happiness, but it still wasn't over. Kenna let me bawl, her own eyes dry now. That's how it worked with us; when one of us was weak, the other was strong. A balance I'd never truly appreciated until that moment. The thought gave me hope. Individually we were strong, but together we could do anything. Even take our kingdom back from an evil witch and an army of the undead.

CHAPTER 26

Mackenna

I bolted into Vee's empty teepee like a hunchback in need of sanctuary. Returning to the Doonian camp had been . . . a lot. Most everyone wanted news of their loved ones, assurances they were alive and well, messages from beyond the Brig o' Doon—but I didn't have that much to offer. Yes, we have your child. Yes, your aging mother is well. No, we haven't seen your brother or your sister.

Alasdair had immediately been accepted as long-lost royalty and was surprisingly good at passing along news from Alloway. He seemed to personally get to know everyone in the camp and had an endless supply of anecdotes to share. He was also quite skilled at comforting those to whom he could offer no news. Who knew he would be such a godsend?

As I plopped onto a floor pallet, Fergus appeared at the entryway. I'd asked him to follow me. I only had one written message, and with so many Doonians hungry for news, I had been waiting to pass the message along. He'd already been given assurances that his wife was well, but that was as much as we'd spoken so far.

Looking like a true hunchback, the big man had to bend in half to fit inside. "How does Fiona fare?"

"She's amazing. I mean, she misses you so much, but she pretty much runs things back in Alloway."

"And ye said that there's hundreds of Destined at your camp?"

"Yes. They're all ready to fight for Doon—and your wife is overseeing them all."

I watched my big friend's chest swell with pride. "She's not one to remain idle when there's somethin' that needs doin'. Especially for her kingdom."

"She sent you a note." I reached into the gym bag I had packed for the trip and pulled out a folded sheet of pale purple paper. When I handed it to Fergus, he frowned and held it up to his nose.

"It's scented," I explained. "Lavender like the color."

Fergus nodded. "Aye. Do ye mind if I read Fee's letter in private?"

He actually looked concerned that I would be offended by the request, which caused me to smile. "Not at all. Go."

With a thankful smile, he shuffled out of the teepee. And as soon as he left, Vee darted in. Since we shared a brain, I knew she'd been waiting outside for the right time to enter. Unlike Fergus, she didn't have to duck at all to fit inside.

She dropped to the pallet next to me with a frown. "Duncan says you aren't going to the mountains with us."

Since our arrival in Doon, the ache in my heart had subsided. Now it returned so fast and hard I actually clutched my chest. "He said that?"

"What's going on with you two? Spill." Vee arched a brow

and hiked up her chin, clearly accustomed to using the Evil Highney to her advantage.

I opened my mouth only to discover that the lump in my throat prevented me from forming words. Tears stung my eyes as I shook my head back and forth. Finally, I managed to squeak, "We broke up—I think." With a gasp, I began to sob.

Vee pulled me to her shoulder and let me ugly cry all over her. As I sniffled and snorted, I choked out the details of my training and Duncan pulling away. "The worst part is—with Jamie alive, it doesn't even matter. Except that it does because he can't take back what he said."

Vee rubbed my arm, comforting me like she had ever since we were little girls. "It sounds to me like it's just a misunderstanding."

All cried out, I rested my cheek against her shoulder as she rocked us back and forth. "I don't think so. He's mad at me for forcing a conversation he didn't want to have. Sometimes when you say things, you can't unsay them. And once they're said, you understand why they weren't said before. You wish you'd never forced them to be said in the first place."

Vee snorted in agreement, prompting me to demand that she spill as well. "Try having the opposite problem."

She went on to tell me about Jamie's escape from beheading and recapture. "I found him when I stormed the castle—thanks for the warning, by the way. But ever since Jamie came back, he's different too . . . Not all the time—but he can change without warning. And of course he won't tell me what happened during that time with Addie."

She lapsed into silence for a moment before continuing her rant. "I'm not just his girlfriend or his queen, we're supposed to be getting married—"

"When?" I demanded.

"Someday . . ." She paused and twirled her hand to indicate the tent and everything that implied. "Before all this, we were going to tie the knot right after the coronation. But I have no idea how we can build a life together when he won't open up to me."

"You want to know his darkest secrets." Vee nodded, which I felt rather than saw, and I continued. "I'd settle for knowing what Duncan's thinking at all. It's like he's made some decision that affects us both, but he won't tell me what it is."

Vee's hand moved from my arm to smooth my hair. "He's just protecting you. And I guess, in his own way, Jamie's protecting me." She sighed. "Why don't they understand that we need to protect one another?"

"Because boys are stupid," I blurted out. Suddenly we were laughing like a couple of deranged lunatics—until our faces hurt and our eyes gummed shut. Wiping my nose on her shirt, I said, "I've missed you."

Her fingers continued to thread their way through my hair. "Me too, Ken."

After another long pause, I sat up to face her. "So how do we convince our princes to stop protecting us for our own good?"

Vee reflected for a moment. "I think we start by going to the mountains as a team."

"But Duncan thinks it's not safe for me to go. I'm sure Jamie feels the same way about you going."

"Actually, he won't go without me. Which is another issue all in itself."

Jamie MacCrae wouldn't do something on his own? That *was* weird—especially where Vee's safety was concerned. But I didn't voice my shock.

"You know," Vee drawled. Her lips twisted into a mischievous grin. "There are perks to being the queen."

"Yeah, I get it. You can do whatever you want. Are you just trying to make me jealous?"

She shook her head, the smile growing wider. "You're the queen's BFF. So if *I* want you to come with me to the mountains, you're going to the mountains."

"Do you want me to come?"

"Of course, Kenna. We're stronger together than apart." She threaded her fingers through mine so that our rings touched. Which gave me an idea . . .

"Hey," I said. "Remember when Addie had Jamie at Dunbrae Cottage, and your ring showed you where he was?"

"Yes." Her brows scrunched together as she tried to fill in the gaps of my seemingly random segue.

"I want to try something. Come outside?"

"Okay." Hands still clasped, I stood and pulled her up.

The afternoon had become almost warm, with the sun shining through the clouds like a long-lost friend. Camp life seemed to be in full swing and everyone scurried around with a sense of purpose. A group of women hung laundry from ropes strung between the trees. Matteo Rosetti helped his father, Mario, roast meat at the cook fire while the older Rosetti brother chopped wood with a fellow ginger nearby. The red-haired guy paused mid-swing and shot my bestie a lopsided grin that in our middle-school days would've rocketed her straight into crush-mode. She lifted her free hand and gave him a wave. He nodded and then arched the ax over his head, grunting as he let the blade fall.

"Good thing Prince *Jekyll & Hyde* isn't around to see *that*."

"Oh, shut it. Ewan's been a good friend." Vee tugged me toward a maze of teepees and tents.

"How good a friend?"

"You know me better than that." And I did. No one could

replace Jamie in her heart. But something told me that Ewan didn't know her as well as I did.

When we reached the edge of the camp, Lachlan and the youngest Rosetti boy raced past chasing a leather ball with two sticks, the Rosetti twins and Blaz on their heels. Twin one and twin two, their moves eerily in sync, flanked the younger boys and stole the ball. With a growl, Lachlan ducked his head and gave chase, his feet moving so fast he looked like the Road Runner. With a powerful swing, he snatched the ball back and wacked it hard toward the makeshift goal.

"Nice move, Lachlan!" Vee called. The boy turned mid-cheer and answered his queen with a smart salute. With a grin, she saluted him back.

I marveled at the unity Vee had created in the middle of the forest, in the midst of such dire circumstances. You'd think the people were at a clan gathering instead of hiding from a wicked witch and her evil minions. "How'd you do it?"

"Do what?"

I swept my arms outward toward the camp we'd just passed through. "All of this."

Not missing a beat, Vee answered, "Believing is half the battle. And we all believe that together we can win."

Together . . . just like with the Destined at the bridge. I was sensing a theme in all of this.

Taking her dainty hand in mine, I turned to face the purple peaks in the distance. Vee's thoughtful eyes followed my gaze. "What are we doing?" she asked.

"We're going to use the rings to locate the people in the mountains." My voice sounded far more confident than I felt. So far my success wielding Uncle Cameron's ring had been spotty.

"You're brilliant!" Vee gasped. High praise, indeed, coming

from a brainiac like her. She tightened her hold on my hand so that the silver of my ring touched the gold of hers. Vee inhaled slowly and then said, "Show us our people in the mountains. That we might find them . . ."

"And save them," I added.

Instead of the red-and-green glow that preceded the white light, the rings flashed yellow and the streak of light zigzagged through the trees. Astonished, I watched it weave across the mountains until it disappeared in a small burst on the horizon.

Vee giggled. "If I didn't know any better, I'd think the Protector of Doon had the Flash working for him. That's where the rest of the Doonians are."

There was no way that Duncan could leave me behind now—despite how mad he was. Our gift, mine and Vee's, would enable us to find the others. And perhaps the journey would give me the opportunity to figure out where Duncan stood. But the truth of the matter was, I was scared I'd already lost him.

Chapter 27

Jamie

One of the songs on Veronica's tiny music box claimed that the best love is insane. As I watched Veronica hike up the mountain beside Ewan Murray, laughing at his jokes, letting him touch her, and help her over muddy patches of earth, I had to agree. Waves of heat pulsed across my skin and I had to keep rolling my neck to loosen the knot between my shoulder blades.

It didn't help that it was my own blasted fault. When we'd first set off, she'd walked by my side, but then she'd begun to probe into my time as Addie's captive and I'd dismissed her, saying we needed to focus on finding our people. Now I walked alone.

Melting rivers of snow and mud made the crag treacherous, so Duncan and I were switching off taking point. We'd all agreed it was best to only use the rings' guidance when absolutely necessary, since their light could attract unwanted attention. Currently, I was guarding our flank, which put me in perfect view of everyone in our small party.

Directly behind Duncan, Alasdair MacCrae hiked the trail like a mountain goat despite being centuries old. Still unsure if we could trust him, we'd surmised it was better to keep him in our sights. Next, Kenna kept pace with surprising endurance and minimal complaints, but Duncan didn't acknowledge her presence except for a brusque order now and then. Their interactions had been thus since their return home. I had a good notion why, and if my suspicions proved true, intended to speak to my brother of his folly.

Eòran trudged on in forced silence. The man had stepped directly back into his role as the leader of Vee's personal guard and since our confrontation at the bridge, spent most of his time watching me. And maybe he was right to. Since my escape from the castle something dark and volatile simmered just below the surface, begging for release.

Murray had been invited along to help old Alasdair, which turned out to be unnecessary, and left the farm boy plenty of time to assist the ladies. Or one lady in particular.

Vee's boots began to slip on loose pebbles. I lurched forward and reached out, but Ewan got there first, wrapping an arm around her waist and then trotting her to the side in a little jig. Her soft laughter floated back to me and I drank it up like ambrosia.

A pain shot into my left eye and I forced my jaw to unclench. I used to make her laugh like that. But now, I felt wrong, different, like I'd never be the person I was before my capture—that confident bloke who had been sure every decision he made was indisputably right. If truth be told, humility had not been one of my virtues. But that was before I'd thought and done things I could never escape—horrendous things. My fortitude had been tested and I'd failed.

I dropped my hand to my side, realizing I'd been rubbing

the witch's brand burned into my skin. What would Vee think when she saw it? She would grieve to be sure, but would she secretly hate me for not being strong enough or smart enough to find a way out sooner?

"Jamie!" Sharp knuckles cuffed my shoulder and on reflex I spun and punched my attacker square in the chest. Not expecting it, Duncan stumbled back, his feet sliding back through the mud before I caught him by the arm.

Once he'd regained his balance, I released him and ran a hand over my eyes. "Apologies, *mo bráthair*. I'm a wee bit edgy."

Duncan stared at me hard as he rubbed his chest. "A wee bit? What on earth is wrong with ye? I said your name three times."

Choosing not to answer, I watched as the girls stopped up ahead and linked hands.

"There's a huge fissure cuttin' the path in two," Duncan explained. "We need to find an alternate route."

The rings ignited and golden light shot up and to the east. Shielding my eyes from the late afternoon sun, I followed the ring's sparkling ray through a dense patch of forest, to a field of boulders that ended in an almost vertical cliff face. The trail had been steep in places, but this would require a whole new level of skill. "Isna Gilgog's Face just beyond that ridge?" I pointed northeast.

Duncan moved to my left to get a better angle. "Aye, it appears so."

"Armpit's Cave," we said at the same time as we exchanged a grin.

We'd discovered Oxter's Cave as boys. Narrow at its mouth, it opened into a domed cavern dripping with thin stalactites that Duncan and I had thought resembled underarm hair—thus the nickname.

"Verranica," I called. "Tha's enough." The girls disengaged the rings and the glittering beam winked out.

Duncan and I trekked into the forest and scouted until we found the trampled grass and broken brush of a narrow deer trail. It wasn't ideal, but it would make the going a bit easier for the others. "I'll take point for this leg. Ye should speak to Mackenna."

My brother spun around, crossing his arms and widening his stance in the classic MacCrae defensive posture.

I ignored it and pressed on. "I'm no' blind, ye know. Ye're pushing her away because you're afraid of losing her." *Like you thought you lost me.* I didn't say the last bit, but I didn't need to.

Duncan's eyes narrowed and his mouth pressed into a flat line, telling me I'd read him accurately. "Why don't ye mind your own affairs?"

"Dinna look so costive." I gripped him by the shoulder, giving him a little push back toward the main trail. He walked ahead. "What ye feel for each other is no' a vulnerability if ye use it to your advantage."

"Ye dinna understand." He wacked at a low branch with his dirk, cutting it out of his path. "She's more concerned for my welfare than her own. She's impulsive and reckless. In battle, tha's a liability for us both."

I shook my head and rolled my eyes to the heavens, glad he couldn't see me. "And how do ye think you'd react if ye saw her get cut down? Would ye continue to fight or drop everythin' and go to her?"

His silence gave me the only answer I needed.

"In unity there is great power." I spoke the motto that accompanied the Doon coat of arms, as I'd done in different situations throughout my life. This time the words cut into my own pain, making me question some of my recent decisions.

Not far from the main trail, Duncan spun to face me. "Ye mean fight wi' her back to back? Keep her close?"

"Aye."

"But if I do that . . ." He stared past me and scratched his brow. "I canna see her."

"Ye canna see me either, when we fight."

"But I trust that ye can take care of yourself. And me, should it come to that."

I was already nodding. "Exactly. Ye've trained the girl, ye love her, now trust her."

My brother's eyes shifted down and he ran his mud-crusted boot through the pine needles at our feet. And I knew the one thing I could say that would taunt him into listening. A mantra that I'd repeated so often in my head during my capture that it had lost all significance. But for Duncan the meaning would still ring true. "You're *not* scairt."

His head snapped up and a grin tilted one side of his mouth just as a scream echoed through the forest. I spun and ran, drawing my sword as I crashed out of the trees and onto the main path. Six of the witch's guards converged on Vee and the others. Eyes glowing incandescent violet, their moves uncannily synchronized, I didn't recognize any of them. Whether they'd once been Doonians, I couldn't say. These men had become soulless beings, irrevocably surrendered to the witch's control.

As if in slow motion, I saw that Eòran was already down and ran toward the soldier raising his sword to the queen. Veronica spun, braid flying out behind her as she hurled an ax into the dead center of the creature's throat.

Make that five.

Another guard rushed her and I rammed into him, knocking him off his feet. The sword flew out of his hand and I finished him quickly.

I leapt to my feet as Mackenna took out another with a left jab, followed by a knife to the thing's gut. Duncan and Ewan fought the remaining three and I rushed to join the fray. Not one to be left out, Alasdair brandished a dirk in front of him. "Come at me, ye witless neffits!"

A guard stepped toward him, and without hesitation the old man threw the knife and it stuck in the creature's shoulder. The wound wasn't deep, but the soldier froze and stared into space before taking off down the path like a shot.

"Murray! Don't let him escape!" I ordered.

Ewan only hesitated a second before sprinting after the defector. Duncan and I fought the two remaining soldiers, but with every clash of bone-jarring steel, it became more obvious that these were no ordinary men. As I'd feared she would, the witch had magically enhanced their strength and skill.

And whether I wanted to admit it or no, I was not yet at full strength after my ordeal. Even as I thought it, a blow drove me to one knee. The soldier raised his sword above me and I gripped mine to block, unsure if I had the balance to hold him off. But before the guard could land the deathblow, an ax whizzed past my head and wedged in the creature's thigh. Without even acknowledging that he'd been hit, the soldier swung at my head. I ducked and rolled away, then jumped to my feet and spun, landing a kick to the guard's ribs. I heard a satisfying crack, and the thing's eyes widened in shock.

Mackenna joined the fight, showing considerable skill as she helped Duncan push his opponent back. I side-stepped my own attacker and caught a glimpse of Kenna's sword being yanked out of her hand. She pulled a dagger, but Duncan jumped in front of her and yelled, "Stay back, woman!"

A fist landed in my face and I stumbled back. Deciding to change strategies and focus on my opponent's weakness, I came in low and managed to slice into his other leg. He didn't even react. Fine. If we couldn't out fight them, we'd have to outwit them. I took quick stock of our surroundings; muddy sloping trail, forest on my left, a wall of boulders on my right. Boulders on my right . . .

I deflected another thrust, but not fast enough. The tip of the blade sliced through my bicep with searing pain. Red clouding my vision, I channeled the rage that lived within me and yelled, "Hurley!" A code word Duncan and I had devised to indicate we needed a distraction.

Duncan's eyes cut toward me and I knew he'd understood. With a growl, I swung my sword with all my strength and succeeded in throwing my opponent off balance a step. Duncan whirled and kicked the soldier square in the solar plexus. The guard's breath whooshed out and he lurched back, giving me the opening I needed.

Sprinting at full speed, I raced up the wall of boulders, then leapt into the air, sword raised. My opponent began to turn, but it was too late. I arched my arm back and brought my weapon down, slicing the witch's monster neck to chest. I landed on my feet and spun, but he didn't get back up.

I turned just as the last soldier smashed his fist into my brother's throat. Duncan's eyes bulged and his mouth gaped open. With a growl of uncontrolled fury, I charged, but the guard smashed his sword into mine, knocking it from my grasp. Duncan, still gasping for air, tossed me his sword. But it flew wide. I crouched and pulled my dagger, knowing it was no match for a magically enhanced soldier with a claymore.

A scream like that of dueling banshees rent the air and a missile zoomed past my ear. A tiny ax thunked into the guard's chest and he lost his footing. I turned to find Veronica and Mackenna swooping in like avenging warriors. Veronica had another ax at the ready, but Kenna raised her sword, and with a violent shriek ran the creature through.

The last soldier fell, and for a moment no one spoke.

Post-fight adrenaline going to my head, I twirled my dagger around my right hand, then re-sheathed it and turned to Duncan, who was bent at the waist sucking in air. "I take back what I said earlier, brother. Perhaps ye should be scared."

The color returning to his face, his lips quirked and he shook his head.

Veronica helped Eòran back to his feet. He'd taken a hard hit to the head, but as luck would have it, the man possessed a skull of concrete.

We all turned to see Ewan returning up the hill. "I lost him. I'm light on my feet, but he was wildly fast."

"Wicked fast," Kenna clarified as she hovered near Duncan, seemingly afraid to touch him.

No such reservations, Alasdair placed a hand on Duncan's back. "Are ye all right, lad?"

Duncan straightened. "Aye," he answered, his voice craggy.

Alasdair then turned to Eòran. "And you?" The guard rubbed his head and nodded. "Then we should hurry. That guard will have gone to alert the witch."

The old man's warning drained the vestiges of my adrenaline, leaving me appropriately sober.

Veronica stepped forward and cleared her throat. "Right. Let's clean up these er . . . clear this . . ." She stared at each one of the bloodied bodies in turn and then looked up at me, her eyes luminous with tears. I reached out and tugged her sleeve, drawing her tight to my chest. I knew what she was feeling; these men may have pledged themselves to evil, but they were her people. It was the sort of thing that left a permanent mark on one's soul.

"I killed them," Vee choked out. "Men that used to be my guards."

My own throat tightened as her sobs shook my chest. I buried my face in her hair, wishing I could cry along with her.

"Laird, look." Murray bent over the first soldier Vee had killed, a pair of empty boots in his hands. The body had disappeared; only the clothes remained.

I turned to the other guards. "Vee, you should see this."

She peeked up from my chest, just as the body closest to us turned from a putrid violet to black, and then shriveled like a raisin before my eyes. Within seconds, the cadaver vanished completely. Creatures, indeed.

Kenna walked up beside us and took Vee's hand. "They were no longer human."

"Aye," Alasdair said as he approached. "These men where long dead, Yer Majesty."

"I'm not sure if that makes me feel better or worse." Veronica sniffed and brushed away her tears. "If Addie has this kind of power, what more is she capable of?"

I had to agree. The witch was growing stronger by the day. Our kingdom was falling apart from the inside, and this time, I wasn't confident we could save it.

CHAPTER 28

Duncan

Growing up, I was always bigger than the other lads, even Fergus. People assumed that because of my size I was brave. The MacCrae brothers were unstoppable, at least that's what our kinsmen believed. And in Jamie's case, it was true.

Whenever I faced an exploit that terrified me, like scaling the castle turret or repelling from a cliff, Jamie would say in a low voice meant only for my ear, "You're no' scairt. You're Prince Duncan MacCrae."

I would reply, "The valiant . . ."

To which, he would add, "The daring . . ."

And I would conclude, "The fearless . . ."

And then he would give me a shove toward whatever it was that was giving me pause and I would go and do it.

We stood at the base of a cliff, contemplating the obstacle separating us from the others—an almost vertical rock face. The ring's guidance had unmistakably led to Armpit Cave. When Jamie and I had discovered the cavern as lads, we thought we were the only ones on earth who'd set foot in it. Apparently, it wasn't only our secret.

Without warning Jamie shoved me in Mackenna's direction and I collided with her, our feet tangling so that we needed to cling to each other to stay upright.

Mackenna's fingers dug into my shoulders as she struggled to regain her balance on the uneven terrain. "Duncan, what the heck?"

"Sorry," I mumbled as I braced us. Looking over my shoulder, I shot my brother a glare meant to wipe the smirk off his face. "I must've tripped."

Balance restored, I continued to cling to the girl who possessed my heart. I stared into her stormy gray eyes as her brow lifted. "Well," she drawled. And for the briefest of moments, I thought she'd discerned my true intent. "Aren't you going to let me go?"

It was a literal question, but I continued to stand there holding her and gawking like a fool. When her brows ratcheted up even more, I released my grip. But as to the question of letting her go, I was afraid that was impossible. I could sooner let myself go than her. But perhaps, as my brother had tactfully pointed out, I'd been wrong about my approach.

Mackenna shielded her eyes against the setting sun and pointed to the fissure in the rock eighteen meters above us. "That's like, sixty feet. How do we get up there? Any ideas?"

Jamie stepped up from behind. "I've one." He lifted his fingers to his mouth and whistled—*short, long, short, short*; our training signal for allies approaching.

After what felt like hours, but was likely only a minute or two, a rope began to snake its way down the cliff. As we watched it being lowered, Queen Veronica chuckled appreciatively. "Where'd the rope come from?"

Jamie and I exchanged grins. "Many of the caves in these mountains are stocked with supplies. Ropes, bedding, dried food, and whatnot from our training exercises. If our people have been moving from one to the next, they would've likely come across provisions."

"Perhaps enough for a small regiment," I added in afterthought. "But scarcely enough to sustain the number of people we estimate are up there, even if they raided a dozen caves."

As Jamie caught the end of the rope, Veronica brushed her hands together. "Then let's not waste any time." She took hold of the rope and began to climb.

"Alasdair will go next. Then me. Duncan and Mackenna will follow an' Eoran will climb last." My brother pointed to Ewan. "Murray, stay down here and secure the perimeter. You know the distress call?"

"Aye, m'Laird." With a nod and a reticent glance toward the queen, Ewan scurried off into the woods. I found myself wondering, not for the first time, what had transpired between them while Mackenna and I were in Alloway and Jamie was captive.

Veronica was already halfway up the cliff with Alasdair close behind. For an auld man bordering on ancient, he was surprisingly nimble. "Rather like a mountain goat, isn't he?" I remarked for my brother's benefit.

"Tha's what I thought." With a chuckle, Jamie handed the end of the rope to me to hold taut, but before he began to climb, he repeated, "You're no' scairt."

Mackenna reached for the rope, but I shook my head to stop her. "We'll wait for them to reach the top," I explained as I pulled on the rope to take up the slack.

"Okay." Her face, which guarded nothing, told me that she wanted to go right away before her courage failed her.

"It'll be all right. I won't let any harm come to ye." I longed to reach out and cup the downy skin of her cheek, but my hands were occupied with the task at hand.

"I know that," she said stiffly. Although she was standing next to me, close enough to touch, the distance between us created a void that chilled me.

Doing my best to take my brother's advice, I said softly, "What's on your mind, woman?"

She raised her brow. "Why would Jamie think you're scared to scale the side of a cliff?"

Looking away from her penetrating gaze, I shot daggers at my brother's backside—thanking the Protector he'd chosen to wear trousers and not a kilt. "It's a long story."

"Of course it is," she replied with a huff. Even though I wasn't looking at her, I could picture the eye roll that accompanied it.

In silence, we watched Jamie disappear into the fissure on the side of the cliff. "Seriously, Duncan. I'm not sure what I—"

"Now's not the time." I cut her off, my words sounding harsher than I intended as I pulled the rope taut. "Up you go."

❁ ❁ ❁

MACKENNA

The Doonians clustered around Vee and Jamie, eager to hear news from camp regarding their loved ones. Vee did her best to calm their fears, but she couldn't answer all of their questions at once. Speaking to Lachlan's parents, who appeared to be in charge of those in the cave, she assured them their son was safe. Mrs. McPhee melted into her husband's arms, both of them crying tears of relief.

And then chaos erupted—people crying out names, others

demanding to know Vee's plan to defeat the witch and take back the kingdom. I tried to shove my way through the mass of bodies, who clearly hadn't had access to running water for a while, but there were too many people between me and my best friend.

A sheer whistle split the air, echoing through the cavernous space and instantly silencing the mob. I could no longer see him, but Jamie's voice carried over the babble. "You will all back up now, unless ye wish to crush yer queen."

Whispers and the shuffling of feet filled the pause as the crowd forced me back until I hit the jagged cave wall. Spotting a higher elevation, I climbed up to a rocky ledge, just as Jamie lifted Vee onto a boulder on the opposite side of the room.

"Give us just a moment," Jamie commanded in his authoritative, prince-of-the-universe voice. "Her Majesty wishes to address you all at once, and then she will meet with ye individually."

Vee dropped her dusty cloak to reveal her Royals jersey and baseball pants. Her hair, coming loose from her braid, fell in thick strands around her dirt-smudged cheeks. Dressed in modern clothes, she looked like a terrified eighteen-year-old girl, not the leader of a divided kingdom. But she could do this. I had faith in her.

After seeing *Wicked*, Vee had adopted Elphaba's anthem as her own. She channeled the song whenever she felt hopeless or scared. If there was ever a time to defy some gravity, it was now.

As the Doonians anxiously waited for her to speak, I lifted my hand and waved until I caught her eye. Then I circled my fingers around my head and steepled them into the image of a pointy hat. Vee cocked her head in question. I repeated the gesture, then pointed to the sky and extended my arms like I was flying.

When she grinned, I knew she got it. The transformation was instantaneous. She straightened her spine and tilted her chin—my bestie becoming a ruler before my eyes.

Queen Veronica raised her hand and silence fell with the hushed expectancy of an opening stage curtain. "I know you all have a million questions, and I will do my best to answer them. What I will tell you first is that many of your loved ones are safe."

There was a collective intake of breath before she continued. "Kenna and Duncan led many of the children and elderly across the bridge to Alloway, and most of the others are camping in a safe location here in Doon. We did sustain some losses during the earthquake, in addition to those who chose to pledge to the witch."

A large man I'd never seen before shouted, "We're almost out o' food. How soon can we leave to join the others?"

"It's good to see you, Mr. MacDonald." Vee granted the man her patented PR smile and his cheeks flushed slightly. "We'll set off as soon as it's safe."

She glanced back at Jamie, who stood near her left elbow. "Sunrise," he answered. "The trail is too dangerous for two-hundred-odd people to traverse in the dark. We canna risk drawin' attention with torch light."

There were a few more logistical queries before an Asian man I recognized from the marketplace called out, "What's your plan, Your Majesty? To take back our kingdom?"

The silence that followed was so deafening, you could have heard a hairpin drop.

Vee's smile faded, her demeanor mirroring the severity of the question as she replied in a clear, strong voice. "As you may know, the witch has taken control of the castle, and we've gathered intelligence that she is attempting to raise an army of the undead."

Everyone began talking at once. Shouts of panic and murmured prayers punctuated the chaos as the acoustics in the cave magnified the sounds of their fear. I saw Vee's lips move; watched as she raised her hand and the Ring of Aontacht ignited in a flash of red that bathed the cavern in bloody light.

When everyone's attention shifted back to her, she lowered her arm, light still pulsing from the ring. "I know you're afraid, but that's exactly what Adelaide wants. If we allow it, she will herd us all like lambs to the slaughter. But I, for one, will not give up Doon without a fight!"

Tears sprang to my eyes as the people cheered and raised their fists with shouts of solidarity. My focus shifted to Jamie, who gazed at Vee with more wonder and love than that of Romeo for his Juliet. I knew in that moment, whatever he was hiding from her wasn't strong enough to withstand their bond.

Oblivious to her prince's adoration, my bestie continued her monologue. "Mr. Chang asked me what the plan is and I do have one, but I will need each of you to do your part to complete it. First, if you choose to pledge your life to Doon, we will hold a brief fealty ceremony. Your vow to the crown and the Protector should earn you a measure of protection against the witch's power. But you must examine your heart, as the pledge will only work if you commit to protect Doon, no matter the cost."

There were murmurs of assent amongst the crowd, which Vee spoke over as she hit her stride. "Secondly, with the help of others and a lot of faith, I was able to sneak into the castle and obtain this."

She raised a tear-shaped vial; the liquid inside shimmered like sunlight on water despite the dreariness of the cave. "This is Saint Sabastian's elixir. It has been blessed from the heavens with the ability to drive out evil—a power that, according to legend, not even the witch can withstand."

She talked about the potion with such conviction that I wanted to believe right along with everyone else that she held the means to destroy Addie in her hand. Could it really be that easy? I prayed it was true.

After tucking the vial back in her pocket, Vee said, "Thirdly, Kenna and Duncan"—she shot me a grin before continuing—"have been training an army of Destined who have gathered from all over the modern world. These Called individuals have specialized skills in combat, weaponry, and battle strategy."

In theory, I amended as the crowd murmured among themselves in reaction to the news. A large majority of them were gamers like Cheska. Yes, there were some Destined with actual combat and/or weapons experience as well as a few survivalists—but I was still at a loss to figure out what the Protector needed with a rodeo champ, or a wildly popular Internet magician.

"They will cross the bridge and join our ranks when the time is right." She stepped to the edge of the rock and braced her hands on her hips. "We are not alone in this fight! The Protector has given us everything we need to win back our kingdom! Now who's with me?"

Amid the applause and shouts of *Aye*, I threw my fist into the air and cried, "For Doon!" The audience immediately picked up the chant, their voices so loud I was afraid they might shake the stalactites down around us.

Jamie jumped from the boulder, trailed by Vee. As soon as they were down, the princes, all three of them, led their people through a mass pledge of fealty to their American queen and to country. As I repeated the oath along with the others, I felt hopeful for the first time since being stranded in Alloway that Doon's story wouldn't end like a Shakespearian tragedy.

Sometime later, after Vee and the MacCraes had spoken to

everyone individually, I nibbled on my supper ration of half a stale roll and some dubious dried meat, and my mind wandered to my own star-crossed love story. I thought I'd done well in the recent battle with Addie's guards, shown that I could handle myself . . . until Duncan had called me off. That moment and his lack of confidence in my fighting ability continued to fester, fueling my ascent to the cliff. Now in the dimly lit space, it was a six-foot, three-and-one-half-inch tall pooka standing between us.

Scanning the crowd for the shadow who stood head and shoulders above the rest, I walked over to where Duncan chatted with a group of men and thumped him on the bicep. "Can we talk?"

Then I turned and wove my way through the large cave toward the back, in search of a little privacy. My heart felt like it was about to beat out of my chest. But as much as I dreaded the impending confrontation, I couldn't allow us to remain in limbo as danger grew all around us.

Ducking into a small recess off to the side of the main grotto, I waited for Duncan to join me. In the space between one breath and the next, he stopped beside me. In the gloom, I rummaged through my bag until I felt a small box.

Inside was a folded scrap of plaid paper, a silly memento I handed to him. "Here."

"What's this?" I watched as he unfolded the paper and then looked to me for an explanation.

"It's your heart," I said without preamble. "I'm giving it back to you."

"I dinna want it back." He shoved the paper back into my hand and crossed his arms over his chest.

"Then what do you want? 'Cause I've been trying to figure that out. You don't want your heart; you don't want me. Do you want me to go away?"

The tension in the darkened alcove was palpable, like an impending thunderstorm or the moments preceding the opening night of a play that's had a bad tech rehearsal. Unable to take the silence, I continued to force the conversation. "Say something. What do you want from me?"

"I want you ta not fight," he hissed. "I want to chain you up in this cave an' leave you here until the battle's over!"

My eyes began to sting as my vision turned glassy—but I refused to cry. Instead, I let the emotion fuel my anger. "You don't want me fighting by your side? Fighting to save Doon?"

His response spewed forth in a heated rush. "Nay. I do, it's jus' . . . if you or Jamie should get inta trouble in battle—I dinna want to have ta choose which one to save!"

I crossed my arms, mirroring his posture. "I guess you won't have to now that we're broken up."

Duncan snorted. "I never broke up wi' you. You're the one who got angry an' broke up wi' me."

"No. You got mad and broke up with me." Suddenly, it hit me. His messed-up, macho, boy logic. "So we're not broken up?"

He shrugged. "I guess not . . . unless you want it to be so."

I gave him an ineffective shove as the emotions of the last couple weeks boiled over. "You self-righteous, stupid ogre. We are stronger together. Haven't you figured that out yet? You've heard that saying about a cord of three strands not being easily broken? Well, you, me, Jamie, Vee, Fergus, Fiona, and the others, we're a tapestry that the witch cannot unravel. So quit being all noble and martyr-like and, for heaven's sake, stop being mad at me. 'Cause I love you!"

"I love you too!" he leaned into my face and barked.

"I know!" Our eyes locked, like lovers from a Noel Coward play, both too stubborn to show vulnerability.

Unable to say more, I turned and stalked away. Determined

to find a quiet corner in this madhouse to decompress, I stomped through the crowd. I got halfway across the cave before Vee intercepted me. "Ken, what's the matter?"

"Duncan and I made up," I growled.

"Oh, that's good . . . right?" Her response took some of the heat from my agitated state.

"Yes." I glared at her for a half a second before cracking a smile. Had I really just had a make-up fight with my boyfriend?

CHAPTER 29

Veronica

You *know ye cannot win . . . I will take everythin',"* the voice hissed through my dreams, sinking deep into my heart. *"Your people will die. Your kingdom will fall."*

I fought to wake up, but the bonds of sleep held me tight.

"And when ye are gone, my weak little queen, your prince will rule by my side. It is what he wants. What he longs for, but cannot say aloud. We've shared experiences that you could not possibly understand.

"I've marked him as my own. Can ye no' tell that he is different? He's not your Jamie anymore . . . He's mine . . . body and soul. Everything ye have is mine . . ."

I jerked awake and blinked at the falling ceiling, its spindly fingers stretching down to crush me. My breath came in short gasps until I remembered we were in Oxter's Cave, the "fingers" stalactites reflecting the glow of multiple campfires. My pulse calmed, but the voice from my dreams still echoed in my head. *Her* voice. The witch. She'd gotten into my head once, long ago, but I couldn't be sure if it had truly been her or my own fears.

I turned over on my pallet of blankets. Jamie lay beside me on his back, eyes closed, hands folded on his chest, dark lashes resting against his cheeks. I studied his profile; strong, straight nose, perfect lips, square jaw covered in light brown stubble. His hair had grown enough that one stubborn strand curled behind his left ear.

Biting my lip, I reached toward him, my fingers tingling in anticipation. My heart beat faster, my skin flushing. But I stopped. Terrified to wake him and see his cold gaze and hear his emotionless voice, I pulled my hand back and tucked it under my cheek. The voice was right . . . He *had* changed.

Jamie twitched, his brows lowered, and his hands clenched into fists. Lips moving, his unintelligible words became more urgent. I reached over and laid my hand on his chest. His heart slammed against my fingers as his limbs began to jerk. I scooted closer and whispered in his ear, "Shh . . . Jamie, it's okay. I'm here . . . you're safe."

"Let me out . . ." Jamie thrashed and I pulled away. "Please . . . no . . . ye're no' Verranica!"

"Jamie, wake up." I leaned over him and shook his arm. "It's just a dream."

His eyes snapped open and locked on my face, fierce and intense, before he grabbed my shoulders and threw me down on my back. Baring his teeth, he snarled in my face, "Dinna touch me. Do ye hear me, witch?"

His eyes fathomless pools, he stared right through me.

"Ja—"

His mouth swooped down, his lips crushing mine. The kiss was demanding, almost painful, but my body didn't seem to care. Powerful yearning rocketed through me, stealing every thought but one—Jamie. I clutched his shoulders and tugged him closer. His skin burned against my fingertips and I couldn't get enough. Slanting my mouth on his, I kissed him with every ounce of love and yearning I'd buried these long, lonely weeks.

I felt the moment he came back to me, his body melting into mine. He cupped the back of my head and took control of the kiss, slowing down to gently worship my mouth with his. Delicious sparks sizzled up from the base of my spine and I pressed into him, needing to get closer to his heat. I ran my hands over the muscles of his arms and back up to the exposed skin of his neck.

Mine. Jamie MacCrae was mine and no shriveled hag of a witch was going to take him from me—body *or* soul. I pulled back and cradled both sides of his face, searching his gaze.

His eyes churned like a dark storm as he gasped for breath. "I dreamt I was kissin' you . . . but . . . I . . ." He rose up on one arm and raked the hair off his forehead.

I lifted on my elbows, trying to hold his attention, but his gaze shifted beyond my head, the impassive mask dropping into place over his face.

I couldn't let him slip away from me again. "What did she do to you, Jamie?"

Without looking at me, he cracked a sardonic smile. "Mind games, imprisonment, torture . . . you know, the usual witchery."

"Don't make light of it!" I gripped his arms, digging my fingers into muscle. "Before you kissed me, you called me witch! You were still trapped in a nightmare . . ."

Several moments passed and I remained silent. Holding my breath on the hope that he would tell me of the memories that lingered just behind his eyes.

His mouth opened and then closed. He searched my face, a muscle ticking in his cheek. "You're bleedin'."

He reached out and brushed a finger over my swollen lips

and then stared at the red stain there. His brows lowered, then his eyes snapped back to mine in horror. "I made ye bleed."

I licked the metallic taste from my top lip. "It's nothing. Really. Probably just left over from the fight with Addie's guards yesterday."

He shrugged off my hands and rolled away. "Maybe it's no' a good idea for ye to be alone wi' me."

I sat up to find him tugging on his boots. "Jamie, I wanted you to kiss me, okay?"

"But I didna have to hurt ye, did I?"

A shadow loomed over my shoulder and I looked up to find Eòran, arms crossed over his chest, feet wide. He couldn't speak, but he didn't need to; his body language said it all. My guard hadn't left me alone for more than five minutes since his return to Doon. But at that moment, I didn't want him hovering like a nanny.

"Eòran, I'm fine. Give us a minute."

Jamie sprang to his feet. "The sun will rise soon. We need to go." Without looking at me, he strode away.

As we made our way down the mountain, I moved from group to group talking to individuals about their family members and asking what their duties had been at their own camp, so I could assign them a job at base camp. Housing would be an issue, but the weather had turned again, the sun shining strong and warm with a slight cool breeze. Sleeping under the stars would no longer be a danger.

Eòran had gone ahead with a scouting team, but Ewan shadowed me everywhere I walked, and I wondered if my guard had put him up to it. I hadn't seen Jamie since we'd left the cavern.

He'd organized the descent down the cliff face and then disappeared. At least Duncan and Kenna had found their rhythm. When she'd told me they made up, she still seemed angry, but now, they walked just ahead of me, hands linked and smiling.

My heart warmed and ached at the same time. What had happened with Jamie this morning had been another setback in a long line of obstacles with him.

"Yer Majesty." Ewan jogged up beside me. "May I speak freely?"

I glanced at my friend, red hair flopping over direct green eyes, and something in the set of his mouth bothered me. I'd never really seen him angry and I wasn't sure this was it, but I hesitated before replying, "Yes."

"Something is no' right with Laird Jamie."

Didn't I know it. But I would defend him until my dying breath. "The prince was kidnapped by the witch . . . we don't know what he's been through, Ewan."

"Well, I realize tha'. But he . . . well . . . I dinna think . . ."

I stepped over a small fissure in the earth before glancing at my friend. He ran a hand over his head and gripped the back of his neck—clearly unused to being at a loss for words. I knew Ewan had developed feelings for me, but I'd figured it was a passing crush, and once I discovered Jamie alive I hadn't given it a second thought. Until now.

Not wishing to hurt him, I searched for the right words to let him down easy. "Ewan, Jamie and I have a Calling. Surely you know what that means."

"Aye, I do. But he doesna treat ye right!"

A few faces turned in our direction at his raised voice. "Ewan, please! Maybe we should talk about this later."

"Nay." His voice had quieted, but was no less passionate. "He's sullen and angry and he ignores ye, but worse, I can tell he's hidin' something. I've known him all my life and this just isna him!"

My chest squeezed at his words. The witch's voice echoed back from my dreams. *He is mine . . .* I set my jaw and focused on the blue sky peeking through the clouds. I *would not* let her into my head.

"And where is he now?" The boy had leaned close to my ear. When I snapped around, he pulled back, but his gaze locked on mine. "I fear he has been bewitched somehow."

My gut clenched as Ewan's word confirmed my own fears. I looked straight ahead, and thought for several moments before I spoke. "Did you see where he went?"

"I was one o' the last to scale down the cliff face. He pulled up the ropes and I never saw him come down."

It was curious, but I still believed in Jamie. Regardless of what Addie had done that he wasn't telling me or my own reservations about his behavior.

"Look, Ewan, I appreciate your concern, but I'm sure Jamie has his reasons for taking off on his own."

"He did." The deep voice gave me a start, and I whirled to find Jamie right behind us.

"Where did you come—"

"I need ye to come with me. Now."

"Wait." Ewan gripped my forearm. "Yer Majesty, I dinna think ye should go on your own."

Jamie inserted himself between us, forcibly removed Ewan's hold on me, and then looped his arm around Ewan's shoulders. He spoke low, but I could still make out the words. "Ye are no' Queen Verranica's guard, or her betrothed. She is none o' your concern, Murray. However, she is mine. Now leave off!" Jamie released him with a push and Ewan stumbled into a group of men who laughingly steadied him on his feet.

"Best no' to anger the laird, young Ewan!" The blacksmith smacked him on the back so hard, he stumbled again.

"Jamie!" Worried he might snap, I followed, reaching an arm out to . . . what? If he decided to hurt Ewan, there wasn't much I could do to stop him.

He returned to me with a rueful grin, and I let out a sigh of relief.

Looping his arm around my waist, he guided me quickly through the slow-moving crowd. "Sorry, love. I've needed to do tha' for several days now."

"If it makes you feel better. But there's nothing going on between us."

"I believe ye, but that doesn't mean I have to sit back and let him disparage me to ye."

"He's only watching out for me." He lifted a brow in challenge and I decided to table that conversation for later. I asked, "What's going on? Where did you go?"

"I need to show ye," he insisted as he made a beeline for Kenna and Duncan.

When we reached them, Jamie gripped his brother's shoulders and said a few urgent words close to his ear. A few minutes later, Jamie led Duncan, Kenna, and myself through the forest at a breakneck pace. It seemed we were headed back the way we'd come. Following a sharp switchback trail, we were forced to climb single file. Jamie took my hand and practically ran the rest of the way. "Almost there!"

We reached the top and burst onto a ridge, the world opening up below us. Fallow fields bisected by low walls and rushing streams stretched out like a patchwork quilt of browns, greens, and blues. In the distance, the castle turrets rose above the trees. The view was breathtaking, but I knew that wasn't why Jamie'd brought us here.

"Wow," Kenna said under her breath.

Jamie stepped up beside me. "I was scoutin' the woods for guards and a place to camp, if tha' became necessary, and I found . . ." His voice trailed off as he took a tubular object out of his pocket and held it to his eye. He muttered a curse and handed me the small telescope. "Look, just north o' the brook."

I focused on what appeared to be a field of tilled earth, but even before I raised the spyglass, I could discern an undulating movement, like worms churning up the soil and figures that looked strangely humanlike, but couldn't've been. Their shape was . . . off. Squinting into the magnifying lens, it took me a moment to find the correct spot. I focused on a patch of ground that churned from underneath, the soil spewing up until a skeletal hand broke the surface, reaching for the sky. "What in the—"

I swung the glass in a slow arc to take in the rest of the field. Skeletons were emerging from the ground. One, half out to his waist, pushed against the dirt with both hands. Another got stuck, snapped off its leg, and then clawed itself the rest of the way out. The creatures who had made it out stood in rows, shoulders slumped, like marionettes without a master. There were rows upon rows of them . . . "Oh no, no, no . . ."

Jamie took the glass from my trembling hands and handed it to Duncan.

"What is it, Vee?" Kenna had slipped her arm through mine and gave me a little squeeze.

I faced my best friend, unable to disguise my panic. "Skeletons . . . zombies . . . I don't know what they are! Gideon said she would do this, but I didn't think . . . this is just crazy!"

Kenna released me and marched over to snatch the telescope from Duncan. "Let me see that." She let out a curse of her own and then said, "Well, I guess that guard made it back to the castle."

"That's why I felt her rage last night in my dreams."

"Aye," Jamie agreed as he took my hand in his and met my gaze, communicating something I couldn't quite grasp. "I felt it too."

"But, how do you think she's doing this? According to Gideon, she needs souls to raise an undead army. The camp is heavily guarded and the people from the cave are with us. So where did she get the souls?" My words dropped off as the realization slammed into me.

Jamie's stricken eyes met mine. "She must be usin' the souls of Doonians who pledged to her. Cannibalizin' them to raise the skeletons."

"What an evil witch!" Kenna spat, but she didn't say *witch*.

I wholeheartedly agreed, but I had to force myself to think. The skeletons were immobile, but I had a feeling they wouldn't stay that way. We needed to get everyone back to base camp quickly, then get a closer look at the zombies while they were still inactive.

CHAPTER 30

Mackenna

In rare instances, life was less like Broadway and more like a horror movie, unless you counted *Evil Dead the Musical* . . . or *Carrie*. Okay, so maybe the recent trend in scary musicals wasn't helping my argument, but I would take the worlds of Rodgers and Hammerstein over Romero and Hitchcock any day.

I crouched with Vee in the brush behind the tree line, watching as one of Addie's skeleton thingies clawed its way up from the field. My heart pounded as the undead pile of bones finally freed itself from the earth like a newborn cicada—minus the baby insect cuteness—and stood unmoving.

When I said as much to Vee, she frowned at me like I'd lost my mind. Considering the freak show in the clearing, maybe I had. "But you hate bugs."

"Sarcasm, geez!"

"Oh. Sorry." Her pale face mirrored the nausea I felt. Her brows knit together as she puzzled something out. "I don't get it."

She trailed off, and before I could ask her to clarify, a bony hand reached for the sky on the opposite end of the field. "Son of a Sondheim! There's another one. How many is that?" I tried to do a little mental mathematics counting the skellies, but lost my place and had to start over, finally giving up.

Duncan, Jamie, and Alasdair knelt behind us, observing in silence. The MacPhees and Ewan had been charged with getting the rest of the people to base camp, while the five of us went on reconnaissance. Glancing in the princes' general direction for a little help, I asked, "How many do you think are out there?"

In a voice not meant to carry, Jamie replied, "Seventy-five or eighty."

At the same moment, Duncan and Alasdair whispered, "Eighty-three."

I clutched Vee's hand to ward off the chill that had nothing to do with the evening temperature. "Why aren't they moving?"

"That's what I don't get," Vee murmured. "What are they waiting for?"

Silence followed, because none of us had an inkling of how to answer the queen, until Duncan mused, "How many bodies do you reckon are buried in that field?"

"No clue," Alasdair grunted. "I dinna know there were people buried here. All our kinsfolk are buried in the cemetery near the castle—all o' the villagers in the kirkyard. This certainly predates the history I know about."

Which raised a good question . . . "Do you think bodies are coming up there too?" Technically, the Doonians burned their dead on a pyre on the lake; I'd seen it once, but after the fire died, the remains were buried. I couldn't imagine us facing what remained of King Angus, or Queen Lynnette—or Duncan and Jamie's folks.

Duncan placed a reassuring hand on my shoulder. "Nay. The cemetery at Castle MacCrae and the kirkyard are consecrated ground. Their souls and bodies are at peace."

"And these, uh, people? How are they different? Besides being skeletons that can dig themselves out of their graves." Something had bitten my right knee. Letting go of my bestie's hand, I scratched at it savagely, grateful to focus on something other than the raising of the undead army.

"They must be Celts," Vee replied as she shifted positions to standing. She realigned herself behind a tree and bent one leg into a yoga pose. But I doubted that all the Zen in the world would help at this moment. "They would've preceded the Doonians. I'm guessing this is a mass grave of some sort."

"Aye—"

Whatever Jamie had been about to say next faded away as the ground directly in front of where we were hiding began to shift. Small, bony fingers wormed their way out of the soil.

A skellie hand continued to dislodge the earth until a yellowed skull wriggled free. The creature continued to writhe back and forth as it squirmed its way up from the ground. Dislodging its hip bones, the thing began to pull itself forward by the hands until its lower body was free. When the monster finally stood, it was about Greta's height.

Vee's very much alive and trembling fingers threaded through mine so that our rings rested against one another. "Does that look like a child to anyone else?"

My "Yup" and the MacCraes' "Ayes" confirmed the unthinkable. Addie's undead army included kids. On a scale of one to ten, my terror ratcheted up to eleven. She was one sick witch!

Thoroughly creeped out, I stood to address my bestie. "How do we kill those things?"

"We use the rings." Vee nodded toward our intertwined hands. "We'll send out a pulse intended to disintegrate evil. That oughta work, right?"

I shrugged; she knew more about how the rings operated than I did. To me, they seemed to have an agenda all their own. But considering what we were up against, anything was worth a try.

When I nodded, Vee said, "Close your eyes and picture a burst of righteous power, like the Force, flowing from the Rings of Aontacht across the field like a tidal wave."

Letting my lids drift shut, I pictured my ring like a lightsaber sending a burst of good energy from my hand and across the field. I imagined it rolling over the skellies, disintegrating their bones into dust. I willed it to happen.

Unsure whether I had felt the power of my uncle Cameron's ring or just wishful thinking, I opened one eye. "Did it work?"

Nope. The skellies were still standing over their graves, waiting for their next order. Vee's eyes blinked open, darted to the field and back to me. "Concentrate harder, Kenna."

"I'm trying," I growled.

"There is no try—"

"Cut the Yoda talk," I hissed. "I'm not Obi-Wan Kenobi. I can't just make the ring go when I feel like it."

"You can," Vee insisted. "Just do it."

"Stop with the slogans, already." I turned to where Jamie, Duncan, and Alasdair hovered. "Can you just step back, possibly? Give us some space?"

As a single entity the princes took several steps backward. Turning back to Vee, I grabbed her hands, squeezing them in mine. "Okay. I'm ready to try again."

I closed my eyes as Vee spoke in a low, hypnotic voice. "Great Protector. We ask you to destroy our enemies. To use our rings to cut them down where they stand—right in this field. We beseech you."

"And we wouldn't ask if it wasn't really important," I added.

"We believe that it is your will to save Doon, and we humbly ask you to destroy these, uh, things—"

"These skellies," I added.

"Yes." Veronica agreed. "Please destroy these skellies."

"Thank you," I intoned. Opening my eyes, I locked my gaze onto Vee's. "Did it work?"

She glanced at the field, where nearly ninety skeletons stood erect and motionless. "Not sure."

A moment later we had our answer, as the tip of a finger bone burrowed its way up from the ground. Letting go of Vee's hands, I grumbled, "That was a bust. What's plan B?"

Alasdair gracefully strode forward, all five-and-a-half feet of him appearing deadly. "I've an idea, Yer Majesty."

"Shoot."

The old guy nodded toward the field. "I figure someone ought ta go out there and try ta engage one o' those abominations, see what happens."

"No," Duncan interjected. He and Jamie stood right behind their ancestor with contradictory frowns. "It's too dangerous."

"Although *mo bráthair*, Alasdair does have a point," Jamie countered. "We've no hope of defeating those skeletons without more information. One of us should go out there."

I watched the shadows move across Duncan's face as he grappled with his brother's logic. The moment he made up his mind, I could read his decision in the set of his jaw.

"Fine." In one fluid movement he unsheathed his sword and strode into the clearing. Slowly, he approached the nearest skellie, the kid. Duncan made a careful circle around it with no results. Moving on to the next one, he stopped directly in front of it. After a moment of hesitation, he reached forward and tentatively poked the thing in the center of its skull. Not even touch could provoke it into life.

"It feels like cold bone," he explained.

Pitching his voice low and projecting so that it carried, Jamie replied, "If you can touch it, you can slay it."

Duncan nodded, never taking his eyes off of the monster. "It's worth a try."

Gripping the hilt of his sword with both hands, he spun in a three-quarters circle, his weapon poised to cut the skellie in half just above the hips. But as the sword made contact, there was a flash of purple sparks and an ear-shattering clang. Duncan's sword ricocheted back toward him as the pulse from Addie's protective magic lifted him off his feet and propelled him across the field. He landed with a thud and rolled several times before coming to a stop against a large stone.

I watched in shock, not quite able to process what was happening or do anything about it. Holding my breath, I waited for him to move . . . but he didn't. By the time my adrenaline kicked in and I felt able to react, Jamie had already scrambled halfway to his brother. When I started to follow, Alasdair grabbed me by the shoulders.

The old guy shook his head and whispered, "Stay tight. The lad's got him."

I held my breath until Jamie reached his brother and checked for a pulse. A few never-ending seconds later, he gave us a nod. My breath and Vee's came out in a collective whoosh.

My best friend looked at me, her turquoise eyes mirroring my fear. She took my hands in hers and gripped tightly. "He's alive, Ken."

I shook my head, unable to speak over the tears lodged in my throat.

The skellies remained inanimate, but that didn't stop Jamie from keeping a watchful eye in their direction as he eased Duncan onto his back. With another sweep of the field and a grim glance at Vee, he began checking his brother for injuries.

After another small eternity, Duncan groaned. That groan was followed by another as Duncan shook his head and opened his eyes. He blinked at the sky for a moment and then, with Jamie's assistance, sat up. They exchanged a few words and then Duncan turned and gave me a little wave.

Alasdair patted me on the shoulder. "See there, lassie. Duncan's a hearty lad. There's no lasting harm."

To underscore Alasdair's words, Jamie hoisted Duncan to his feet and helped him make his way slowly across the clearing.

Who did that witch think she was? Anger pulsed through me, and I turned to my bestie. "Let's try the rings again." I reached for her hand, but she pulled back.

"No. It's not working for some reason." She stared at the ruby ring as if it had betrayed her and then, shaking it off, returned her determined gaze to mine. "We will try again, just not yet. Maybe after the skellies are animated, they'll be more vulnerable. For now, we need to get back to camp and warn the others."

She gave the skeletons one last glare, and then turned and stalked back toward the path.

Clearing his throat, Alasdair followed. "Yer Highness. I'm wondering if I might have a word with ye." Keeping my eyes on the field, I sensed rather than saw Vee stop.

"Yer Highness," Alasdair began. "I know how you can destroy Adelaide once and for all."

"You do?" Vee's tone pitched up in her interested-but-skeptical voice.

"Aye. You must first make her mortal."

"How?" I could almost see her brow arching.

"Ye must strip her of her magic. In my figurin', there's a couple o' different ways ta accomplish it."

"Go on."

"She's usin' up her magic with this army. If she spends it all, the only thing left will be her human form. And if that doesna do it, there's a good chance that the elixir will strip what remains."

"So what you're saying is that you really don't know the best way to make her mortal." I was fairly sure I could hear Vee's arms crossing in front of her chest.

"Nay, Yer Highness. I know of one surefire way ta accomplish the task. But the method is so extreme, I'm reluctant ta mention it."

Before Alasdair could say more, Duncan and Jamie emerged through the tree line. Other than a little limp, my boyfriend seemed all right. And he was still clutching the hilt of his sword in his free hand. "Blasted magic broke my blade in two."

Jamie chuckled. "He's fine. That thick skull o' his has saved him yet again."

Vee returned and searched both princes. When she was satisfied they were truly okay, she said, "Any insight on how to kill those things?"

"We're calling them skellies," I interjected.

Duncan lifted his broken weapon for us to see. "Definitely not with swords."

"And there's no way to predict when the witch might activate them," Vee clarified.

"Nay."

She frowned. "How soon do you think the Destined army can be ready?"

"Soon as Mackenna and I are able to go get them."

"You should go first thing in the morning. But talk to Oliver first. If we can't cut the skellies down, maybe we can blow them up. See what type of explosives Oliver thinks we should use and what he'll need from the modern world to make them. Let's get back to the camp." She turned on her heel, expecting us to follow. And we did. "I want eyes on this field twenty-four seven, and if one of these skellies so much as jiggles, I want to know about it."

As I finished packing my duffle bag for the return to Alloway, Vee slipped into the tent. Holding a finger to her lips, she motioned for me to come outside without waking the other sleeping girls.

"Take a walk with me." There were bags under her eyes and I suspected that she'd spent much of the night worrying about the skellies and how quickly we could return with the Destined army.

The pink and orange sky had already begun fading to blue in the growing dawn. As my bestie led me out of the camp, I noted the signs of spring bursting from the earth. Delicate buds poked up from the grass and the trees were beginning to flower.

Just beyond the camp, we stopped in a small clearing near a line of wilted black petunias. On the other side of the zombie fungus ravaged earth, stood the ruin of the witch's cottage. Just as I remembered, the place stank of rotten meat and death—being near the place gave me the heebie jeebies.

Vee faced me, taking both my hands in hers. "All night long, I've been thinking about how we can protect the camp while you're gone. I have an idea—it's a longshot but I want to try anyway."

"Okay . . ." I couldn't keep the skepticism from coloring my voice. Yes, we'd used the rings to find the people in the mountains, but wielding them to defeat the skellies had been a bust.

Ignoring my tone, Vee explained, "When we entered the limbus, our rings united and formed a protective bubble around us. I want to try to create a force field like that around the camp. If my theory is correct, it will allow our people to pass through, but will keep evil out."

"Including Addie's minions?"

"Exactly." She let go of one of my hands. Turning toward the decaying building, she took a deep breath. "If we enter the cursed grounds, the protection will form around us."

Together, we took a step and then another and another, until our rings glowed fiery red and brilliant green. At the point of no return—the rusted gate—we paused. As one, we reached toward the gate, opened it, and stepped across evil's threshold. Immediately, the light from our rings morphed into a dazzling white bubble that surrounded us, blocking out the worst of the stench.

"Now what?" I panted.

"Close your eyes and envision the protective bubble expanding from us to the camp—along the stream that flows from the River Doon, to the Murrays' fields, to the livestock pen in the east pasture." Her words were soft, almost hypnotic, and I could see everything she described in my mind's eye. She went on, painting a picture of every aspect of camp, and as she did, I envisioned the bubble covering it.

After a few minutes, I couldn't take it. I cracked an eye and then two, unable to believe what I was seeing. A shimmering dome arched over us as far as I could see. "Vee, look!"

She opened her eyes and her jaw dropped. "We did it."

"We sure did." As much I wanted to stand around

crowing about her cleverness, I was more anxious to get back on uncursed ground. "Let's get out of here." I tugged her back across the witch's garden and through the gate.

As soon as we hopped over the row of dead petunias, she stopped. "Hold on. There's one more test. We need to make sure the protection will stay without us."

She released my hand and I held my breath as the bubble around us faded from white to a red and green glow and then winked out completely.

As I stared at my ring, Vee muttered something very unqueenly followed by, "It's gone!"

I gazed up at the treetops to where a faint glow shimmered, sparkling like dust moats floating in a sunbeam. "No, it's still there. I can see it."

"Really?" She stood on her toes and blinked, but the moment I'd released her hand, she could no longer see the enchantment. Clasping her hand in mine, I asked, "Can you see it now?"

"Yes." Vee nodded toward the glittering dome and then turned to me with a watery smile. "See, stronger together. Which is why you need to hurry back."

CHAPTER 31

Duncan

I loved my brother. But when it came to the MacCrae portion of obstinacy, Jamie had received a triple share. He was more pigheaded than the rest of my clan combined. While that trait lent itself to an irreproachable code of morality, it oft as naught led to masochism when my brother made up his mind to punish himself.

I waited until Fergus left the tent so I could speak to my brother alone. Jamie stood behind a makeshift table of weapons, cleaning them. I joined him, picking up a small dirk and sharpening the blade with a whetstone. When I finished I replaced that dagger and picked up another.

"Mackenna and I are nearly ready to leave for the Brig o' Doon." My brother and the queen were to accompany us, not only so that Veronica could open the portal, but also to test the Calling between our lasses once we'd crossed. It would be extremely beneficial if they could communicate with one another as needed. "I'm wondering what to do about the auld man."

Whatever fault made Jamie blind to himself, he was an excellent judge of character where others were concerned. Pausing in his work, he turned to me. "I believe Alasdair's on our side." He went on to tell me about the conversation my kinsman had had with Queen Veronica at the skeleton field.

"Shall we leave him here then?"

"Aye." Jamie nodded.

"The fewer people to cross the bridge, the better," I replied.

"An' Mabel?"

At the mention of my beloved horse, I frowned. "What of her?"

"Will you bring her back wi' ye?" Jamie asked casually.

"Nay." I'd given the matter much thought during my time in Alloway. Mabel was the one creature I could keep safe; therefore, she would stay behind under the meticulous care of our solicitors.

Changing the subject, I opened my sporran, selected the MacCrae family ring, and presented it to Jamie. "I thought ye might want this back," I said.

As he stared at the lion-headed ring in the palm of my hand, he flinched. For several moments he stood by in silence, lost in thought.

At length he said, "I want you to have it."

"Nay." I made to give him the ring, but he snatched his hand away like I held a burning coal. "That ring is meant for a ruler, a king . . . not for me." Intending to put an end to the discussion, he resumed weapon cleaning.

"So what? You're no longer royalty? You're the firstborn MacCrae and your intended is the queen. I think that more than qualifies you ta wear it."

Jamie shook his head. "If you knew what I've done, you'd think otherwise."

"Then tell me about it."

Still avoiding my gaze, Jamie lay the sword on the table. "We should leave for the bridge."

He tried to step around me, but I blocked his path. "When it comes to advice, you're all bum and parsley." He glared at me to back off, but I persisted. If Jamie was to have any chance of moving forward—to heal—he would have to face his demons. "I see the wedge you're driving between yourself and the queen."

His body stiffened, telling me that I'd struck a nerve. Avoiding my eyes, he said flatly, "She deserves better 'n me."

"So that's it, then—you're just going ta freeze her out. You *want* ta see her with Murray? King Ewan—has a nice ring to it, dinna ye think?"

Coiling like a lion about to pounce, he growled, "Get out of my way, Duncan."

I stepped aside and then turned to regard his retreating form. Just before he reached the tent entrance, I said, "All hail, King Ewan!"

With a sound more like a bull than a lion, Jamie spun around and charged. Before I could brace for impact, I was flat on my back with my brother's fists pummeling me.

Snaking a hand around his throat, I rolled until I was on top of him. Normally with my size advantage and his quickness, we were evenly matched, but his raging emotions made him wild, allowing me to stay out of his reach as I squeezed just enough to subdue him. The instant he stopped struggling, I let go.

"Now, canna we—" Jamie's fist connected with my diaphragm, knocking the breath out from underneath my words. Squirming onto his stomach, he started to crawl away, but I grabbed ahold of his boot. He kicked back, narrowly missing my jaw with his free foot.

Pulling him toward me, I rammed a fist into his head and anchored a knee in the small of his back, pinning his arms. As I loosened my grip, he started to roll out from under me. I scrambled after him, putting him in a headlock before he could get away.

As boys, I spent many a fight on the receiving end of Jamie's headlocks, and as much as one might think to the contrary, it gave me no pleasure to turn the tables. "Now I've something to say and you're goin' to listen." I tightened my grip as he struggled in vain to get free. "I canna claim ta know what happened when ye were Adelaide's prisoner, but I see the demons you're carrying around because of it.

"You have to find a way ta let them go. For the sake of our kingdom. For Veronica's sake—because she needs you. And for your own sake."

"You dinna understand."

"Then help me," I pleaded. Jamie had stopped struggling, but I dared not let up. "Tell me what happened."

"I did things . . . things I thought I'd never do. There's blood on my hands and I canna get them clean." He sobbed a single dry heave. "I don't deserve ta be king and I certainly dinna deserve Verranica."

"What about what she deserves? Does she no' deserve to be with the lad she loves?"

He grunted in answer.

"And what about what you deserve?" Slowly, I released my hold. As I suspected, the fight had left him and he didn't move. "Don't ye deserve forgiveness? And happiness?"

"Not anymore." He shook his head and I moved to face him.

"I know you, brother. Whatever you've done, ye had your reasons."

He looked up, the pain in his eyes hard to witness. "I had a choice, Duncan, a moment in time when I could've . . . *should've* made the right decision and I failed."

"Right or no', you're entitled ta forgiveness. Stop punishin' yourself."

"How?"

"Start by takin' your own advice. Tell Veronica everythin'. Do not let this darkness come between you."

After a moment, his jaw hardened and he straightened his shoulders. "Ye're right, I need to face the consequences o' my actions and let my queen decide."

I opened my hand, where I still held his ring. "Will ye take this now?"

With a tight nod, he lifted it from my palm. Although he slipped the ring into his pocket instead of putting it on, his acceptance of the imperial symbol heartened me.

He stood and extended a hand to help me to my feet. "My thanks, *bráthair.* I know what I need ta do now." He clasped a hand on my shoulder. "After we see ye off at the Brig o' Doon, I'll find a way to tell Verranica the truth. All of it."

CHAPTER 32

Veronica

Mending one's cloak didn't seem like the best use of time when others prepared for battle all around me, but I found the mindless kinetic activity calming. Even if I sucked at it. I stared at the uneven stitches tugging the gaping edges of the rough-hewn fabric together, and inexplicable tears stung my throat. Addie had torn a hole in Jamie, one I had no idea how to fix.

We were headed into a fight that we may not survive, but instead of facing it as a united front, the gap between us grew wider by the day. I needed him whole and by my side. Puncturing the fabric, I yanked the thread up and then down again, tugging tight. If only I could bring Jamie and me back together so easily.

"Will ye please come with me, Yer Majesty?" I started and pricked my finger, blood surging in a scarlet bead. I stuck it in my mouth and glanced up to find Gabby Rosetti's pale green eyes sparkling with mischief.

The girl likely had some diversion planned and I'm sure she

meant well, but I had a million and one things on my to-do list; after I finished sewing my cloak, I had a meeting with Oliver to discuss a strategy for his explosive devices, then target/self-defense practice with Ana, followed by a gathering to resolve several disputes that had cropped up around camp. I took my stinging finger out of my mouth. "Thank you, but I can't—"

Before I could finish, Sofia appeared and took my arm, lifting me to my feet. The girl was tiny, but mighty when she set her mind to something. "Queen Veronica, Prince Jamie has requested your presence."

My gut clenched. Jamie's unpredictability made me nervous, and I hated to admit it, even to myself, but I'd been avoiding him.

"And we're ta prepare ye!" Gabby took my other arm and tugged me away from the fire circle.

I didn't like the sound of that. "What do you mean, *prepare me*?"

Gabby squeezed my arm and whispered, "'Tis a surprise."

We entered the laundry tent, where huge pots of clothing boiled over a fire, the scents of lye and pine coating my throat. I raised my hand to cover a cough. Women scrubbed fabric against washboards and then dunked them into the vats, stirring with long poles. Lines were strung above our heads, draped with clothing of all shapes and sizes in various states of dampness. The laundry shelter had been set up to protect our clothes from the frequent rain showers. Doc Benior had advised that dry clothes were essential to keeping illness at bay.

"Ma, did ye find what we requested?" Sofia asked.

Sharron Rosetti appeared, swiped a strand of sweaty, gray-blonde hair off her forehead and grinned. "That, I did." Then she hustled away.

"Sofia, what's going on?" I hated surprises. In my experience, they never turned out well.

"Here it is!" Mrs. Rosetti said in a singsong voice as she held out two garments—something that resembled a short sundress in a faded plaid and a pair of lacy pantaloons in a matching seafoam green.

"What in the heck is that?" I yelped.

The Rosetti sisters giggled, but didn't explain.

"Oh, and I found the matching bonnet!" Sharron said in triumph as she pulled a ruffled cap from her pocket. She leaned in and whispered, "Embrace this second chance ye've been given."

I wanted to. I really did, but apprehension squeezed my chest and stilted my breath. At first, it had been enough that Jamie lived. Now I worried the boy I'd fallen in love with was gone forever. And since he wouldn't talk about what he'd gone through, I had no clue how to help him. To reassure the woman who'd become like a mother to me, I pasted a smile on my face, thanked her, and accepted the weird outfit.

Once we were outside, I hissed, "Please don't tell me this is the Doonian version of lingerie."

That elicited further giggles as we entered the teepee we shared. "Don't be such a prude, Ver—I mean, my queen," Gabriela admonished.

I had to laugh at that. These girls would faint dead if they saw modern-day underwear, or swimsuits for that matter. And then it hit me—the garments were vintage swimwear! What was Jamie thinking? The weather had turned a bit warmer, but low sixties with a cool breeze was by no means swimming weather.

Blasted Scotsman!

His audacity reminding me of the Jamie I knew, I deciding to play along by wearing the swimsuit, but rejected the hideous cap. The girls helped finger-comb my hair and then wound the waist-length strands into a loose bun on top of my head. Wishing I had a mirror, I glanced from my bare legs up to the lace-edged shorts and the A-line plaid dress, fitted in the waist and bodice. It looked a bit like a ballet tutu with frilly spanks underneath. I felt ridiculous.

Gabby clapped her hands together beneath her chin and exclaimed, "Ye look lovely!"

"Please don't make me wear this. I'll meet Jamie wherever he wants, but if he sees me in this, he won't be able to stop laughing."

"My friend." Sofia grasped my shoulders and stared me in the eye. "In our world, this is considered provocative. Believe me when I tell ye, Jamie will no' laugh."

Extremely grateful that my BFF was not around to crack Ethel Merman jokes, I allowed them to slip fur-line moccasins on my feet and a light cloak over my shoulders. I was ready, but trepidation still rolled through me at the thought of being alone with Jamie for the first time since his return.

Gabby exited the tent. As Sofia followed, I reached for her hand to stop her. "Can I talk to you for a minute?"

She turned. Her wide, dark eyes examined my face and her expression sobered. "Of course." After telling Gabby she'd meet her later, she joined me back inside the shaded warmth of the teepee.

"You dinna want to go?" As usual, the girl saw more than I'd intended.

"I . . ." Instead of answering, I asked, "Where's Eòran?"

"I've occupied him elsewhere. Ye need this time alone." She cocked her head. "Or are ye afraid?"

"It's not that . . ." I turned and faced the fire, not wanting her to read the pain on my face. "Since Jamie came back he's . . . he's not the same. It's like something is eating him up from the inside . . . turning him into someone I don't even know. He can be fine one moment and then something triggers a change and he snaps. I never know which Jamie I'm going to get, moment by moment, and it makes me . . . leery of being alone with him."

"Veronica, when you first came here—to Doon—ye were broken, were ye not?"

I thought back to the abandoned, insecure girl who'd crossed the bridge looking to escape the pain of her life. She was right. This place, the miracles I'd experienced, and Jamie's love had healed me. But it had taken many ups and downs. Just a short time ago, in Indiana, I'd had a hard time accepting that men weren't all like my father—that they wouldn't leave when things got hard. Jamie had said he would choose me no matter what the future held. That he would choose me over and over until I understood that he always would.

Unable to speak around the scorching in my chest, I faced my wise friend.

"He's hurting, Vee. I've known him all my life and I've never seen him like this either. But I ha' to believe the Jamie we know and love can return to us."

My eyes stung and I couldn't be sure if they were tears of hope or shame. It was my turn to choose him. To show him that, despite his broken places, I wouldn't give up. That I would do whatever it took to heal him. To heal us.

I pulled Sofia close and hugged her tight. "You're so right. I have to show him that I haven't lost faith in him. Thank you, my friend."

She pulled back and met my gaze, her eyes swimming with unshed tears. "Dinna let the witch win this battle. The great love you share is worth fighting for."

Then I remembered—in the confusion of the last Centennial, Sofia's Called soul mate hadn't crossed the bridge. She'd lost her chance to find her own great love. Silently, I vowed that when this was all over, I'd find a way to complete her Calling. But for now, I needed to fix my own. "I'll do whatever it takes, I promise."

The path Sofia sent me down wound through the trees, past the witch's property, and through a rock tunnel. I heard the water before I saw it, a rush and splash like a fountain. No longer caring about my earlier fears or my strange swimwear, I picked up speed.

When I emerged, a gasp escaped my lips. Jamie sat in a milky-blue pool, bare-chested to his waist, arms outstretched on the rocky ledges to either side. Clusters of candles drove back the darkening sky and steam rose off the water in tendrils, forming a sheer curtain between us. It was a geothermal hot tub.

"Hello, love." Jamie smiled, drawing a dimple out in his right cheek. "Will ye join me?"

The sight of his half-nakedness, all golden skin and rounded muscle, had me fidgeting with the toggle on my cloak. He was male beauty personified, and I looked like a clown from the Mesozoic era. I shifted my eyes up to the rock walls stretching around us, the only break a narrow opening where water fell over the side and into the stream below. "I had no idea hot springs existed in Doon."

"'Tis the only one, that I'm aware of. It's so close to the witch's cottage that most Doonians avoid it."

"It's . . . amazing," I said, tucking my cloak tighter around my waist as a cool breeze blew down the tunnel behind me.

"Even better if ye get in. I promise I won't bite."

I studied him. His right hand clenched into a fist, his bicep flexing. Despite his smiles and casual words, he radiated tension and a bit of my trepidation returned.

"Considerin' my brother near pounded my mule head into the ground this afternoon, this location is somewhat o' a necessity for my sore muscles." He rubbed his shoulder, temporarily covering the intricate loops of his tattoo.

For the first time, I noticed the dark shadow on his jaw. And there was an even darker smudge on his pectoral muscle— black, like an open wound. Concerned, I dropped my cloak and laid it next to his on a nearby rock shelf.

Jamie stood, water cascading over his bare skin as he extended his hand.

Knowing he, like most Scotsmen, had little modesty, I breathed a sigh of relief to see he wore a pair of cut-off trousers.

I dipped my toe into the steaming water and watched his eyes glaze over as they flowed up my bare legs. I almost laughed, realizing Sofia had been right about my antiquated swimwear.

As I stepped all the way in, delicious warmth enveloped me like a blanket, relaxing my muscles. The bottom of the pool was smooth, slippery rock. I clutched Jamie's hand harder as he led me over to a ridge that served as a seat. Raising my head to thank him, I froze in horror. Eye-level with his chest, what I'd thought was a wound stared back at me with a black, serpentine stare. I swallowed a gasp and lifted my finger to trace the impression in his flesh of the snake swallowing its own tail.

He grasped my hand and tugged it to his right arm, where I felt an indentation around his bicep. "The witch's brands."

My gaze shifted to the identical serpent circling his arm. I couldn't breathe. She'd marked him. Burned her symbol into his flesh. He pulled me down to sit beside him and the water slid around us like a living organism.

Gently, he lifted my chin with the tips of his fingers and his solemn eyes melted into mine. "There is much I need ta tell ye, and I want ye to know that after I'm finished ye will have a choice." His gaze cut away as he lowered his hand from my face.

"What do you mean?"

A furrow appeared above his left brow. "Whether ye want to revoke our Completing."

My heart slammed painfully in my chest. His words confirmed my worst fears that the rift between us couldn't be mended. "You mean end our Calling?"

"Aye. As the chosen queen, the completion of our Callin' makes me a king. Which I am no' sure I deserve."

I swallowed, hard. The thought had occurred to me in my worst moments of doubt. "Jamie—"

"She made me do things, Verranica." He shoved his face into mine, then pulled back and raked the damp hair off his forehead. "Nay, tha's wrong. She didna *force* me to do anythin'."

I gripped his arms. "I don't care what she did to you, or made you do."

The grief tightening his eyes fissured my heart. "Dinna assume . . . just hear me out."

I nodded, my throat squeezing closed.

He took a deep breath and then began, his voice barely a whisper. "When Adelaide recaptured me, she figured out I would make a better weapon alive than dead. But she knew with the protection afforded by the fealty, she could no longer control my mind wi' magic, so she tried to break me."

He jerked his gaze away and I clasped his hand beneath the water.

Without looking at me, he continued. "She chained me in the antechamber off the throne room and had Sean MacNa—" His words cut off and a muscle jumped in his jaw. "Had Sean MacNally beat me to within an inch of my life, and then she would swoop in like Satan's angel and heal me. Only to have Sean return and beat me again, so that she could heal my wounds. This cycle went on for days, weeks . . . I'm no' sure, but at some point, I began to anticipate her arrival like a starving man craves meat."

He shook his head, his fingers tightening around mine. "But I refused to show her my weakness. Through prayer, and memories o' you, I was able to resist her efforts to condition me . . . to make me inta her monster. That's when she burned the ouroboros into my skin. It was the worst pain I've ever felt."

His throat contracted as he swallowed. "She moved me to the dungeon after that. I tried to escape. But Sean . . . he . . . came back before I could. I could see in his eyes that he'd lost his mind. I tried to reason wi' him and I thought it was workin'. He remembered things from our childhood—things he was still angry about. He didn't appear to be enthralled. But I think Adelaide's obsession with me drove him to the edge, and he stabbed me."

I started, my muscles tensing as I searched his face.

Refusing to look at me, Jamie withdrew his hand from mine and leaned his elbows on his knees. "I had to defend myself. So I took him down. Wrapped my chains around his neck and drove him to his knees." Lost in memories, he shook his head. "I'd beaten him. He was barely conscious. But I . . . I pulled the blade from my own side . . . and with Adelaide's encouragement . . . slit Sean's throat." He dropped his head into his hands.

He'd committed murder. That witch had driven my noble prince to do the unthinkable. I reached over and rubbed his back in slow circles. "Jamie, no one would blame you. He'd tortured you for weeks. He tried to kill you first."

"It's just, I thought I was better than that . . . my ma raised me to temper my power with mercy. To live by a code of honor. But I learned I'm worse than Sean was. I *murdered* one of our people, Vee." His eyes shifted to mine, their dark anguish cutting into my soul.

"It's war, Jamie. We do what we have to. I killed at least two of those guards on the mountain path."

He sat up and turned to me. Beads of moisture dotted his skin, mixing with his sweat and the tears leaking from his eyes. "But Sean didn't disintegrate. He was still a man. Still had his soul, and *I* took it from him."

"You don't know that—he pledged to the witch. We don't know what that did to him."

As if he hadn't heard me, he said, "There's more."

I nodded. Ready to hear it all—every horrible thing he'd buried that was cutting at his insides like a dull knife.

"I was moved to a bedchamber, given clean clothes and food. But every time I closed my eyes, I saw your face. You were the only thing keepin' me sane. And then ye were there."

I waited. Confused.

"Or I thought it was you, until . . . I kissed her."

"Kissed her?" Chills swept over my arms and I began to shake.

"Aye. She wore your body. Spoke wi' your voice. But when our lips met, I knew . . . She begged me to join her, ta rule by her side. And for a fraction of a second, I considered it—if only to gain her trust and infiltrate her confidence. But I knew I didna dare."

I rubbed my chilled arms and then dipped them into the heated water, emotions battling for control inside of me—rage, jealousy, fear, and sorrow. The witch had taken my form and touched Jamie. Kissed him. Tried to seduce him to her side, and she'd almost succeeded.

Jamie let out a deep sigh. "Ye should know, she imagines herself in love wi' me."

I clasped my hands and stared at their wavering image beneath the water. "That much I know."

"How?"

"In my dreams, she's claimed you as her own. But I think it's less about love and more about destroying me. Ever since I thwarted her plan with the journal and outwitted her by using the ring to save you and take the throne, she's seen me as her greatest obstacle."

I paused and after a moment raised my eyes to his beloved face. "When I believed you dead, it almost killed me. There were moments I knew I wouldn't survive without you. Eventually, I found my strength in the Protector and decided to honor you by becoming the queen you always knew I could be. But if she stole your heart from me . . ." I shook my head, the thought filling my eyes with tears. "I fear she'll come for you before the battle."

He clasped both my hands, his face set in hard lines. "I'll die before I let her take me again."

Our gazes locked, steam rising between us in swirls that reminded me of the time he'd appeared to me in Aunt Gracie's cottage, the mist stealing him away across the Brig o' Doon. This time, he wasn't going anywhere. I wouldn't let him. I moved closer, so that our knees intertwined. "Jamie, do you really believe that after all we've been through, I would abandon our Calling? That I would abandon *you*?"

"Vee, I dinna deserve to be by your side. I was tested and I failed. How can I lead Doon when I've committed the gravest sin of our faith? If the people knew, they would never trust me. Never follow me."

The tears flooding his eyes shattered my heart. And I knew

Sofia was right; Addie had done her best to destroy Jamie's confidence and pull us apart. But her plan would fail. There was no way I was letting him go without a fight.

I squeezed his hands and forced him to look at me. "Jamie, that's the witch talking. Everyone falls sometimes. If anything, that makes you more qualified to lead. If you didn't care, that would be different. But your remorse wipes the slate clean. I forgive you and the Protector has not abandoned you. He rescued you! Brought you back to me." I clutched his hands tight. "If you let that one mistake stop you from achieving your destiny, then you've let Addie win. Doon needs you . . . I need you!"

His eyes searched my face, tears spiking his lashes. As quick as a blink, he grabbed me and pulled me to his chest. I threw my arms around him and held him with all my strength. "I'm sorry, Vee. I'm so verra sorry."

"You said I had to make a choice." I leaned back and took his face in my hands. "I choose you. I choose our Calling. I will always choose you." I kissed his mouth and lowered my hands.

A slow smile spread across his face as he tucked a wet strand of hair behind my ear. "We have only this moment, sparkling like a star in our hand and melting like a snowflake."

"I know that quote. Sir Francis Bacon, right?"

"Aye. Marry me, Verranica. Tonight! Before the moon rises."

With deliberation, he unleashed the dazzling, full-dimpled grin that stole my breath. He wasn't quite the churro-eating, ball cap-wearing guy I longed to see—we still had a battle to win, after all—but his smile told me his heart was lighter and he was on his way to becoming the confident boy-king I'd fallen head over heels in love with.

He looped an arm around my waist, and the buoyancy of the water did the work for him as he tugged me onto his lap.

His lips brushed my neck, then moved to my jaw, his fingers threading into my hair. "Say yes, love," he murmured against my ear, sending sparks all the way to my shriveled toes.

I'd never wanted to say yes to anything more in my life. We needed to take a tangible step to solidify our commitment to each other. But my mind warred with my heart. I scooted back to face him. "I would gladly bind myself to you for eternity, Jamie MacCrae, but we can't marry in the shadow of evil. And I don't want to rush to the altar without all of our family and friends."

His face fell. "Ye're right. I couldna marry wi'out my brother by my side."

"However . . ." I brushed the scruff on his cheek with my thumb and dropped a quick kiss on his mouth. "The people *could* use something to lift their spirits. A handfasting ceremony, perhaps?"

His eyes burned into mine. "Aye. First thing in the morn. I willna face another day without makin' you mine."

I laced my fingers into the damp hair curling against his neck and kissed him until my head spun and the pool practically boiled around us.

If the witch had sought to drive a wedge between us, she'd failed. Our connection could not be severed, short of death.

CHAPTER 33

Mackenna

Fiona Lockhart folded the slip of paper containing words of love and encouragement written by her husband and tucked it into her bodice. Her hazel eyes glistened with unshed tears as she said, "Fergus is right. We shall be together soon. And when we defeat the witch, all the sacrifice shall be worth the sweet victory."

The fierceness of her words reminded me that the petite, strawberry blonde with a smattering of freckles across her button nose was also a Celtic warrior, prepared to fight to the death for her kingdom . . . as we all were. But how many of us on the modern side of the bridge knew anything about battle except in video games, where opportunity for a new life took the finality out of dying?

I'd witnessed the skellies with my own eyes. They appeared invincible. As of now, we had no idea how to defeat them. How many of us would die trying? And how many, when faced with a seemly unbeatable foe, would run away?

Fiona's dainty hand covered mine. "What's troubling ye, Kenna?"

"What if I'm not brave enough?" The question spilled out before I could stop it. I knew how important it was for me to put on a courageous face for the sake of our people. It was like being the lead in a show. No matter how unprepared you felt for opening night, the entire cast and crew looked to you to guide them through to the other side. But unlike theater, where a botched performance resulted in a bad review, a botched campaign would eradicate us from the planet.

Quietly studying me, Fiona waited until I met her empathetic gaze to respond. "You're one of the bravest people I know. When it comes to following your heart, you're fearless. Now, what's got ye in such a state?"

"You know how Duncan and I told everyone about the skeleton army that Addie's raising?"

"Aye."

"Well, they're protected by Addie's magic. They appear invincible." I explained about Duncan's futile attack on the skellie, how he was thrown through the air and knocked unconscious.

"And?"

"*And?* How do we stop something that can't be defeated? What if we all die trying?"

Fiona made a noise of disapproval. "Mackenna Reid. The good Protector dinna call forth a Destined army just to lead us to the slaughter. He dinna bring you and a queen from Indiana just to have you fail."

"Why did he call us, then?"

"Fer the same reason he chose Cheska, Ezekiel, Jerimiah, and the others—to have ye stand with him. Make no mistake, you've been called to be Doonians. You're one of us and we're his. The Protector already has a plan in motion that will end in triumph."

I shook my head in frustration. "But Vee and I were right there, on the edge of the field. It was the perfect chance to destroy those creatures before they could do any damage. We tried to use our rings, but they wouldn't work. We even appealed to the Protector and nothing happened." I huffed, knowing that I sounded like a spoiled kindergartner but unable to stop myself. "It would've been so much easier if the rings had just zapped the skellies."

I expected more lecturing, but instead Fiona challenged in a gentle voice, "When has this journey ever been easy? The Protector's ways are not always our ways. Events may not happen the way we think they should, but they will always work out for our best if we have faith."

"But the newcomers, some of them are just kids. They're not soldiers. No matter how much they train, they're not ready to fight a supernatural war."

Fiona squeezed my hand. "I've seen Duncan do a lot more with a worse lot."

Duncan had taken a small group into Glasgow to get supplies for Oliver's explosives. At the suggestion of a blue-haired girl from Vancouver, they were also picking up nylon rope, fishing line, and duct tape. Her idea—and it was a good one—was to set traps in the tree lines that didn't appear to be threats, like trip lines and sticky barriers, in hopes that the skellies would walk right into them and destroy themselves. But a good idea didn't make us warriors.

"I promise ye, Kenna. When this is over and we're standin' on the other side, you'll see how everythin' worked out exactly as it should've and better than anything ye could've asked for."

"I hope so."

"I *know* so."

She was right. I had to trust that the Protector wouldn't lead us into a bloodbath. Regardless of how we got here, the path would lead us to a final showdown with Adelaide Blackmore Cadell. Too much had happened to believe we would not win. That didn't mean there wouldn't be casualties. Some would surrender their lives for the sake of the cause. Fiona was prepared to do so—so were Duncan and Jamie and Fergus. So was Vee . . . and I was as well.

But that battle was in the future. Right now, in this moment, I needed to cherish my life and the people in it, especially one thick-headed ogre who had traveled across worlds more than once to find me.

CHAPTER 34

Jamie

The morn dawned in an eruption of larks heralding the new day. Clouds, like flames shooting across the sky, filled the landscape with brilliant hues. Each sound, each color, moved over my skin like a master painter's brush on canvas. The overall portrait was one of joy, almost as if Doon rejoiced along with us.

Our ceremony was set to begin within the hour, with a celebration breakfast to follow. I stretched my sore limbs and breathed the crisp air. Duncan had near beat me senseless the day before, but I'd take the pain again and again if it led to the same outcome—Veronica's absolution.

I felt as if I'd been carrying a devil on my back, its lies sinking into my flesh, clouding my every thought, and now it was gone. I was *free*. The storm had passed, but another brewed just over the horizon. I stretched my arms to the sky, power buzzing through my muscles. Adelaide may have plotted and schemed for centuries to gain vengeance and sit on the throne of Doon, but vengeance was not hers to take and I would defend the throne with my life—fighting for something you believed in was a blessing. My father had taught me that. But I knew everyone I loved would fight alongside me, and therein lay the heart of my fear.

Finding a quiet spot in the forest, I dropped to my knees. The Protector had proven over the centuries that he used the weak to defeat the strong, and I asked for him to do this once again. For an army of peace-loving Doonians to defeat Adelaide's supernatural soldiers, it would take a miracle. Fortunately, Doon had been built on miracles.

After concluding my prayers, I returned to my tent to finish dressing. There was much to be done in preparation for battle—weapons forged, strategies and counter-tactics finalized, squadron drills . . . the list went on, but first, I would make the girl who ruled my kingdom and my heart officially mine. A handfasting before the Divine Ruler bound a couple body and soul; the marriage rite just a slip of parchment. For me, this meant forever. And I wouldn't have it any other way.

When I entered the clearing, my heart swelled at the sight of our people, all five hundred of them packed elbow to elbow in the glade we'd been using for training. Rushes had been laid on the ground to control the mud and someone had created an altar of sorts. Reverend Guthrie greeted me from the other side of a trellis made of sticks and vines with white flowers cascading down the sides.

Sharron Rosetti's beaming but tired face gave me a strong notion that the woman had been behind the lovely decorations. I gave her a nod of thanks, just as the pipes and fiddle began to play. Turning, my heart thumped into my throat. Escorted by Eòran, Veronica entered the clearing to the sounds of gasps and exclamations of her beauty.

I could do nothing but stare. Her hair hung in loose waves

down her back, topped by a crown of white and yellow pansies. The ivory gown she wore was a simple medieval style that hugged her body as if it had been made for her—and perhaps it had. She glided forward and I took in every detail, determined never to forget this moment. The neckline was wide and ended in a point, beveled sleeves draped over her hands, and a delicate silver chain sat low on her hips, the length of it trailing down the center of her skirt.

She smiled and I sucked in a gulp of air, realizing I'd forgotten to breathe. Sofia and Gabriela followed behind, holding the train of their queen's dress off the ground. Vee turned to face me and I nearly lost myself in her incandescent eyes.

The sound of a throat clearing forced my gaze to Eòran. The big guard, who'd become a father figure to my queen and protected her with a doggedness that forced him to distrust even me, had tears welling in his eyes. He couldn't speak, but as he met my gaze and gave a solemn bow, he didn't have to—he was giving his consent. Veronica must have shared our conversation with him. "Thank you, sir. I vow to protect her heart wi' my life."

Reverend Guthrie signaled and the music rose to a crescendo, then cut off. "Yer Majesty. M'Laird. Are ye ready to begin?"

As Eòran joined the crowd, I stepped closer to my intended and grinned with every bit of love I felt coursing through my veins. "Aye!"

The passion of my response provoked catcalls, cheers, and laughter from the people around us—our people. I pumped my fist in triumph, and the unmistakable voice of Fergus yelled, "Pipe down, lad, or the lady may change her mind!"

Veronica leaned around me and responded, "Why, Fergus Lockhart, are you jealous? Just wait until I tell Fiona!"

The crowd roared and I smiled proudly. "A proper Scotswoman, she is."

She arched a flirtatious brow as a gentle breeze blew her hair back from her face. Something low in my gut tightened and my pulse pounded in my ears. I leaned in close, her scent of honeyed berries filling my senses as I cupped her cheek and ran my thumb over her full lips.

When the pastor cleared his throat, I jerked my hand down and stepped back, hardly able to believe I'd lost my head and almost kissed her in front of the holy man and five hundred spectators. "Pardon me, Reverend."

He gave a solemn nod, but his eyes twinkled. "Laird, please take your betrothed's hands. Right ta right and left ta left."

"You're wearing your ring," Vee whispered.

"Aye, my brother kept it safe for me." I guided Vee to cross her arms and she placed her hands in mine, forming the traditional infinity symbol. "Are ye sure ye're ready for this?"

"I've never been more sure about anything in my life."

Her smile ignited tiny explosions in my heart and I squeezed her hands as the Pastor began the ceremony, projecting his voice for all to hear. "Just as the Protector brought the two o' you together and will form everlastin' ties between you, we bind your hands in a symbol o' your commitment to one another." He took the multicolored ribbons from his pocket, tied in a knot at one end, and looped them around our hands. "These cords represent the Calling, a sacred bond that draws two hearts together through time and space. A divine union, tha' once accepted, intertwines the two souls throughout their lives."

He wound the cords again, completing a figure eight. "Ye may now state yer intentions."

I hadn't prepared what I would say, but smiling into my love's eyes, the words came easily. "Verranica, you are the holder o' my heart. The stealer o' my breath. The light shining in the darkest corners of my soul." Her gaze softened, and for a moment I was struck speechless by gratitude for this magnificent creature who knew my worst and loved me still.

"Ye are my perfect match. The one I was born to stand beside. And I vow to spend ever' day o' my life showing ye how absolutely, indescribably I love you."

Tears glistened in Veronica's eyes and it was all I could do to hold back my own as she began to speak.

"Jamie, destiny brought us together, but even if it hadn't, even if there were no such thing as a Calling, I would have found you. You're my compass, the one who guides me home. You're my strength when I want to fall apart. You're the hero from every dream I've ever had." Her throat constricted, tears leaking from her eyes. "I choose you, James Thomas Kellan MacCrae, to be my co-ruler and partner for life. As I am bound to Doon, I am yours forever."

Reverend Guthrie wove the cords around us once more, laid his hands atop ours, and bowed his head. "We ask for the Protector's blessin' upon his chosen servants, James and Veronica. As the rulers of our great kingdom, these cords also symbolize their Completing. They have accepted the call ta rule side by side, to balance, support, and challenge when need be. We ask that ye give them wisdom and guidance ever' day o' their long lives. Amen." He lifted his hands to the sky. "In this unity there will be great power!"

As all of Doon roared their approval, something buzzed through our joined hands, and when I met Vee's startled gaze I saw that she felt it too.

"Ye may kiss your queen!"

Our hands still bound and tingling, I leaned down as Vee rose on her toes, and I brushed my lips against hers.

"Laird MacCrae!" a distance voice shouted.

I jerked back and spun to find Gideon half dragging someone toward the clearing. I squinted and recognized the man as one of those we'd sent to guard the skeleton army. Blood darkened the side of his head and he appeared barely conscious.

Our hands still bound, Vee and I raced to meet them at the edge of the field.

"Gideon, report!"

"The rest o' the guards are dead, m' Laird." Gideon stopped before us and bent at the waist, sucking in ragged breaths. "Adelaide has mobilized her army."

The reverend, who had followed us, began to unwrap our bound hands as Doc Benoir rushed forward to help the injured guard.

"Where, Gideon?" Vee asked as she shucked the last of the ribbons from her fingers. "Where is her army headed?"

"To the bridge, Yer Majesty. To cut off the Destined from enterin'."

"She knows about that?" I questioned.

"Aye. From the guard. It's no' his fault, m'Laird. She flayed the others right in front o' him."

Gideon straightened and I clapped him on the back. "You've served the kingdom with great honor this day, Captain. Thank you for warnin' us."

"I would do it again, if need be."

Fergus began to yell orders, attempting to mobilize people into squads, but mass chaos reigned. I ran back to the field and leapt onto a nearby boulder, put my fingers in my mouth and blew. The whistle had the desired effect, everyone freezing to look in my direction. "Do not panic! We're safe under the ring's protective shield. Assemble your weapons and be ready to move at the queen's order. Now go!"

As I turned back to where Vee stood, the wounded soldier leapt up from the ground, brandishing a wicked looking blade. With an ungodly shriek, he lurched at my queen. She threw up her arms and her eyes flared in terror. I jumped from the rock, but even as my feet hit the ground, I knew I was too far to stop the knife as it descended in a wide arch toward her heart. I screamed her name, but couldn't hear my own voice over the roar of my pulse.

I willed my legs to move faster, and as I pulled my dirk, a body flew through the air, tackling the rogue soldier to the ground. With a burst of speed, I reached Vee and caught her as she tumbled back, a horrified gasp passing her lips. "Gideon."

The soldier pushed a body off him as he rolled to his feet. My commander's lifeless eyes stared back at me, a blade protruding from his chest. I palmed the dirk and charged, but as I knocked the soldier to the dirt, his figure flashed and then transformed into Veronica. "Jamie, wait!"

Vee's wide, aqua eyes stared back at me in terror and my arm froze mid-stab. In that split second, my brain *knew* it was the witch, and yet, I hesitated. I'd almost killed the real Veronica before. Forcing out my fear, I plunged the weapon toward the Vee-Addie thing's heart. And she disappeared, my blade slicing harmlessly into the damp earth.

My gut clenched and I rammed my fist into the mud. What a blasted idiot! How had I let her fool me again? As I rose up, a tickle of purple smoke drifted past my ear. "Aww . . . ye *do* miss me."

I spun around and sprang to my feet, yelling as I moved. "Vee, get back inside the shield!"

Unwittingly, we'd stepped just outside of the ring's protection in our eagerness to get to Gideon and the fake wounded soldier. Veronica turned and fled, and it only took two steps for her to make it back inside. Wicked laughter buzzed around my head as I helped Doc Benoir drag Gideon's body back to safety.

The witch was playing with me. Quite literally, getting inside my head, trying to steal my joy. Now she knew about the handfasting and that I was bound to Veronica for eternity—a fact that would surely inflame her wrath. And worse, she knew the Destined army assembled on the other side of the bridge. We had lost the element of surprise, our strongest advantage.

Inside the safety of the bubble, my head clear of Adelaide's taunts, I knelt beside Gideon and checked his pulse, but Doc Benoir was already shaking his head. Fergus ran to join us and dropped to his knees with a gasp. He'd become Gideon's apprentice at the tender age of ten, and had told me many times the man was like a father to him. With a quiet sob, Fergus closed his mentor's eyes for the last time. Vee knelt beside him and held his hand.

Reverend Guthrie spoke a quick prayer for the commander's soul as tears streamed down Fergus' ruddy cheeks. I felt his pain. As a lad, Gideon had been my hero—and today, despite my doubts about him in the last months, he'd proved worthy of the title. He'd died to save the queen's life, and in turn, mine.

Grasping Fergus's trembling shoulder, I whispered the only words of comfort I could. "He died with honor, my friend."

I stood and helped Veronica to her feet, my mind turning to Gideon's last warning. "Ye need to reach Mackenna through your Calling. Tell them no' to cross until we can hold off the army."

She swiped tears from her cheeks and nodded. "Our connection is shaky at best . . . I don't know if it will work."

"Try, love. Use your emotion—your fear for our people, your anger at the witch."

She searched my face and then closed her eyes. People

surged all around us. Men arrived and helped Fergus carry away Gideon's body. The doc and Reverend Guthrie left to attend to their various duties, and finally, Vee opened her eyes.

"I can't reach her," she squeaked. "It's like she's just on the other side of a curtain—I can hear her, but she can't hear me."

A hand clamped onto my shoulder. I turned to find old Alasdair. "Hold her hands, lad. Her connection with Mackenna is fading now that ye've committed your souls to one another."

Vee's eyes appeared to take up half her face as I took her hands. "How do we—"

"Just do what ye were doin', Veronica," Alasdair instructed. "Jamie, lend her your strength."

Vee closed her eyes and I held tight to her hands, doing the same. With all my will, I projected power into her and suddenly I could hear Vee's voice in my head. "Ken, don't cross the bridge yet. The skellies are on their way. It's an ambush. Kenna, can you hear me? It's a trap!"

CHAPTER 35

Mackenna

Birds."

Duncan raised his eyebrows in disbelief. "Are you sure?"

"Yep. I'm getting birds . . . and sunshine." I shrugged. "Like a Disney princess montage. That's it."

My boyfriend and I stood in the middle of the newly restored bridge just after sundown. Doonians and Destined, packed and armed to the teeth, waited restlessly on the riverbank for me and my best friend to open the portal. "Let me try again."

Crouching Tiger to Hidden Dragon—Come in, Hidden Dragon. I shook my head to indicate the Calling still wasn't working. *Hidden Dragon, if you can hear me, we're at the bridge. Waiting for your cue.*

I closed my eyes and held my breath as Vee flickered like a hologram and then materialized with Jamie at her side. *What's he doing here?*

Um, that's a long story. She blushed. The three of us were standing on the Brig o' Doon in early evening, and although I

281

could feel Duncan next to me, I could no longer see him or the hundreds of people waiting to cross.

Spill. I raised my brows, doing my best imitation of the Evil Highney.

Later, she promised. *Did you hear me about the skellies? They're assembling at the bridge.*

How many? I asked, doing my best to estimate how many we'd seen in the field.

Adelaide's army has grown into the thousands, Jamie answered. *Pushin' them back without the Destined army as reinforcements is unlikely. And even with your troops, we're out-numbered two to one.*

So not used to this, I interjected. *Hold on . . .*

Opening my eyes, I quickly filled Duncan in on the skellie situation and the new three-way Calling. Duncan frowned as he absorbed the news. "Tell Jamie not to face them without us."

"'Kay." I shut my eyes again and relayed the message to Jamie.

Vee's apprehensive gaze darted between her boyfriend and me. *Could we try the mountain pass?*

Jamie shrugged. *There's no guarantee that rebuilding the bridge also restored the portal in the pass. That's a long way to go, and a lot o' lives to risk without assurances.*

Vee wound a strand of hair in her hand, one of her "thinking" tells. *Maybe there's a way we could check.*

And what if the skellie army goes on the offensive? We have to at least try to lure them away from the bridge.

As I waited for them to get on the same page, Duncan tugged at my sleeve. *One sec, guys . . .*

I blinked up at Duncan's anxious face. "Is he listenin' to ye?"

I shook my head. "He wants to try to lure the skellies away from the bridge."

"Nay." Duncan invaded my space as if he were actually talking to his brother instead of me. "Tell Jamie—"

"Stop." I was tired of being the MacCraes' personal go-between. Squeezing my eyes shut, I turned my focus back to Vee. *How did you connect Jamie into our Calling?*

We got handfasted. The Completing, they answered at the same time.

I held up my hand, indicating that they should hold on. Turning my attention back to Duncan, I asked, "You love me, right?"

"Aye."

"Quick, now tell me you're mine."

"Mackenna, what—"

"Just do it, okay?"

He shrugged. "Mackenna Reid, you may be daft in the head, but I am completely yours."

"And I'm yours. For always. Forever. Now, take my hand and close your eyes." I grabbed Duncan's hand and let my eyelids drift shut. Vee and Jamie were waiting on the bridge under the stars right where I left them, and Duncan . . . was definitely not with us.

Nuts!

Opening my eyes, I regarded Duncan with a sigh. "What do you want me to say to your brother?"

Duncan's brows pinched together like I was truly cuckoo for Cocoa Puffs. "Tell him not to confront the skellies in some misguided suicide mission. Tha's a terrible idea."

I held up my hand indicating he should hold on while I relayed the message. After listening to Jamie curse for several minutes, I opened my eyes, and replied, "I'm not going to repeat your brother word for word. But he does want to know if you have a better idea."

"Tell him I do." My boyfriend chuckled sheepishly. "But he's no' gonna like it."

CHAPTER 36

Veronica

I crouched at the mouth of the miniature bridge in the castle gardens, ring hand extended. Waiting. The minutes ticked by, and my arm began to shake. Were we crazy to think that hundreds of people would be able to cross into Doon on a tiny five-foot wide bridge without being noticed? Probably so, but it had to work. We had no time for an alternative.

Where are you, Ken?

There was a soft touch on my shoulder before Jamie whispered, "Any sign from Mackenna?"

I shook my head. "I'm going onto the bridge."

"Nay, ye'll be too exposed," he hissed under his breath.

"Then use that big bad arrow machine of yours to cover me."

Staying low, I crept farther up the incline of stone. We'd decided on a small party to accompany us: Ana, Fergus, and a small unit of royal guards. We were all armed to the teeth, including the crossbow Jamie had purchased back in Indiana. Oliver had wanted to come and "kick some skellie-bum," but he was still too weak from his injuries. As a compromise, I'd agreed to bring a few of his smaller explosive devises. One of them jangled in my right pocket, ratcheting up my nerves. The round metal ball had a pin like a grenade, but I didn't entirely trust the bomb not to detonate and blow me to smithereens.

I stopped at the top of the arch, hunched behind the stone balustrade, and fingered the tear-shaped bottle in my right pocket. Some thought it was a useless vial of lake water—Fergus among them—but I had to believe it would work. Why else would Jamie have come to me in a dream to lead me to it?

The ring pulsed, buzzing up my arm, and I yanked my hand out of my pocket, just as two quick whistles sounded behind me. The warning signal. Still crouched, I held out my glowing hand and glanced over my shoulder. Jamie and the others had moved into the formation that we'd practiced—the royal guardsmen fanning out and moving forward, while Jamie, Ana, and Fergus hung back to guard the mouth of the bridge.

I strained to see the threat through the dark, but heard them before they came into view.

Click-clack. Click-clack. Click-clack.

Bone against bone. To use Kenna's analogy, they sounded like a thousand giant cicadas moving as one. Jamie raised his bow, signaling Fergus and Ana to do the same as the four guards pulled their swords and disappeared into the darkness.

"Come on, Kenna."

As the words left my mouth, I turned to find the air flickering in front of me, the light of my ring transitioning from red to white. This was exactly the scenario we'd hoped to avoid. The Destined greeted by an army of creatures as they crossed into the kingdom. I rose slightly and whisper-yelled back to Jamie, "The portal's opening!"

"Ready. Aim. Fire!"

The swish of arrows filled the night as Kenna and Duncan shimmered into view.

I raced forward to warn them and lost my power of speech as I saw the hundreds of unfamiliar faces lined up behind them. Recovering quickly, I grabbed Kenna's hand. "The skellies are here!"

"We're ready for them," Duncan assured me. He put his fingers in his mouth and made three sharp whistles. Did they train all princes to whistle like that?

Without turning, Jamie directed our crew to split down the middle. They moved to either side of the bridge, still firing. The skellies moved into the light, and I watched in horror as arrows bounced off of them like Nerf darts. Addie's protection spell guarded them from being harmed. We weren't even slowing them down.

Clearly realizing they were wasting ammunition, Jamie ordered a ceasefire and unsheathed his sword, but I feared it would do little good. I spun to face Kenna and Duncan. "The force field is protecting the skellies. Maybe you should turn back."

"Nay." Duncan's brows crouched over his eyes. "We're prepared to defend Doon or die tryin'."

I glanced past him to the people waiting—Destined who'd been called from all over the world, some of them barely older than children—and all I could see was an impending blood-bath. I opened my mouth to order them back, when Kenna stepped forward and fully into Doon. "Vee, let them do what the Protector called them to do. If nothing else, we can help you get safely back to camp."

The *click-clack* had grown louder and I knew the army would soon be upon us. "Okay. But hurry!"

I rushed off the bridge just as the skellies reached the front line of royal guards. One of the men swung his sword in a wide arc, aiming for the closest creature's head, but when he made contact his arms bounced back and he stumbled. Not quite the blow Duncan had taken when the creatures were immobile, but still devastating. It was just as we feared; we couldn't touch them.

As the Destined swarmed off the bridge and divided to either side, the skellies began to attack. The guardsmen raised their swords to defend themselves, but could do nothing to stop the creatures from surrounding them.

Jamie yelled, "Retreat!"

I rushed to Jamie's side as one of our men fell and the creatures swarmed him. Jamie tensed to move, but I stopped him. "No, we have to be smart. Find a way to slow them so we can escape back to camp."

Another guard fell as he was trying to run back to us. The skellies fell on him, swords first, while the army swarmed around them and kept coming.

Jamie pulled a bomb from his pocket. "I dinna dare try this, but what if—"

"We can try to use the rings to weaken the protection spell first!" I finished for him.

I spun to find Kenna directing the last of the Destined off the bridge. "Kenna!"

She raced to my side, and I was so intent on my goal to take down the witch's barrier spell that our rings began to glow before she even reached me. "Take my hand and focus on the protective spell around the monsters."

She nodded and, hands linked, we moved forward. Fergus and the others flanked us, but there was little they could do as we drew closer. I didn't dare shut my eyes to focus as the creatures advanced. They were within twenty feet of us now, close enough that we could see the pale violet glow of their eyes.

Fear knotted my gut as I remembered the rings' ineffectiveness against the skellies in the field. But in that moment I'd let the witch get in my head and my belief had wavered—my faith in myself and the Protector. I wouldn't make that mistake again.

"Envision it, Ken . . . the rings' magic taking down the skeletons' protection, just like we envisioned the force field around camp."

We raised our linked hands above our heads and a beam of scalding golden light blasted from the rings. I raised my other hand to shield my eyes, but could see the monsters falling back. The two remaining guards raced toward us, bleeding but alive.

Fergus, who was the best shot among us, let an arrow fly. I think my heart may have stopped as it sailed through the air and struck home in a skellie's eye socket. The creature stumbled back, regained its feet, and kept coming. The shot proved we could now hurt them, but one arrow at a time would not do the trick.

"Jamie, the bomb!" Before the words left my mouth, he had the device out of his pocket. Taking aim, he pulled the pin, drew his arm back like a bowler, and flung it forward. It rolled in a steady, straight line into the midst of the advancing creatures, who didn't pay it a bit of attention.

"Retreat! Everyone get behind the bridge," Duncan cried.

Hands guided Kenna and me away. In unspoken agreement, we lowered our hands and unlinked our fingers, letting the beam from our rings fade. The explosion that followed shook the ground and we fell back, heat washing over us.

A cheer rose behind us. And I sat up to find the creatures had turned into a pile of fiery bones. With the few partially intact, hobbling around in circles. Then the bones dissolved, as if they longed to return to the earth where they belonged.

Kenna leaned over and helped me to my feet. "All right, Highney?"

"Yes, but . . ." My voice trailed off as I watched Jamie and Duncan rush to check the fallen guards. Duncan placed two fingers on the first man's neck and then shook his head with a frown. When Jamie reached the second guard, I could tell by his body language that he still lived.

"He wishes a word, Yer Majesty!" Jamie called.

"Ken, have Fergus and Ana lead the Destined back to camp. And tell them to hurry before Addie's reinforcements show up."

She nodded and I jogged to where the MacCrae brothers leaned over the young man who'd just crossed the bridge with Kenna and Duncan—it was Rabbie MacGregor, Duncan's apprentice. Slowly, I knelt beside him and took his blood-soaked hand.

Duncan knelt on his other side. "Yer gonna make it, Rabbie. Just hold on."

His dark gaze bore into mine. "Yer Majesty, please tell . . . my sister, Hannah, I love her." His eyes closed and a sick gurgle bubbled in his throat.

Choking on a sob, I felt Jamie place a hand on my shoulders for support. I swallowed and forced the words past my burning throat. "Of course, Rabbie, I'll tell her. Is there anything else?"

He turned his head toward Duncan, his eyes flickered and then cracked open. "Hannah wishes . . . ta become a . . . royal guard." A tiny smile tilted his mouth. "Like me."

Tears coursed down Duncan's face. "I'll make it so."

Rabbie clutched his hand. "'Twas an . . . honor to . . . die . . . protectin' Doon."

A last breath shuddered from his chest and then he was gone.

"Well, isn't tha' touching. Another useless death caused by the American simpleton who fancies herself a queen."

Addie's unmistakable, hideous voice froze my grief. I whipped around to find the witch holding Kenna in front of her, a knife pressed to the front of her throat. Raising my hand, the ring blazed to life. Jamie and Duncan flanked me on either side, swords drawn, Duncan practically vibrating with anger.

"No need to pull out the big guns, dear. I'm just here to make a trade." Addie lifted her hand and crooked a finger, and in *my* voice, said, "Jamie, come to me."

After a moment's hesitation, he took a step forward. My brain told me to stop him, but I couldn't move. Was he really going to her willingly? Or did she have some sort of hold on him? As he took another step, shock buzzed through my limbs and I lowered my ring, afraid to catch him in the crossfire.

"Release Mackenna and I'll come wi' you."

At Jamie's words, relief washed through me. He wasn't entranced, just attempting to rescue my best friend.

Jamie lowered his sword and took another slow step forward. "My friends leave here unharmed and I'll do as ye ask."

"See, little queenie, he really does want me," Addie boasted, no longer using my voice. "He just needed the right . . . incentive. Together, we will take Doon piece by piece, until ye have nothin' left ta rule. Then I'll watch as your *true love* kills you and bathe in your blood!"

I fingered the handle of one of the axes hanging from my weapons belt, calculating whether I could bury it in the witch's face before she could slit Kenna's throat. It wasn't worth the risk. Kenna's gaze caught mine and I could tell she was trying to communicate. Suddenly her words slammed into my brain. *"I've got this. Back off!"*

Jamie stopped. He must've heard it too.

She might think she could handle the witch, but I wasn't taking any chances. Mustering every ounce of acting skill

I'd absorbed from my best friend over the years, I rushed to Jamie's side and gripped his arm. "Jamie! Please don't do this! Don't leave me for *her*!"

He stared down at me like I'd lost my brains. "Vee, get back."

I glanced quickly at the witch to see if she was buying my act. Her chin tilted as she watched us with narrowed eyes, her lips curling in satisfaction. *Perfect.* Jamie tried to take my arm to push me behind him, but I flung myself against his chest and moaned, "She can't make you happy! We can win this fight together."

And then I slipped the bomb into his pocket. I felt the tension in his body the moment he understood.

Giving my hand a quick squeeze, he shoved me away from him. "'Tis over between us! I'm sick o' bein' on the losing side!" He glanced at Addie, whose smile had grown huge. "I'm in love wi' someone else now."

As he spoke, I dropped my hand into my pocket and flicked the cap off of the elixir. Jamie turned away on his heel as if to join Addie and gave Kenna a quick nod.

In a seamless sequence of motion, Kenna threw her head back into Addie's chin, pulled the knife away from her neck with both hands, and bent forward, forcing the witch off balance. Then with a screech, she rammed her elbow into Addie's stomach and twisted her knife arm painfully to the side.

Seeing my opening, I leapt forward as I pulled the vial from my pocket and splashed Saint Sabastian's elixir into the witch's stunned face.

"Kenna, get clear," Duncan shouted.

Kenna knocked the knife from Addie's hand and grabbed it out of the air before sprinting toward us.

I waited. For what, I didn't know. Addie's skin to boil and blister like a vampire in the sun. Her old, haggish self to appear the way a werewolf morphs back into a man. Perhaps for her body to shrivel away to dust like her monsters. To shriek, "I'm melting!" and disappear into a puddle of fabric. Something.

What I didn't expect was for her to throw her head back with a resounding cackle. "You stupid, stupid girl, I've been immortal for hundreds o' years, and ye think a bit o' holy water will hurt me? This isn't Oz!" Violet light blasted from her eyes. Her hair whipped around her head like Medusa as she raised her palms directly at us. "But you have given me a wonderful idea."

CHAPTER 37

Mackenna

Purple orbs of magic began to gather in the center of Addie's outstretched hands, writhing like agitated serpents in small glass bowls. "I always thought that Frank L. Baum was a ninny for creating a world where his witch could be killed with something as basic and necessary as water."

Kenna, Vee's voice buzzed inside my head. *Addie gets sloppy when she's antagonized.*

Got it! Squaring my shoulders, I leveled my gaze at Addie and projected that I found her pathetic. "Do you have a point you're eventually going to make? Or are you trying to soliloquize us to death?"

My bestie stepped into me and grasped my hand, covering up the movement with a chuckle. "Good one, Ken."

I watched the rage move across Addie's face. "Acid. That's my point, dearie. Acid is a much more effective way to melt someone." The slithering balls in her hands began to secrete liquid. A single drop fell from her hand. With a sickening hiss, the spot blackened as the grass turned to zombie fungus. "Not me, of course. But I'm thinking it will do the trick on the two of you nicely."

Without a second to spare, Kenna and I raised our hands, using our rings to put up a shield as two purple balls flew through the air. The orbs expanded into a gelatinous web that coated our protective bubble. As it oozed to the ground around us, the earth decayed and blackened.

My head began to buzz as Jamie's voice ordered, *Take cover now!*

I looked to Vee who clarified, *Bomb!*

A moment later, a metal ball rolled past, coming to a stop against Addie's boot. The witch glanced down and her eyes flew wide. In unspoken agreement, Vee and I expanded our protective bubble to include the MacCraes right before the garden exploded.

Duncan wrapped me in his massive arms as a wave of heat pushed us back several steps. Thanks to my boyfriend's ogre-like stature, we managed to stay upright. But just barely. Vee and Jamie weren't so lucky.

The moment Duncan loosened his grip, we rushed over to where Vee and Jamie lay in a tangled heap. As Duncan reached for his brother, I knelt next to my best friend. Both of them were alive, but dazed.

Jamie impatiently pushed Duncan's hands away. "I'm fine. Tend ta the queen."

"I'm fine too," Vee insisted in sloppy speech. She looked about her without focusing on anything specific. "The protective bubble?"

"Gone." I stuck my hand under her nose. Uncle Cameron's ring no longer emanated any light; neither did its counterpart on Vee's hand.

"An' the witch?" she slurred.

Holy Hammerstein! With the explosion, I'd forgotten all about Addie. I stood and swiveled around, fighting against the sensation of vertigo as I looked toward where I'd last seen the Witch of Doon.

The miniature bridge had been blown to bits. Stone fragments littered the garden in all directions. In the middle of the rubble, Adelaide struggled to sit up. The skin on the right side of her face, from cheek to jawline, hung down from her skull in a loose flap. The gross combination of tendons, arteries, and bone that it exposed lent a nightmarish quality to the scene as the witch shakily stood up.

"Is that the best ye've got, love?" She directed the taunt to Jamie, the loose side of her face undulating as she spoke. "I dinna mind a quarrel now and then. Not when the prospect of making up is so sweet."

Vee, who'd gotten to her feet and was being held back by Jamie, growled, "You're delusional, witch."

Addie just chuckled. "Where were we? Oh, yes . . . acid. For all but my sweet prince."

Magic began to ball in her palms as I reached for Vee's hand. Unfortunately, the rings didn't respond.

We're defenseless! Vee's voice buzzed through my brain followed by Jamie's. *Make a run for it. Duncan and I will hold Adelaide off while the two o' you get away.*

I'm not leaving you. We're stronger together, Vee and I responded, our replies overlapping as we refused to cooperate.

The gathering magic in Addie's hands began to sizzle. "Time's up," she sneered. The ground shook as she arced her arms up over her head. The magic in her palms became a supercharged, violet black hole. Debris from the bridge began to fly through the air as it got sucked into her magical void.

The wind caused by the witch's vortex snatched my hair

and clothes and pulled me painfully forward. Unable to resist, I searched for anything I could use to anchor myself, but the scorched, spongy earth offered no help. Vee, Duncan, and Jamie fought their own futile battles against the witch's power.

Link arms! I commanded as I reached for Vee. She, in turn, grabbed hold of Jamie, who clung to Duncan. Step by unwilling step, the witch dragged us closer. As we struggled to resist her tug, chunks of stone and branches battered our heads. A small twig became a projectile that pierced my brow. I could sense the blood from the wound it created streaming into the corner of my eye.

When we were about twenty feet away from the witch, the force of her magic began to lift us off our feet. As we flew toward her, the vortex began to crackle like a speaker with a short. Losing its fury, the black hole began to dissipate. All around us, things caught in its pull began to drop to the ground. We were no exception.

Hitting the ground with a smack, I felt Vee as she crashed into my hip; heard Duncan and Jamie groan in what I could only assume was a collision of princes. Scrambling toward the others, I grabbed on to Vee as Duncan and Jamie reached for us. Huddling together, the four of us watched Addie drop her arms. Outraged, she stared at her hands in disbelief.

Then, murmuring an incantation, the witch lifted her hands and focused. Purple magic flickered in her palms but failed to manifest into anything more. With a scream, she tried again. This time, she couldn't even cause a spark. As she howled in outrage, the ground began to come apart. Little vein-like fissures crisscrossed through the garden.

Suddenly Addie and the earth stilled. Her eyes, which always contained a bit of craziness in them, gleamed with a new level of insanity—one that chilled me to the core of my being. "More souls," she muttered to herself, ignoring us as if we no longer existed. "I need more souls." In a dramatic poof of purple smoke, the witch disappeared.

For several seconds, Vee, Jamie, Duncan, and I lay in a heap, unable to process what had occurred. Finding my voice, I asked, "What just happened?"

"Hopefully, a way to kill Adelaide Blackmore Cadell," Jamie replied.

"Or," Duncan countered, "the death o' us all."

"Either way," Vee said as she struggled to sit up, "we need to get back to camp and prepare for the next wave of attack."

As if they agreed with Vee, the Rings of Aontacht sparked to life in their red and green brilliance.

CHAPTER 38

Duncan

Rabbie was dead—but my grief would have to wait. Our camp was in trouble. If we didn't act quickly, I would be mourning many more lives than that of my apprentice.

The sounds of panic, intermingled with the cries of the wounded, wove their way through the trees to meet us long before we reached camp. Such fearsome sounds superseded the golden dome of protection that with Kenna's hand in mine, I saw as clear as day. If not for the noise, I would've marveled that I could now see the world as Mackenna did. But there wasn't time for that either.

Instead, I began to run. We all did.

Chaos reigned in our makeshift headquarters. Wounded Destined and Doonians lay just inside the protection, the least wounded tending to those with more severe injuries. I singled out Fergus supporting Alasdair as they limped their way into the weapons tent.

With a burst of speed, Jamie sprinted past me. I followed my brother into the tent, Mackenna and the queen close on my heels. Jamie took Alasdair's other arm and with Fergus, gently lowered the auld man to a log serving as a bench.

Once our kinsman was settled, Jamie demanded, "What happened?"

"We were ambushed, m'Laird." Fergus sank onto the log next to Alasdair. Other than a bleeding bite mark on his bicep, my dear friend seemed physically none too worse for wear. But I couldn't help noticing the subtle tremor in his hand.

"Where's Fiona?" Mackenna asked as she and Queen Veronica settled across from the two injured men.

Fergus blinked at her as if she were speaking another language. In the awkward silence that followed, Alasdair croaked, "She's tendin' to the wounded."

"Aye," Fergus agreed. He shook his head as if to clear it of cobwebs. "She's fine."

"But others are not?" Veronica probed. Her shrewd eyes narrowed in comprehension even before the words were spoken.

"Nay, Your Highness." Fergus offered the queen an account of what had transpired. In the darkness of the tent, shadows accentuated the angles of his face like the teller of a creepy story at a sleepover. "We were escorting the Destined back to camp when skellies attacked. There were too many of them and they were surrounded by evil magic, so's that we couldna touch them. I sounded the alarm and our troops rushed to aid us. Even with the advantage of numbers, the skellies were unstoppable."

He rested his head in his hand and took a deep breath. "Then, quite unexpectedly, the magic around them failed. Suddenly, our broadswords could knock them inta pieces."

The queen's startled eyes met mine before seeking Jamie's. "I wonder if that's when I threw the elixir on Addie?"

Alasdair nodded gravely. "Mayhap, Yer Highness."

Veronica turned her attention back to our friend. "Then what happened, Fergus?"

"We were having some impact against the skellies, our troops were taking over the fight so we could get the Destined out of the thick of things. Tha's when the earth began to shake. All of a sudden, the skellies dropped their weapons and each took hold of a person." Fergus trailed off, looking as if he were going to be sick. "Then they just disappeared."

Jamie's alarmed eyes briefly met mine. He refused to comprehend what Fergus was trying to say. I felt the same way. There was a short pause as each of us struggled with our own desire to remain ignorant of the awful truth.

Mackenna wrapped her arm around the queen's shoulders. She looked around the room and then asked Fergus in a small voice, "The skellies just disappeared?"

"Aye," he replied. "With the people they were holdin'."

"How about the rest of the Destined?" Vee asked. Her eyes were riveted on him, willing herself to not fall apart.

"Alive." Fergus shook his arm, flinging little drops of blood across the floor. "Several are injured. They're frightened but they'll live."

"And our people?"

Something closed behind Fergus's eyes, a shutter blocking out his feelings like any veteran soldier would do when delivering horrific news. "Several casualties," he replied matter-of-factly. "But considering that we're fighting a war . . . we got off easy, Your Highness."

The flaps to the tent rustled, and I swung 'round with my sword at the ready. Fiona's startled face saw the tip of my sword and she paused. "I'm lookin' for Fergus," she stated.

Lowering my weapon, I nodded and she flew across the tent and onto her husband's lap. Fergus and Fiona kissed as I averted my eyes and moved to stand behind Mackenna, resting a hand upon her shoulder. In light of what had transpired, I needed to feel her close to me.

Jamie came to stand next to me, behind the queen. "How many people did they take?" he asked.

Fiona swiveled in Fergus's lap, but made no move to get up. "A hundred and forty-seven Destined. Thirty-one Doonians."

The image of Adelaide Blackmore Cadell as she'd looked with half her face in ruin and her magic faltering came back to haunt me. "She said she needed more souls."

The queen's face turned to look up at my brother, horror and remorse emanating from her blue eyes. "We did this," she whispered. "We provoked Addie and she took our people."

Jamie knelt and embraced her from behind. "This is war, love. There will be casualties."

Beneath my touch, I could feel Mackenna bristling. I reached down to take her hand, but she evaded my grasp. "We led them across the bridge like cows to a hamburger factory. They had no idea what they were facing." Springing to her feet, she paced away.

I followed, attempting to be the voice of reason. "They were called ta Doon same as you and Veronica. They knew there were risks."

"How can you say that?" The pain in her eyes rent me in two. She raised a fist and struck my chest. Followed by a second strike. I offered no resistance, letting her pummel me back across the tent. Tears glistened in the corners of her eyes as her blows grew in force. She broke with a sob, and I gathered her into my arms.

"I don't get it," she wailed. "I don't get why the Protector doesn't *protect* us. Why sometimes the Rings of Aontacht work and sometimes they don't. If the Protector wanted, Vee and I could use the rings to turn the skellies into dust. This could all be over."

"It's my fault," Veronica added in a haunted voice. "I keep doubting that we—that *I* can really do this. My lack of belief is causing the rings not to work."

Alasdair cleared his throat. "Nay, lass. I mean, Your Highness. Some things need goin' through. Tha's simply the way life works." Holding Mackenna, my face buried in her strawberry-scented hair, I couldn't see Alasdair as he spoke, but his voice held an authority I'd never noticed before. "If I've learned anything from my millennia on earth, it's that the human race gains nothin' from takin' the easy way out.

"The Rings of Aontacht were created for unity across the portal. They were forged to protect the bearers, not as offensive weapons. They're no' like your culture's mythical lightsabers."

I lifted my head and watched as Jamie helped the auld man to his feet. "You all are so young. And ye've lived so little o' life. I canna explain to ye why things dinna always happen the way we want, or the easy way. But I kin attest that the Protector's plan is a far better one than we could ever devise, and that, when this is all said and done, ye'll be able ta look back and see the purpose in all o' it."

Mackenna buried her face in my shirt. "If I don't believe there's a reason for all of this, I'm going to go crazy." Then she straightened up. "So you better be right, Alasdair."

The auld man laid a gnarled hand on her arm. "I kin assure ye lass, I am."

Veronica, Jamie, Fiona, and Fergus all stepped in, surrounding us in something that was half hug, half rugby scrum. It was then, in the midst of this breakthrough, that I heard it. *Click-clack. Click-clack. Click-clack.*

Like thousands—nay, millions of crickets. The sounds of

the undead army swarmed the tent. Queen Veronica let out an exhausted sigh. "Sounds like the skellies are back."

Mackenna scrubbed at the tear tracks on her ruddy cheeks. Her face, leaner since she began training, bore the traits of a fierce warrior, unafraid and uncompromising. "Duncan, if there's even a chance our people are still alive, someone has to go after them. Before Addie breaks them and strips them of their souls."

CHAPTER 39

Veronica

Like a thousand robotic dancers in an undead tap recital, the uniform *click-clack* of the skellies droned on until I thought I would scream. But breaking down was not an option for a queen. I had to remain calm as I waited at the fire circle for word of the army's position. One by one, the scouts returned with the same report—skellies waited just outside our protective shield, hundreds of them on every side. We were surrounded.

The camp was organized chaos as Doonians scrambled to locate weapons, to find their assigned squadron, and to tell their friends and family one last "I love you."

Fear thickened the air like a humid August morning. The skellies had been stopped by the bubble, but for how long? Why had the witch sent them here if there was no way for them to get in? I had a feeling I didn't want to know the answer.

Kenna had just spent the last thirty minutes arguing that a rescue team needed to go after the missing people. I'd asked her to leave me so I could think it through. Who could we spare?

I'd experienced Addie's version of the castle firsthand, and there were magical traps and supernaturally enhanced guards at every turn. How could I send a rescue party knowing the chances of them surviving the mission were marginal at best?

I adjusted my thick leather breastplate and strapped my axe belt across my chest, then picked up the round shield Jamie had custom-made for me. Hefting its weight, I marveled at how he had managed to make it feel light and yet strong at the same time. Maybe not Captain America strong, but still, perfect for me.

Fergus approached, his skin blotchy, his blue eyes swimming with emotion.

"What is it?"

"The Destined are hurtin', my queen. Fee's doin' her best to encourage them after the loss of their friends, but I think they need ta hear from you."

Shame washed over me until I was sure my face matched the color of my big friend's mottled cheeks. He shouldn't have had to tell me to speak to our newest Doonians. I'd talked to some of the Destined in passing, but I hadn't even thought about how frightened they must be.

"Fergus, did you know that I've always thought of you as my guardian angel?"

His cheeks went from pink to flame-on. "No, Yer Majesty."

"From the moment I set foot in Doon, you've been watching out for me and Kenna. I thank you for that and for calling my attention to this matter. Please gather the people. I'd like to speak to them immediately."

Before he turned away, I grabbed his sleeve. "And thank you for being such a great friend."

He gave a quick nod, his eyes misty. "Always, Veronica."

A short time later, I balanced on a log and looked out over

the crowd. Interspersed among the Doonians, hundreds of unfamiliar faces, those of teens and young adults, wearing modern clothes, some with piercings, tattoos, and dyed hair, stared back at me. Not soldiers, but ordinary, terrified people waiting for some great wisdom to spew out of my mouth and take away their pain and fear. Realizing that was impossible, I decided to speak from my heart.

I raised my hand in greeting and projected my voice above the incessant clanking. "Hi. My name is Veronica Welling and I wasn't always a queen. Like you, I'm not from Doon, but a small town in Indiana. And like many of you, before I was Called here, I lost the security of home and family. When Kenna and I first arrived here, the Doonians believed us in league with the witch and threw us in the dungeon." There were a few incredulous laughs, and Fergus wandered up and shouted, "I'm not proud of it, but 'tis true!"

I nodded. "It wasn't exactly what I'd imagined my reception in Doon to be like. So I know how scared and confused you all must feel to have lost so many of your friends."

More Doonians began to gather round, many of them mingling with the crowd and taking a hand or putting an arm around one of the new Destined. Alasdair moved toward the front and clapped a hand on each of the African boys' shoulders. I met his penetrating gaze and remembered something he'd said to me long ago.

"A wise man once told me that what is seen as light will forever be coveted by the dark. And as I look out at your faces, all I see is blinding light. A light so brilliant that it cannot be quenched by the darkness. And in your eyes, I see hope. Hope for a better future, for the home that many of you have never had. If we each hold tight to that hope, there is no darkness strong enough to defeat it."

Trying to make eye contact with as many individuals as possible, I continued. "I'm not saying that we'll all make it through this battle unscathed, but I do know that the Protector is faithful and he will be with us. I also know that if there's anything in this world worth fighting for, it's a place we can call home. You are part of that home." Clarity struck and in that moment, I knew what I had to do. "And since we don't give up on family, I'm asking for volunteers to send on a rescue mission." Confusion and hope mingled on nearby faces. "I cannot believe the Protector would bring any of you here to feed the witch's power. Our people who have been taken *must be* alive. It will be terribly dangerous, but I need volunteers to sneak into the castle and bring them back to us."

Hands flew into the air. Analisa, Sofia, Ewan, and a young Filipino girl who hopped up and down shouting, "Me, me, me!" I nodded to my friends as each one came forward and then turned to the Destined girl. "What's your name?"

"Cheska Ann Santos, and I've been training for this exact moment."

"How so?" I arched a brow. The girl couldn't be more than fifteen.

"I'm a gamer, Yer Majesty. I specialize in a war game that puts me in a position to strategize and spy on other groups." Her voice grew higher as she spoke. "Sneaking into castles is what I do! I've dreamed of this moment!"

My eyes shifted to Ana, who gave a barely perceptible nod. She would watch out for the girl. "All right then, you're in."

She pumped a fist in the air as the brothers from Africa, Jeremiah and Ezekiel, stepped forward. "We're going too." Ezekiel lifted his chin and met my gaze with such confident determination that I didn't question them further. Kenna had shared a bit of their horrifying and heroic past. These boys were perfect for the job.

"We have our group then." Catching Cheska's enthusiasm, I threw a fist into the air and shouted, "Today, we will take back what is ours! Today, we fight for Doon!"

Fists flew up around the group as they shouted in unity, "Fight for Doon!" The chant grew so loud, it drowned out the skellies' clanking.

My chest burned as I yelled along with them, the mantra echoing from all corners of the camp as Doonians joined in. After several moments, the people began to disperse to their duties, some still chanting. Now that I was alone, the tears I'd held in splashed down on my cheeks.

A hand extended in front of me and I looked down to see Ewan Murray. *Perhaps not so alone.* Accepting his help, I grasped his fingers and hopped down.

"Tha' was inspiring, Yer Majesty."

He handed me a clean handkerchief, and after I'd wiped my nose and eyes, I turned back to him. "Thank you for volunteering, Ewan."

He plunked his shield into the dirt at his feet and turned to face me. "Of course. I'm takin' point since I know that castle best. And I know how to get around the witch's protection spell."

"Watch out for Sofia. I know she's desperate to help, and feels like she would be useless in a battle, but this will be just as dangerous." As I finished speaking, his summer-green eyes drilled into mine. He'd avoided me since the handfasting. I knew there were unresolved feelings between us, but I'd had too much on my mind to seek him out.

"Veronica, please forgive me."

I started, not expecting those words to come out of his mouth. "For what?"

"Ye have a Calling with Prince Jamie and I disrespected

that." He swiped a hand over his fiery hair, but it flopped back down over his right eye as he let out a deep sigh. "When we thought he'd passed on, I couldna bear to see ye so sad and alone. I determined to help any way that I could. I didna expect ta fall for ye."

I opened my mouth, but he kept talking.

"The Laird is a good man and the perfect one ta lead by your side."

As I searched his sweet face, a realization struck me—this reckless boy had been my friend when I needed one most, and despite Jamie's doubts, I wanted Ewan in my life. "Thank you for that. Your support means a lot to me. When this is all over, I'd like to ask that you join my royal guard."

His eyes sparkled with excitement and I knew I'd said the right thing. "Aye, Yer Majesty! It would be an honor."

"Murray!" Ana called from nearby. "Get your scrawny hide over here!"

"I will protect the others and bring the Destined back no matter what it takes. I swear it!" Ewan dropped into a quick bow, picked up his shield, and ran to join Ana and the others. He would leap headfirst into danger, but I knew he would do everything in his power to keep his promise to me.

"Verranica!" I turned to find Jamie jogging up, metal breastplate catching the sun, and in one quick glance I memorized the way he looked in that moment—black boots laced tight, daggers strapped to both strong calves exposed below his blue-and-green kilt, metal braces on both of his wide forearms, a bow strung across his chest, a sword swinging at his side. One word entered my mind: Powerful. My eyes landed on his face and I had to swallow a sudden blast of terror. I could *not* lose him again.

"There's something ye need to see, love." He linked his

fingers through mine and we set off at a quick pace. "I told my brother and Mackenna to meet us there."

"Are the bombs set up?"

"Aye. Oliver created a trippin' mechanism, so if the skeletons cross they'll detonate within thirty seconds."

"How many?"

"At least six. We're keepin' our squads away from those areas. We also have the Crew divided. They wound the tape that Duncan brought from Alloway through the brush and now they're waitin' in trees with animal nets in the east and west. Tha' should slow the bags o'bones down a bit."

"And the trenches?" I asked as we climbed a grassy hill.

"Coming along nicely, but we'll need at least an hour to get them deep enough. And I dinna think we'll have it."

We rounded the top of the knoll and my breath stopped. Hundreds of skellies, in perfect formation, spread out below us, their legs pumping in unison like wind-up toys. Beyond, approximately two football fields away, Addie sat astride something that looked like a horse, but its size made her appear the size of a doll on its monstrous back. Black with snow-white hair on its legs, the animal stomped the ground and shook its massive head. "Is that a . . ."

"A Clydesdale. They're native to this area, but tha' creature is somethin' else . . ." His voice dropped off and he shook his head in horrified awe. "'Tis at least twenty-five hands tall."

"Seven feet at the shoulder," Duncan clarified as he stepped up beside his brother.

Kenna looped her arm through mine and handed me the spyglass. "And I wouldn't compare that *thing* to the majestic Clydesdales in the beer commercials, at least not anymore . . ."

I raised the small telescope, and when I found the horse and rider I gasped out loud. The animal's flesh was the sickly black, brown, and purple of a deep bruise. Large shards of hide hung off its bones in bloody chunks. It stamped and turned to expose a gaping hole in its side, and I could see its ribs and pulpy organs beneath. I shifted the glass up to the rider, and it was Addie's face that gave me the biggest shock; the skin on the right side had completely disintegrated, bones and tendons exposed from eye socket to jawbone, while the other half still held the beauty of a surgically enhanced trophy wife. Why hadn't she healed herself after the explosion?

Then, as if she could see me, she stared straight down the lens of my telescope and mouthed the words, "It's over."

In a move so quick I could barely see her hands, she formed a ball of purple flame and hurled it in our direction.

"Take cover!" I screeched.

Jamie grabbed my hand and we dropped, sliding down the grassy hill, just as the sky exploded.

CHAPTER 40

Jamie

The violet ball struck with a boom that vibrated the ground beneath us. Vee squeezed my hand as we looked up at the point of impact. Because of Mackenna's gift, I could see the purple ooze of the witch's magic melting the white shimmer of our protection buffer. The disintegration was slow, as if Vee and Kenna's barrier fought against Addie's spell.

We have to stop it. Veronica let go of my hand and rushed to Mackenna's side. "I don't know how. The rings—"

"We can do this, Ken. Just like in the castle gardens when we took out the skellies force field. We have to *believe*." Mackenna nodded and they raised their joined fists to the sky and began to call on the Protector's strength.

Protect our people, we ask. Defeat the witch's magic and repair the shield that you so graciously granted us, Vee's voice whispered through my head. The girl's eyes remained closed and suddenly the strength of their will smashed into my mind, almost dropping me to my knees as I felt their belief, their resounding faith.

The rings sparked, shooting white flame that pushed back the purple darkness. The crystalline dome sealed once more and the lasses lowered their arms. But the moment the white beam from the Rings of Aontacht disconnected, violet sparks began eating another hole in the protection.

Veronica and Mackenna linked hands again, and this time my brother and I joined them. Placing a hand on each of their shoulders, white-hot fire burst from the rings. Raising our consciousness together, the shield began to rebuild itself once again. This time, the lasses didn't move, but kept their hands linked and raised.

At first, it seemed to work, but then another purple globe hurtled down, this one breaking into smaller orbs before smashing into the dome. Each hole grew larger by the second. The power of the rings was unable to keep up, and soon both sputtered and winked out.

"No!" Vee cried. "Kenna, try again!"

But the rings did not spark again. And the purple continued to eat away at our shield.

Duncan put his hand over the lasses' joined fingers and gently pushed their arms down. "One of the most important aspects o' bein' a soldier is knowin' when you're bested. Knowin' when to retreat."

The girls' eyes met and with a solemn nod, they let go.

I pulled Vee tight to my chest. "We need to go and warn the others. You and Mackenna head west and raise the alarm. Duncan and I will go east and north."

Releasing Veronica took herculean effort, but I'd accepted that we couldn't stay together through this fight. She'd proven she could take care of herself. I glanced up; the holes had met in the middle and the purple sparks were making their way down the sides of the shield. We had little time. With one last squeeze, I let her go and we all took off at a sprint.

Duncan and I ran in the same direction. Before splitting up, we agreed to meet at the horse paddock.

I reached Lachlan and the Rosetti twins perched in a tree first. Cupping my hands around my mouth, I cried, "Sound the alarm!"

Fabrizio's shaggy head leaned down from a branch. "What's happening?"

My gaze flicked up to see the dome almost halfway gone. "The shield's comin' down."

Farther up the tree, Luciano raised a cow bell above his head. He rang it back and forth with a resonating gong.

I moved on, going from group to group, and the bells quickly multiplied until their clangs drowned out the skeleton's march. When I reached the horse paddock, I retrieved my shield and mounted Crusoe. Duncan arrived right behind me, grabbing his own shield from the dirt. "Did ye see the lasses?"

"Nay." He shook his head, frowning as he entered the pen and mounted the horse I'd prepared for him.

Reaching out with my mind, I said, *Verranica, the shield's almost down. Where are you?*

For three heartbeats there was no answer, and then, *Protection . . . Over . . . Cave . . . children.*

"They're puttin' a shield up ta protect the children in the tunnel," I told Duncan. "The connection must be shaky, because they're usin' the rings."

Duncan opened his mouth to respond, but an explosion cut off his words. I jerked around to see that the shield had fallen. The clash of steel meeting steel reached us before another bomb detonated, this one close enough to shake the leaves from the trees. With a nod to my brother, I galloped out of the corral and toward the border. At the sight of Addie's approaching army, we pulled up at the edge of the forest.

Eyes glowing with an ethereal violet light, hundreds of skeletons marched in mechanical unison, their feet ringing out a symphony of death. Tremors coursed through my body, wave after wave of tightly leashed adrenaline causing my muscles to vibrate in anticipation. Some carried swords, some small knives, some were weaponless except for their bony-sharp fingers and teeth. The bitter taste of dread coated my tongue as the rhythmic clacking drew closer, vibrating in my chest.

I glanced at Duncan and he met my gaze with grim determination mixed with a deep dread that twisted a knot in my gut. Nothing gave me courage faster than when I saw my brother afraid.

Shaking the numbness from my hands, I pushed down my own fear and tucked it deep inside. Then, recalling a scene from the movie I'd watched with Veronica where an elf and a dwarf made sport of how many monsters they could kill, I drew my sword and flashed a cocky grin. "Bet I can take down more skellies than you can, *mo wee bráthair.*"

His mouth curled as he unsheathed his own weapon. "I'll take that bet."

With a battle cry, we galloped out to meet the skeletons. I swung my sword and slashed at the first creature, cutting through its spiny neck. It collapsed in a pile of lifeless bones. Somehow, the shield around the skeletons had fallen. Perhaps the witch couldn't hold their protection while decimating ours. Or maybe the elixir had weakened her permanently. I could only hope.

All suppositions left my head as I blocked a blade with my shield and then smashed it into the creature's skull, exploding it to dust. Swinging to my right and to my left, I sliced heads from necks while keeping a rough count.

One creature climbed up my saddle and sank its claw-like fingers into my leg. I elbowed it in the head and it flew backward, knocking several of its mates off their feet.

The sound of Duncan fighting not far from my side was heartening, and as I swung my sword in a wide arc, taking out at least five at once, I called, "Tha' makes twenty-five! How about you?"

"Closer ta thirty!"

I grinned and booted one in the face as it climbed up Crusoe's neck. My brother was nothing if not efficient. I swung and slashed and kicked and punched until my arms ached. Unfortunately, the creatures just kept coming. Looking up to see how many were left was not an option. I had to hold out hope that we could make a dent in their numbers.

Duncan's voice sounded strained as he shouted, "Tha's fifty!"

Pain pierced my back and I pulled a dagger, whipping my hand back and driving the blade into the face of a creature attempting to stab my kidney. Then I rammed my sword into its gullet and sent it flying.

"Fifty-one!" I bellowed. But I knew I'd only knocked it down temporarily.

Exhaustion set in as minutes or hours passed. I couldn't tell. The only thing that kept me going was knowing we were holding this line of monsters back from the camp. Grasping the reins, I swung to the side and met the sword of a skeleton, but he feigned and drove his blade into Crusoe's flank. My horse was so well trained that his only reaction was a wheeze and side step.

"No!" Red squeezed in on my vision as I lobbed off the creature's head. Crusoe had been a gift from my parents for my thirteenth birthday; more like family than a horse. I slashed and hacked at the skeletons, until my legs and arms were covered in lacerations. But they kept coming. Crusoe, losing blood, faltered a step, and just as I was about to call the retreat, cries sounded behind us.

Someone yelled, "For Doon!" And a chorus of voices repeated the chant.

I turned to see a group of forty-some Destined, brandishing ropes and whips, rushing into the fray. Relief flooded me even as I felt my horse shudder. I bent forward and smashed my shield into a creature's face before murmuring, "It's okay, boy. I'll get ye back to safety soon."

The Destined's weapons of choice took out the creatures more efficiently than our swords, and soon the forest was littered with skeleton parts. Once the newcomers had pushed Addie's minions back, I dismounted and jumped to the ground. Hooking my shield onto my back, I leaned down to inspect Crusoe's wound. It was long, but not too deep. If I got him help soon, he might survive it.

The skellies have breached the camp. Need reinforcements! Vee's voice shouted in my head.

Before I could respond, Duncan shouted, "Jamie, to the camp!" And he took off at a gallop.

I rose and whipped around, sword ready to slash some skeleton bum, and froze. The thing that stood before me was flesh and blood, with gory bits of meat hanging from his arms and face, exposing bone and sinew beneath. Yet I still recognized who he had once been . . . Sean MacNally, risen from the dead, and back for vengeance.

CHAPTER 41

Duncan

Confident that Jamie would be right behind me, I raced toward Mackenna and the queen. Addie's magic had completely disintegrated our shield. Without protection, hundreds of skellies overran the camp, destroying everything in their path.

Slowly, I picked my way through the enemy, slashing and chopping at their bones. In the middle of the chaos, I spied Queen Veronica throwing axes with deadly precision. At her back, in a blur of steel and auburn hair, Mackenna held her own against the skellie army. But my brother was missing.

Shutting out thoughts of losing Jamie again, I hacked my way forward, my attention divided between my own situation and the plight of Mackenna and Veronica. Beyond their line of sight and moving fast was a creature several hands larger than the other skellies. Perhaps it had been a giant in its former life.

Ignoring the fighting around it, the gigantic skellie locked onto Mackenna like a bull fixating on a red handkerchief. Terror gripped me as I considered what a creature like that could do to her, and for a moment, I froze . . . until Jamie's voice reverberated in my head. *You're no' scairt!*

Fleshless hands clutched my foot, spurring me into action. As I booted away a skeleton that tried to unseat me from my mount, I watched the giant undead thing uproot a nearby tree. It brandished the stump with the roots in the air, like an improvised cat-o'-nine tails. In heavy, earth-shaking steps it continued its advance toward Mackenna, who, occupied with the skellies in her immediate vicinity, seemed quite oblivious to the approaching threat.

Spurring my horse into action, I galloped forward and called her name. For an instant, her eyes met mine as I hurtled past. About to charge the giant creature, my horse shied. It reared up on its hind legs, while bony fingers dug into my clothes, clawing at my skin. Unable to maintain control of my mount, the horse leapt one direction while I went the other. Before I could right myself, two dozen skellies surged and dragged me to the ground.

In that moment, I had no doubt I was about to die in a frenzy of claws and teeth—and, strangely, I was at peace with my lot. As long as I'd been able to save Mackenna from meeting a similar fate, my sacrifice would be well worth the cost.

Pain arched through my body as fangs tore at my face, neck, arms, and legs. Searing hot agony pierced my abdomen, caused by what I suspected might be a dagger. Whispering my good-byes as if my loved ones could hear, I said to Jamie and Veronica, "Rule with compassion and mercy."

Then to Mackenna, "My heart will be yours forever."

I longed to see my fiery red-haired lass so much that I imagined her reply. "Don't you dare leave me, Duncan MacCrae!"

"I'm sorry, woman."

"Stop apologizing, you infuriating ogre!" This time, the response was definitely not in my head.

The skellies covering me began to fall back. I first became aware of my legs being freed from attack. Then my torso. One of the monsters on my head, digging into my scalp, rolled away, leaving its bony fingers still embedded in my skin. With my sight restored, I saw that the creatures were not in retreat but under attack by someone wielding a staff—someone with cornflower blue nail polish.

The staff smashed into the remaining skellies covering my body. They split apart, scattering bones across the brush. Breathing a prayer of thanks, I blinked into the severe, bloodied face of Mackenna as she pointed her staff at my chest. "Can you move?"

"You came for me," I breathed in a shaky voice.

"Always. We're a team." Her wide eyes flitted over my battered body. "You look awful. Can you get up?"

"I think so." I reached for the end of the staff and held on with all my might as Mackenna hoisted me to my feet. Scared and trembling with shock, I took a deep breath, willing myself to regain my equilibrium. After another breath, I nodded and took the spare sword she offered me. "I'm all right."

"Good. We need to get back to Vee." She tipped her head toward where the queen was driving skellies back with a small axe. Before moving, her radiant eyes locked on mine. For a moment, time stood still as her lips twisted into a smile. "I'll kiss you senseless later."

chapter 42

Jamie

The first time I'd killed Sean MacNally had been a mistake. I'd repented and accepted forgiveness for that sin. But it wasn't until this moment that I realized I'd yet to forgive myself. As I watched my greatest sin rise up in front of me, I knew if I didn't move on from what I'd done, I would die here.

"Fight me . . . man . . . on man . . . I will . . . kill ye . . . MacCrae." The words garbled out of zombie Sean's damaged mouth like his teeth were made of glass. If he had any teeth.

Darting my attention to the field, I watched the Destined knock down another row of skellies with the rope stretched between them. The second wave finished the creatures off with axes and scythes. And yet, the creatures kept coming.

As I turned back, zombie Sean raised a claymore and shield. "I'll fight ye, if that's what ye wish." I twirled my sword around my hand and then caught the hilt. "But this ends here and now."

Reaching for the shield on my back, I secured it to my left arm and bent my right elbow so my sword pointed at my adversary's throat.

The monster roared, his half-decayed mouth opening unnaturally wide, and then he charged. I blocked his first strike with my shield, but the power behind the blow forced me back a step. His strength had been supernaturally enhanced, just like the guards we'd encountered in the mountains.

Leaping forward, I struck. Our swords clashed together, the impact forcing mine out of my hand. I sprinted to the weapon, slid on my knees, and scooped it up. When I stood back up, Sean had only covered half the distance. Strong, but slow. *That*, I could handle.

He charged and smashed his shield into my sword hand. Pain raced up my fingers, but I managed not to let go. I parried and he countered, our swords tangling. Eye to eye with the monster, I struggled not to gag. He smelled of rotting meat and defecation. I shoved him away, but the creature didn't budge.

Trying a bit of psychological warfare, I baited, "Adelaide must be verra angry wi' ye."

Sean's bloodshot eyes widened a fraction.

"Ye've failed her so many times, and this one will be no different!" I slammed my shield into his head and freed my sword.

The monster stumbled back and then surged forward with a growl, his brain leaking out of his split skull. It went against all logic, but while physically strong, his body was frail. I sidestepped, spun, and sank my blade into his gut. He froze, but then a hideous grin split his decomposing face as he took hold of the blade and yanked it out of his stomach. His shield smacked into my shoulder before I could move, knocking me on the ground.

The thing lumbered toward me. "Addie . . . hat . . . hates . . . ye . . . kill . . . ye . . . kill."

"Ye really shouldna try ta speak." I scrambled backward until my shoulders bumped against a wide tree trunk. Biding

my time, I let Sean close the gap between us. As he readied his
weapon, I sprang to my feet and lunged, arching my sword over
my head and bringing it down with all my strength. The blade
sliced into the crook of his neck, but he batted the weapon
away, dislodging the blade from his flesh. The wound would've
stopped a mortal man. It appeared I'd have to take him apart
piece by piece.

I ducked around the tree, narrowly avoiding Sean's next
strike. As the monster followed, I raised my shield to defend
myself. Making him angry seemed to increase his strength.
His sword beat against my shield again and again until a final
slam sent it flying into the dirt. I whirled and kicked the vile
thing square in the chest. The blow pushed him back, but
when I brought my sword around he blocked and then went
on the offensive. Our weapons crashed together over and over
until I struggled to block his strikes. With a massive swing,
he knocked me off my feet. I fell on my back, the sword flying
out of my hand. As he raised his sword over his head to deliver
the final blow, I pulled a dagger from my belt, buried it in his
thigh, and rolled away.

Scrambling on my hands and knees, I grabbed the sword,
swung around, and slashed blindly. The blade cut halfway
through his calves, bone breaking through skin. With a bellow
of rage, he toppled face-first. I leapt to my feet and swung, my
blade slicing into the monster's neck as he fell.

I circled his prone body, sword pointed at his head. I had to be
sure. Reluctant to touch the unholy creature, I grasped his sleeve
and rolled him onto his back. He still blinked, his jaw working
as he tried to speak. I straddled his chest, grasped the sword in
both hands, and hesitated. Could I kill him all over *again*?

The answer flashed through my mind in a moment of seamless clarity. This was not Sean, but another mental torment sent

from the witch. If I let it, my guilt would destroy me from the inside out and Adelaide would win. What I'd done could not be changed, but I could accept absolution and move on. When I freed this soulless abomination from his torment, this time it would be out of compassion, not anger.

"I forgive you, Sean." I raised my sword and lifted a prayer, "Deliver him, Lord, for he knows not what he does."

And then I slammed the blade through his throat. His eyes flew wide, but it wasn't until I lifted his head and dislocated it from his body that he stopped moving.

Exhausted, but finally free, I dropped the monster's head and glanced to the field. The Destined had defeated the last of the skeleton battalion and were making their way toward me. As my head cleared, I began to hear snippets of words. Veronica's voice. *Ja . . . you . . . army . . .*

I snatched my shield out of the dirt, grabbed Crusoe's reins, and began to run.

CHAPTER 43

Veronica

Jamie! Where are you? Addie's army has us surrounded!
The skellies swarmed and I threw my last ax. End over over end, it hurtled through their ranks, knocking three . . . four . . . five creatures down like bowling pins, three of which lost their heads completely. Arms shaking, I raised my sword as Ken knocked down a row with her staff, blowing them apart with the impact. Working as a team, Duncan stepped into the void she created and decapitated the following row with his claymore.

"I dinna understand," Duncan mused. "What's the witch's end game? The skeletons are almost too easy to take down."

"Good point." Kenna moved into position as we fought back to back.

Another group scuttled forward, and I turned away, letting my friends take the lead under the pretense of readjusting my shield. Jamie hadn't responded to my mental calls and I could tell Duncan was also concerned his brother had yet to return.

Knowing Kenna would hear my desperation, but unable to

care, I projected, *Jamie, if you can hear me, please answer. Say something to let me know you're alive!*

Silence met my call, and then I heard his voice echoing through the trees. "Save some skellies for me!"

Jamie ran into the clearing bloodied, bruised, and the most beautiful sight I'd ever seen. He charged the last cluster of skeletons from behind, using his shield and sword to knock them to bits. Then he raced over and we threw our arms around him in the best group hug in the universe.

"What kept you?" Duncan asked.

"Zombie Sean," he replied matter-of-factly.

"What?" I growled, my voice hoarse from shouting orders.

"Aye," Jamie answered. "He can rest in peace now."

I pulled out of the tangle of arms and searched Jamie's face. Dirt and sweat streaked his skin, but his eyes were clear and golden brown. In truth, he seemed lighter than he had in a long time.

In unspoken agreement we moved into the fire circle and slumped against the log benches. My whole body shook with fatigue as I reclined next to Jamie, laying my head on his shoulder. Without the incessant *click-clack* of skellies, the camp seemed eerily silent.

Addie's undead army was gone. Although there were casualties all around camp, I couldn't think about that yet. I needed this one moment to regroup.

"Is it possible tha' we've defeated them all?" Alasdair strode into the fire circle, appearing spry as usual. Only a slash on his arm and a slight limp betrayed that he'd just fought the battle of his life.

"Let's hope so."

None of us spoke the question that was surely on all of our minds: Where was Addie?

A horrid thought broke through my exhaustion, causing me to straighten up despite my protesting muscles. "We need to get everyone into base camp and restore the shield. Addie'll be looking for more souls to rebuild her army."

"Or she could just do that . . ." From Kenna's weary tone, I couldn't tell if she was trying to make a joke or on the verge of hysteria. But as I processed what had captured her attention, I had no urge to laugh.

In the center of the fire circle, a bone that had once been part of a skellie's leg twitched. "Please tell me I'm not the only one seeing this!" Her voice pitched higher with every word as several more bones came together.

I leapt to my feet as all the bones around us began to rattle. "They're regenerating."

Everyone rose, warily watching the bones dancing toward each other and fervently hoping it was just a bad dream.

"You mean we've got to fight those things all over again? You've got to be kidding me. It's like *Groundhog Day* from hell!" Kenna moaned. She tugged the tail of her braid, her eyes wide. "Maybe I can wake myself up."

The ground vibrated as hundreds upon hundreds of bones around us convulsed, trying to reunite with their former bodies.

"We can't last another round!" Panic gripped my chest. "We've lost too many already."

The upper half of a skeleton dragged its way through the dirt, its violet eyes intent on my face. I scuttled back on my hands and it sparked.

"What in all that's holy?" Jamie raised his sword to the laboriously advancing skellie.

"Wait!" Kenna shrieked. "It's glowing . . . with dark magic. Igniting . . . like a sparkler."

"Maybe they're about to disintegrate," Duncan suggested.

"Tha's no' what happened to them in the castle garden." Jamie backed away from the creature that seemed to have stalled in place.

"Tallyho!" a call sounded from some distance away.

I shot to my feet. "Ewan?" I jumped onto a log and my heart squeezed. The missing Doonians and Destined, led by Ewan and Ana, raced toward camp. "They saved them!"

Kenna hopped up beside me. "Oh my . . . there's Cheska, and Jerimiah, and Ezekiel." Her voice thickened with emotion as she gripped my arm.

As they ran, I made out Sofia's tiny form next to Ewan. Kenna and I jumped off the log and raced to meet them, Jamie and Duncan on our heels. We dodged sparking bones as other Doonians joined us. I couldn't keep the smile from spreading across my face. Even if the skellies did re-form, we had reinforcements. The Destined were our second chance!

Jamie looped his arm through mine and we pulled ahead, jumping over rattling bones and debris. A whistling sound drew my gaze up to where a violet orb of magic streaked across the blue sky in a perfect arc. Robbed of words, I yanked Jamie to a stop and pointed at the ball as it whizzed over our heads toward camp.

A low cackle rang in my ears, raising the hairs on my neck as the voice from my nightmares resounded inside my head. *Checkmate, Queenie.*

CHAPTER 44

Mackenna

Click. Boom!

The explosion launched me through the air. I slammed into the ground, gasping for breath as debris rained down around me. My ears rang and I could barely hear the chaos in the camp. Rolling to my side, I pushed myself into a sitting position.

The bomb had created a car-sized crater where Calum Haldane had stood seconds before. Scanning the carnage around the blast, I saw Oliver face-down in the grass. Whether he was alive, I couldn't say—but there was no sign of the storyteller. Something wet landed on my cheek. I swiped at it and my finger came away with a hunk of bloody flesh, confirming my suspicions that the man was gone.

For a brief moment, I felt nothing . . . . The next thing I knew, I was on my feet, screaming at the top of my lungs. Duncan charged through the mass of downed people at full speed. When he reached me I tried to bury myself against his chest, but held me firmly at arm's length.

"Where are ye hurt worst?" he demanded. His alarmed eyes darted from my face to my abdomen and back.

The terror in his eyes made me wonder if I was missing something vital, like an arm. But my limbs felt connected. "I'm okay," I gasped loudly.

I followed his gaze as it moved downward to my stomach. My tattered shirt revealed a pulpy mess of mangled flesh and blood. Although I could see the injury, I still couldn't feel anything.

Duncan let go of my shoulders. His trembling hands reached for my wound. As he touched me, hunks of flesh fell away. Startled, he jumped backward as I realized the terrible truth. I was covered from head to toe in blood and gore, but none of it was mine.

"It's Calum." My stomach roiled and I choked back a gag. "I got Calum on me!"

I hunched over and spewed my meager breakfast. My ears were ringing ferociously, but my hearing was coming back. Shouts and cries of distress came from all around the camp.

Bent over, trying to collect myself, I noticed the debris around my feet—bones mixed with the remnants of Addie's witch bombs, sizzling with the acidic remnants of violet magic. I watched the skellie remains and magic dissolve, leaving an oozy black bog in their wake.

Straightening up, I met Duncan's concerned gaze. "The residue from the bomb is mixing with the skellies."

Pointing to the spot where the ooze had sprung from the magic, we watched as a small patch of black petunias sprouted in the aftermath. *Zombie fungus!*

"Duncan—"

"Aye. I see it." He did a quick scan of the surround area. "It's coming up all over."

"So I smell." I crinkled my nose as the smell of decay permeated the air.

"Incoming!" Analisa's shrill warning cut through what was left of the camp. I spun around to see her running from the field toward the camp. As she looked up at Addie's projectile, she stumbled and fell. Getting to her hands and knees, she started to scramble forward but it was too late. The explosion landed directly in her path, engulfing everything around it in purple fire.

The force of this explosion knocked me backward. Just as my feet came out from under me, Duncan grabbed me in a bear hug and we crashed into the ground.

"Are you okay?" I asked as I scrambled off of him and onto my stomach.

"Aye," he replied as he turned over. "But the others?"

We military-crawled toward the battlefield, avoiding the glowing bones and oozing flowers. Doing the same thing, Vee and Jamie made their way over to a log that provided cover as long as they remained flat. We scuttled up next to them just in time to witness the ensuing chaos.

Shouting Ana's name, Giani Rosetti ran toward the blast. He struggled forward until the heat singed his hair and his sleeve burst into flames. His father and second-oldest brother fought to pull him away—his brother beating at his smoking clothes as they forced him back. At a safe distance, Giani dropped to the ground. Mario and Matteo knelt beside him.

The other Rosettis—Sharron, Sofia, Gabby, and the other brothers—were crouched in a tightly knit group at the edge of the clearing to avoid the heat. Next to them, Lachlan crouched over Blaz, soothing the terrorized pup.

"They're too exposed," Jamie murmured, nodding in the direction of the Rosetti clan.

"Aye," Duncan confirmed. "An' the witch knows it."

Jamie turned his face toward Veronica. "Duncan and I will fetch them. You lasses stay here."

At the far end of the field, Addie, seated atop her decomposing steed and looking even more like something from *The Magical Walking Dead*, began to form another bomb between her hands. That's when an arrow lodged into her horse's eye socket.

Without warning the horse turned in an agitated arc causing Addie's magic to untether. The girl responsible for the shot, the Olympic archer from China, continued to sink one arrow after another into the unholy beast from a nearly impossible distance.

The witch's mount faltered beneath her, going down on its forelegs. Addie lurched forward and the magic ball flew out of her hands, detonating a few yards away. The blast threw her off her undead horse and the thing collapsed, convulsions racking its enormous body.

"The witch is down," Veronica hissed. "Go now!"

"And avoid the zombie fungus," I insisted.

"Zombie fungus?" Vee glanced over the log and for the first time noticed the little patch of black flowers popping up all around us. As we watched, the flowers expelled a puff of purple mist.

"Oh, snap," she moaned. Only she didn't say *snap*.

"We'll be fine. Stay put." Duncan shot me a pointed glance that meant *Listen for once in yer life, woman* and then scrambled away.

The MacCrae brothers crawled along the edge of the camp like G.I. Joes on fast forward. Avoiding the patches of black flowers, they got as close as they could to the Rosettis while still keeping cover.

Jamie whistled in a short series of bursts. Lachlan turned

toward the noise. Using gestures, the prince indicated that the group needed to get out of the open.

I watched the comprehension dawn on Lachlan's face. He whispered something to the youngest Rosetti boy, who in turn murmured something to his mom and siblings. In unison their heads swiveled toward Giani and the others.

Sharron Rosetti cupped her hands around her mouth and then whispered, "Andiamo!" Mario and Matteo hoisted Giani to his feet and ran just as the other group dashed for the cover of the camp rubble, scattering as they went.

Hunkered down behind the log we had no vantage point on the witch but her shriek of triumph reached us as clear as Lady Day. Unable to help myself, I peeked over the log toward the archer's last position. There was a minimart-sized crater where the Olympian had been.

When I looked back at the witch, I could see the grin stretching across her ravaged face with homicidal intent as she zeroed in on our not-so-secret hiding place. The violet energy gathering in her hands began to solidify, this time in a bomb intended for us. There was nowhere to go. We'd never make it out of the blast zone before impact. Duncan and Jamie were too far away—there was no time to say good-byes, except to my bestie.

Reaching for Vee's hands, I said, "I love you!"

"Wait." She shook her head, refusing to deny the inevitable. We were about to die. Tears coursed down my cheeks as I tried to get out all that I needed to say.

"I'm not sorry for any of it. Doon was the best thing to ever happen to me. I'm not afraid."

Please, I prayed, shutting my eyes. Peace washed over me as I clung to Vee. *Don't erase us from the narrative. Let Doon survive to tell our story . . .*

CHAPTER 45

Veronica

I love you too, but this isn't over. Look."

The moment our hands had joined, the black ooze of the zombie fungus rising around us had prompted our rings to form a bubble of protection.

Kenna blinked at the shimmering light surrounding the two of us like a cocoon. Just as her shoulders relaxed, we took a direct hit. The magic bomb Addie had cooked up especially for us hit with the force of a thousand sledge hammers. On impact, we fell into a heap of tangled limbs on the ground, just managing to keep our hands clasped.

A groan nearby drew my attention to Alasdair's prone figure. The old man struggled to sit up as fresh petunias sprouted all around him, their toxic mist permeating the air. He began to choke and gag.

"We have to save him! Crawl to the right." We hobbled to our knees and scooched toward Alasdair. He spotted us just as we reached for him with our free hands. The moment his fingers linked with ours, he became encased in safety.

Another bomb hit close by, knocking us into one another like bowling pins. After we'd regained our balance, I glanced around at the chaos of camp; people on fire running, crying, others tending to the wounded. Calum, Ana, Oliver . . . I'd seen all of them go down. My heart throbbed, pushing against my lungs until I couldn't breathe. Were they all gone? How many others? I hadn't seen Eòran or Fergus in ages.

I sucked hard to draw in air, my head like a balloon floating above my shoulders.

"Vee!" Kenna pushed her face into mine, so close our noses brushed. "Pull it together. I can't do this without you!"

I blinked. Once. Twice. Three times. My heart slammed into my throat as my vision started to dim and I wobbled on my knees.

"Come on, use your yoga breathing. Deep breath in." Kenna pulled air into her lungs, her spine straightening. I followed suit. "Slow breath out." We both exhaled, our shoulders slumping.

And I could think again. "I'm good. I'm good."

A bomb smashed into a nearby tree and it burst into violet flames. The same tree where . . . "Lachlan! The twins!"

"I saw the twins wi' their family," Alasdair reassured. "And the other boy was wi' yer dog, Blaz. They're safe—" His voice fell off and he didn't have to say the rest. *For now.*

I had to think of something. These people were my responsibility—and I knew there was no way we could win. *Unless . . .*

I gripped Alasdair's hand with all my strength, tugging him closer. "Back at the field where we first saw the skellies, you said there was a way to beat Addie. A last resort."

"Aye, but ye aren't goin' ta like it." His watery blue eyes met mine, their intensity making them as brilliant as the sky. "Ye have ta break the Covenant."

I raised my brows and waited for the punch line. No way was that the secret he'd been keeping. But instead of laughing it off and giving me the real, more plausible way to defeat the witch, he said, "Ye have ta breach the borders."

Something inside of me snapped. "Are you insane? There is no way we're giving up and committing mass suicide!"

Eyeing the old man, Kenna asked, "What are you saying exactly?"

"If ye break the Covenant, the witch becomes mortal. The fact tha' she canna restore her appearance while usin' her magic to attack tells me ye weakened her. I believe that Saint Sebastian's Elixir is continuing to weaken her and will strip Adelaide of any remaining magic as the Covenant breaks. Ye see, it's harder to hang on ta magic in the modern world than it is in Doon. Once she's mortal, ye will be able to kill her. It's the only way."

"If we do this"—I cringed as another magic bomb crashed into the camp—"can you guarantee it won't kill us all and end Doon forever?"

"Nay, but I have faith. I believe the Protector knows our intentions and would never abandon us."

Addie hurtled a seemingly endless supply of magic explosives at our camp and the zombie fungus grew larger by the second; soon it would begin to swallow our people and eat their flesh. When I looked at it from that perspective, we had little to lose from Alasdair's last resort. If we did nothing, we were dead anyway.

"Even if I believed you, and I'm not saying that I do, there's no possible way we'd make it to the border before Addie blew us all to kingdom come."

"Aye," Alasdair agreed. "It would take a miracle."

As the old man and I stared at each other, the air between

us began to stir. I watched in disbelief as a small funnel formed. It swirled away from us, devouring the zombie fungus and ripping the petunias from the ground. Three more funnels were sweeping through the paddock, sucking up skellie bones before they could create more fungus.

"Verranica!" Jamie's face appeared just outside our bubble. Relief smacked into me and my knees buckled.

He clasped my shoulder, keeping me on my feet. "Ye're no' going to believe this!"

Duncan ran up beside him and we joined hands with them, looping them into our shielded circle. "A cyclone just smacked the witch back into the treeline! She's too busy fightin' it to throw any bombs."

"Miracle enough for ye, Yer Highness?" Alasdair asked with a chuckle. "I'd say tha's a sign."

Nodding in agreement, Duncan said, "The weather has always played a role in Doon's protection."

Jamie squeezed my hand. "We need ta get the people to shelter while she's occupied."

"Alasdair has given us another option." Quickly, I explained his theory about breaking the Covenant. It didn't sound any more plausible coming from my mouth.

"I'm willin' to try it." Duncan's gaze locked on Kenna. "What do ye say?"

My best friend nodded, but I could read her like a book and she was two seconds away from changing her mind.

I turned questioning eyes to Jamie. "I believe it's our best option. But it's your choice. We await your instruction, my queen." He raised our joined hands and kissed my knuckles.

Alasdair was right. When stepping out in faith, there could be no guarantee. But faith had brought me to Doon in the first place; had made me its queen when I would have gladly given my life. If we were to do this, we needed to act as one—step out in faith as a kingdom united.

Withdrawing my hands from the group, the bubble disappeared and wind tore at my hair and clothes as the mini tornados spun around the camp, ridding it of all traces of zombie fungus. Jumping up on a stump, I put two fingers in my mouth and whistled as I'd seen Jamie do.

Everyone within hearing distance gathered around. I couldn't allow myself to search their weary faces for those who could be missing. They were too many to name, and if I had any hope of saving the rest of us, I had to stay focused on rallying the Doonians to our next impossible mission.

Raising my voice over the wind, I spoke the words I knew would plant further fear in their hearts. "Spread the word for every able-bodied Doonian and Destined to rally at the Brig o' Doon. And for those too weak or injured to make the journey to gather at the auld Kirk and join us in spirit and in prayer."

I took a deep breath and made sure my next words were sure and confident. "Tell the people we are going to break the Covenant and unite our kingdom with the modern world in order to make the witch mortal. We need to believe that breaching the borders will not kill us, but save us. For Doon!"

CHAPTER 46

Mackenna

Rally at the Brig o' Doon!"

The cyclones had cleared away the majority of the fungus, making a path for us. Jamie and Duncan raced among the people shouting orders and lending a hand while those able began to make their way toward the bridge.

I dashed across the field alongside my best friend, doing my best not to have a clumsy moment on account of the uneven terrain. As we neared the tree line, someone shouted, "Incoming!"

Acting on impulse, I stopped to look at the magic bomb hurtling through the sky. *Duck and cover!* my addled brain shouted at me. And I did. I dropped to the ground and wrapped my arms over my head.

What are you doing? Vee demanded. *Get up!*

She hoisted me up from the ground, but it was too late. The bomb was headed right for us. Quite suddenly, a bolt of lightning cut through the heavens like a missile and intercepted the bomb. The sky exploded in a shower of purple and white fireworks.

"Holy Hammerstein!"

"You can say that again," Vee murmured.

A second witch bomb flew toward us, only to be stopped by another lightning bolt. As sparks fizzled around us, a blood-curdling screech rose from the opposite end of the clearing. Although the hair on my arms stood on end, I couldn't help reveling in the moment. "Guess Addie wasn't expecting that freak storm."

Vee grinned back at me. "Guess not. To the bridge!"

Doonians took the lead, escorting Destined through the tree line toward the bridge.

Jamie and Duncan waited for us within the cover of the forest. As Vee and I approached, Duncan said, "The people are spent."

"An' many are injured," Jamie added.

Ignoring the sinking feeling in my chest, I pasted a cheerful expression on my face. "Fiona told me that the journey wouldn't be easy."

"That I did," Fiona called as she and Fergus came up from behind. Next to them were Sofia and Gabby Rosetti, each with an arm around Oliver.

When Vee saw Oliver, she frowned. "You're injured. You should be back at the church."

"And miss all the fun, Your Highness?" He grinned, and for the first time I saw the Aussie's resemblance to Iron Man. Other Rosettis guided a group of Destined, including Cheska, who grinned like Ralphie in *A Christmas Story* despite the fact that her head had been wrapped in an improvised plaid bandage.

Vee searched the crowds, standing on her toes to see through the people. "I don't see Ewan."

Taking her hand, I tugged her forward, giving her a reassurance I didn't feel. "I'm sure he's around, but right now we have a bigger problem to solve."

"You're right. We'll find him later."

As exhausted and wounded people rallied around their queen, Vee turned to Jamie, Duncan, and me. "How should we do this? Should we split up or go together?"

As I contemplated the distance we still had to travel to reach the bridge, an involuntary groan slipped from my mouth. "I don't suppose we could ask for another miracle? Like the ability to wiggle our noses and automatically appear at the bridge."

Vee took my hand. "I don't see why not."

I glared at her, wondering just how many skellie hits to the head she's sustained during the battle, but she laughed. "Just hear me out."

Then she clapped her hands, gathering the people to her in a tight cluster. "We're tired, and even as we stand here the witch is rallying. As you've heard, we're going to break the Covenant that keeps Doon protected. We believe it's the best chance to make Adelaide mortal."

"Won't that kill us all?" someone shouted as heads nodded all around us.

Vee shook her head. "We don't believe so. The Protector knows our intent. We must have faith."

I looked about at the dirty, bloodied faces regarding their queen with subdued hope. In addition to being frightened, they were exhausted. "I think we should try to use the Rings of Aontacht to transport us to the bridge."

Vee slipped back into full ruler mode. "Everyone close your eyes," she instructed. I slipped my hand into hers and clamped my eyes shut, focusing on my bestie's voice. "Picture all your family and friends, all the new Destined, the children and older people in the caves—everyone you can think of. Now picture us all standing on the riverbank at the Brig o' Doon."

Eyes closed, I felt our rings heat up. Then I could hear the

River Doon rushing by. Duncan gasped and I blinked into his astonished face. We were standing at the mouth of the Brig o' Doon, not just those of us that moments ago had been gathered in the forest, but also the Doonians from the cave.

Next to him, Jamie scooped Vee into his arms and spun her in a circle. "You did it, love!"

"We did it." She pressed her lips to Jamie's in a brief kiss before turning to me. "Ready to bring Doon into a new age?"

Even as I nodded my agreement, confusion puckered my brows. "But, what if we don't—"

"Ken." Vee placed her hand on my shoulder. "Don't even say it. The Protector's brought us this far. We have to trust, even when we can't see the outcome."

I nodded, pushing away the suspicion that breeching Doon's borders would kill us all in order to focus on a more positive outcome. "How will this work exactly? What are we going say to explain Doon appearing in the middle of modern Scotland? What if Castle MacCrae gets turned into a theme park like Harry Potter World?"

"I have no idea. But if this is what it takes to defeat Addie once and for all, Doon becoming the next Disney World is a price I'm willing to pay." She dropped her hand from my shoulder and slipped Aunt Gracie's ring off her finger. "Now, take off your uncle Cameron's ring and slip it into your pocket."

Hoping she knew what she was talking about, I did as she instructed.

"Everyone, join hands." With me on one side and Jamie on the other, she intertwined our fingers. I, in turn, grasped Duncan's. As he fit his hand into mine, he reached over and captured my face. Time stopped as his lips pressed against mine in a kiss that was at the same time savage and heartbreakingly sweet.

When the kiss came to an end, he whispered, "Forever."

"And ever," I agreed. I gave him a final, quick peck and then as he reached for Alasdair, I turned to my best friend. "I love you, Vee."

She squeezed the heck out of my hand and smirked. "I know."

Vee looked left and then right at the united line of Destined and Doonians stretching along the riverbank as far as the eye could see in both directions. "On the count of three," she announced, patiently waiting as the word spread down the line.

"Ready? One . . . Two . . . Three . . . FOR DOON!"

We stepped forward. Duncan, Jamie, Vee, Alasdair, and I walked onto the Brig o' Doon, which, from the kingdom side, ended mid-arch in ruins. The others stopped at the very edge of the river. Mist began to form on the surface of the water, becoming as thick as a winter whiteout in seconds. With a rumble, it devoured everything around us. It swirled around our legs, blocking out the ground and swallowing the sounds of the river.

On the far side of Duncan, Alasdair groaned. Searching his face in the fog, I wondered at how much older he looked. Seeming to be in intense pain, Alasdair's clear, blue eyes shone with joy. "Thank ye, lad," he said to Duncan. "For bringing me home one last time."

The old man's voice bore the evidence of strain as he turned to Vee. "Yer Highness, it's been a pleasure to fight alongside o' you. Yer a credit to our kingdom."

With those words, the suspended man disintegrated into the mist, trapped between worlds no longer. Had Alasdair known that this would happen when he suggested that we breach the borders? Was this the sacrifice he'd been prepared to pay? I clung tightly to Duncan and Vee, praying that this was not the end, but a new beginning.

Chapter 47

Veronica

The mist churned in opaque swirls, a sudden wind sweeping Alasdair MacCrae's remains away as if he'd never existed. I squeezed Jamie's hand, and then Mackenna's, as Duncan looped an arm around her shoulders. I didn't need to hear their voices in my head to know we were all thinking the same thing: *Are we next?*

Kenna's gaze met mine as her lips tilted in a tremulous smile. "See you on the other side, bestie."

I didn't know if she meant in the modern world or somewhere beyond. My experiences in Doon had proved to me the undeniable existence of a greater being who loved and cared for us. Therefore, I didn't fear death. But I wasn't ready. I had so much more living to do—a kingdom to rebuild with the boy I loved, with our family and friends around us. I'd pictured our future children more times than I cared to admit. We'd have twins; a little girl with my coloring and a little boy with soulful brown eyes, dimples, and golden hair. Our daughter would boss him around, but the little prince would take it in stride. My throat constricted at the thought of the life we could've had.

But even if this was the end, I took comfort in the hope that since Alasdair was gone, that meant Adelaide Blackmore Cadell had most likely disintegrated into the earth along with the bones of her skellies.

The fog shifted, the breeze stinging my tear-filled eyes. Jamie squeezed my hand as a gust of cool, sweet-smelling wind pushed down on our heads and the mist parted to reveal a wide expanse of blue sky. Releasing my friends, I spun around, staring up at the soft orange glow of the sun's fiery rays peeking through the clouds. My ears began to buzz, accompanied by a low rumble vibrating in my chest. "Do you hear that?"

Without waiting for the others to reply, I backtracked across the stones, onto the spongy earth of Doon, and whirled around. A cylindrical shadow moved across the ground, then tilted, revealing its wings. I threw my head back, just as the plane flew over and I stumbled forward. In the distance, gleaming white turrets rose into the sky, framed by gray, snow-capped mountains. Just visible on the far side of the bridge a lamppost glowed with electricity. Doon on one side and the modern world on the other—we'd done it!

I turned around to run back to the riverbank and congratulate the others, but froze mid-step. The Witch of Doon stood before me, alive in all her terrifying glory.

A wall of solid indigo vapor fell like a curtain behind her, blocking me from my friends on the bridge and the others on the riverbank. Immediately, I sent out a frantic call to Kenna and Jamie, but received no response. Another unexpected sacrifice of breaking the Covenant; our Calling connection had been severed.

Addie's face had further disintegrated, the flesh appearing

to melt off her bones. She raised her hands and magic swirled in her palms. "Well, well, little queen, we meet one last time."

"Why are you still here?" I marched toward her, fuming that we'd merged Doon with the modern world and yet she still lived. "You should be dust!"

She sauntered forward, the violet sparks growing into orbs. "My magic has sustained me for a millennia. Do ye really think yer little trick could finish me off?" She threw her head back and let out a cackle like icicles shattering on concrete.

Shoving my hand into my pocket, I slipped on the ring and whispered a quick prayer of protection. But when I raised my hand, nothing happened. The ruby remained as lifeless as an ordinary stone.

"That willna work, Queenie," Addie goaded as she moved closer. "Ye've broken the Covenant, ye see. You're just a weak little human."

The ring would be of no use to me now. But if its power was no longer viable, Alasdair had been right. I squared my shoulders and stared into the face of evil personified. "Then magic will leave you too. You're dying, Addie."

The spell in her palms pulsed, and then faded. She grimaced and pushed her hands against the air, the violet sputtering before it blazed again. "Just a temporary setback."

Her lidless eyeballs glowed purple, giving me the warning I needed before she hurtled a globe of fire. I threw myself to the ground, tucked, and rolled. As I peeked up, something moved out of the corner of my eye, but before I could get a good look she threw the second orb. I scrambled to the right, the magic catching the hem of my cloak and sizzling up the fabric. I unhooked the fastening and stood, dropping it to the ground.

I frantically searched the curtain for help, but it was as if every last Doonian had disappeared. So it would be a showdown to see if I could outwit her long enough for her magic to fade for good.

Addie's whole body trembled and she chanted into her hands, the bones of her fingers poked through the end of her flesh as she worked to summon another blast of magic.

Emboldened by her growing weakness, I circled, staying on my toes, ready to dodge her next attack. "It's over, Addie. But it's not too late to turn from evil. Make the right choice before it's too late."

With an unearthly wail, she leveled her hand at my chest. Suddenly, I couldn't move, only watch in horror as she lifted her other hand to the sky. Purple-black lightning flashed into her palm and her mouth twisted into a lipless gargoyle smile. "I suppose I should thank you for breakin' the Covenant. Ye see, while it protected Doon, I couldna touch you—well, not the way I wanted to. But now, let's jus' say it's a dream o' mine about ta come true.

"Ye've been a worthy adversary, Veronica Welling. In fact, yer soul is so strong and pure that once I drink it and take over yer body, not even your delicious prince's kiss will be able to tell the difference."

I strained against her hold with every ounce of will I possessed. No way would I let her take my soul and steal my identity! But I couldn't even move a finger. My chest tightened as cold sweat dripped down my back.

Addie stepped closer, her voice a gravely hiss. "And when an infant mysteriously dies every six months, we'll chalk it up to natural causes. No one needs to know their sweet little souls will sustain me and fuel my magic until I'm restored to my former power . . . It's worked verra well for me the last millennia." She lowered her voice to a whisper. "The beauty of it all is that I won't even need to take Doon. When I'm you, those simpletons will just hand it over to me."

Even as she boasted, her arm shook, the purple lightning she held in her hand flickering. While her power faltered, strength surged back into my muscles. I lunged, scrambling to the right and heading for the cover of the nearby trees. But she froze me again mid-leap.

"Appears my fun is endin'. Or should I say yours!" she crowed in triumph. "Adieu, Queenie. I'll enjoy livin' yer life, wi' relish!"

She lowered her arm and electricity shot from her hand. I braced myself for death as a body flew in front of me, the bolt slamming into him as he fell.

Addie shrieked.

In that instant, my movement returned, and I flung myself to the ground beside the boy who'd sacrificed himself for me. Ewan Murray's summer-green eyes stared lifelessly at the clear sky. *No. No, no . . . Not Ewan!* Not the passionate, energetic boy with the mischievous smile and enormous heart. Not my friend.

My eyes traced his body for any signs of life and I noticed a huge gash in his right side—not from magic, but a blade. The injury must have put him a few minutes behind the rest of us. Now he was dead.

Because of me.

Tears flooded my eyes as a scream built in my chest like thunder. Grabbing the dagger from Ewan's belt, I sprang forward and flung the blade. In slow motion, it flew end over end toward the witch. Addie's lipless mouth widened in a scream. Her hands moved frantically as she tried to summon magic that she no longer possessed.

The blade hit her square in the chest, knocking her back on her feet. Impossibly, she stayed upright and stumbled forward, arms out, eyes wide. "Ye think . . . a blade can . . . stop me . . . how quaint."

I tripped backward, unable to look away from the black sludge bubbling out of her chest. With effort, she brought her hands together to form a ball of magic. Terrified that she'd already drained Ewan's soul and regenerated her power, I turned to run just as she toppled back.

Stunned, I stared for long minutes. Waiting. When she didn't move, I crept over to her body on wobbly legs. I reached her just as the last breath shuddered from her chest and her head lolled to the side, my gold filigree and ruby crown falling into the grass. I reached for it and then drew back. Addie had commissioned that crown for herself—it had never been mine.

I took a step back and waited for her to disintegrate or melt, or whatever wicked witches in Doon did after they were dead. I had to see it. Had to be sure she was gone for good. And I wasn't disappointed.

A sharp sound rent the air, like a pickax cutting rock, and the ground began to tremble. I stumbled back as dark forms, blacker than a starless night, emerged from the ground. Their shapes continually changed in a morphing impression of horns, gnashing teeth, and vicious claws, so that I couldn't focus on them individually. They howled and it was as if all sound left the earth.

Before the scream of terror could escape my throat, the indigo curtain collapsed and my friends rushed into Doon calling my name.

I turned back as the demons sunk their fangs into the witch's arms and legs, lifting her into the air. Unlike Alasdair's majestic end, they forced her body into the ground with an earth-shattering boom that I felt in my soul.

And just like that, the Witch of Doon was gone. Forever.

I raced to meet my loved ones and threw myself into Jamie's arms, wrapping my legs around his waist. Over his shoulder, I saw the beautiful face of my best friend. We reached out and linked our fingers. "I killed the witch, Ken."

"I saw those demon-things take her down," she replied with a shudder. "How did you do it?"

"She ran out of magic and I threw a knife into her chest. But . . . but Ewan . . . he died saving me." Tears burned my throat as I said, "We need to take him back to the castle. Give him a proper hero's send-off."

"Of course, love." Jamie's arms tightened around me as I watched Doonians and the Destined flood off the Brig o' Doon. Around them, people still on the bridge snapped pictures and held up their phones—likely taking video. "The modern world can see us?"

Jamie set me on my feet and I met his penetrating gaze. "Aye. 'Tis the price we must pay. But watchin' those devils drag the witch to the underworld will make the sacrifice worthwhile."

He was right, of course, but that didn't stop the deep sadness filling my chest. It was over. Our fairy-tale kingdom would become nothing more than a tourist destination. I could almost see the advertisements replete with dancing highlanders in plaid pants and tams. *Come see the mythical Brigadoon come to life!*

Proving that we still shared a brain, if not a Calling, Kenna commented, "I was right, wasn't I? Doon's going to become the next Harry Potter World."

Duncan placed a hand on her shoulder, his mouth dropping open as his eyes flared. "I wouldna be so sure." As I turned to follow his gaze, the blast of trumpets filled the air, their sound so mighty and unexpected that my knees buckled beneath me.

CHAPTER 48

Mackenna

Catching Vee mid-swoon, I tried to take it all in: the trumpets, the blinding gold light, and the awe-inspiring creatures heralding from the Brig o' Doon. Angels, just like the ones so many of the Destined had described seeing, lined both sides of the bridge like a celestial chorus line.

Along with the sound of trumpets, their terrible voices were lifted in song. Feeling like Dorothy and her companions about to meet the wizard, Jamie, Duncan, Vee, and I stepped onto the bridge and slowly walked to the center. Doonians and Destined, filling both sides of the riverbank, watched in breathless reverence.

Suddenly, the modern world—the tourists and the streetlamps—faded away as a voice as quiet as a blade of grass in the wind and more booming than a thousand giants pronounced, "Choose."

My friends and I looked at each other uncertainly. "Choose what?" I asked.

"The modern world," the voice replied. "Or a new covenant."

As much as I vowed to accept the cost of breaching the borders, my heart leapt with this new proposition. After everything, would the Protector offer a new covenant that would safeguard the kingdom of Doon and its inhabitants from becoming the eighth wonder of the world?

Beside me, Duncan murmured, "The choice of the suspended man."

I squeezed his hand and sought Vee's gaze. "Doon," she said in a clear, musical voice. "I choose Doon."

"Me too!" I added.

Jamie and Duncan spoke over one another, choosing Doon, followed by Fiona and Fergus. One after the other, both Destined and Doonian made their choice—all of them chose the new Covenant—until a last person, a boy with blue-and-green streaks in his hair, stepped forward.

"That's the magician dude," I whispered to Vee. "The one with his own YouTube channel."

Eyes shimmering with the force of his conviction, he addressed the queen. "Your Majesty, have you thought about how we're going to explain what happened here today? The modern world will be looking for a plausible explanation. And I think I have one to offer."

Vee nodded. "Go on."

"You see, Majesty, I'm an illusionist. Although I'm only eighteen, I'm fairly well known. And if you'll allow it, I'll take credit for this. I will make Doon my greatest illusion. If people think it was a magic stunt, they'll be more likely to let it go. News will eventually fade away, and this will become part of urban legend, just like the story of the bridge before."

Vee gawked at him. "You'd sacrifice your Calling to protect Doon."

The boy tucked a wayward strand of colorful hair behind

his ear with a shrug. "I think this is what I've been Called to do. I'm supposed to protect Doon from the outside. Is that okay?"

"Yes." She hugged the boy. "And thank you!"

We watched Jeremy walk resolutely into the mists toward Alloway. Once he had disappeared, my friends and I joined hands and set off in the opposite direction with assurance of a new Covenant and the promise of a bright future.

chapter 49

Veronica

Sunlight tumbled through the leaves, creating muted patterns on the carpet of moss under my feet as I trudged up the steep trail. A sweet, verdant breeze pushed the hair off my face, causing me to pull the shawl tighter around my shoulders. Morning in Doon was my favorite time for a leisurely stroll, but this day I was headed toward the hunting lodge on a mission. Jamie had been conspicuously absent the last two weeks, showing up for the occasional dinner peckish and exhausted. Whenever I'd question him about his day, his answers were evasive at best, and the night before, he'd fallen asleep at the table with his head propped in his hand.

The business of rebuilding the kingdom kept us both busy, and Jamie had taken a special interest in getting our latest Destined settled into their new lives; not to mention the fresh crop of kids he'd recruited for the Crew.

However, his recent preoccupation and secretive smiles told me he was up to something unrelated to restoring order to his land. As I still viewed any surprise as a bad thing, a few days ago I'd begun systematically searching the kingdom. The exercise and the alone time gave me an opportunity to reflect on what we'd been able to do and where we were going next.

It was amazing what we'd been able to accomplish in the six months since we'd defeated the witch. The Protector, in his infinite mercy, had reestablished Doon's separation from the modern world. The first covenant had been formed against an immediate threat—an evil witch. This time we'd been shielded from a much subtler, but no less sinister fate: the corrupting influence of modern civilization on the kingdom and its people. Or as Kenna put it, becoming *Brig o' Doon World* . . . or worse.

There were still so many things we didn't know about the new covenant—would Doonians still experience Callings? Would there still be a Centennial? Would the portal ever open again? Since the battle, the Rings of Aontacht had remained silent—not even giving off so much as a spark—and I wondered if they'd served their ultimate purpose.

All the damage from Addie's black magic had been restored, all traces of her spells erased—except for the numerous friends we'd lost in the battle. Their loss had left a permanent hole in all our lives.

Gideon and his staunch determination to protect Doon at any cost. Calum, whose animated narrative was lost to us forever. Analisa, who had challenged and supported me in perfect measure. And of course, Ewan. I'd known him the least amount of time, and yet missed him most of all.

I kicked a pinecone with the toe of my boot and braced for the blinding pain to close my throat, but it never came. Time had begun to heal the open wounds of grief. Day by day, I was learning to live with gratitude that we'd been given the chance to build a new world.

My only lingering regret was that with the portal closed, I no longer had a way to bring Sofia's Called mate across the bridge. Kenna, refusing to believe that not everyone has a happy ending with a bow around it, flung her in the path of every eligible Destined boy in the futile hope that she'd find "the one."

When she wasn't busy dodging Ken's setups, Sofia threw her energy into restoring the kingdom with a clarity of purpose that bordered on frightening. Every time I turned around she was there working to help someone else get their life back. When I pulled her aside to discuss it, all she would say was that she trusted the Protector had a plan.

A tiny fur-covered animal squeaked across my path and I paused, took out my flask of water, and turned to look back at how far I'd come. Raising a hand to shield my eyes, my breath caught at the sight. The bucolic scene was a far cry from the cracked, concrete landscape of my childhood. Hills rolled out below me covered in waves of golden gorse and wild heather, giving way to a patchwork of flatter geometric fields. A surge of puffy, white sheep returned from the high pasture, and just beyond, the spire of the Ault Kirk rose above the colorful buildings of the village.

Doonians, like tiny dolls, moved around the marketplace. But they were not faceless figures to me, as I knew every one of them by name; had fought beside them, cried beside them, and worked beside them. No longer their American queen, I was one of them. The fragile girl who'd crossed the bridge searching for her prince had found more than romance—of course, Jamie was the love of my life, but I'd also found a family, faith, and purpose.

From far below, a strain of fiddle and pipe caught the wind and wove through the trees. Joining my people in spirit, I picked up my skirt and danced a quick jig, swishing the fabric around my calves. A giggle bubbled out of my throat as I twirled in a quick circle.

"Tha' be the most bonny sight I've seen in days."

Choking on a laugh, I spun to face my prince leaning against a shade tree, arms crossed over his chest. Broad and strong, disheveled gold hair sticking out at odd angles, his tan cheeks streaked with dirt, he still managed to look magnificent. With determined strides, I climbed the path toward him. His dark eyes glinted, before a wide smile spread across his face, pulling out the dimple in his right cheek.

Ignoring the funny things the sight of him was doing to my heart, I poked a finger into his chest. "What are you up to, Laird MacCrae?"

He raised a brow. "*Up to?*"

"Don't play dumb! You know what I mean. What have you been doing every day?"

Jamie raked a hand through his hair, taming one side. "I dinna know what ye're referrin' to."

"You know I hate surprises." With a frustrated growl, I balled my fist and hit his arm as hard as I could. It was like punching rock.

He rubbed his bicep. "Och, lass, ye pack a wallop for such a tiny thing."

Covertly rubbing my stinging knuckles on the inside of my elbow, I crossed my arms again, and tapped my foot in impatience. "I order you to show me what you've been doing . . . as your queen." I lifted my chin and arched a brow, unleashing the Evil Highney.

"Oh do ye, now?" His gaze intent, Jamie pushed off the tree and took three long strides toward me.

With a half laugh, half squeal, I backpedaled fast, but he

reached out and clasped my arms, stopping my retreat. He tugged me against his chest and then lowered his mouth to mine. I raised my arms and threaded my fingers in his hair, the world spinning around me as his lips ignited sparks all over my body. It took every ounce of my willpower to end the kiss and push out of his arms. "Your distractions won't work this time!"

"Then let me try again." He quirked a wicked grin and reached for me. "I know I can do better, Yer Highness."

As tempting as that was, I shook my head. "No. Show me now."

Our eyes clashed as we stared each other down. Birds tweeted, crickets chirped, wind rattled the leaves, and finally he huffed out a sigh. "Fine. If you really must know . . ." He pulled a clean handkerchief from his pocket. "And knowin' you, I'll get little peace until ye do." He spun me around and wrapped the cloth around my eyes. "Ye'll need ta let me blindfold ye."

As he tightened the knot at the back of my head, I blinked and strained my eyes, but couldn't see a thing. "Wait! I didn't agree—"

"Hush! If ye insist on ruining the surprise, ye'll let me have my way on this." He looped his arm around my waist and guided me up the trail.

"Do ye remember the mornin' after our night in the huntin' lodge?"

That twenty-four hours—our first kiss, the revelation that I loved him enough to let him go, and watching him be crowned king while believing the title would separate us forever—was burned into my brain. "Yes."

Jamie's grip tightened on my waist. "Step up over this log."

Blindly, I lifted my foot, probing the air with my toes until I felt something solid. I tapped my foot against the log, measuring its height. Impatient, Jamie scooped me into his arms and continued on. "What about on our way down the mountain, when I guided you off the path?"

The sound of voices and banging filled the air, followed by a grating noise like someone cutting wood. I searched my memory of that long-ago day, but my overwhelming heartache that those would be our last moments together clouded everything. "Um . . ."

As we walked, the construction sounds grew louder, punctuated by occasional laughter.

"I teased you about needin' a wee bit o' privacy if I should take a queen . . ."

Then it hit me. The spot with the spectacular view where I'd suggested someone should build a house. "Jamie . . . you didn't!" Realizing we'd stopped moving and the noise had quieted, I reached up and tugged the blindfold off my head.

Blinking the sun from my eyes, it took me a moment to see the cabin made of wood and stone, perched on the edge of the mountain. My friends and half the Crew stood outside of the cottage holding tools and grinning from ear to ear—Gabby, Sofia, Duncan, Eòran, Cheska, Fergus, and even Fiona with her "wee" baby bump ballooning out her skirt. Blaz sat beside my pregnant friend, his tongue lolling out of his enormous head. My dog had taken to following Fiona around, as if he sensed the tiny life within her needed his protection.

Jamie set me on my feet and then leaned close to my ear. "The house is yer wedding gift, love. A place of our own."

"No' until after the wedding, mind," Eòran admonished with a chuckle. Since my guard had regained his power of speech, he rarely shut up—especially where my virtue was concerned.

Lachlan and the Rosetti twins waved, drawing my attention to where they perched on the roof.

"How did you . . . I . . . a place of our own?" Words tumbled out of my mouth as I wiped my wet cheeks.

"Aye, for when ye need some peace and quiet ta read, or just be." My prince, who was soon to become my co-ruler and king officially, tucked me against his side and pressed a kiss on the top of my head. "This is a place where ye dinna need to be a queen."

Kenna poked her head out of a side window and waved a paintbrush dripping dark stain onto the grass.

"You knew about this?" I accused with a laugh.

"Of course I did! You helped build my theater, I couldn't miss out on bringing your dream to life."

My vision swam as I rushed forward and embraced my best friend. Only she knew how much my chaotic childhood had made me long for a safe haven, a home where I could cross the threshold and put distance between myself and the world; a place of comfort and security.

"Ekk . . . Ninja girl, you're about to cut me in half."

I let her go as Jamie chastised his construction crew. "What are ye all starin' at? Back ta work!"

"Aye, aye, Captain," Duncan quipped as he snapped his brother a salute and then turned to me with a teasing grin. "He's only buildin' ye a house to keep up wi' me."

"I'm no' so ostentatious." Jamie rammed his fist into Duncan's shoulder. "If I'd wanted to outdo ye, *bráthair*, I would've had to build her a cathedral."

Duncan returned his brother's punch with a shove then rubbed his arm and gave Jamie a nod, accepting the compliment.

Jamie was right. Kenna's Broadway Theater had been an effort of love by the entire kingdom; a project to bring us together after our losses. Everyone had a job, from sewing the massive curtains to constructing the elaborate pulley system, or staining the scrollwork that surrounded the stage like an enormous frame—the names of those we'd lost in battle carved into the curves and eddies of the design. The resulting structure was nothing short of spectacular.

And there hadn't been a dry eye in the house during Kenna's inaugural one-woman show. I'd seen her perform many times, but the naked adoration on Duncan's face as he'd watched her had tugged at my heart. Perhaps he shared my memories because he leaned down, cradled the back of my best friend's head, and kissed her thoroughly.

"I need ta get back to work, love. An' so does my besotted brother, if he knows what's good for him," Jamie threatened as I turned to face him. "It's no' finished, but go inside and let Mackenna show ye around."

Not ready to let him go, I grabbed his hand, emotion thickening my voice. "What would I be without you?"

He lowered his eyes to the ground, a lock of hair falling over his forehead as color stained the slopes of his cheekbones. When he looked up, his gaze drilled into mine and a muscle rippled in his cheek. "Lost. Just as I would be."

"Well, I'm glad we never have to find out." I rose on my toes and planted a quick kiss on his mouth, before turning to go into the cottage.

The door stood open as I stepped onto the small covered porch where Fiona sat on a bench planting bluebells and yellow primrose in a flowerbox. "Any names yet, Fiona?"

She closed her eyes and shook her head. "If tha' dunderheaded husband o' mine suggests *Eunice* one more time . . ."

"Do you think it's a girl, then?" I could already picture the baby with wisps of strawberry blonde hair, pink cheeks, and Fergus' clear-blue eyes.

"I couldna say, but—" Her entire face appeared to glow from within as she placed a hand on the rounded curve of her belly. "Either way, this baby is perfect."

"Vee!" Kenna called from inside. "Come here, you've got to see this!"

Giving Fiona's shoulder a squeeze, I said, "Don't work too hard, that baby needs all of your strength."

"No worries. It's nap time for me soon."

Following Kenna's voice, I stepped through the doorway and my breath caught in my chest. A wall of windows at the back of the cabin made it feel as if it were suspended in the sky. I turned a slow circle to see the room; a small kitchen, a wood-burning fireplace made of stone, and a set of narrow steps leading to a loft that I assumed would contain the bedroom.

"Jamie wanted to have it all finished and decorated before you saw it, but I knew he couldn't keep it a secret until the wedding. Not from Queen Nancy Drew." Kenna grabbed my hand and led me through a narrow door leading to a deck that stretched the length of the cabin.

"Oh my—" Doon spread out below us. Slate blue and white castle turrets soared into the clouds, their splendor reflected in the crystal blue water of the loch. I could just make out the winding cobblestone streets of the village, and beyond, the gentle curve of the Brig o' Doon.

I'd once thought of Doon as my Christmas village, a place I wished to stay in forever. Now I would get my wish to see it during the holidays. In fact, Jamie and I would be married on Christmas Eve.

I threaded my fingers through my best friend's and pointed west to the tournament stadium. "Remember sneaking up that hill . . ."

"And you stood on my shoulders to see into the arena! Oh my gosh, how stupid were we?"

We both laughed and then grew quiet as we watched the breeze pull whitecaps through the water, waving the reflection of the castle.

"Our adventures have been better than anything we ever dreamed up for the Reid-Welling production company," Kenna mused.

"Yeah, we do drama pretty well."

She leaned over and we tilted our heads together. "We made it, Vee. We got our happily ever after."

"We did." I melted against her just like when we were kids. "I have a feeling that with the two of us together, this is just the beginning of our *once upon a time . . .*"

EPILOGUE

Mackenna

[NARRATOR]

Once upon a time . . . there were two best friends

[VEE]

A dreamer from Indiana

[KENNA]

And a diva from Chicago, by way of Arkansas.

[NARRATOR]

Together, they discovered a secret kingdom outside of time and place.

[VEE]

The dreamer met a young prince with a Jedi complex and became a queen.

[KENNA]

And the diva was enchanted by an ogre who built her a theater.

[NARRATOR]

Using the strength of their epic friendship and a pair of special rings, they saved the kingdom from an evil witch who plagued the land with zombie fungus and an army of undead skellies.

"Kenna—you know I love you, but your chronic narration is driving me crazy—especially when you play all the parts."

"Hold your war horses, Your Highney. This is important."

"Fine. Finish telling our story."

[NARRATOR]

And while their lives were never perfect or even necessarily easy, they lived happily ever after. And it was enough.

ACKNOWLEDGMENTS

Much like Vee and Kenna, Carey and I are two very different, and strong-willed, individuals, which can make for an interesting partnership. We've laughed and fought and sometimes clawed our way through, but we never gave up on DOON. This series is born of our shared passion, sometimes competing visions, and our unshakable faith in The Protector. Doon exists because we never held anything back. Our hearts and souls were poured ferociously into every line. In short, Doon is magical because we wrote it together.—Lorie Langdon

---

The magic of a story grows exponentially through its readership. That our words can enable someone to be braver or kinder, inspire them to create instead of tear down, or persuade them to love when others would hate is humbling. If even one person is challenged to make the world a little bit better because of something they read, that is magic, indeed. Thank you for giving Doon life and for encouraging Lorie and me to be our best-selves as authors and as human beings. As proud as we are of the Doon series, we are even prouder of our Doonians!—Carey Corp

Check out this excerpt from *Gilt Hollow*,
the new novel from Lorie Langdon.

CHAPTER TWO

The familiar squeeze enveloped Willow's chest as she ducked behind the cappuccino machine. Sweat coated the back of her neck and a chill raced across her shoulders. She peeked out, searching the faces in the one-room café until she found the petite blonde perusing the shelf of organic pastas and sauces. Why did she have to come in *here*?

Mrs. Turano hated Willow with a passion that bordered on psychotic. Avoiding the woman did Willow little good. In such a small town, their paths continued to cross.

The room began to shrink.

No, no, no! Not now! She lifted her eyes to the paneled ceiling as she attempted to shake the tingling from her fingers. Her second day on the job; she *so* did not need this right now.

"Willow!" her manager barked. "I asked for a slice of carrot cake to go."

Wishing she could disappear, Willow ruffled her bangs so they fell over her eyes, rushed to the display case, and squatted behind it. Her arm shook as she slid the spatula under an icing-coated wedge, and she barely managed to wrangle the cake into a plastic container before she heard the voice like nails on a chalkboard.

"Margaret," Mrs. Turano snapped. "I thought you had better judgment."

Reluctantly, Willow stood and met pale blue eyes—the same shade as the woman's late son Daniel's—lined with a road map of red. Mrs. Turano had been drinking again.

"I refuse to be served by the girlfriend of a murderer!"

A hard silence descended on the room, every set of eyes darting between Willow and the poor woman who'd lost her son. Which, by default, made Willow the villain.

She longed to defend herself, to yell that she'd had nothing to do with Daniel's death. That she'd never been Ashton's girlfriend. But she knew from experience that denial wouldn't help. The woman would only insist that Willow admit Ashton's guilt. Demand that Willow denounce the only true friend she'd ever had. And Willow would walk away without saying a word. As always.

"Claire, I—" Willow's manager sputtered, her face flushing a deep red.

"There's no excuse, Margaret! If *she* works here"—Claire Turano pointed a trembling finger at Willow's head—"then you've lost my business. Which includes catering the annual art fund-raiser *and* the Sleepy Hollow Ball!"

The panic attack in full force, Willow's airway constricted as if she were breathing through a straw. Wheezing, she backed away from the counter.

Margaret glanced over her shoulder. "Willow, take a break, *now.*"

Gladly.

Willow spun on her heel and ran through the kitchen and out the side door to the shaded patio. She could feel people staring holes in her back, but she didn't care. She fell into a chair and searched for her focus color. Directly across from her, above a sign advertising the CC Café, she found a sky-blue flag with a peace symbol in the center. It would have to do.

Gasping for breath, she concentrated on the blue fabric and blocked everything out. The loud chewing of the woman beside her. The scrape of iron chairs against cobblestone. The mumble of voices . . .

Inhale through your nose.

1, 2, 3 . . .

Fall into the blue.

Exhale through your lips.

After three repetitions, the fog in her brain began to clear, but the pain in her chest persisted. Her shrink had given her a "panic script"—phrases to talk herself down. Unfortunately, it only worked when she said it aloud.

"Here goes nothing." Still focused on the flag, Willow recited, "This is an opportunity for me to learn to cope with this problem."

Cue the furtive glances and scurrying away.

Deep inhale.

"I have survived this before, and I can survive this time too."

Slow exhale.

The slam of her heart gentled to its normal beat. She could feel eyes on her, hear them gathering their things and whispering to one another, but she didn't dare look. She knew what she would see—condemnation and fear with a sprinkle of pity that equaled nothing but ignorant judgment.

Willow stared up at the fluttering green and yellow leaves and then drew a strong, clean breath before chancing a glance at the woman beside her—the only one who didn't leave. But the old lady's unwavering gaze made her swallow and look away.

"It's all right, dear. I talk to myself all the time."

Willow didn't respond, hoping the lady would get the hint and go away like everyone else.

The woman lifted half of her sandwich in arthritic fingers. "Want some? It's ham and cheese." The woman grinned, her cheeks plumping and eyes glittering in sweet enticement.

Willow blinked. Everyone knew you didn't accept food from strangers, especially not old women with stained dentures, but she'd made the sandwich herself not ten minutes ago and she hadn't eaten since breakfast. Her stomach growled like an angry beast, making up her mind for her. "Sure."

Accepting the offering, she peeled back the paper and sank her teeth in for a bite. The salty ham and creamy cheese melted in her mouth, dissolving the last of her anxiety. Willow slumped against the back of her chair.

"So, why are you so upset?"

Willow chewed, her eyes darting in search of an excuse not to talk to a complete stranger about her screwed-up life. But they were the only two left on the patio. When she glanced back at the woman's expectant face, she shrugged and answered, "Old decisions coming back to haunt me, I guess."

"I see." The woman's eyes narrowed. "Well, do you have a friend you can talk to?"

A lump of bread and lunchmeat lodged in Willow's throat. How much of the truth did the lady really want to know? That after Ashton had been convicted of killing Daniel Turano and was sent to juvie, he hadn't responded to any of her letters? That her one true friend had abandoned her and left her here to defend his innocence? That everyone at school either treated her like she was invisible or a freak of nature? Would she want to hear all that?

Willow rolled the sudden tightness out of her shoulders and attempted a light tone. "Not really."

"I see. Well, you can talk to me if you like."

Willow concentrated hard on her sandwich. When she finished, she folded the empty wrapper into a perfect square. She didn't want to confess the evil weed that had sprouted in her heart as Mrs. Turano yelled in her face—that her life would've been much easier if Ashton had been the one to die that day at the falls. Then *she* would be the martyr of the story.

But even so, she couldn't wish it were true, and she certainly couldn't tell a complete stranger. "Thank you, but—"

"Oh, there you are." Margaret stopped in front of her.

Saved by her not-for-long boss.

"We need to chat." She patted down her dyed blonde hair and retied her apron strings before meeting Willow's gaze.

Of course we do.

Reluctantly, Willow rose and followed her manager's retreating form but then turned back. "Thanks for the sandwich." Willow extended her hand. "I'm Willow Lamott."

"I'm Mrs. McMenamin, but everyone calls me Mrs. M." They shook hands, a red plaid sleeve falling across the woman's papery skin.

Willow glanced down and saw scuffed cowboy boots peeking out from the ruffled hem of the woman's flannel nightgown. She remembered then that Mrs. M had taught English at the high school but retired years ago. Everyone said she was a few clowns short of a circus. Though after her meltdown moments before, Willow didn't feel qualified to judge.

Mrs. M. held her gaze and leaned in close. "All heartbreak fades with time. Don't be afraid to move on."

The woman shuffled away, calling over her shoulder, "And don't be a victim!"

■ ■ ■

Willow lugged her overloaded backpack up the winding, cobblestone walkway to her new home. Three stories of Gothic Victorian loomed above her, blocking out the setting sun. Sagging wrap-around porch, chipped gingerbread trim, wood siding stained a dirty gray, and, like the topper on a Tim Burton wedding cake, a rusted-out weathervane leaning precariously from the third-floor turret room. She shifted her backpack to the opposite shoulder and walked into the shadow of the dilapidated mansion.

Everyone in town believed Keller House was haunted, and for Willow it was true. But the specters that disturbed her were not of the ethereal variety.

"Willow, bet you can't do this!" the boy with the shaggy dark hair and smiling eyes chants as he leaps over the porch railing and jumps to the ground.

"Seriously, Ashton," Willow muttered, "if you can't get out of my head, I'm not living in your stupid old house. Even if this is my mom's dream job." When her mom had landed the job of caretaker to Ashton's rundown family estate, you would've thought they'd won the lottery. But for Willow, living in her ex–best friend's house was a form of slow torture.

She jerked as the double-arched doors swung open with a baleful creak. But her fright was short-lived. Her mom posed in the doorway like a character in an old movie, hands on gypsy-skirted hips, heavy salt-and-pepper dreads looped in a lopsided bun. She spread her arms wide. "Velcome home, Villow! Hov vas your day?"

Willow bit her lip to trap a laugh. "Awesome, Count Chocula. How was yours?"

Her mom's face fell into a pout as she dropped her arms. "I was trying to be Elvira."

"Who?"

"You know, Mistress of the Dark?"

"That old chick with the black wig and the low necklines?" Willow asked.

Her mom nodded and stuck out her chest, making Willow giggle as she slipped into the foyer. "You've made some progress in here." The dust cloths had been removed from the entry table and parlor furniture. The cherry wood floors gleamed, and the bright scent of lemon filled the air.

"Only one problem," Mom huffed, pointing up.

Willow tilted her head back and stared at the centerpiece of the two-story foyer, a massive chandelier dripping crystals and cobwebs.

"Can't find a tall enough ladder," her mom grumbled.

"I don't know, I kinda like it." She met her mom's dark-chocolate eyes, the exact shade of her own. "Could go a long way for the Elvira image."

"I want to keep it for Halloween!" A four-foot ball of energy in the form of her little brother sped past, his bony elbow knocking the backpack off her shoulder.

"Hey!" Willow called to the boy who'd sped around the corner. "How was school?"

Rainn poked his head out and threw a sock at her head. "Good!"

Willow flicked the tiny stink bomb from her shoulder. For such a little kid, his feet sure packed a punch. Rainn's satisfied snigger echoed back to her as he disappeared into the house.

"Oh, I almost forgot." Her mom walked to the entry table and returned with a wooden picture frame. "I found this while cleaning out Ashton's old closet."

Willow gaped at the intricate pencil drawing of the tree house at the back of the Keller property. She and Ashton had spent so many hours there in the summer months, their parents had jokingly referred to it as their vacation home. It brought back happy, uncomplicated memories of before— before her best friend went to jail for manslaughter.

She took the picture and opened her mouth to make a witty remark about the property value skyrocketing after the scandal, but only managed to mumble, "Thanks."

Her mom bent to pick up the discarded sock. "I'm working at the soup kitchen tonight. Want to come?"

"Not tonight." Willow hefted her bag back onto her shoulder.

"What happened? Something's bothering you."

"I'm fine." Unwilling to admit she'd lost another job, she turned and began climbing the wide wooden staircase. "Tons of homework—trig, lit, chemistry . . ."

"No one told you to take all those honors classes!" her mom called after her.

If Mom had her way, Willow would stay home and attend Annherst next year. With no traditional grading system and classes like Experimental Body Art and Media Conspiracy Theory, the liberal arts college attracted freethinking societal anarchists from all over the country. And while the school infused the town with an eclectic mix of people and produced an inordinate number of famous musicians and actors, it didn't offer undergraduate degrees in biochemistry.

Willow opened the first door at the top of the stairs and inhaled a cloud of dust and powdery Shalimar. A sneeze rocked her chest, and she slumped against the mahogany wood frame, pushing her glasses up on her nose. This had been Kristen's room . . .

Ashton turns, shoots Willow a wink, and sets the baby-blue glass bottle on the vanity table. She reaches out and adjusts it to the proper angle, even as butterflies war in her stomach. "What if she gets it in her eyes?"

With a drawn-out sigh, he says, "Why would she

spray perfume in her eyes? Besides, it's only vinegar. The perfect complement to my sister's sweet personality."

The click of high heels echoes in the hall, and he grabs her arm, tugging her deeper into the room.

"We have to go!" she hisses.

"No time." He ducks and slides under the dust ruffle of the bed, and she scrambles after him just as the door opens.

Lying flat on her stomach, she watches Kristen apply fresh lipstick, run a brush through her long blonde hair, and lean into the mirror. "Flawless," she says to her own reflection before reaching for the blue bottle.

Three squirts, and a screech rents the air.

Willow jerks and shrinks farther under the bed, but Ashton's face is right there. Flashing a broad crescent of straight, white teeth, he squeezes her hand, and something like an inflating balloon fills her chest.

"Ugh." Willow's ribcage expanded as if her fingers were still entwined with his. She took several slow breaths and blew the dark veil of bangs out of her eyes. By sheer force of personality, Ashton had imprinted on this house—and on her.

She forced her feet to move. In theory, her own massive bedroom should make her ecstatic with joy. But in her heart, she wished her mom hadn't accepted the caretaker job. Willow preferred their cozy two-bedroom cottage to this abomination of hardwood, stained glass, and endless memories.

But even if she could convince her mom, it was too late to go back. A couple of newlyweds had rented their old house and turned it into a tattoo parlor/holistic healing center—as if Gilt Hollow needed another one.

Willow flopped down on the king-sized bed and tucked a pillow under her head. Most of her homework wasn't due until the end of the week. She could afford to close her eyes for a moment . . . A chill of awareness tiptoed up her spine, like when a teacher caught you texting in class. She twisted around, ready to yell at Rainn for sneaking up on her. But there was no one else in the room.

■ ■ ■

Willow couldn't sleep.

There's no such thing as ghosts, said the scientific part of her brain. But the little girl, the one who'd listened to all of Ashton's spooky stories, the one who used to have nightmares about the ghoul who lived in the attic, shivered under the covers. Ashton had sworn for years that he'd seen things in this house. Lights flickering. Chairs rocking in empty rooms. Doors swinging open by themselves. And as she lay straining to hear every sound, a part of her believed him.

She rolled onto her side and clutched a pillow to her stomach. The harsh digital display seemed to throw the time in her face—3:04 a.m. Propping up on an elbow, she spied the drawing of the tree house leaning against her lamp. In the moonlight, she could just make out the shape of the tiny dwelling that she and Ashton had helped her dad build the summer before he passed away. They'd scouted for weeks for the perfect spot. When they'd found the sprawling oak on the back of the Keller property, her dad went to Mr. Keller for permission, hoping he'd join them in the project. When he'd granted them the land but declined to help, her dad had made a big deal about Ashton being the architect.

Willow flopped onto her back. The dark paneled walls and twelve-foot ceilings loomed, stretching and contracting in the shadows as if they had a life of their own. She should go downstairs and make some warm milk or peppermint tea, but the thought of walking through the spook factory of a house in the dead of night kept her glued to her mattress.

A low groan sounded from somewhere close, followed by a clacking like metal against wood. A shiver skittered across Willow's shoulders, and she tugged the comforter up to her chin.

Ugh! She needed to relax. The noises were just the house settling.

Working to calm her thoughts, she pulled a long breath in through her nose and blew it out through her mouth. Her eyes drifted shut and she pictured a white-sand beach, turquoise water, the gentle rush and ebb of the tide, the warm sun on her skin . . .

Bam!

Willow sat straight up and held still, waiting for the sound to come again. Had it been a door slamming or something heavy crashing to the floor? Visions of Rainn falling out of Ashton's old four-poster had her springing out of bed. Without turning on a light, she ran around the corner and down the hall, the slap of her bare feet the only sounds. She rushed into Rainn's room and found her brother sleeping peacefully, his stuffed ninja turtle clutched to his chest.

Breathing a sigh of relief, she tiptoed to her mother's room and heard her snores before she even reached the door. So what had made that loud slamming noise?

She wrapped an arm around her waist as she crept back into the hall and toward an arched picture window. There were hundreds—maybe thousands—of trees on the five-acre property. The noise could've been one of them falling against the house.

When she reached the window that faced the overgrown back garden, a cloud obscured the moon, turning the yard into a tangle of dark shapes and twisted silhouettes. Leaning close to the glass, she didn't see any broken limbs or branches close enough to scrape against the siding. She recalled the sound and realized it had seemed to come from below her on the first floor.

And then something moved.

She jumped back from the window, her heart pounding into her ears. The quick, furtive movement had been a living being. Something large. Gathering her courage, she stepped closer to the glass. It was probably a deer. She'd seen plenty of them leaping through the woods between their old cottage and the Keller property.

Capturing her nightshirt sleeve in her fingers, she wiped a circle of dust from the window pane and peered into the yard. Directly below, a circular stone walkway bisected the unkempt lawn overrun by tangles of weeds and wildflowers. Beyond, the trees stood sentinel in a thick line, their leaves rustling in the wind.

Willow scanned the edge of the woods, skimming broad trunks and sweeping pines. Her eyes darted back to a group of narrow birch trees. The gloom between their silver trunks moved, and she pressed her nose to the cool glass. Had it been a trick of the light? Or . . .

Then the clouds shifted and revealed a figure. A midnight shade between ghostly white trees—tall and solid, its features in shadow—it turned and disappeared into the forest.

Willow stumbled back. Had he seen her watching? Her pulse ratcheted into overdrive. Had that person tried to break into the house?

She ran. Not caring if she woke her family, she ran down the creaky staircase and through the drafty, cobweb-infested hallway, flipping on every light switch she came to. When the first floor blazed like daytime, she ensured all the doors were locked. But there were too many windows to check. Should she wake her mom? Call the police?

And tell them what? She heard a noise and thought she saw a shadow in the yard? The cops would laugh all the way back to the precinct, joking about the girl who lived in the haunted house of her ex–best friend, the murderer.

Willow stood in the middle of the kitchen shaking, the room spinning around her. Maybe she was losing it. Her chest tightened as the panic attack tried to steal her breath. *Not again!* Determination pushing back her fear, she poured a glass of milk and gulped down her anxiety with the cold, soothing liquid.

Her equilibrium restored, she wandered from room to room, switching off all the lights, and then climbed the stairs. After checking on her mom and brother once more, she went back to Kristen's room—*her* room—and locked the door.

Gilt Hollow

By Lorie Langdon

Willow Lamott's best friend is a convicted killer, and no one in the small town of Gilt Hollow will let her forget it. Over four long years, she's tried to fade into the background—but none of that matters when Ashton Keller comes striding into school, fresh out of juvie and fueled by revenge. The moment their eyes meet, Willow no longer feels invisible. Drawn to the vulnerability behind Ashton's mask of rage, she sinks deeper into his sinister world and begins to question whether he's a villain, a savior, or both.

Ashton thought he wanted vengeance, until Willow Lamott stepped back into his life. Now he longs to clear his name and become the person she sees in him. But the closer they get to uncovering the truth, the darker the secrets become, and Ashton wonders if his return to Gilt Hollow will destroy everyone he loves.

The Doon Novel Series

By Carey Corp and Lorie Langdon

Softcover: 9780310742395

Hardcover: 9780310742333
Softcover: 9780310742401

Hardcover: 9780310742357
Softcover: 9780310742418

Available in stores and online!

BLINK